TREASON AT HANFORD

A HARRY TRUMAN MYSTERY

SCOTT DENNIS PARKER

Treason at Hanford
A Harry Truman Mystery
By Scott Dennis Parker

Copyright © 2023 by Scott Dennis Parker

Cover Concept by Scott Dennis Parker
Cover Design by SudevVp
Quote on cover by Harry Truman, from *Plain Speaking: An Oral Biography of Harry S. Truman* by Merle Miller, Berkeley Publishing Corporation, 1973.

ScottDennisParker.com

All rights reserved.

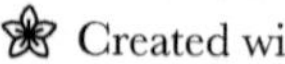 Created with Vellum

To Doug Warren,
who asked me a simple question
and helped create this story

1

At 3:30 a.m. on Saturday, April 8, 1944, armed forces of the Empire of Japan landed in the state of Oregon.

The new moon cast no light on the shore. The sea lapped the sandy beach with white-capped waves visible on the dark water. Astoria, Oregon, the closest town, was five miles to the north, its lights extinguished during wartime. The closest road was nearly two miles away but gas rationing kept most of the cars off the roads. Only a fifty-yard expanse of beach separated the water from the dense, natural forest. And it was across this open area that five figures carried an inflatable raft.

They reached the edge of the forest and vanished inside the wooded curtain, swallowed by the near-complete darkness. A few more yards into the forest and they set down the raft. One man withdrew a black canvas tarp from a knapsack and, with a quiet flourish, threw it over the raft. The other men helped him. Within seconds, the yellow raft disappeared.

One figure stood off to one side, a night flashlight shining on his compass and a sheet of paper. The red beam spread just wide enough on his uniform to reveal his captain's insignia. His four soldiers stood on guard, rifles at the ready, waiting for his orders.

He had been given specific instructions on where the meeting was to take place. He was to land just to the south of the rock outcropping that jutted into the ocean. After finding the broken tree, he was to travel approximately one hundred yards inland to the rendezvous.

There he was to meet the American.

Satisfied with his directions, the captain turned to inspect the covering of the raft, walking around the entire perimeter. He nodded his approval and directed two men to lookout points about ten yards to either side. The remaining two soldiers stood with the captain, rifles ready.

The captain and his guards started walking away from the shore. Their footfalls, though light, still cracked a few small limbs on the ground. The sounds of the waves obscured most of their ambient noises. The smell of pine and oak was strong and, for a moment, the captain's mind ventured beyond his current circumstances and back to his childhood, playing in the woods outside Kyoto. He had always loved the smell of the forest. Ironic that he joined the Imperial Navy and was never able to smell anything organic.

After three minutes of cautious walking, the captain smelled something else. At first, his mind dismissed it. Surely, it could not be here. Not in the forest. It required a fire and a fire would give away the American's position.

Nonetheless, as he kept walking, the smell grew stronger and he relented to what his nose was telling him: he smelled green tea. The distinctive aroma wafted through the trees, intermingling with the other natural smells, to create something intoxicating. His mouth began to water at the thought of tasting green tea. The tea rations on the submarine had run out weeks ago. So had most of their other rations despite the previous supplies delivered by the American.

The odor of tea got stronger and stronger until the captain and his men stopped just inside a small clearing, no bigger than the captain's quarters on the submarine, about seven feet square. His guards immediately crouched into a defensive position, aiming their rifles at the center of the clearing.

In the middle of the clearing was a tent. One flap was open and tied back. From inside, a blue glow underneath a cast iron pot vaguely illuminated the interior of the tent. The captain could see a man, kneeling on the ground inside the tent, his hands on his thighs. Directly in front of the person was a small cast iron pot from which the green tea smell emanated.

The person on the ground spoke first. "You might want to order you men to focus their attention elsewhere. I am unarmed and pose no threat to you."

The voice was softened by smoking. But what struck the captain most was how well the man spoke Japanese.

"Plus, Captain, why would I go to such extraordinary lengths to bring you here just to kill you? If I wanted you dead, I would have alerted the United States Navy to your presence." The man paused to let this fact sink into the captain's thoughts.

The captain, still uncertain, stood up straight. His soldiers, however, didn't move, ready to attack at moments' notice. The captain nodded to his guards and spoke softly. One soldier left his battle-ready stance and turned to watch the forest. The second one, however, remained ready to shoot the man in the tent.

"Please, Captain, come inside. I would like to pour you a cup of tea." The captain's eyes, wholly adjusted to the dark, noticed the American's face vaguely outlined by the soft blue glow of the heat source. The American was kneeling on a small blanket. There was another blanket for the captain, directly across from the American.

The captain walked forward, stooped, and stepped inside the small tent. The smell of the tea was spirituous. It had been too long since he last tasted good tea. He kneeled on the blanket set out for him. The American's face was now more distinct.

The American smiled at him. "Am I what you expected?"

It was the captain's turn to smile. In English, he said, "Since your message to me was written in Japanese, I assumed you spoke my language."

The American's smile grew wider. "I had no idea you spoke my language. I apologize that our current circumstances do not allow us to perform the traditional *cha-no-ya* ceremony. To compensate, I have provided the best tea from my personal collection." He bowed to the captain. The captain reached out to accept the offered cup of tea.

The captain put the cup to his lips and drank. It was blessed. He closed his eyes at the taste. "Genmaicha, a good selection."

The American took a sip from his cup. He let the steam wash his face and, again in Japanese, he spoke. "There are a large number of Americans who speak Japanese. In fact, it is wonderful to be speaking Japanese with another citizen of the Empire after so long. " He paused and savored another mouthful. "But they are all almost entirely being held as *de facto* prisoners of war." He spat out these last words with fierce anger.

"You speak of the relocation camps." It was not a question. "I have read about them. Somehow, the government who professes democracy and freedom decided American citizens who just happen to be of Japanese ancestry are a security threat? And this despite written statements of loyalty?"

The American scoffed. "Yes, that would be my country. At least your Empire is ruled by a legitimate emperor. We have Roosevelt who just thinks he is one."

It was the captain's turn to frown. "I would not characterize your president as an emperor. That would be an insult to His Majesty."

He sipped his tea. "When you discovered my submarine during your civilian patrol, you had the opportunity to reveal my position to your government. You didn't. Instead, you made contact with me. You supplied my men with provisions. You even presented me with your name and your history, all in an effort to gain my confidence. Finally, you requested to meet me here, on your soil. Well, I am here and, while I enjoy your tea, I am understandably curious as to why you arranged this meeting." The captain drained the last of the tea and motioned to the American with his cup. "You are, after all, my enemy. I am under orders to kill all Americans I meet."

The captain set his empty cup down on the small crate situated between him and the American. The American reached over to the teapot and refilled the captain's cup.

"Captain, I am here to help you." The American looked up at his guest. "Why would you want to kill an ally?"

The American reached into his breast pocket and withdrew a pack of cigarettes. The captain took the offered cigarette and ran it under his nose. The sweet smell of fine tobacco reminded him, yet again, of the dwindling supplies for his men. After the American lit both cigarettes, he gave the pack to the captain.

"I would imagine that your supply of cigarettes is as low as your rations, if not altogether gone," the American said as smoke plumed out of his nostrils. He motioned with the cigarette hand to four small boxes in the shadows next to the captain. "There are three cases of cigarettes and one case of tea for your men. I do not know how many men your submarine holds so I just had to guess." He exhaled again and looked at the captain. "Tell them it is from a friend."

The captain dropped ash on the dirt next to him. "So you offer me tea and cigarettes for me and my men and you say it is from a friend. You also say you are an ally of mine. Well, if you are an ally of mine, does that not make you an enemy to your own people? Are you not a…what is the name of that man from your revolution?"

"Benedict Arnold," the American said after a moment. "Yes, that thought has crossed my mind more than once. But I do not consider myself a traitor to a country and a government that has betrayed me and the ones I love."

The word 'betrayed' was spoken with such venom that the captain was taken aback. The other man seemed to be truthful, he thought, but he was still an American, still capable of deceit.

The American caught the captain's glance and put his hands out toward the captain. "But where are my manners? I am the host and you are my guest. As you have stated, you already know my name. Whom do I have the honor of addressing?"

The captain considered a false name but then thought better of it. How would the American know any difference? "My name is Hiroyuki Morimoto."

"And what classification is your ship?"

In Morimoto's mind, he remembered how beautiful his ship

looked in the bright morning sun as it splashed into the Pacific. He remembered the ship's first shakedown cruise and how flawlessly his men followed his orders. And he remembered how his commanding officer had delivered to him the secret orders Morimoto was expected to carry out. He was instructed not to tell the crew until they were underway.

The orders were simple and straightforward: bring the war home to the mainland of the United States.

No, thought Morimoto, he would not tell this American of his mission or his submarine's secret weapon. But the American could be used to achieve greater victories in this mission. "My ship is a standard submarine. Undoubtedly your military has intelligence regarding submarines of the Imperial Japanese Navy."

After a moment of strained silence, the American ran a finger across his lips and continued. "Very well. My personal issues with my government are mine alone. What I want to achieve will deal a blow to America that will strike fear deep into the heart of this people like nothing since Pearl Harbor. With any luck, the additional resources in men, material, and public outcry needed to deal with the 'Japanese invasion of mainland America' will be enough for your forces to rebuild and prepare yourselves for withstanding the onslaught of the ultimate violation: the invasion of the Japanese home islands."

Morimoto actually let out a laugh at the idea. "I do not think the American people have the willpower to withstand the devastating loss of life on such a futile effort." He raised his cup to his face and looked at the American. "It is not in the American character to fight to the death. Surrender is in your cultural core."

"I would not underestimate the character of the Americans in this war, Captain. Pearl Harbor did something to the American people. Some say that your attack awoke the sleeping giant. Most feel it is only a matter of time before they win."

Morimoto chuckled softly again. "Not at the cost we will inflict." He drained the cup and placed it back on the crate. "No, my kind sir, you have overestimated your country's chances of victory in this war."

It was the American's turn to chuckle, a dry rasp. He placed his cup next to Morimoto's and rested his hands on his lap. "What if I told you that the United States Army is working on a weapon so powerful that it might make an invasion of the Japanese home islands unnecessary? A weapon powerful enough to bring to mind the possibility of something heretofore inconceivable: the surrender of the Empire of Japan."

Morimoto's movements were so quick that the sound of the knife leaving its sheath arrived in the American's ears only after the blade was on his neck. The captain noticed some of the confidence left the American's eyes but not all.

The American's hands stayed still on his lap as he softly spoke. "I do not believe that the Emperor will ever surrender, Captain, but that is the talk in the secret groups associated with this weapon." His Adam's apple bobbed over the knife's edge. "These American generals are certain that this weapon will change the course of the war."

The American looked directly into Morimoto's eyes. "That is why I need your help. I want to sabotage the effort to create this weapon. I want to assist Imperial Japan and defeat the United States."

2

Monday
April 17, 1944
7:25 a.m., Pacific War Time

Without even looking at his watch, Senator Harry Truman knew it was time for breakfast. He put down his pen across the unfinished letter to his beloved wife, Bess, and stood. The train's sleeper car was cramped so he barely moved three feet before he was in front of the mirror. He studied himself and made sure he was presentable.

His white shirt remained neatly pressed. His tie sported the perfect Windsor knot he made an hour ago. His hair, now more salt than pepper, was still in place. The eyes that stared back through his thick spectacles showed signs of tiredness but still lit by the fire he felt for his job. He reached over to his suit coat, withdrew the handkerchief, and began to clean his glasses. He squinted out the small window to see the sun beginning to rise over the Idaho mountains. And, after he put his glasses back on, he noticed a farmer already at work in his fields and he remembered his old life.

All those many years ago, he thought. Had it really been thirty years since he awoke before dawn to till the fields, being one with the land? He sighed at the thought of so many years passing through him.

He slid into his gray suit jacket and replaced his handkerchief in the breast pocket, making sure that five points rose gracefully from the lip of the pocket. It didn't matter if he was in Washington D.C. attending Senate meetings or out here in the American west on an investigation, he was a United States Senator and he always looked the part wherever he went.

As he made his way from the sleeper car to the dining car, one of the stevedores saw him and tipped his hat. "Good morning, Senator. Did you sleep well last night?"

"Tom, the clickety-clack of the train was like a lullaby and I slept like a baby."

"And your room?" Tom the stevedore looked nervous as he spoke, scratching his chin absently, eyebrows raised in anticipation. "When your office called, we didn't have the first class car available."

"Don't fret about it, Tom. Since when do I need first class?" Truman slapped Tom's shoulder as he eased by the stevedore. "I may be a senator but that shouldn't entitle me to extra attention." And, in a stage whisper, he said, "Besides, can you imagine the stink I'd get myself into if I made you kick out the actual first class passengers just so I could get a first class room? With my luck, it would be a constituent." Truman winked and started again for the dining car.

When he got to the dining car, he was not at all surprised to find Carl Hancock already seated at the table, waiting for him. Hancock, who had been looking out the window when Truman entered the car, turned to face the senator and smiled.

"Beat you again, Senator," he said as he ran a hand through his dark brown hair. He, too, was dressed as if he were in Washington. His brown department-store suit was not as nice as Truman's hand-tailored double-breasted one. The western cut suit fit his stocky frame too snugly in the shoulders and chest. His coat sleeves were about an inch too short, prompting Hancock to pull at them constantly. Despite Truman's continual insistence that his investigators act as an extension of him, the senator could not convince Hancock to get hand-tailored suits. It was just not in the family budget was Hancock's standard answer, a rationale to which Truman could certainly relate.

"Carl," Truman said as he took the chair across from Hancock, "I hope you got enough sleep last night. I didn't plan on meeting over breakfast. We still have nearly a full day's travel ahead of us." As he said this, he made a mental note to put another notation in Hancock's personnel file.

"Gotta eat, Senator," Hancock said as he raised his coffee cup to his mouth. "And they only serve breakfast from seven 'til nine." He sipped his coffee as a waiter appeared and poured Truman a cup of coffee.

"Good morning, Senator Truman. I hope you've enjoyed your journey with us." The waiter, having finished pouring, stepped back, waiting for the senator's word.

"Yes, Jack, you and your train company have done a remarkable job for me." He looked sidelong at Hancock, a barely suppressed grin cracking his stoic features. "I just hope Carl here can say the same. You know, he's so used to first class." The grin broke free of its restraint and lit up Truman's entire face.

All three men laughed. The waiter was the first to regain his composure. "Would you like the same breakfast as yesterday, Mr. Truman?"

Hancock looked up at the waiter. "Bring me the same, please. I want to know what keeps this man going." The waiter nodded and withdrew.

Hancock noticed that, after the waiter had left, he and Truman were the only two people in the dining car. He put his elbows on the table. In a low voice, he said, "So, can you at least tell me what's so important that you ordered me to stop my investigation in Denver and fly up to Helena just so I could get on a train after midnight and have you tell me 'we'll talk in the morning'? I slept alright. But it was the last thing I thought of before I fell asleep and the first thing that entered my mind when I woke up." He paused and let his eyes fix on Truman's. "I'm dying here, Harry."

Truman matched Hancock's position and whispered, "I'll start but will shut up tight when Jack comes back or anyone else comes in here. This is strictly confidential, more so than our other investigations."

He leaned back and took in some of his coffee. He placed the cup back on the saucer and folded his hands. With seeming reluctance, he said, "It's Hanford again."

Hancock all but dropped his cup, coffee spilling over the rim and filling the saucer. His eyes went wide. "Holy Cow, Harry! What the hell are we doing with that? I thought you and Stimson[1] had an agreement that we wouldn't go there."

Truman sighed. "I know, I know. We have an agreement. We had an agreement even before Fred[2] went out there last November. You were in North Carolina at the time." Truman stared out the window. "I think I really angered Stimson by sending Fred out there. The secretary hasn't spoken to me since. He probably thinks I'm trying to hamper the war effort." His manner took on a sudden air of sadness. "That's the furthest thing from my mind, Carl."

"Okay, I got all that. Fred even told me about the memo."[3] Hancock sopped up the spilt coffee with a napkin. "So, I say again: what are we doing out here?"

Truman looked back at Hancock, drawing three envelopes from his inside coat pocket. He handed them to Hancock and waited for the other man to read them.

Hancock looked at the three envelopes, read the postmarks, and realized without surprise they were in order. He opened the first one.

MARCH 9, 1944

Seattle, WA

Senator Truman, US Senate:

My name is Horace K. McLeod, attorney, representing Donald Bumble. As you know, the US Government has been seizing land near Richland, WA, since 1943, including land owned by my client. A number of the farmers and citizens whose land was condemned have filed suit in court against the Government but the process is slow and prone to obstruction.

I am writing to you in your position as the chairman of what has become known as "The Truman Committee." My client suspects illegal business practices are being conducted in this area, undoubtedly costing the Government money, and may even be hampering the war effort.

I would like to request a meeting with you to discuss these issues. Please contact my office and I will make arrangements to travel to Washington, D.C.

Sincerely,

Horace K. McLeod

HANCOCK RAISED HIS EYEBROWS. "Okay, so we get lots of letters like this. Did you tell him that we'd put his complaint on the list and we'd look into it?"

"Yes."

"Did you tell him that we just don't go off half-cocked into investigations just because someone writes us a letter like this?"

"Yes." Truman's eyes were fixed and steady behind his lenses. With each answer, Hancock's brow furrowed deeper.

"Why is this one so special that it's got you and me on a train to Washington?"

"Read the next one."

Hancock sighed but Truman could tell the other man was curious. With Hancock's police background, he analyzed things in a different way than Truman's other investigators.

Hancock opened the second letter and read the following, handwritten letter.

MARCH 24, 1944
Richland, WA

Senator Truman, US Senate:

Thank you for your letter of the 17th. I certainly understand that you and your committee have too many letters like my first with my particular complaints. I also understand that you have procedures you must follow so as to promote a fair and honest investigation.

But something has happened. Two days after I sent you my letter, a very agitated Mr. Bumble called me at my house. I asked him to tell me what was wrong.

Mr. Bumble had been noticing missing crates at the Richland branch of Moore Shipping and Warehouse. He asked the head foreman about it and was told, in no uncertain terms, to mind his own business.

Not wanting to be a part of any criminal activity, Mr. Bumble talked with the sheriff about his suspicions. My client even said he could get evidence of the missing crates. A few days later, a gang of men accosted him, beating him enough so that he had to go to a clinic.

Needless to say, Mr. Bumble was shocked. He called me the same day and told me what happened. He asked that I come to Richland and promised that he would get some hard evidence.

Senator Truman, I am wondering if, perhaps, my client's case can be moved up in rank on your list? An investigation by your committee would certainly shine the light of truth into this matter.

I am staying at the Hurley Hotel in Richland, WA. Please direct any letter to that location.

Sincerely,

Horace K. McLeod.

TRUMAN COULD TELL that Hancock had to read it twice before looking up at him. Hancock's look was of interested skepticism.

Before he could respond, the waiter returned with their food. Hancock quickly slipped the letters into his coat pocket. On their plates was a hearty Midwestern breakfast of sunny-side up eggs, bacon, toast, strawberries, and grits, a pat of butter melting in the center.

Truman's smile was as wide as his face. The chagrin that had permeated his face seconds before was all but a memory. "Jack, if this is even half as good as yesterday's, I think I'll get double the work done today." He leaned back in his chair, took a deep breath, and genuinely looked as happy as possible.

"Thank you, sir." Jack's face beamed with pride at the senator's compliment. He looked at Hancock. "And I hope you'll find our food equally as good."

Hancock took the cue from Truman. He put on a huge smile, slapped his stomach and rubbed a circle. "Jack, my mouth is watering just lookin' at it. And, you know what, I can't wait." He plucked a strawberry from his plate and popped it in his mouth. He closed his eyes as he chewed. Opening his eyes, he looked at the waiter. "Jack, this might be the best damn strawberry I've ever tasted. Don't you worry. I'll be more than satisfied."

Wearing a thin smile, the waiter nodded and returned to the adjoining car.

Truman looked back at Hancock after confirming that the waiter was out the door. "Don't give me that look, Carl. You haven't even read the third letter."

Hancock stared at Truman, his fork poised in midair, another quizzical look on his face. He put down the fork and fished the letters out of his pocket. Finding the third one, this one a telegram, he began reading.

April 7, 1944

Richland, WA

Senator Truman, US Senate:

I received your letter of 30 March in response to my second letter. I thank you for your increased interest in my situation and your promise to promote my client's case higher on your priority. But I must convey to you that the situation has become more dire.

Mr. Bumble has been drafted into the Army. In our last meeting, just yesterday evening, he told me that he was fearing for his safety.

He said he wouldn't be surprised if he got silenced, one way or another.

I discovered what had happened when he didn't show for lunch. I went to his row house to see if he left some sort of note for me. Everything had been taken. Last night, as I was returning to my hotel room, two men assaulted me, saying only, 'Why don't you go home?'

Senator Truman, you are the only one with whom I have confided my suspicions. At this point, I do not trust the Army or the sheriff. Will you please help me discover why my client was silenced?

I am also going to call Washington State's two senators and implore them to ask for your assistance. Please let me know what you decide.

Sincerely,

Horace K. McLeod

TRUMAN'S FACE was serious when Hancock finished reading and returned the letters to the senator. "Convinced yet?"

"Well, I'm certainly convinced there's something going on out there." He began to eat his bacon. "But still, why us? Why you and me? Why not call some state policing agency?"

"You read the letters, Carl. Something's going on out there and Mr. McLeod has no one else to turn to. The local sheriff certainly seems to be in on something or else he would've investigated Mr. Bumble's complaints." He paused as he cut his eggs, the yolk flowing around his plate. "What I don't get is the military connection. How did Mr. Bumble's suspicions elevate to where he was drafted?"

"Harry, we're at war. Loose lips sink ships. No matter what's going on out there at Hanford, it's still under the Army's jurisdiction. And Stimson asked you not to poke your nose out there." Hancock pointed at Truman with his fork. "And that's exactly what we're about to do."

"Still, Carl, doesn't it bother you that the government can just draft someone it finds offensive? That's smacks of Hitler."

"Hey, desperate times require desperate measures. If someone's trying to hamper the efforts of our boys over there, take 'em out. Now, I ain't sayin' that's what's going on." He paused, swallowing some coffee. "Frankly, I don't know what to make of this little situation you've got us in."

"It's an investigation into a claim of embezzlement with possible criminal overtones." Truman's voice was one of a person stating a simple and obvious fact.

"Yeah, I know that, Harry," Hancock said, his voice not quite a whisper. "But since when do we get off being all Nero Wolfe and such? This is a *law enforcement* issue. This ain't our bag. We investigate whether or not a company is sticking it to Uncle Sam. The hardest thing we do is to tell some jackass executive that he'd better shape up and do what's right for our GIs overseas or we'll bring the might of the U.S. government on his head. We *don't* investigate crimes. *Cops* investigate crimes. We need to hand this off to someone else." Hancock stabbed a piece of bacon with his fork, popped it into his mouth, and began to chew.

"You used to be a cop, Carl," Truman replied through a mouthful of eggs. "Has your time with the committee softened you?"

"That ain't it, sir. I was *supposed* to look into crimes: break-ins, robberies, assault, larceny. Now I'm an investigator for the Senate Committee to Investigate the National Defense Program. I look into contractor mismanagement. I ain't supposed to work on crimes no more." Hancock stopped, nearly laughing at the sound of his last words. "Well, not crimes like that."

"But you helped your cousin, the sheriff, solve many cases back in Texas. There was even that famous one back in '41." Truman sipped his coffee. "Don't forget I was there when the case was solved. The sheriff gave you lots of credit for bringing down the suspect." Truman paused, absently sopping up egg yolk with his toast. "Besides, you know how to use a gun."

Hancock stabbed his fork in Truman's direction. "Ha! That's why you called me, isn't it? Because I know how to use a gun and I ain't afraid to use it."

Truman's eyes hardened. "I need you, Carl. All the other investigators are out on investigations and…"

"*I* was on an investigation," Hancock interrupted.

"Yes, I know, but you were closest. All the others are working mainly on the east coast right now. Matthew's[4] the only one who's remotely close and he's in Chicago. I actually met with him on the way out here. I was already thinking about you and he confirmed you're the best man for the job."

As Hancock was about to retort, other passengers entered the dining car. Both Truman and Hancock fell silent for a few minutes, content to finish their breakfasts. Gradually, they began to discuss the war, the weather, and the latest books each was reading. More and more diners arrived so the two men decided to go to Hancock's cabin to continue their discussion. As they made their way toward the door, they were interrupted by a loud voice.

"You're damn right that's where they're supposed to be."

Truman turned toward the voice. It belonged to a large jowly man sitting next to a window. The face of the woman next to him was a deep red, her embarrassment palatable. The man and woman sitting opposite them, their backs to Truman and Hancock, were nodding.

The man's wife placed a hand on his forearm in an attempt to calm him. "Honey, can we please not discuss this subject here?"

"Why not?" Now his face was turning red and a piece of egg flew out of his mouth and landed on his plate. "This is a room full of Americans, isn't it? I'm still an American who can say any damn thing I want to, right? Last I checked FDR runs this country, not Adolph."

Truman and Hancock exchanged glances, neither really knowing what the fuss was all about. The man helped them by pointing his fork at the window. "Stinkin' Jap traitors! That's where they belong. Right there, behind fences and barbed wire with armed men guarding them. After we kick Tojo's teeth in, I hope FDR sends 'em back to Tokyo."

By this time, everyone in the car had stopped eating and talking, their ears trained to listen to the man speak. They were also looking out the windows. Since they were standing, Truman and Hancock had to stoop to peer out the window to see where everyone's eyes were fixed.

What Truman saw made his heart sink. It sank not only because of what he saw but also for the man's words now had context.

Not one hundred yards to the north of the rail line was a chain-link fence with barbed wire rimming the top. Every so often, a guard tower rose above the fence and overlooked the neat rows of white tents and shacks. Even from this distance, Truman could see the faces of the occupants turned toward the sound of the train. In the center of the compound, an American flag flew.

It was the Minidoka, Idaho, Japanese-American Internment Camp.

---

1. Henry L. Stimson, Secretary of War.
2. Fred Canfil, investigator for the Truman Committee.
3. Canfil discovered a secret memo from the War Department giving orders that no one from the Truman Committee or anyone connected with the Senate was to be told or given any information about the project.
4. Matthew J. Connelly, chief investigator for the Truman Committee, made all assignments for the various investigations.

3

Monday
17 April 1944
12:00 p.m., Pacific War Time

Captain Hiroyuki Morimoto looked up when he heard the knock on the door to his cabin. He got up and opened it. "Come in, Okada-san."

Morimoto's chief engineer entered the captain's quarters and shut the door. As befitting a sailor on a submarine, Okada was a slight man. Thin but with muscles rippling under his skin, the sleeves of the engineer were rolled up and stained with grease. His pants displayed the wrinkles of one who had just spent a long time kneeling. Sweat beaded on his face, and he wiped it with a rag that left a smear of black on his forehead. Space being what it was, he stood at parade rest while the captain stood in front of his bunk. "You wanted to see me, Captain-san?"

"Yes. I have been thinking about our plans with the American." He pointed at a logbook on his bunk. "The American's plans are, how shall I say it, amateurish."

Okada nodded. "Yes, sir. And he clearly doesn't know our full capabilities." He paused, unsure of how to say what he wanted to say.

Morimoto noticed the silence. "You have something further to add, Okada-san?"

Okada cleared his throat. "Yes, sir." With the delicate nature of what he was about to say, he stood at attention. "Sir, you are the captain and I do not question your orders. But I am surprised that in the three meetings you have had with the American, you have allowed him to lead you." He looked at the captain. "I think we have the upper hand, sir, and I think it is time not only for you to reveal the true nature of this vessel but to change the plans accordingly."

Morimoto wanted to smile but kept his face impassive. He had been a junior officer once and always wondered what it was the senior officers knew that he didn't. Now, as captain, he was privy to all knowledge regarding his ship and he finally realized the discretion a captain had. And now was a time to let some of that discretion loose. "I agree with you, Okada-san. Thank you for speaking your mind. At ease, Lieutenant."

Okada shifted back to parade rest.

"The American's plans call for the sabotage of the military facility inside the state of Washington. Since he has no idea about our extra ability, he has created a plan that is nothing more than a large-scale raiding party that, in all likelihood, will be totally lost. I find his approach to be typically American: go in full-force, the consequences be damned." He picked up a pencil. "I prefer a more tactful approach."

"What do you have in mind, sir?"

"I think you can guess that, Lieutenant. I want to use all the means at our disposal to cripple this 'super bomb' as the American calls it."

Okada smiled as did the captain. The engineer then furrowed his brow. "Will you be making any attempt to radio the rest of the fleet or the homeland?"

Morimoto sighed and shook his head. "No, not now. The Americans do not even know we are here. To send any type of signal would alert them to our presence here and jeopardize our mandate." Morimoto patted Okada on the shoulder. "No, my friend, this time we will have to do this on our own."

Morimoto handed Okada a sheet of paper. "Review this, Okada-san."

The engineer looked at the folded sheet of paper. "What is it, if I may ask?"

Morimoto smiled. "It's my recommendation for taking control of the unique situation we have with the American and using him for *our* objectives."

He let his engineer review the plans for a minute. "What is your assessment of my plan? Speak as freely as necessary."

"Yes, sir. In short, your plan is the best one under our conditions. It accomplishes all we require: sabotaging the American bomb plant and saving as many lives of the crew as possible." Okada looked directly at the captain. "But there is a tertiary plan that may also be beneficial."

Morimoto raised an eyebrow. He considered himself a good, if not great, military strategist. That Okada had considered something he had not troubled him.

Okada took Morimoto's silence as permission to continue. "It is odd that our contact says that the engineers who are building this bomb do not even know its power. But, if what the American, or Koishii, as he wants us to call him, says is true, then this "super bomb" may change the course of the war. And it would change in favor of the Americans."

"Obviously."

Okada began to talk more quickly as his enthusiasm increased. "But what if we could find a way to get this bomb and use it *against* the Americans? Or, at least, let them know we have it. If they have it, they will use it. But, if we both have it, they may not use it for fear that we would unleash our bomb on the American Marines." Okada paused. "It could prevent the attempted invasion of the home islands."

The captain pursed his lips. "That is a possibility. However, I think this war is such that each side will use all the means at their disposal to win the war. If both sides have this bomb, then both sides will use it. It's as simple as that. I know I would."

Morimoto reached into his shirt pocket and shook out a cigarette for Okada and himself. They lit them and blew smoke toward the ceiling. Morimoto said, "How do you propose we get this super bomb?"

"Having detailed schematics would be the ideal situation. However, I do not think Koishii can obtain any schematics, as they are undoubtedly guarded quite closely by the Army. I do not think the American has that kind of access, despite his claims to the contrary." Okada pulled on his cigarette and stared at his captain. "No, Captain-san, I think we need another way to get the bomb ourselves. We need someone who knows all about the bomb, how it works, how to build it, what to build it with, things of this nature."

Morimoto cocked his head. "Who do you propose we need?"

"We need someone like me, an engineer or a scientist. Someone who works for the Army and, with the proper…motivation, would tell us anything that we want to know."

Okada stopped talking and just smoked, allowing Morimoto to mull the proposal. The captain was silent for half a minute, pondering the varied possibilities. Finally, he said, "I like your idea. It has many facets that can be exploited. Who do you suppose we should get and how?"

"The question of who we will leave to the American. He certainly has special access and can probably get close to anyone at a high level."

Morimoto paused. "Do you think he will be able to simply go in and, what, abduct a scientist and bring him to us? That seems too simple. Remember, his plan as it is now demonstrates basic thinking."

Okada nodded. "True, but he did find our ship and that was a particularly ingenious way he contacted us."

Morimoto smiled ruefully at the memory. "Yes, it was." He stubbed out the cigarette in the ashtray next to his bunk. "And, I suppose, you think that my new plan for sabotaging the bomb plant will act as a diversion?"

Okada beamed. "Of course, sir. We launch our raid on the bomb factory and the American brings us a scientist who can help us build our own bomb."

Morimoto gave a curt nod. "Okada-san, we shall move forward with our combined plans. I will tell the American tonight when I see him. I will inform the officers of our plans."

Okada bowed to his captain. "Thank you, Captain-san." He exited the room.

Morimoto sat on his bunk. His mind raced with the ideas of this new strategy. He smiled. It would take precise timing. It would take the dedication he expected from his crew. But it could be done. He could change the course of the war.

He opened his logbook and made a note of special commendation for Engineer Okada.

4

Monday
April 17, 1944
4:13 p.m., Pacific War Time

Horace K. McLeod stood on the platform at the Pendleton, Oregon, train station and held his hand over his eyes to block the late afternoon sun. His brown suit showed the wrinkles from sitting too long in the station and he tried to smooth them out. The blue striped tie matched the handkerchief in his breast pocket and his shoes showed barely a scuff.

He looked down the tracks for any sign of the incoming train and saw none. He pulled a shiny gold pocket watch from the vest pocket of his three-piece suit and checked the time. It was 4:13, two minutes past when he last checked it. He sighed, put the watch back in his pocket, inwardly vowing not to look at it again until after the train arrived.

He walked over to the ticket booth. "You're sure the 4:15's on time?" he asked, glancing at the clock on the back wall above the ticket taker's head. The man wore a blue uniform, a brass nametag on his lapel with "Dan" etched in block letters.

"Mr. McLeod, as I said a few minutes ago, the 4:15 is on time. If you just go get yourself a drink at the water fountain inside, the train will be here by the time you get back." Dan lowered his head and began reading his paperback, ending the conversation.

McLeod took a deep breath and let it out slowly. He was by himself on the platform, the rest of the patrons waiting inside the station. He pushed open the door leading into the station. As the door was closing behind him, he heard the approaching whistle. He caught the door before it closed and ran out to the platform.

The train made its slow approach to the station. When it finally stopped, McLeod glanced at the clock above Dan's head again. The clock read exactly 4:15 and Dan wore an I-told-you-so expression. As the train doors opened, an airplane squadron roared overhead. No one but McLeod looked up, so used to the sound were the local residents.

He stood just to the right of the door leading into the station. Senator Truman had wired McLeod asking that he search out the senator since the lawyer knew what Truman looked like. What the senator was too modest to include was the fact that his face had graced the cover of *Time* magazine the previous year. The news-magazine had run a cover story on the work the Truman Committee was doing in ferreting out companies and men who thought it was a good idea to skim money from the government while American soldiers died overseas.

The lawyer stood and scanned the disembarking passengers. Behind a family of four strode Harry Truman. His walk was brisk, a suitcase in his right hand, his hat set firmly on his head. Truman was so smartly dressed that McLeod thought that he looked as if he had just stepped out of a tailor's shop.

Keeping pace with Truman was another man wearing a suit of the western variety. The Stetson was kicked back on his head and the man's boots clonked on the wooden platform. Taller than Truman's five foot nine by a few inches, the man looked totally out of place in Oregon.

McLeod raised his hand and walked toward Truman and his

companion. McLeod extended his hand. "Senator Truman, it is so good to meet you. I'm Horace K. McLeod."

Truman shook the extended hand. "Thank you, sir. It's good to meet you, too, although I wish it were under other circumstances." He motioned to the other man. "This is Carl Hancock. He's one of the investigators assigned to the committee."

Hancock's hand clamped down around McLeod's. In McLeod's profession, a handshake with opposing counsel was the opening volley in the warfare that was litigation. He was accustomed to meeting or exceeding the grasps of his opponents. It was all he could do not to grimace with pain at the bigger man's grip.

"Howdy. Pleased to meet you."

"I see you have your bags," McLeod said as he opened the door and let his guests precede him into the station. "My car's out front."

* * *

AFTER THE THREE men disappeared into the station, the ticket taker put down his book and picked up the telephone in his booth. He gave the operator the exchange and waited. After a moment, he said, "Yes, this is Dan Morgan. I work at the Pendleton, Oregon, train station. I need to make a report." He waited while the person on the other line spoke.

"No, it's not about him. It's about Horace McLeod, one of the other names on that list." A pause. "Yeah, him. He met Senator Truman from the 4:15. Is he a state senator?" Another pause. "Really? From Missouri? Wow."

Morgan picked up a pencil and made a note. "Oh and there was some other guy with Truman. Didn't catch his name. He wore a cowboy hat, though." Morgan began to chew on the eraser end of the pencil. "Yeah, okay then. Just wanted to do my part, ya know. Well, you're welcome. Bye now."

Morgan hung up the telephone and hunched his shoulders, lost in thought. *A United States Senator out here in Pendleton,* he thought. *I should have gotten his autograph.*

* * *

McLeod led Truman and Hancock out into the parking lot after the two travelers had refreshed themselves. As McLeod was getting his keys from his pocket, Truman said "This is your car?"

"Yes, it is," McLeod said, a hint of pride in his voice as he admired how the sun shone off the chrome grill and the midnight blue paint. "It's a 1941 Lincoln Continental, the last major line produced before the war started." He ran a hand along the roof on the driver's side. "This baby really purrs, too. Smoothest riding car I've ever known."

He opened the back door behind the driver's seat and placed both suitcases on the seat. He leaned in and unlocked both passenger doors. The other two men climbed in, Truman in the front. McLeod slid behind the steering wheel and started the engine.

He paused with both hands on the wheel and looked over at Truman. "I deeply appreciate you both coming out here. I know you don't know me from Adam and I'm not even a constituent. But it's reached the point where I don't trust anyone official over in Richland."

"Well you can trust us," Truman said, his finger idly tracing the curve of his hat, now on his lap. "Your letters, taken as a whole, amount to something we've not encountered. Usually, we get the company cheating the government and hampering the war effort with cheap products. Yours was, well, unnerving." He glanced back at Hancock. "Carl?"

"It's certainly *unusual*, I'll give you that," Hancock said. "But I'd like to hear some more details, if you don't mind."

"We have the time," McLeod said, putting the car in gear and backing out of the parking space. "We have a little drive back up to Richland."

Hancock said, "That reminds me. Why'd you have us meet you here in Oregon? Ain't there a train station in Richland or some other town near there?"

McLeod looked at him in the rearview mirror. "I think I'm being watched. Those two hoods convinced me of that. I wanted to get out of the spotlight and meet somewhere where no one knows who I am."

"You give your name to anyone here?" Hancock asked.

"No." McLeod thought. "Yes, to the ticket man. I introduced myself and asked whether or not your train would be on time. Why, was that wrong?"

"Not necessarily, no, but it might've been better if you hadn't."

McLeod frowned. "But we're more than an hour away from Richland. Why would it matter if I gave my name down here? Besides, I live in Seattle so Richland's not even my hometown."

"But you've been in Richland for a few weeks working for your client." Truman said, seeing where Hancock was going. "You're probably known around town, too. You aren't just some worker. You're the attorney for a man suing the federal government. Word spreads in small towns when out-of-towners come in. Back in Independence, the whole town would know if so-and-so's uncle or aunt were visiting almost as soon as they arrived."

Hancock said, "Mr. McLeod, I've come late to this party. I just read your letters this morning. And I don't know what else you and Harry've talked about. Why don't you fill in some details while we're driving?"

"I didn't leave much out of the letters. I had to make a compelling case to get some help out here. As I wrote in the last letter, I've gotten to where I don't trust anyone official out here, even Ira, the local sheriff." McLeod shook his head. "Ira. That one's hard to explain. He's such a straight arrow. Nothing bad ever happened to him except for the loss of his wife back in '37. My wife and I were at Donald's house for Christmas and he'd invited Ira over so he wouldn't be alone on Christmas. He'd even…"

"Why were you at Mr. Bumble's house for Christmas?" Hancock asked, his gaze never leaving the passing scenery outside his window. "I thought you were just his lawyer."

McLeod's face reddened at the question and Truman, half facing McLeod, leaned in closer. "Is there something you've left out of your letters, Mr. McLeod?"

"It's not important, really," McLeod said, "and it doesn't have any bearing on my standing as Donald's attorney." He eased off the gas as he approached a slow-moving truck carrying crates of apples. "I didn't think you'd come out here if I wrote it in a letter."

"What is it, Mr. McLeod?" Truman asked, a bit more firmly.

"Donald, or Donnie, as my wife likes to call him, is my brother-in-law."

Truman sat back and Hancock let out a little chuckle. "Let me guess. Your sister didn't want to live on a farm for the rest of her life so she got outta there as fast as she could. 'Cept that left Mr. Bumble as the only one to tend the farm when dear old mom and dad went to the great orchard in the sky. Then, when the government took the land, your wife got all guilty and 'persuaded' you to represent her brother." The word "persuade" was said in such a way that each man, husbands all, exactly knew the meaning.

McLeod eyed the Texan sitting in his back seat. "That's about eighty percent correct. How'd you know?"

"Because I was in a similar situation. Me and your wife played the same part and my sister and Mr. Bumble played the other part. 'Course, in my case, it was the other war. Took me away from the farm and I never went back, despite what I told my sister. She hated me for a while, too. Spent the first Christmas after the war stuck at my podunk apartment in Austin." Hancock turned from his window and looked at McLeod through the rearview mirror.

"What changed your sister's mind to invite you back the next time," McLeod said.

"Oh, she didn't. After that, I met my future wife and she invited me to celebrate Christmas with her family." Hancock's voice sounded like it was far away. "Fact is, it wasn't until I went into law enforcement that Edna finally came around."

McLeod had sat up straighter. "Did you say 'law enforcement'? Are you a cop?"

Truman jumped in. "I recruited Carl straight out of the sheriff's office in Texas." He shifted in his seat so that he faced McLeod. "That's beside the point, Mr. McLeod. Aside from the many details of dates, times, witnesses, et cetera, is there anything else you need to tell us before we proceed?"

McLeod shook his head then stopped. "Well, as Donald was feeling the heat, I took steps to get him to dictate and sign an affidavit. We actually drove all the way to Walla Walla to see one of my law school buddies we could trust. He's a county judge out there. We got the affidavit four days before Donald was drafted."

Truman noticed that Hancock was nodding. "Okay, that's good," he said. "Anything else? Anything at all?"

McLeod, finally realizing the fruit truck was not going to turn anytime soon, downshifted the Lincoln and sped past the truck. "No," said McLeod, settling back into his casual driving position, the open highway before him.

"Tell us about the warehouse where Mr. Bumble worked."

"Moore Shipping and Warehousing? They have branches all over the Columbia River, from Spokane to the Pacific, as well as Portland and Seattle. I didn't know anything about them but my firm represented them once, before I was on board. The owner is Edward P. Moore, avid hunter and outdoorsman. Real Hemingway type, if you know what I mean."

The conversation went on in this manner with Truman and Hancock asking questions about Richland, other people McLeod represented, and other theories the attorney had. Hancock, his eyes rarely leaving the view outside his window, caught the first glimpse of a river he assumed was the Columbia. He also was the first one to see the police lights.

McLeod slowed the car and stopped at the junction of two roads. Both he and Truman saw the police cars, now clearly visible about fifty yards away to their right.

"That the direction we're going? Hancock asked.

"Yes."

"Good. Let's stop and say hello."

5

Monday
April 17, 1944
5:30 p.m., Pacific War Time

McLeod turned his Lincoln onto the highway and drove the short distance to where the Umatilla County, Oregon, patrol cars were parked, end-to-end along the river side. The three cruisers had their lights flashing and were half parked on the shoulder of the embankment leading down to the river.

As McLeod pulled his car over on the opposite side of the highway, Hancock had his door open before the car stopped. With a trained hand, he put on his Stetson and looked both ways. No other cars approached. The one sound that drowned out everything was that of rushing water.

"That the Columbia?" Hancock asked McLeod.

"Yes."

Hancock began to cross the highway. "The troopers must be down by the river." Truman and McLeod hurried to keep up with Hancock's eager steps.

The three men reached the patrol cars and walked around it to the river side. Down the sloping embankment, about twenty feet away, were the four uniformed police officers. One officer, taking notes on a small notepad, stood next to a man and a canoe. The other three officers were in a semi-circle around something on the ground, obscured by small shrubs and rocks.

Hancock walked a short distance to his right to get a better view. After he cleared the shrubs and rocks, he saw them: two bodies. Even from this distance, Hancock could tell that the bodies were floaters. The three officers around the bodies had their hands over their noses, trying to keep the stench under control. A sudden gust of wind brought the smell up the embankment. Truman and Hancock just grimaced. McLeod gagged and brought out his hand-kerchief.

Truman pointed down to the bodies with his chin. "That what I think it is, Carl?"

"Certainly looks like it," Hancock replied and started down the embankment. Truman followed close behind. Starting to get queasy, McLeod hesitated, but followed.

"What do you think it is?" McLeod's voice sounded small out of his own throat. Neither of the two men answered but, as McLeod got closer to the scene, he didn't need anyone to tell him. Both bodies were wearing khaki shirts and fishing vests. On the chests of both bodies were large dark blood stains.

Hancock was half way down the slope when the officer with the notepad noticed the newcomers. He excused himself and plotted an intercept course.

"Hold on a minute," the officer said. He limped over the uneven terrain. "Duncan" was stitched on his uniform. "Just where do you think you're going?"

Hancock tipped his hat to Duncan. "Howdy. We were just driving by and thought we'd stop and see if you boys needed any help."

Duncan, a young man whose uniform seemed to just hang on his slight frame, outwardly bristled at the comment. "This is official police business, sir. We do not need any *civilian* assistance."

"Well, I'm a civilian now," Hancock replied, easing his hand inside his coat pocket, "but I used to be…"

Duncan's right hand went to his service revolver, gripped the handle, and pulled the gun halfway out of its holster. His left hand, still holding the notebook, extended straight out in Hancock's direction. The Texan froze, his hand still in his coat. Truman had seen the aggressive move by the officer and stopped cold. McLeod, still staring at the dead bodies, ran into the back of the senator.

"What the…," McLeod started to say but was overwhelmed by Duncan's shout.

"Freeze right there!" Duncan's voice cracked. " Sheriff!"

The other three troopers had not noticed the newcomers until Duncan's yell. Now, two of them broke off and headed over to where Duncan stood. Hancock's eyes never strayed from the deputy's.

The sheriff, a stout, but not fat man, had easy eyes. Under his trooper's hat, his hair was trimmed neatly, the blond hair catching the sun's ray. The creases of his uniform looked crisp even if his black lace-up boots showed mud splatters. He stopped next to Duncan and looked at the newcomers. "What seems to be the trouble, Deputy?"

Duncan's hand didn't move from his gun. "These three men think that we need some help, sir. This *cowboy* here started reaching into his coat for something. What I don't know. I thought it best to bring this matter to your attention."

The sheriff eyed Hancock, Truman, and McLeod in turn and then returned to Hancock. "What've you got there in your pocket that's so important?"

Hancock's eyes still didn't leave Duncan's but he could tell the sheriff didn't feel threatened. "Deputy Duncan mentioned y'all wanted no civilian assistance. I was merely going to show him my badge."

The sheriff nodded. Hancock withdrew a small black leather case. The edges were worn and faded, and some of the stitching was frayed on the edges. He opened the badge case with one hand and showed the sheriff and Duncan its contents.

Truman was surprised when he heard the sheriff read the words on the badge. "Deputy Sheriff Carl Hancock, Harrison County, Texas." Truman wondered why Hancock still carried his deputy's badge.

"You're a long way from Texas, Deputy Hancock. What brings you and your friends out to Oregon?" The sheriff placed a hand on Duncan's right shoulder and gave it a small squeeze. Duncan eased his grip on his revolver and let his hand fall by his side.

"We're on some other business north of here, Sheriff," Hancock said, replacing his badge back in his coat. "We're traveling up to Walla Walla and, like I mentioned to the deputy, we saw lights and decided to stop." Hancock gave a small laugh and lowered his voice. "I don't know 'bout you, Sheriff, but whenever I see the red lights, I'm always itching to see what's going on. My wife hates it, especially when we're on our monthly date." He sighed and smiled. "It's a cop's curse, I guess."

Recognition crossed the sheriff's expression. Evidentially, Hancock had hit the nail on the head with his attempt to ease the tension. Another commendation for the record, he thought.

"Yeah, I'm right there with you," the sheriff said. He extended his hand. "Lester Blaine."

"Carl," Hancock replied and clasped Blaine's hand. He turned to Truman and McLeod. "This here's Harold Bruman and," he pointed to McLeod, "Hiram McLean."

Truman smiled inwardly to himself. Hancock's smooth delivery of even the most blatant of lies made him an excellent poker player.

McLeod, however, didn't get the hint. "This is Sena…"

"What do you have here, Sheriff Blaine?" Hancock asked. He glanced sharply at McLeod. It was a look so fierce that McLeod instantly shut his mouth.

Blaine eyed Hancock but said, "I'll let Deputy Rendell fill you in."

Rendell stepped forward and shook hands with everyone. He was Duncan's senior by five years and he looked at Hancock and the others through thick glasses. Unlike his boss, Rendell's uniform appeared wrinkled, perhaps from too much sitting behind a desk.

One knee was damp with water or mud, evidence, perhaps, that he knelt on the wet ground. "I was the first one who saw that canoer waving for help." He pointed over to where the other man was sitting on his overturned canoe, idly drawing shapes in the sand with a stick.

Blaine patted Duncan's back. "Joe, why don't you ask Mr. Morton if he has any extra details he might've forgotten?" It was a soft dismissal.

Duncan looked again at Hancock, turned, and all but marched back to the river's edge.

Blaine looked sheepishly at Hancock. "Sorry about that, Mr. Hancock. Joe's a good kid. Desperately wanted to join the Army in '41 but his limp kept 'em out. Farming accident. Now, he plays soldier in a deputy's uniform. Good cop but a little overzealous."

"I understand completely, Sheriff," Hancock said. "I was a young cop once, too. Always trying to impress the boss."

Blaine continued. "Plus, with the Army up there across the river, this whole area's under tight security. Everyone gets a little edgy, you know? We don't even know what's going on up there, really. Most say it just a big RDX plant. At least, that's what the Army says. Of course, they won't confirm or deny it's the secret explosive or not." Blaine motioned his head to Rendell, indicating for the deputy to continue his story.

"So, I saw Mr. Morton waving his hands frantically and stopped," Rendell said. "When I get out, Morton's eyes are all frantic and wild. 'Officer' he says, 'there's two dead men down by the river!' And he shows me." He kicked at the dirt with his boot. "I radioed the sheriff. We weren't here fifteen minutes before you showed up."

Blaine tipped his hat back. "We haven't had a murder in this county in thirteen years. I ain't even worked one." He let out an exasperated breath and shook his head. "And these two seem especially vicious."

Hancock deferred to Blaine. "Mind if we go take a look?"

"Worked murders before?"

"A few."

"Let's go," Blaine said and started walking. The five men made their way down to the river's edge where the two bodies were lying side by side on the shore. The fourth officer—Deputy Caldwell— had removed the vests from both bodies and placed them over the dead faces.

Hancock stopped at the head of one of the bodies and got down on his haunches. Truman and McLeod stood off to the right. Blaine kneeled next to Hancock and nodded to Caldwell.

Caldwell removed the vest from the first body. The dead man was probably about forty and his eyes were frozen open and bulging. Rigor mortis had formed his mouth into a tight O. Pieces of river grass were inside the mouth. The man's shaggy beard was matted with mud and the blood that had escaped from the massive cut on his neck.

At the sight of the open wound, Truman outwardly grimaced. McLeod just stood and stared, his mouth agape.

Blaine asked, "What do you think?"

Hancock pointed as he spoke. "Well, obviously, the man didn't die of drowning. That cut is clean with a well-defined line. No animal I know of, not even a bear's claw, could make a cut that clean." He poked at the dead man's hand with a stick. "He's got two broken nails and what appears to be blood under another." He nodded at the other body. "How about him?"

"Same stuff," Blaine said. "Caldwell, take that vest off the other one."

While Caldwell removed the vest from the other body, Truman asked, "Do you have any idea who these men are?"

Blaine shot a thumb back toward Duncan. "Duncan thinks it might be part of our very own local myth, the 'Mountain Men.'"

"Mountain Men?" Truman repeated.

"Yeah, that's what people took to calling them. Back in Forty when that peacetime draft law went into effect, there was a large group of people out here who didn't take kindly to the government drafting our boys when we weren't even in a war." He rested his right hand on his gun. "The way I see it, FDR saw the handwriting on the wall and thought we best be ready. Some folks here decided to escape to the mountains and hide out from the law. Remember those days, Ed?"

Caldwell nodded. "We had whole squads of men searching for those folks. They didn't want to be found and we got tired of looking for 'em. Then the Japs bombed Pearl Harbor and most of them came back."

"Why do you think most?" Truman asked, fascinated by the story.

Blaine said, "Because when some of the men came out of the woods and walked directly into the Pasco Naval Station to sign up, they told us there were still some in the woods but would never say where." He picked up a rock and began to turn it over. "Most of the unsolved burglary cases in this area are attributed to the Mountain Men. They've become local legends around here, especially since the Army came in last year. They sent out a big search party last year. Didn't find a single one."

Blaine hauled off and threw the rock into the river. He motioned at the second dead body. "So, what do you think? I got my ideas but I'd like to hear an outside opinion."

The face of the second body reflected surprised pain more than anger. The eyes were open and there were cuts on both hands between the thumb and forefinger. Unlike the first body, this man's throat was not cut. Instead, the bloodstain on his chest came from a single gash in the middle of the chest.

Hancock said, "Shoot, I even wonder if these two deaths are related." He sighed. "My guess is that whoever did this killed this one first. Explains the clean cut. The other one saw it all and tried to stop it, as evidenced by the struggle marks on his body." Blaine nodded as Hancock spoke. "Yep," he said, "I'd say you got murder one. No way these two killed each other. They were killed by someone else." He stood. "Any suspects?"

"Not a one," Blaine said and stood. "And I'm going to have the devil of a time trying to investigate."

"Why's that?" Truman asked.

"Because of the Army. They got everything within ten counties all but tied up. Sure, the big facility's in Hanford but all the surrounding counties support it. And that includes all the local law enforcement: sheriff, state patrol, city police, everyone that isn't off fighting."

Hancock laughed in commiseration. "Once, back in Texas, the governor came through our town during an election. Every single law man in the county was ordered to attend the speech, all dressed in our finest uniforms." He narrowed his eyes. "You know what happened during that speech?" He paused for effect. "Three robberies." He slapped his knee for emphasis. No one jumped except for McLeod.

Blaine laughed. "So you know how it is." He screwed up his face. "We even have lists to keep up with."

Hancock was suddenly interested but feigned otherwise. "Lists?" Truman held his breath and even McLeod perked up.

"Yeah, lists. Names of people we're supposed to look out for. The government wants to know who goes into that facility up there and, in the past few months, has expanded the perimeter to all the surrounding counties. We get updates wired to us every morning. Oh, that reminds me"—Blaine turned to Caldwell—"you got the list, right. Check it for 'Hancock,' 'Bruman', and 'McLean.'" He turned back to Hancock, looking awkward. "Regulations. Plus, sometimes we feel it's all we can do to help our GIs."

Truman, Hancock, and McLeod all steeled themselves for what might be on that list.

Caldwell retrieved a yellowed wrinkled paper from his pocket. He scanned it and said, "No Hancock or Bruman. There's a 'McLeod' but not a 'McLean.'"

Truman was actually proud of McLeod for not visibly reacting in front of Blaine. He knew that McLeod was probably screaming inside.

"Where'd you say you boys were going?" Blaine asked.

This time, Truman was the first to speak. "We're on the way up to Richland. We're insurance adjusters and, with all the dislocation of the folks up there and the growing population, there's more than enough of a market for life insurance. Our boss in Denver sent us up here to make an assessment."

"Insurance," Blaine said, wiping his forehead with a bandana and glancing at Hancock. "How'd you go from the sheriff's office to insurance?"

"The wife. She didn't like the idea of people taking shots at me during my workday so she convinced her uncle to hire me on." He shook his head, plaintively. "Can't argue with the mother of your children but I sure miss the excitement."

"Well, this is about as exciting as it's been in a long time and, frankly, I don't need this kind of excitement." Blaine nodded at the two bodies. "I hope these two had insurance."

They all heard the sound of an approaching car and turned to the highway. A coroner's van pulled up behind the patrol cars.

Truman saw an opening and took it. "Well, Sheriff, we don't want to keep you any longer. You've got some work to do and we've got to get to Richland." He shook Blaine's hand. "I hope you catch the ones that did this. And soon."

Blaine shook Truman's hand, then McLeod's, and finally Hancock's. "I know it's not your job anymore but do you think I might call you up and run things by you, if you've got a minute? Kinda let you live vicariously for a few days."

Hancock smiled warmly but his heart began to beat faster. He knew he was about to be trapped.

"Where are you staying in Richland?" Blaine asked.

Without thinking, McLeod said, "The Hurley Hotel." Even then, he didn't realize his error. Hancock and Truman both wanted to slug him.

"Fine hotel. Be sure to eat at Grover's Restaurant just two doors down. Best damn steaks in this part of the world. I take the missus there on our special dates."

"Will do," Hancock said and all three turned and began walking up the slope. As they reached the road, two men from the county morgue began to make their way down the slope carrying two stretchers.

6

———————

Monday
17 April 1944
5:55 p.m., Pacific War Time

As soon as the three men got in the car, McLeod's emotions burst out.

"Did you see those bodies? They were all bloated and white and…and…the blood. Holy cow! And the neck on that one guy. And their eyes, they were so dead, clouded…. And the grass in the mouth." He shuddered at this point, a full body shudder.

"Horace, will you please shut up!" Hancock's voice was louder than he wanted it to be but it was just as well. It was like a slap in the face and McLeod stopped speaking in mid-sentence.

Truman took the silence as an opportunity to get the discussion going on their next move. "So, Carl, you're upset that you let Sheriff Blaine trap you into revealing where we're staying. And you don't like that Mr. McLeod let slip the name of the hotel. So, where does that leave us? Are there any other hotels in Richland?"

McLeod shook his head. "The owner, Mrs. Reta Hurley, has two rooms for you. Other than that, nearly all the hotels in the area are booked." He glanced over to Truman. "So, what do we do? Use the names Carl made up?"

"No, that won't work," Truman said "because you've already registered under your own name. Sheriff Blaine knows Carl's name so that leaves me as the only one he doesn't know. And, I assume, since you know the owner by name, she also knows you by name."

McLeod nodded. "She's a real nice lady. She took over the hotel when her husband went off to war. He died in Italy last year."

There was a moment of silence in the car. In his own way, each man said a silent prayer for the woman and the husband she lost. It was a common occurrence for those on the home front.

"Senator, you can at least sign in using the Bruman name," Hancock said. "That would keep your identity from getting out. The folks out here are used to seeing the military. We don't know what they would do if they knew a U.S. Senator was in town."

"They ought to be damn glad a senator is taking notice of their plight." Some of the righteous indignation returned to McLeod's voice. "And that reminds me," he said, eyeing Hancock in the back seat, "why didn't you want me to let the sheriff know who Mr. Truman is? I'd think that a man of his stature would command some respect. He's not just some senator, you know. He's the chairman of an important committee."

Truman said, "The reason we want to keep our presence as quiet as possible is that when the business people I'm investigating find out who I am, they clam up. You can't get one word out of their mouths without a crowbar." His mouth was a hard line and he shook his head in regret. "I can never get them to understand that I'm looking out for what's best for America. And, by damn, they shouldn't be sticking it to Uncle Sam. We're at war, by God, and all they want to do is make a lousy buck." Truman's voice had grown sharp with anger.

"Take it easy, Harry," Hancock soothed. "You're preaching to the choir here."

The rest of the trip to Richland passed with talk of the war. The land, unlike other areas of Washington State, was arid and desert-like. From a distance, Richland appeared to literally rise out of the ground. Beyond the town, mountains rose from the flatland. Closer in, there were only mountains of brick and mortar. The tallest things in the town were the electrical poles sticking out of the ground. In the distinctive downtown area, a few buildings were three stories tall but not many.

"That where the government is?" Hancock asked, motioning to an area across the river.

"Yes, that's Hanford," McLeod said.

Northward, paved roads lined the flat sandy soil. A railroad track disappeared into the distance. Most of the roads linked separate neighborhoods, literally carved into the ground. In one area, there was row upon row of what looked like cylinders buried in the ground. A second section appeared more like a traditional neighborhood, with houses and small yards. Closer to the river were scores of trailers, parked side-by-side. In all the areas, streets formed a neat grid.

Along the highway leading into Richland, there were a series of billboards at regular intervals. None of them sponsored a product or a service. All of them extolled the citizens of Richland to their patriotic duty. "Keep Kiddies Clear of Construction" read one while another was "Minutes Mean Men's Lives." Other, more pointed billboards featured "Smash Japan! 6th War Loan." The last billboard before they entered downtown read, "Don't Open the Book with Careless Conversation." It featured a book that looked like a girl's diary with a padlock to keep out prying eyes.

Truman chuckled. "That's a good variation on the 'Loose Lips Sink Ships' theme."

McLeod drove through the warehouse district next to the Columbia River. There were a few structures five and six stories tall but not many. Truman and Hancock didn't need McLeod to point out which warehouse Edward Moore owned. In the late afternoon sun, the five-story tall warehouse cast a long shadow across the river. On the roof, in giant metal letters, rose a sign of the owner's name. The word "Moore" appeared in reverse on the calm waters of the Columbia.

McLeod parked the Lincoln in front of a three-story red brick building. From the outside, it looked no different from the general store two doors down or any of the one-story structures along the block. A large sign reading "Hotel" was the only thing distinguishing the building from being a typical business establishment.

The three men got out of the car and looked around. People were walking up and down the sidewalk, talking, laughing, and generally passing the time. There was a general hustle even now, at a few minutes past six o'clock. Hancock commented about it.

"Oh, it's shift change from four to six. There's always a lot more people around. We might need to wait a bit before we go to eat."

A few doors down from the hotel entrance, Truman noticed a small line forming at the door to a restaurant. "That the restaurant Sheriff Blaine talked about?"

"Yup," McLeod said, reaching in the back seat and retrieving the two suitcases. "It's the best place in town by a mile. Like I said, let's check in and give the crowd some time to leave. It starts to thin out after seven."

He came around the car and handed the suitcases to Truman and Hancock. "So, let's go over this again. I can't use the fake name Carl gave me and I can't change my name because Mrs. Hurley knows me. Carl gave the sheriff his own name so the only person who can still be incognito is Mr. Truman. So," he lifted his eyebrows to Truman, "you going to go along with it?"

The senator thought for a moment and looked at Hancock. "I don't have a problem with me using an alias. Might even help the matter. What do you think, Carl?"

Hancock nodded and started walking to the door. "C'mon, let's get in there. I'm starving."

McLeod hurried ahead of Truman and Hancock and held the door for them. They entered a small foyer. The check-in desk was to the left. On the deep mahogany counter sat a ledger and a small bell. Behind the counter, a sign in wooden letters read: Hurley Hotel. Beside the sign, in a small alcove, was a shelf with sixteen numbered slots. McLeod tapped the bell.

From the back office, came a rustling and the squeak of a chair. A woman appeared in the doorway. Her green dress was plain, but she wore it as if she were headed off to church. She was tall for a woman, a couple inches shy of six feet. Her brunette hair was pulled back from her face and fashioned into an exquisite bun. Her hair framed her face which was marked by a smooth forehead and high cheekbones. Her blue eyes appeared like sun hitting the ocean. Her nose was thin but her mouth was wide. The only sign of age were the slight wrinkles under her eyes.

She glanced once at McLeod, then Hancock, and rested her eyes on Truman. She broke into a smile that was not entirely genuine, McLeod noted. Odd, he thought, Mrs. Hurley was usually so buoyant.

In a move that caught the three men by surprise, Reta Hurley, staying behind the counter, walked over and stood directly in front of Truman. "Senator Truman, glad you finally arrived. I trust you had a good trip from Washington, D.C." She stood there with a look of absolute power over the situation.

Truman was stunned but missed barely a beat. "Thank you, Mrs. Hurley. My trip to Richland was uneventful. The long train ride allowed me time to answer constituent letters and read up on the bills I have to vote on next week." He turned his head looking around the foyer. "And I must say you have quite a fine establishment here. This is nicer than most places I stay. You must be very proud." His gaze returned to her. "Do you get a lot of out-of-town guests?"

She was unfazed by Truman's attempt to change the subject. "We certainly do. Pasco's got a naval air station just up the road. Hotels up there fill rather quickly. We get the overflow as does Kennewick. Now we have the Army just up the road." She smiled without humor and looked at McLeod. "I can imagine Mr. McLeod has told you all about that."

McLeod shifted his feet and looked at the alcoves behind the desk. "Do I have any messages?"

Without looking back, Hurley said, "Yes. One from your wife and one from your law firm." She turned, retrieved two slips of yellow telegraph paper, and handed them to McLeod.

Returning her gaze to Truman, she said, "Mr. Truman, you will be in Room 8, just down the hall from Mr. McLeod. Your friend can stay in Room 9. Mr. McLeod has already taken care of the fee."

Truman stepped forward and placed his hat on the counter. "I'm afraid that'll be impossible. I'm here as an official representative of the United States government and I'll pay my own way. And I'll need receipts, as well, if you don't mind." His tone was formal but friendly.

"Very well," she said, turning the ledger around so that it faced Truman. "Will you please sign in?"

Truman picked up the fountain pen and scratched his name in the ledger. He scanned the other names and found McLeod's ten names above. He turned and gave the pen to Hancock.

The Texan walked up and nodded. Intentionally, he signed his name using one of his more illegible signatures. He placed the pen back on its pedestal and smiled. "Thank you very much, ma'am, for giving us a room."

Hurley looked at the Stetson in his hand. "Are you from Texas, mister…?"

Hancock grimaced. "Hancock, ma'am, Carl Hancock. I work for Senator Truman."

"You work for the American people, Carl," Truman said. "We both do. You work *with* me."

"Certainly, sir."

McLeod saw an opportunity to jump into the conversation. "Well, Mrs. Hurley, I know our travelers would like to settle into their room before we have dinner at Grover's. What's the special tonight?"

"Salmon, I think," she said, handing Truman and Hancock their keys. "Enjoy yourselves and welcome to Richland." She put on her best professional smile.

"Right this way, sirs," McLeod said as he led Truman and Hancock to the stairs.

* * *

SHE WAITED until the three men reached the landing of the second floor before she picked up the telephone. "Reta Hurley of Hurley Hotel," she said to the question from the other line.

"Yes, they just arrived. Yes, there were three of them: McLeod, the senator, and a Carl Hancock. He's a Texan judging by the cowboy hat. It won't be hard to follow him. He's a tall one." She listened. "No, they're going to eat at Grover's, the restaurant, just a few doors down."

She idly smoothed her blouse as she listened. "Yes, I understand. I'll call you whenever they leave and when they return. Don't worry, sir, I'll do my part. Yes, sir, it's an honor and Charlie would be proud. Good-bye."

Mrs. Hurley hung up the telephone and moved her hand to the photograph of her husband, posing proudly in his Army uniform. As she ran a hand along its frame, she began to cry.

7

Monday
17 April 1944
7:20 p.m., Pacific War Time

It didn't take long for Truman and Hancock to put away their bags and settle in their rooms. Truman took care to hang his suit so that the wrinkles would fade.

After twenty minutes, the two men met McLeod in the hallway and walked down the stairs. When they reached the foyer, Truman walked over to the counter where the manager sat reading a newspaper. "Mrs. Hurley," Truman said, placing his hand on the counter, "the room is splendid. I'm sure we'll be well rested every morning. Where do you recommend I get my shirts pressed?"

Hurley closed the paper but kept a finger in it to mark her place. "You can give them to me, Senator. I do the laundry around here. How heavy on the starch?"

"Heavy," Truman replied. "I like my shirts to stay fresh and looking neat. I'll drop them off tomorrow after we leave on our business."

"And what business brings you all the way across the country?"

Truman was nonplussed. "The American people's business," he said and softly tapped the counter. "Good evening, Mrs. Hurley."

The three men exited the hotel and turned left to walk down to the restaurant. She waited a full minute before she picked up the telephone. Again, she stated her name and told the person on the other line what time Truman, Hancock, and McLeod had left and where they went.

After hanging up the telephone, she dropped the newspaper on the counter and went into the supply closet. She retrieved furniture polish and a towel and began to clean the lobby.

* * *

SHERIFF LESTER BLAINE sat at his desk and looked at the two pieces of paper in front of him. On one was the typewritten list of names issued by the Army. On the other was the handwritten names the three men had given Deputy Rendell: Carl Hancock, Harold Bruman, and Hiram McLean. Under those names Rendell had scrawled "Hurley Hotel."

Blaine scratched his chin and looked down his nose at the names. That Hancock was a smooth customer. But then again, he used to be a deputy in Texas. They probably had some wild men down there to make Hancock seem ordinary.

Still, there was something there about those three men, something just under the surface. The one guy, McLean, who seemed positively green at the sight of the floaters, kept wanting to say something the other two didn't want him to mention.

Blaine picked up the telephone and asked the operator to connect him to the Hurley Hotel in Richland. After waiting a few seconds, he heard a woman's voice on the other end.

"Hurley Hotel."

"May I speak with the manager, please?" Blaine asked.

"This is Reta Hurley, the owner and manager. How may I help you?"

Up until that moment, Blaine had not decided whether to go the official route and identify himself or the unofficial route and pose as a customer. He chose the former.

"This is Sheriff Lester Blaine of Umatilla County, Oregon. I'm calling to locate a man I met today. He said if I needed his assistance, I could call him. His name is Carl Hancock."

"Yes, Sheriff, Mr. Hancock and Mr. Truman checked in this afternoon."

Blaine frowned. "Truman? You mean Harold Bruman?"

"No, Truman. With a T. And I've never heard the senator referred to that way but that might be his Christian name."

Blaine's eyes widened at the mention of a senator. "I'm sorry, did you say 'senator'?"

"Yes, Senator Harry Truman. He and Mr. Hancock are in town from Washington, D.C. for an inspection or something. Shall I tell Mr. Hancock that you called?"

Blaine's mind whirled and he couldn't think straight. "No thank you, ma'am. I'll call him tomorrow. Thank you for your help. Good-bye."

Blaine hung up the phone and didn't move for a minute. He sat there, thinking. A United States Senator out here on an inspection? It had to be a part of the giant construction site up north of Richland. But why did they not just tell him who they were and why they were here?

He sighed and stood. He was just a county sheriff. Why should a federal man even give him the time of day? He had better things to worry about, namely two dead men.

Still, information never hurt. He called for Deputy Joe Duncan and assigned him the task of finding out what he could about Senator Harry Truman.

8

Monday
17 April 1944
7:45 p.m., Pacific War Time

The walk to the restaurant was brief. They only had to wait a few minutes before being seated. Hancock and McLeod ordered coffee, served in thick white porcelain cups. Truman opted for iced tea. A waitress came and took their orders. Truman and Hancock decided to take Blaine's recommendation and ordered the steaks. McLeod ordered salmon. While they waited for their food, Truman and Hancock surveyed the room.

The wall facing the street was all glass with the painted words "Grover's Restaurant" seen in reverse from the inside. There were about thirty tables on the floor and twenty booths crowded both walls. The kitchen was in the rear but the patrons could see the cooks toiling away through the three-quarter wall that separated the kitchen from the dining room. The sizzle of food filled the air.

The patrons of Grover's were a mixed bunch. Many were construction workers, their coveralls caked with dirt and grime. Truman also noticed quite a few men in uniform.

McLeod was finally in familiar surroundings and it showed in his disposition. He was smiling and quite happy to be playing tour guide. He filled in some minor details that had slipped his mind when he was questioned earlier that day. While he was putting sugar in his coffee, McLeod said, "Okay, what's our first step tomorrow?"

Hancock deferred to Truman. "Well, Mr. McLeod, I think the first thing we do is pay a visit to the Moore Warehouse. I expect we'll meet with Mr. Moore and see if we can get to the bottom of your little issue."

"Senator Truman," McLeod said, setting his cup back on the saucer, "please call me 'Horace.'" He sat there, expecting the reciprocal from Truman. It didn't come.

Hancock stifled a smile and jumped to McLeod's rescue. "You mentioned Edward Moore is often traveling to all his different warehouses and factories throughout the state. Do you know if he's here now?"

McLeod shook his head. "I don't, but the Richland warehouse is the biggest one he owns. He expanded it just last year to accommodate the Army. And then there was that sign. What'd you think of that sign?"

"Screams vanity to me," Truman said. He gestured with his hands as he spoke. "This is a town with very few buildings over three stories and this man put his name atop a building that's five stories tall. I just don't understand that kind of ostentatiousness. And believe me, I work in a town with plenty of that. I know about half the Congress would like to put their names up between the porticos of the Capital building." He shook his head. "It's barons like this that give the honest man such a hard time trying to do right."

Hancock said, "Harry, that doesn't sound like you. It's like you have pre-judged Moore and..."

"Of course I've pre-judged him," Truman retorted. "Why else would we be out here?" He signaled the waitress for more tea and returned his gaze to Hancock. "Now, that doesn't mean I can't change my mind. Hell, it could be just some misunderstanding coupled with our active imaginations."

McLeod shot Truman a stern look. "You don't really believe that, do you, Mr. Truman? I mean, don't get me wrong, but our imaginations didn't draft my brother-in-law."

"No, not really. But there still might be a simple explanation."

Hancock said, "Yeah, like 'How can we get rid of this guy? Hey, let's draft him.'"

The waitress arrived with their dinners. Up until that moment, they didn't realize how hungry they were. All conversation stopped as they devoured their food.

After a while, Hancock sat back in his chair and rubbed his stomach with both hands. "I think I'm going to have to call up Blaine myself and let him know that he was right about…Harry, what is it?"

At that, McLeod looked up from his plate at Truman. The senator sat frozen, his fork halfway between plate and mouth. His mouth was set in a hard line. His eyes, magnified behind his glasses, were not kind. "Gentlemen," he said quietly, "our supper is about to get very interesting."

Hancock, his back to the door, turned around to see where Truman was looking. McLeod, to Truman's left, turned his gaze toward the front door.

At the entrance to the restaurant stood two men. They garnered no attention from the other patrons as everyone was accustomed to seeing men in uniform. The two men wore matching Army uniforms: khaki shirts over khaki trousers. Their ties, also khaki, were tucked into their shirts just below the second button. As they stood in the doorway, scanning the room, each man tucked his garrison cap through his belt.

One man spotted the senator and began walking toward their table. The other man followed close behind, nodding at people he knew.

Hancock turned back to Truman. "Well, that was quick. Who you reckon they are?"

"The older one I know. He's Colonel Franklin Matthias. He's the local man in charge of this project. I don't know the other one."

McLeod, still facing the approaching men, said, "What are we going to do?" There was clear tension in his voice.

"See what they have to say," Truman replied. He dabbed his mouth with a napkin.

The two Army officers made their way to the table and stood facing Truman. Only thirty-six years old, Matthias's hair was cut and combed like a soldier. His hair was dark on top, but the temples already had started to gray. He had a small mouth with a dimple on his chin.

The former civil engineer smiled as he extended his hand. "Senator." Truman shook the offered hand, half rising in his chair. "Colonel."

Matthias motioned to the other man with him. "This is Major Nicholas Lynch, security and counter-intelligence officer for Hanford."

Unlike his superior officer, Lynch's uniformed looked as if it had been tailored to his body. His shirt was ironed, the cuffs peeking out from his jacket sleeves at a fashionable length. His black shoes all but sparkled. His dark hair was not cut in the Army style, but swept to the side, almost like a movie star. His clean-shaven face looked chiseled, with hard cheekbones and a thin mouth. But his most distinguishing feature was his eyes. His deep, penetrating stare bore into the senator and Truman got the instant impression Major Lynch missed nothing.

Truman gestured to Hancock. "Carl Hancock, special investigator for the committee and this is…"

"Oh, we know who this is," Lynch cut in. His voice sounded educated, like he had attended a prestigious university in the east, and likely led the debate team. "Horace McLeod, attorney at law. He came all the way from Seattle to cause trouble and slow down the war effort with his excessive litigation."

McLeod's ire rose quickly. "Listen here, Major. The Army is the one who's at fault here. It didn't offer a fair compensation for my client and all the other farmers and homeowners who were summarily booted off their own land. To think we're fighting tyranny abroad and right here in our own country, the government acts like…"

Truman put a hand on McLeod's arm to calm him and prevent the lawyer from saying anything stupid. "What can we do for you gentlemen?"

Truman noticed the fire in Lynch's eyes didn't go out as Matthias spoke. Lynch, and everyone else, knew where McLeod was going with his statement. That it was unspoken didn't matter.

"We'd like to talk with you for a few minutes, Senator Truman," Matthias said.

"Sure," Truman said. "Why don't you pull a table over here and join us?"

"Alone, Senator."

Truman read Hancock's expression: don't do it.

"Carl," Truman said, "would you and Mr. McLeod mind excusing us for a few minutes? The colonel and I have some things to discuss."

Hancock glanced up at Matthias and Lynch. The two men didn't move. With a sigh, Hancock said, "C'mon, Horace. Let's leave 'em to talk." He got up from his chair, not too subtly brushing Lynch as he did so. "Y'all got a newsstand around here?"

McLeod downed the rest of his coffee and rose from his chair. "Sure. A block and a half down the street. Next to the movie theater." All the time McLeod was getting up and moving toward the door, Lynch constantly watched him.

"Great," Hancock said and looked at Truman. "That's where we'll be, Harry. Meet us there after y'all's pow wow." Hancock nodded at Matthias but not at Lynch.

Hancock and McLeod made their way to the front door and exited. Truman motioned for Matthias and Lynch to have a seat. Matthias sat in the seat next to Truman while Lynch sat in the seat vacated by Hancock. Truman motioned for more iced tea.

"No, thank you," Lynch said.

Truman smiled. "I want some more. Colonel?"

Matthias nodded and Truman held up one finger. The waitress arrived with one extra cup, and filled it as well as Truman's glass.

Truman caught the small smile she threw in Lynch's direction and made a mental note.

"Gentlemen, what would y'all like to discuss?" Truman said.

"Well, Senator," Matthias said, "for starters, why don't you tell us what you're doing out here? You and Stimson had an agreement that your committee would look the other way."

"He probably thinks he can talk the government out of its money and hurt our boys overseas," Lynch muttered.

Truman realized that he didn't like Lynch. "Far from the truth, sir," he said looking at Matthias and ignoring Lynch. "Investigator Hancock and I are looking into alleged embezzlement at one of the warehouses in Richland."

Lynch let out a sardonic laugh. "You see? We're trying to beat Hitler and the Japs and he's worried about money." He leaned on the table and gave Truman a penetrating stare. "At what price freedom?"

Truman turned to face Lynch. "At what price integrity with the people's money? Our government has a duty to be honest with the American people. And part of that honesty is how their money is spent. Lincoln had the devil of a time with Congress poking and prodding his every move. That's not my aim when I created this committee." He started chopping the air with his hands. "You may not realize it but I proposed the creation of a committee to help *win* the war and bring as many of our boys back alive as possible." He paused and softened his tone but not his rhetoric. "There is more than one way to beat the enemy."

Lynch was trying to form a retort but none came. Matthias broke the silence. "I see. I guess we all want to do our part." He paused to lend his next words more resonance. "And what we're doing here will help win this war. What we're doing here needs absolute secrecy, with no outside interference from anyone. That's why you and Stimson agreed that you and your committee wouldn't look into anything we're doing here."

"I understand, Colonel," Truman said, "and that's why I am not asking about it. Secretary Stimson said it was very important, that it would help win the war, and it needed to be conducted with the utmost secrecy, and that was, and is, good enough for me." He drank some iced tea and set down the glass. "I won't be responsible for sabotaging this project."

Truman looked over at Lynch. "I must congratulate you, Major, on finding us so quickly. With security like this, I know you'll get your job done as quickly as possible. I supposed Mrs. Hurley called you?"

Lynch didn't reply.

Truman nodded. "Thanks for the clarification." He turned his attention to Matthias. "But do your tactics have to include the drafting of innocent civilians?"

"There are no civilians in this war, Mr. Truman," Lynch said. "We are all combatants."

Matthias said, "We do what we have to do to keep the project secret. If the Germans or the Japs found out about any aspect of it, the outcome of the war might be different. Look, Senator, people are instructed not to have idle conversations about their work here. We don't even want husbands to talk to their wives about the work they do. Everyone, everyday is reminded of their duty. If some folks still don't shut up, we shut them up."

"Just like that?" Truman asked.

"Just like that," Lynch said. "Since you're with McLeod, I assume it's about that farmer that we drafted last week?"

"Yes. His name is Donald Bumble. He lived on a farm in this area before the Army came in. The issue about the price of his land is not my concern. What is my concern are his suspicions of illegal activities going on at the warehouse where he worked."

Lynch nodded and leaned back in his chair. "From what we were told, he was becoming a security risk. And that doesn't even include the shitstorm his lawyer was kicking up."

Truman looked puzzled. "From what you were told?' You mean you didn't have firsthand knowledge of Mr. Bumble's actions?"

"We don't have to," Lynch said. "We have good patriotic Americans living and working around here. They keep their eyes and ears open for any sign of trouble." He smiled without humor. "You might want to let Mr. McLeod know that even though he's forty-seven…" He let the unspoken words hang in the air.

Truman brushed aside the threat. "Colonel, I would very much like to know who recommended Mr. Bumble be drafted. Based on what you told me and what I've been told by Mr. McLeod, you might have been duped." Truman related the gist of Bumble's story.

After Truman finished, Lynch snickered. "Boy, that's a story. You think the old farmer came up with that himself or did he have help from the lawyer?"

Truman's blood was beginning to boil at Lynch's insolence. He was about to retort when Matthias said, "So, I assume your first trip tomorrow will be to the warehouse?"

For once, Truman was not happy at the diversion but inhaled deeply. "Yes, Mr. Hancock and I will be there in the morning."

"You wouldn't mind, then, letting me know what you find out, will you Senator?"

"Colonel, I would be happy to. It's my standard operating procedure to let those companies under investigation read and respond to any report before my committee makes the report public. I'll share my findings with you. Like you said, we all want to do our part. Now, if you don't mind, I'm going to turn in for the evening. It's been a long day." He motioned to the waitress and pulled his wallet from his coat pocket."

As she walked over, Matthias waved his hand toward Truman. "Senator, please, let the Army pick up your tab."

"No, Colonel, the Senate will pay my bill." To the waitress, he said, "And I'll need a receipt."

9

Monday
17 April 1944
8:15 p.m., Pacific War Time

Truman exited the restaurant and inhaled the fresh air. He knew that Matthias and Lynch were watching him and decided to give them a show. He placed his hat on his head, making sure the brim was situated just so, and began to walk briskly toward the newsstand.

As a man who grew up in a small town, he was accustomed to being out at night, visiting neighbors or watching the local brass band in the town square of Independence, Missouri. Richland was certainly larger than Independence even before the Army arrived. Now that the federal presence was here, the town of Richland felt like a city. As a failed businessman, he envied the owners of the establishments he passed along his stroll. All the businesses—five-and-dime stores, drugstores, and barber shops—were open for business and thriving. The war was changing everything.

He reached the newsstand and found McLeod reading a Seattle newspaper, the latest copy of *Time* under his arm. Hancock noticed

Truman. "So, Harry, they kicking us out?" McLeod, upon hearing Hancock's question, folded his paper and tucked it next to *Time*.

Truman allowed a smile to come across his face. "No, Carl, they aren't kicking us out. They just wanted to know what we're doing here."

"Did you tell them?"

"I did. I figured honesty was the best course of action. Matthias seemed mildly interested, even wanting me to report our findings to him directly. But that Lynch fellow…he's a real piece of work. I already don't like him."

Hancock grinned. "He's just the bulldog, Harry, like I am for you."

McLeod said, "How did they find us so quickly?"

Truman looked at the lawyer. "With the secret government operation just up the road, the Army, justifiably, has its eyes and ears everywhere. Mrs. Hurley told them."

"What?" McLeod said.

"Don't be too hard on her. Her husband died overseas and she was just doing her part to help the war effort. Now as to how she knew we were coming, I'm not quite sure. She certainly could have recognized me but I doubt it. I suspect Lynch called her to let her know Carl and I were coming. The only way that could've happened was if someone was watching you pick us up at the train station."

"You mean someone followed me to Pendleton?"

"No," Hancock said. "It means that the 'eyes and ears' of the Army extend that far south. I bet that ticket guy heard your name and called Lynch. He put two and two together and bam, they knew that Harry and I would probably stay with you." Now he tapped McLeod's arm with each word. "You have got to start watching what you say." He looked over at Truman. "Of course, that probably doesn't matter now. I bet the whole town knows we're here."

Truman pondered the statement. "No, I don't think so. You see how many folks they have here? There must be thousands. We might still be able to do some good work here without too much trouble. Right before I left, I asked Matthias not to give the people at Moore's Warehouse any advance notice of our arrival tomorrow. He agreed as long as I report to him what we find."

Hancock sighed. McLeod looked at him and then at Truman. "What?"

Truman looked to Hancock, giving him leave to voice his own opinion. "You see, Horace, the military don't like what we're doing much. They'd rather be left alone and run the war as they see fit. What they don't realize is that Harry's committee has saved the people millions of dollars and the military a large headache. We have the same objectives. The brass doesn't often see it that way. So they mess with us and make it more difficult to do our job, like reporting to them while we're here. We represent the United States Senate, not some military bureaucracy."

Truman hid his grin by speaking. He loved it that Carl could be so passionate about his job. "Carl certainly has some opinions about our business. But, suffice it to say, we'll follow Matthias's request because, to do otherwise, might get us kicked out of the area and we won't have resolved your problem."

Truman held up the back of his hand to hide the yawn that suddenly escaped. "Which reminds me, I'm going to turn in. Railroads can be comfortable if that's all you have but I'm looking forward to a bed that doesn't move. What about you two?"

Hancock and McLeod exchanged glances. Hancock spoke. "Actually, Harry, I'm gonna buy these"—he held up the stack of periodicals in his hand—"and me and Horace are going to catch the feature next door at the theater. They're showing the latest Bugs Bunny cartoon called Nip the Nips and Spencer Tracy's A Guy Named Joe."

Truman pointed at the stack of material in Hancock's hand. "What've you got there?"

Hancock beamed with pride. "The latest issues of *Batman, Detective Comics, Superman,* and *Captain America.*" He stopped when he saw Truman's broad smile. "It's for Tom." To McLeod, he said, "That's my son."

"But I imagine his father might've read over every page by the time you get back home, huh?"

Hancock gave a sheepish smile. "Hey, it's good entertaining reading."

Truman patted Hancock on the back. "I know how it is, Carl. I'm expected to bring Margaret back something, too." He shook McLeod's hand. "Well, Mr. McLeod, it's good to meet you. I hope we can get to the bottom of this. Breakfast at seven. We'll meet in the lobby so Mrs. Hurley can see us. Good night, gentlemen."

Truman turned and walked down the street, his pace brisk despite his tiredness.

The two men stared at the retreating figure of the senator. McLeod said, "He certainly is persistent and direct. You would never guess it by the looks of him."

Hancock chuckled. "Just you wait. If the people at the warehouse start obstructing us, they will see an entirely different side of Harry Truman. C'mon. Let's get some tickets."

10

Monday
17 April 1944
10:30 p.m., Pacific War Time

Hancock and McLeod emerged from the theater with the other moviegoers and into the darkened night. They stopped under a street lamp and McLeod fished out a pack of Lucky Strikes he had purchased at the newsstand. He shook one out and offered it to Hancock who took it.

"I don't usually smoke," Hancock said, "I prefer chewing my tobacco but my wife doesn't care for it much. So, I chew gum." He put the tip of the cigarette against the flame of McLeod's Zippo and inhaled deeply. "Damn, that's good."

"I've got it easier," McLeod said. "My wife smokes her Chesterfields and I have my Luckys."

"That's all well and good but I suggest you not light up around Harry. He doesn't like smoking."

"I'll try and remember." The two started walking slowly back to the hotel. After a moment, McLeod said, "Do you believe in angels, like Tracy was in the movie?"

"What, guardian angels?" Hancock asked.

"Yeah."

"Boy, I'd sure like to, you know? But it's a little difficult to believe in angels when you've got men dying all over the world. I bet each one of them think they have a guardian angel, especially the ones who live through battles. But what does a man think about after he's shot and dyin' right there on the battlefield? You think he thinks his guardian angel left 'em?"

McLeod looked thoughtful. "Perhaps their guardian angel is the first thing they see as the heavens are opened and they see the great beyond."

Hancock nodded. "Kinda like the angel saying 'I've watched you through your entire life and, now that you've died, welcome home.' I think you got something there, Horace."

They both heard the sound of an airplane high in the sky. It was faint and far away but distinct.

"That's odd," McLeod said.

"What?"

"Well, there's the naval training station over in Pasco, about thirty miles to the south. Ever since I've been here in Richland, these past two weeks, whenever I hear planes, they are usually lower, like they're readying to land. This one is either far away or very high."

McLeod was looking up and Hancock did as well. He saw nothing but the stars in the moonless sky. "I bet these buildings around here make everything sound funny. That's the way it is in D.C. Too much marble and concrete does strange things to sound."

Hancock tapped McLeod's shoulder and started walking. "C'mon, Horace, I'm tired. Besides, you never know. Maybe what they're building up there at Hanford's a big new plane."

"I heard it has something to do with RDX," McLeod said, keeping stride with Hancock.

"The explosive? Why would they build a huge complex out here, in the middle of nowhere, just to make more RDX? They do that down in Tennessee."

"Don't know. That's just what I heard." McLeod tossed his

cigarette butt to the pavement and ground it out with his shoe. "You're probably right. I'm a lawyer. What the hell do I know about planes?"

As the two men started walking again, Hancock noted the puzzlement on McLeod's face.

* * *

THE JOB of radar operator Jack Bower in south central Washington State, sixty miles west of Hanford, was one step up from complete boredom. Grounded because he wore thick glasses, the blonde-haired young man had many hours to kill sitting in front of the radar screen, waiting for something to appear. He spent much of this time reading his favorite magazines: *Amazing Stories* and *The Magazine of Fantasy and Science Fiction.* Many of his fellow soldiers ribbed him. "Did you see any UFOs today, Jack?" Bower would just smile, his head a million miles away.

As part of the daily routine, Bower was always provided with the flight schedules of the surrounding airports and air bases. He enjoyed watching the radar screen as the squadrons practiced their flying techniques or training new pilots.

Every time a blip appeared on his radar screen, he referenced the flight schedules. There were quite a few so it would take him a little time to locate the actual flight. He would then put a checkmark next to the flight in question and watch the blip until it disappeared off the screen.

And so it was, on the evening of 17 April a blip appeared on his screen. He put down his magazine and picked up the stack of papers listing the known flights from all the surrounding airfields.

As he did this, the blip moved across his screen. The screen was situated like a standard compass so that the top of the round screen was north, the bottom south, the left was west, and the right east. The blip was moving left-to-right across his screen, west-to-east.

Bower finished scanning all the flight schedules and frowned. He found no regularly scheduled flight at this time of night on this day.

Thinking that he must have missed the listing, Bower scanned the lists again, this time more slowly.

The blip continued to move east.

He finished his second review of the schedules and was convinced, more so this time, that he had made no error. There was no scheduled flight. It was then that he realized he no longer heard the blip.

Bower looked at the screen and watched the sweep line turn around the screen. He did this for ten sweeps and no more blips appeared. Whatever it was—bird, cloud, plane—it was now out of range of his radar. Shrugging his shoulders, he picked up his magazine and began to read again.

Five minutes later, a blip appeared on his screen. Again, he put down the magazine and looked at the screen. This time, the blip was moving right-to-left, indicating an east-to-west movement.

Having just reviewed the lists, he glanced at the clock above his station and noted the time: 11:36 p.m. He made a record of the blip on a notepad. He was all alone in the duty station. The rest of the crew were in their barracks, sound asleep.

Bower thought for a moment. He could rouse his commanding officer and let him know what he saw. But, he thought to himself, what had he seen? A blip on his radar screen, two blips actually. He had no proof of anything, really.

He decided to note the blip in the official log. Tomorrow, during his off-time, he would call the neighboring airfields and inquire about any unscheduled flights. Just to satisfy his own curiosity.

He watched the blip pass out of range and off his screen. The audio blip was hypnotic, especially with no one else around. After the blip passed out of range, he began reading.

11

Monday
17 April 1944
10:45 p.m. Pacific War Time

In their three previous meetings, Captain Morimoto's movements on American soil had been tentative. He had brought guards with him during the initial meeting, his first mate on the second trip, and his munitions officer on the third. Tonight, the man with Morimoto had a seemingly incongruous insignia on his uniform. There was a plane stitched on a patch on the man's left sleeve. Why, thought Koishii, did Morimoto have someone from the Japanese air corps onboard a submarine?

The two submariners were kneeling opposite the American in the makeshift tent, the airman to the captain's left. As was now a custom at these meetings, Koishii had prepared tea. He apologized for not providing any additional provisions. He could not see the two guards stationed outside the tent but felt their presence through the calm demeanor of Morimoto.

The captain's disposition was different tonight, Koishii thought. He appeared calm, calmer than he had ever been, but there was something different. Koishii had seen behavior like this before, in poker games he played with some of his friends. This was the behavior of a man with an ace up his sleeve.

"Good evening, Koishii," Morimoto said. "You honor me again with your attention to detail of the Japanese tea ceremony." The captain bowed to Koishii. The American returned the gesture.

Morimoto gestured to the Japanese sailor sitting next to him. "I have brought with me a most special officer from my ship." He paused and looked playfully at Koishii. "I have found you to be a most observant man, especially when you deduced that the first officer I introduced you to was none too pleased that I am working with you. Please, humor me: what do you observe about my comrade here, Lieutenant Sato Niigata?"

Koishii didn't want to insult the captain by pausing here, pretending to study Niigata. Morimoto would have known that Koishii had been studying the new man since he arrived. The young soldier stood about five foot six, shorter than Koishii but on par with the other sailors from Morimoto's command, the captain included. He stared at Koishii, the look in the soldier's eye unreadable, but the American discerned a hint of hostility and smugness.

"The insignia. It shows a plane. I assume he is part of naval aviation but I cannot, for the life of me, figure out why he is part of your crew."

"Precisely," Morimoto said, picking up the pack of cigarettes from the small table. He shook one out of the pack and lit it. As the smoke rolled across his face, he said, "It is now time for me to let you in on a little secret that will help us achieve our goal: my submarine carries an airplane and Lieutenant Niigata is one of its navigators."

In all of Koishii's time on earth, nothing he had ever heard sounded so preposterous. He actually laughed. "Surely you jest, Captain. Submarines cannot carry airplanes."

Morimoto's eyes hardened and his voice took on an icy timbre that Koishii remembered from their first meeting right after Koishii suggested Japan surrender. "When it comes to war, I do not joke."

He held Koishii's gaze, the cigarette smoldering in his mouth. Niigata kept staring at the American.

After a few awkward moments, Koishii bowed. "I apologize, Captain-san. I didn't mean to dishonor you." He wiped at the edges of his mouth with an index finger and thumb. "It is just that I have never heard that a submarine can carry an airplane, at least not in the U.S. Navy."

"You Americans are not innovative thinkers. You dream up a design, a simple design, and then manufacture thousands upon thousands of the same thing. You have the luxury of supply." He stubbed out the cigarette on the ground and fished another one out of the pack. "We do not have the abundance of supply." He struck a match and lit the cigarette. "We have to be innovative." He shook the match dead and tossed it to the ground.

Koishii felt something in the air shift. The captain's tone had not lost the ice it had taken on and Koishii reached over and got a cigarette. "So what are you saying: The Empire has developed a what, some sort of submarine aircraft carrier?"

Morimoto's eyes softened and he smiled. "Exactly."

Koishii still seemed incredulous. "But how is it that Japan built such a vessel and the Americans know nothing about it?"

Without missing a beat, Morimoto replied, "The same way that you Americans are building some huge bomb and my government knows nothing about it."

Koishii nodded a touché.

"Nonetheless," Morimoto said, "Niigata is a navigator on my seaplane and I will prove to you that what I speak is the truth. When the time comes, I will want you to step outside this tent with me. Then, we can reevaluate our objectives and how best we might achieve them."

Koishii didn't move for a moment, trying to decide what had just happened. He felt less in control than he had since he first met the captain. He felt as if he were now about to go down a road from which there was no turning back and to which he didn't want to go.

The American signaled Niigata to close the flap on the tent and ignited a Coleman lantern. The harsh glare blinded the men and it took a few seconds for their eyes to adjust to the light.

Koishii retrieved a leather notebook from his canvas knapsack and withdrew several sheaves of paper. He moved the teapot from the crate and set the papers on the empty space, turning the orientation so that Morimoto could see the map on top of the pile.

"Okay, when we last met a week ago, I didn't know you had a seaplane. So, the best plan I had was for your men to travel cross-country to Hanford and stage a series of raids. It is risky and, understandably, there might be near 100% casualties—either captured or killed—but I thought it would pose the best chance of disrupting the construction." He looked over at Morimoto. "But I guess we are going to change these plans now?"

"Do not sound so hurt, my friend. I purposefully kept this information from you. I had to assure myself that you are indeed what you are."

Koishii began to fume. "What, exactly, do you think I am?" In his mind, the American worried what the captain might say. In Japanese culture, a traitor was to be mistrusted at best. But the fact that they were talking boded well.

The captain's face remained impassive for a few moments, some of the longest moments in Koishii's life. Finally, Morimoto broke into a genuine smile. "A misplaced Japanese patriot."

Koishii seemed mollified but still harbored doubts, doubts he kept to himself. "So, as I was saying, I am assuming we are going to change those plans?"

Morimoto nodded. "Initially I did approve of the idea but I cannot sacrifice that many men, even for a cause as grand as this."

"There is another option," Koishii said, "one that could be modified from this initial plan." Koishii was getting excited at the potential for regaining control of this excursion. "In Walla Walla, a town about seventy miles from Hanford, there are some German POWs being held in a hospital."

Morimoto frowned. "How important is this construction site to your government if they put enemy soldiers so close to it? Do they not even fear an escape?"

"I do not think so. And that would make it perfect. We could break them out of the prison, arm them with rifles, and drive them over there with your men. I'm sure that they would follow us. They have nothing to lose."

Morimoto glanced over to Niigata whose face remained impassive and then back to Koishii. "Forgive me this question but have you ever served in the military?"

Koishii swallowed. "Infantry."

Morimoto sighed. "I'm afraid it shows, my friend. You are thinking like one of your Hollywood movies. You would probably not get twenty kilometers before your Army would destroy any convoy of trucks carrying those Germans. And where are you going to acquire rifles for all these men? And who is going to drive the trucks, assuming we could even get the Germans out? No, Koishii, we do not have the abundance of supply that an operation of that magnitude requires. We are going to have to be innovative." He turned to Niigata. "And that is where Niigata comes in."

Morimoto picked up the pack of cigarettes and offered Niigata one. The younger man accepted the offer and lit the cigarette with a lighter he pulled from his breast pocket. "*Merushi, kyaputen,*" he said.

Morimoto said to Koishii, "Niigata doesn't speak any English so, if you have to say something that you do not want him to hear, just speak English. Now, let me tell you what we are going to do."

Before he could begin, one of the guards outside said, "Captain, the plane is approaching."

Morimoto stood and walked to the flap serving as the front door. "Come outside, my friend, and I will show you my plane."

Koishii was hesitant but also quite eager to see what Morimoto wanted to show him. He extinguished the lantern and followed the captain. The soldier gazed up into the moonless night.

Outside the tent in the clearing, the stars were bright, and the Milky Way lashed across the sky. Koishii heard the sound of an engine far away and approaching. He could see nothing.

Then, as the sound got louder, he saw a red light seemingly floating in the air, about three hundred feet above the treeline. It moved with the sound of the plane. The red light began to flash. At first, Koishii thought the light was just flashing in the normal manner of tracking lights. Slowly, he noticed a pattern in the flashes and the duration of the flashes. Some were short and some were long.

His heart skipped a beat when he realized the pilot was spelling something out using Morse code. It had been awhile but Koishii remembered most of the alphabet. Slowly, he pieced together what the pilot was communicating. He felt Morimoto's eyes on him and the message became clear to him. And his heart sank.

The pilot spelled out Koishii's real name.

The American traitor swallowed hard and watched the light pass overhead and in the direction of the ocean, a hundred yards away. He saw the red light fleetingly through the trees and then the light was extinguished. The sound of the airplane grew more distant and then faded altogether.

They all stood still—Koishii, Morimoto, Niigata, and the two guards—listening. The faint sound of the crashing surf was constant but no other sound could be heard other than the rustle of the wind through the trees. After a few minutes, the three men returned inside the tent.

With the tent flap closed, Koishii relit the lantern. His mind raced with this new turn of events and the new possibilities. He looked to Morimoto who was beaming with pride. "How many planes do you have?"

"Just one," Morimoto said, his beaming face still alight, "but that is all we will need."

"I will set aside the obvious question of how you get a plane in and out of a sub for now. You said it was a seaplane, right?"

Morimoto nodded. "Of course. Go on."

"And I've seen pictures of the American aircraft carriers and how the planes' wings fold-up. I would imagine that something like that is how you store this plane on your sub?"

"*In* the submarine." Morimoto reached over, took out another cigarette, and lit it. As he smoked, he gave Koishii the basic over-view of how it was that the submarine could carry a seaplane, launch it from the foredeck, have the plane land on the water, and the submarine's crane retrieve the plane from the water. "Since you have already expressed interest in coming with us, you will see it first hand. But let me ask: are you convinced?"

It was Koishii's turn to nod and he bowed to the captain. "It certainly seems that Japanese innovation has served its country well." He looked over to Niigata. "Now that I know what weapons you possess, please tell me of your plan."

Using the map, Morimoto described the plan. He became quite agitated in his zeal to describe just how much damage they intended to inflict on the target. Only one thing made Koishii uncomfortable. "Why are you not just going to bomb the target as opposed to landing a commando and conducting covert operations?"

"It is a simple matter of space and size," Morimoto said. "While it is an engineering feat to be able to have a submarine that houses a seaplane, it is understandably small. The primary mission of this plane is reconnaissance. It is not a bomber. And, as I mentioned to you, we launch this plane from a catapult located on the forward deck. There is space for a bomb on each wing. But they are small. So, we must adjust to our surroundings and circumstances. And we have adjusted." He paused and looked pointedly at Koishii. "What are your impressions?"

Koishii inhaled deeply and let out his breath slowly. "I agree with the overall thinking. The site itself is too big to destroy even if we had access to a bomber, which we do not. Moreover, the government has put this project on such a fast track that the usual red tape is not there. So, by doing what you propose, the entire operation will slow down to a crawl. That should be quite effective." A smile broke the American's face. "And then I will rendezvous with you and…"

The captain held up his hand and cut off Koishii. "There is one other thing I require. It is something for which you are uniquely suited." He waited for a moment to let the American get ready. Koishii's face stiffened at the mention of something else.

Morimoto continued. "I mentioned earlier that the Japanese people do not always have the benefit of supply and that we have to rely on innovation. Well, I would like to augment our supply."

Sweat broke out on Koishii's face. He made a stab in the dark.

"What, you want me to smuggle something out, like plans or something? Look, I have to tell you, I have access to a lot of the people around there but I have never even seen a blueprint."

"The information we need is not in any blueprint."

The statement hung in the air until Koishii figured out what Morimoto was asking for. "You want me to kidnap a person?" For the second time that night, Koishii's stomach lurched into his throat, which was suddenly dry. He reached over to take a sip of tea but the cup was empty. He put the cup down and said, "Who?"

"A scientist. One who knows enough about this project of yours and who will tell us all he knows…with the appropriate persuasion."

Koishii was staring at Morimoto with a blank expression on his face. He managed to get out one word. "How?"

"I assume you have someone who trusts you, someone who knows about this bomb, and who would come with you on, say, an urgent matter? From what you tell me, this bomb is so secret that most of the people who work there do not know what they are working on. And, yet, you know." He left the question unspoken: how is it that you know about it?

Koishii's insides felt hollow. He had found out about the true nature of the Hanford project by pure mishap, one little lapse in judgment on the part of another person. And Koishii had sworn to the other man he would never tell another person.

And that's when Koishii made his decision. He had leverage on Burt Osborn, the scientist who let slip the true nature of the project up at Hanford. Yes, he thought to himself, I can get Burt. But the look in his eyes will haunt me for the rest of my life. Burt is my best friend. But this is war and, in war, sacrifices had to be made.

"I have someone in mind."

"Good," Morimoto said. "Now, let me tell you what you are going to do and how you and your guest are to rendezvous with me."

12

Monday
17 April 1944
11:15 p.m. Pacific War Time

Three hundred feet above Koishii's tent, Toshiro Ishihara considered the seaplane an extension of himself. While he reviewed the instruments directly in front of him, he preferred a more spiritual way to fly. He kept his mind open and allowed the wind to guide his actions. He communicated with the seaplane, allowing its sounds and vibrations to tell him how to fly. But most of all, he accepted the spirits of his brethren who had died defending the Empire to flow through him and let him see what he needed to see.

And what he had seen tonight was the vulnerable Americans contentedly going on about their business, knowing no attack on their homeland would ever come. Ishihara burned with rage at the mere sight of the unblemished land beneath him. Why was it, he thought, that the Americans could sleep peacefully in their beds at night without fear from air raid sirens while his kindred slept in constant fear?

His kindred. Oh, how he longed to see them and talk with them and just be in their presence. The American Marines had killed them, not even sparing the women and children. The murderous Americans deserved to be awakened from their veil of complacency. And Ishihara was the one to do it.

But Ishihara could not comprehend the captain confiding with the American traitor. It was shameful enough to have allowed the traitor to live and to put the ship in danger just to meet with him. But the captain was confiding with a man who was betraying his own country. How could such a man be trusted? It was not honorable.

Ishihara, however, possessed the utmost faith and loyalty in his captain and the orders the crew was to execute: bring the war to the shores of the United States mainland. It was a mission Ishihara relished from the day he heard about it from his uncle, the captain's commanding officer. Ishihara knew that he could have used his uncle's influence to get a commission on the I-40 submarine but Ishihara relied on his piloting expertise to earn him a spot on the one ship destined for America.

Morimoto had noticed the young pilot's vigor in carrying out orders and Ishihara was proud that he was in command of the aircraft hanger on board the submarine. With his efficiency training, Ishihara and his men could assemble the plane and launch it within eight minutes, a record among the fleet.

But Morimoto didn't know Ishihara's desire for revenge. He didn't know how much it burned Ishihara to fly his plane with the insignia of Imperial Japan covered so as to avoid any alarm before the time was right. *It is for the good of the mission*, Morimoto had said, placing his hand on Ishihara's shoulder and looking directly into the pilot's eyes. I know you want to avenge your family's murder, but there will be a place and there will be a time.

Ishihara smiled in the cockpit. The captain didn't know Ishihara had already satisfied some of his bloodlust on his previous reconnaissance mission. Those two weak Americans on the river put up no fight. It was so easy, like slaying dogs. Ishihara particularly enjoyed the look of horror on the first one's face as Ishihara sank his blade deep into the man's chest.

It was an unscheduled and unauthorized landing and, had the captain known about it, Ishihara would likely have been killed himself. As such, Ishihara didn't leave any markings on the bodies, as he would have wished. He just dumped them in the river and let them float away. The entire exercise took less than five minutes but Ishihara had slept soundly that evening, as sound a sleep as he had ever had since boarding the submarine eight months ago.

Ishihara's thoughts were interrupted when his navigator seated behind him, spoke over the radio. "Ishihara–san, we are here. Initiating the message."

Ishihara groused to himself. His usual flying partner, Niigata, was down on the ground with the captain. Although Niigata had been present when Ishihara killed the two Americans and had expressed deep concern for the unauthorized landing, he was the type of soldier who only followed orders and never questioned them. Ishihara was a different type of soldier and that was what made their partnership unique. Niigata and Ishihara had flown together for nearly two years. They had a rhythm and a knowledge of each other that transcended friendship. Even though they didn't agree on everything, Ishihara would fly with Niigata to the grave if necessary.

As Ishihara guided the plane past the coastline, the navigator spelled out the American traitor's English name in Morse code. The captain had told Ishihara that he, Morimoto, wanted to put a little fear into Koishii's heart and let him know that Morimoto was commanding this operation.

Ishihara only wished the captain could see the face of the second man he had killed. That was the face of fear Ishihara relished.

Ishihara glanced at his watch and saw the time was 12:07 a.m., Tuesday, 18 April. Ishihara inhaled deeply and closed his eyes. A smile broke across his face as he thought about the mission and the plan to strike at the heart of America.

"One more day."

13

Tuesday
18 April 1944
7:10 a.m., Pacific War Time

"When are you going to tell him?" Hancock asked Truman.

The two men were in the lobby of the Hurley Hotel waiting for McLeod. Reta Hurley, a feather duster in hand, made her way around the room brushing the previous day's dust from all the surfaces.

"I think it's only proper for a man to have some food in him before he hears some bad news," Truman replied. He glanced over at Hurley. Her back was to them and she kept dusting.

Hancock nodded. "Yeah, that makes sense." He held on to his Stetson by the brim and began to rotate it in his hands. "He ain't gonna be happy about it, you know? He'll say it was his case to begin with and then the same government he's fighting comes in and snatches it from him."

"You're starting to sound like him, what with that 'government' talk."

"I'm just thinking about what he's gonna say. He's going to want something to do. What do you want him to do, just go back home to Seattle or sit here all day? Besides, how do we ask a guy to back off a case *he* brought to us and also ask him for the use of his car?"

"That's not really my problem, Carl," Truman said. "I don't want even the whiff of impropriety in our investigation. If we show up with McLeod, that makes our investigation all the more difficult. I want this to be clean, precise, and honest."

"I can use him." Hurley's voice surprised both men and they both turned to where she was standing.

"I beg your pardon," Truman said.

"I said I could use his assistance. He's a lawyer and, frankly, I need one." She walked over to the two men lightly tapping the duster on the side of her dress as if it were a riding crop.

"What for?" Hancock asked.

She looked at him. "That's personal, Mr. Hancock. Suffice it to say, I need a lawyer and you need to get rid of one. I can do that for you." She looked back at Truman. "I'm just trying to do my part."

Truman's mouth formed a tight smile and he nodded. "Thank you very much, Mrs. Hurley. We'll take you up on your offer."

"And, if he balks, you can use my car."

"Thank you again but I still want to tell him over breakfast."

"Tell me what?" McLeod said as he entered the lobby.

"There's been a new development in the case, Horace," Hancock said, putting his arm around McLeod's shoulder and turning him toward the front door. "Hungry?"

* * *

"Is this all of it?" Blaine asked.

"Yes, sir," Duncan said. "This is everything that was in the dead men's pockets. I sorted them. This pile here is from the blond man. That pile is from the bearded one."

Blaine nodded and motioned for his deputy to have a seat opposite him. Duncan sat down and crossed his hands.

The sheriff looked at the items on his left, the pile Duncan identified as that of the blond man. "This was the one that had no defense wounds, right?"

"Yes, sir."

"Okay." Blaine slid a sheet of paper over to Duncan. "Joe, read this while I double check that everything's here."

Duncan took the paper and began to read. "Swiss Army knife, eyeglasses, pencil, notepad, bag of peanuts, and a partial invoice."

Blaine picked up the crumpled and wrinkled piece of paper and smoothed it out on the table. "Everything here is what you'd expect from a couple of guys going camping…except this. What do you make of it?"

"The invoice itself is not unusual. It's for powdered milk. That's certainly something campers might have." He pointed to the invoice. "But fifteen cases are a bit of overkill unless you're planning to stay out for a long time."

Blaine grinned. "You think? Did we find any powdered milk packages on the bodies?"

"Yes, one package, unopened. It's here in the other pile."

Blaine looked at the other pile. It contained almost identical contents except there were no eyeglasses and there was a bag of powdered milk. "We have an invoice listing fifteen cases of powdered milk and yet we have only one bag." He looked up from the invoice. "Where's the rest?"

Duncan shrugged. "We don't know. If you'd like, we can start a search for them."

Blaine shook his head. "No, that won't be necessary. I can't see asking for manpower just to search for a few crates of powdered milk. Did the coroner confirm what all the evidence pointed to at the scene?"

"Yes, sir. Both men died of repeated knife wounds. The blond man, apparently the one caught by surprise, has only two cuts on him. The bearded one, the one with the defensive wounds, had many cuts and scrapes."

Blaine nodded. "So, our assailant took these campers by

surprise, managed to kill one and then had to fight the other one for a time before he killed him." He paused for a moment. "Have we called all the hospitals in the surrounding area to find out if anyone was treated for wounds that would be consistent with a fight?"

"Sam's on it now. So far, we've turned up nothing."

"It could be a hunting dispute," the sheriff said. "Both groups see game, shoot at it, arrive at the kill site at the same time, a discussion turns into a brawl and then murder."

Gingerly, Duncan said, "But that doesn't explain the invoice." Looking down at the table and steeling himself for Blaine's reaction. "It could be those Mountain Men."

Blaine let out a sigh. "Joe, after four years with nary a sign of them, that should tell you something. They don't exist. Yes, they once did but they all came in from the wilderness after Pearl."

Duncan sat up straighter. "Sir, think about it. Who else would need fifteen cases of powdered milk? Someone who was going to be out in the wilderness for a long period of time."

"What, so they live on powdered milk and anything they kill in the wild? That doesn't sound realistic."

"Doesn't have to be. The powdered milk was probably just one provision. They probably get other provisions as they need them."

Blaine leaned back in his chair. "You speak of provisions. How do they get them?"

Clearly Duncan had devoted much time to his theories. He didn't pause before answering. "Someone gives them the supplies they need. Or they steal them. Remember, some of those shops and warehouses up in Washington have armed guards. It's probably to keep out the Mountain Men."

Blaine thought for a few moments. Duncan sat in silent anticipation. Finally, Blaine said, "Okay. I can't say that I agree with your theory but it's the only one we have right now. I'm going to call all the sheriffs in the surrounding counties, both here and in Washington. I'll ask them if any recent burglaries have occurred in the past month. That'll at least narrow down our choices if we have to follow up."

Duncan smiled and stood. "Good idea, sir. I'll go get the telephone numbers." He exited the sheriff's office.

Blaine sat at his desk and shook his head. He let a derisive sigh escape his mouth. "Mountain Men."

14

Tuesday
18 April 1944
7:55 a.m., Pacific War Time

"Well, that went worse than I expected." Hancock sat behind the wheel of McLeod's Lincoln. He had commiserated with McLeod when Truman broke the news to the lawyer that he would have to stay away during the investigation. But there was a fringe benefit of McLeod staying behind: Hancock got to drive the car, something he had been itching to do since he laid eyes on the Lincoln.

Truman sighed. "It's a good thing Mrs. Hurley had something for him."

"Don't worry about Horace," Hancock said. "As soon as he begins to calm down and think logically, like a lawyer, he'll understand our position. Shoot, you never know, we might just deliver him a better case without him." He looked over at Truman. "What do you think Mrs. Hurley has for him?"

Truman shook his head. "I don't know but we'll owe her one. But now, we've got to focus on our investigation."

Hancock was immediately attuned to Truman's mood change. "How do you want to play it?"

Truman was thoughtful. "The way I see it, Mr. Bumble stumbled onto something. I don't know how deep it is or if it's even illegal but it's certainly fishy. We're going to find out what's going on and report it. We're going to treat this like any other investigation. We're going to walk up to the warehouse and see if anybody notices us. If not, we'll just nose around and see if we can't learn something from the workers. If someone meets us right off the bat, we'll be upfront with who we are and why we're here. Either way, I certainly want to see the books."

Hancock nodded and smiled. "Yeah, fraud is a nice and easy way to nab someone."

"It is, but that's not our aim here. It's entirely possible that nothing untoward is going on here and that Mr. Bumble and Mr. McLeod both have overactive imaginations. Or they're simply looking for some easy money. He *is* a lawyer." He tapped his hand on the dashboard. "But let's not make enemies of these folks. If they make a fuss, we'll stay calm." He looked over at Hancock with a twinkle in his eye. "You'll know if we need to change our approach."

The parking lot of the Moore Warehouse was little more than an open dirt field. As Hancock turned into the lot, a huge cloud of dust followed the Lincoln. The lot was almost full but Hancock found a spot next to the highway. Both men got out of the car and met at the front. They looked up at the south façade of the building, now obscured by the floating dust.

"It's a good thing this wasn't a surprise attack," Hancock said, "or they'd know we're coming a mile off."

Truman took out his handkerchief and began to clean the dust off his glasses. "With all the informers Lynch has around here, I wouldn't be surprised if Mr. Moore already knows we're coming."

Hancock toed a line in the dirt. "Well, McLeod's not been exactly subtle in his efforts here..." His voice trailed off, the unspoken truth apparent to both of them.

Truman put his glasses on and folded his handkerchief. As he placed it in his suit pocket, he started walking. "That's what I'm afraid of. C'mon, let's see what they give us."

The warehouse was shaped like a large "L." The main area was five stories tall. It was through this area that all shipments were received through two large thirty-foot bay doors. The lower, two-story office area was to the right of the main warehouse floor. It was on top of this part of the warehouse that the new "Moore" sign gleamed in the early morning sun.

As Truman and Hancock approached the open bay doors, a large truck sat idling, its flatbed now vacant of its cargo. An old beat-up forklift, its yellow paint only hinted at amid all the scrapes and rust, ferried the last crate of supplies into the warehouse.

"Looks like flour from Iowa," Hancock said.

Truman grunted. "At least you can still read small print from a distance."

They arrived at the bay door in the forklift's cloud of dust. A man in blue coveralls and a John Deere cap walked out to meet them, a cup of water in his hand. "Hey, I already left my invoice at the office."

"Thanks," Hancock said, not missing a beat at the driver's mistake. "Good work." He and Truman kept walking into the warehouse.

The man walked past them and climbed into the cab of the truck. He ground the gears, honked the horn twice, and began driving through the warehouse.

At the sound of the grinding gears, Truman and Hancock both turned, saw the truck, and sidestepped out of the way. Hancock nodded to the driver as he passed. The driver raised his cup to Hancock in salute.

The truck left the interior of the warehouse thick with gray smoke. The smoke rose and floated out through the open window high above the floor. After the truck had passed, Truman saw a man standing across the warehouse, staring at them. His khakis were heavily pressed, as was his shirt. His work boots poked out from the bottom of his khakis but they showed no scuff marks. The man's close-cropped hair resembled those worn by the soldiers in the field.

He was not smiling.

As the pair approached, a large scar running along the man's left cheek became visible. The doctors had done a good job but the wound still marred an otherwise handsome face.

"Can I help you?" the man asked.

Hancock deferred to Truman. The senator walked across the center of the warehouse floor and extended his hand. The other man shook Truman's hand with a firmness that almost hurt. Hancock noticed Truman suppressed his pain and kept his senatorial smile intact.

"Good morning, I'm Harry Truman."

The younger man just nodded. He held onto Truman's hand a second longer and then released it. He didn't break eye contact with Truman until Hancock walked up. About the same height as Truman, the man had to look up to meet Hancock's gaze. He took the Texan's hand and began to squeeze. Hancock was ready for it and met the young man's grip with equal power.

"Howdy," Hancock said, giving the new man his best Texas smile, "I'm Carl Hancock." His Stetson was still on his head and the overhead lights shielded his eyes.

When the man didn't offer his name and tried to extract his hand from Hancock's grip, Hancock didn't relent and tightened his grip. Still smiling, he said, "Where I come from, if a man gives his name, it's good manners to reciprocate."

It was the younger man's turn to grimace. "Christopher Moore," he said and Hancock released his hand. Moore did his best not to show the pain he was experiencing. Some of the arrogance disappeared from his face, replaced by anger that he had been brought down a notch.

"Christopher Moore?" Truman asked. He was searching his memory but could not remember McLeod mentioning a 'Christopher Moore.' Having never seen Edward Moore, the owner of the warehouse, Truman took a shot in the dark. "Are you Edward Moore's brother?"

The corner of Moore's mouth curled slightly. "Why do you want to know?"

"We're here to see Edward Moore."

"He ain't here," Moore said.

"Then perhaps you can help us."

Moore looked at Truman, up to Hancock, and then back to Truman. "Not likely. What do you want?"

Before Truman could reply, another man approached the trio. Unlike Moore, this man's clothes looked the worst for wear. His boots had scratches all along the toe and sides. The knees of his green pants were nearly white either from kneeling in dust or years of wear. His work shirt was soaked with sweat and his rolled up sleeves barely contained his massive arms.

"Mr. Truman," the man said, offering his hand, "so good of you to come by. I'm Larry Watson, head foreman." He turned to Hancock and repeated his greeting.

Watson stepped back, put his hands on his hips, and nodded to Moore. "I take it you've met Chris, here? He's in training to learn the ropes and take over the old man's business."

Moore looked downright irritated. Truman could tell from the young man's face that he had enjoyed having the upper hand and hated that he lost it.

"I assume you're here to conduct one of your famous inspections, Senator," Watson said. "Well, I gotta tell you, you won't find anything wrong here. We run a tight ship and, as you can see, we're quite busy." His face was beaming with pride.

Another flatbed truck, loaded with three layers of crates, approached the entrance . Watson yelled an order to a man standing over by the loading dock and the man jumped to comply. Watson then offered the clipboard he was carrying to Moore. "Chris, why don't you take care of this shipment while I show Mr. Truman and Mr. Hancock around." He had to shout to be heard over the din of the truck's diesel engines. "And remember to note *everything* on that shipment. This is probably the A-frames for the prefab houses and Mr. Moore'll want a precise count."

Moore glared at Watson. He glanced over once more at Truman and then walked toward the truck. The three men stood watching the younger man as he approached the driver and began noting the contents of the crates.

"You'll have to forgive Chris," Watson said, scratching his chin. "If he had his way, he wouldn't be here, working in this warehouse for the rest of his life. He had dreams, big dreams. Fancied himself a movie star. And he had the looks for it, too. The war took care of that." He pantomimed the place on his own cheek where Moore's scar was.

"What happened?" Truman asked.

"Shrapnel. His unit was part of Ike's invasion of French Morocco in '42, you know, the area around Casablanca. Chris's unit attacks a barricade and a shell lands smack dab in the middle of his unit. Five men just cease to exist. The other twenty—Chris was one of these 'lucky' ones—get ripped apart by shrapnel. Seventeen of them died within two days of their wounds."

Watson took off his hat and ran his hand through his hair. "Of the remaining three, Chris's injuries—his right hand doesn't work too well, but that's okay because he's a lefty—lands him in a hospital for two months and an honorable discharge soon after that. One of those three dies a few months later. Too much internal damage. The last guy, a man by the name of Zach Abraham, a Jew from Brooklyn, nearly got his leg sheared off. He survived the war but shot himself last year. Said he couldn't stand to see half a man."

All through Watson's retelling of Moore's war experiences, Truman and Hancock remained silent. As the details emerged, both men relived their war experiences of twenty-six years previous.

"As you can imagine, the war cost Chris his dreams and, well, he's bitter." He replaced his hat. "But you didn't come all the way out here just to hear war stories." He swept his arm around in a grand gesture, grinning all the time. "Want the grand tour?"

"Yes, we would," Truman said. "And we're also going to need to meet with Mr. Moore."

Watson shook his head. "Mr. Moore ain't here right now, but he's supposed to be back after lunch."

Hancock chuckled. "Now, those are hours I could get used to."

Watson laughed but it came across a bit forced. "Mr. Moore has many different branches of his company. He likes to check on them personally at least once a month."

"How many branches does he own?" Hancock asked.

"Ten. Most of 'em are located along the coast even though this one here was his first and it's the one he considers his pride and joy."

As they started walking, Watson gave what Truman considered 'the spiel.' He almost felt like Watson was treating them as potential customers rather than inspectors. The information was interesting but perfunctory.

After a few minutes, Truman decided to interrupt. "By the way, Mr. Watson, we're also going to need to see the books, if you don't mind. Can you provide that information while we wait for Mr. Moore?"

Watson had a moment of hesitation and the investigators both caught it. But, almost as soon as the concern flashed on his face, Watson recovered.

"Actually," he said, "I don't have access to the books." He smiled sheepishly. "I'm just the foreman."

"But, surely, you have something to do with the accounting of what comes in and what goes out," Truman said.

"No, not really. Folks like Chris usually take the inventory as they come in. I just make sure everything works and runs smoothly."

They had stopped at the foot of a flight of stairs that led to the main office and a door marked 'Private.' Truman assumed this was Moore's personal office. Watson didn't make any motion of going up the stairs.

Truman waited for Watson to start up the stairs and, when he didn't, said, "Who has access to the books other than Moore?"

Watson leaned his arm on the railing, effectively blocking the stairs. It was a none-too-subtle suggestion. "Benjamin Riley is the accountant but he's not here either. He's home sick. His wife called yesterday. Said Ben and a few of his buddies all came with some food poisoning or something."

"Where does he live?" Truman asked.

"Richland," Watson said, jabbing a thumb over his shoulder in the direction across the river. "He managed to get one of the prefabs located outside the base. The big medical building is inside Hanford. But that shouldn't be a problem for a senator. I bet you have all sorts of access." He leaned closer to Truman and feigned a conspiratorial stage whisper. "Heck, you might even know what's going on up there." He leaned back and smiled.

"You don't know?" Hancock asked.

"Don't know, don't care. As long as the government keeps sending all their supplies through this warehouse. Keeps me employed. They say it'll help win the war and that's good enough for me."

Truman smiled. "Just like those billboards, huh? 'Loose lips' and all that." He gestured up to the office. "You mind showing us the office?"

Watson hid his obvious reluctance with loud speech. "Sure, if you don't mind the short tour. Only thing up there is Ben's desk and file cabinets I don't have a key for." Watson started up the stairs and Truman started to follow him when Hancock said, "Mr. Watson, I noticed the head next to the side door. Y'all go on ahead and I'll meet y'all up there."

Hancock looked up at Watson who was three steps up the flight. The foreman clearly didn't want either of his two guests to be out of his sight but was helpless. "Well, depending on how long the Senator takes to look at a desk, we might just beat you back."

Watson turned and raced up the stairs. Truman and Hancock exchanged glances and Truman followed Watson up to the top of the stairs.

The landing was about ten feet long with iron railings on all sides. The wooden slats that served as the landing showed the warehouse floor through gaps between the pieces of wood. There were two doors. The main office door had a plate glass window. The other door, marked only with 'Private,' was of solid wood.

"Is that Mr. Moore's private office?" Truman asked.

"Yep," Watson said as he swung open the office door and entered. The office was just as described. Three-drawer filing cabinets lined the entire length of one wall. A desk sat in the middle of the room. It was neat and tidy with a desk pad, a coffee can full of pencils, and an ashtray. The wall facing the warehouse had a window running the length of it. On the wall facing the front of the warehouse, Truman made out the parking lot and McLeod's Lincoln.

On the walls, Truman noticed a portrait of President Roosevelt, a calendar, and four maps. One was of Washington State, one of Oregon, one was of the Pacific Theater, and one was of the European Theater. Truman walked over and inspected the war maps. There were blue and red pencil marks noting battles and lines of territory occupied by the Allies and the Axis. He nodded in appreciation.

"Ben avidly follows the war," Watson said. "His eyesight prevented him from joining so he fights Hitler and Tojo from here."

Truman nodded as he looked at the common wall between this office and Moore's private office. In the middle of the wall was a small door, about a foot square. Watson answered Truman's unspoken question. "Mr. Moore got tired of having to walk out of his office and into this office just to tell Ben something so he decided to make the little 'speakeasy' door." He grinned. "That's what we call it. Mr. Moore just thinks of it as a time saver."

Watson spread his hands. "So, was I right? There ain't much to see without Ben or Mr. Moore here." He was standing with his back to the door, obviously wanting Truman to take the hint and exit the room.

"You say Mr. Moore will be back after lunch? Does he know we're here like you did?"

"Of course. He's the one who called me this morning."

Truman made a mental note to chastise Colonel Matthias. Seeing nothing else that interested him, Truman decided to appease Watson and walked out of the office. He started as Watson barked an order to one of his men across the warehouse floor. As he reached the ground, he noticed that Hancock was not there. Watson realized this, as well, and the expression on his face showed his displeasure.

But, just as Watson was starting to get antsy, Hancock walked up beaming. "Man that coffee ran through me like nobody's business. So, what's up, Harry?"

"Mr. Watson's correct. There is not much to see without Mr. Moore or Mr. Riley here. Moore's coming back after lunch and we'll be back here at 1pm." With a look, Truman told Hancock to play along.

Truman turned to Watson and extended his hand. "Thank you for the tour, Mr. Watson. We'll see you later today."

Hancock shook Watson's hand as well and both men walked out through the same door they entered. Hancock tipped his Stetson as he passed Christopher Moore, the young man's face now drenched with sweat and dust. Moore just glared.

15

Tuesday
18 April 1944
9:30 a.m., Pacific War Time

Larry Watson watched as Truman and Hancock left the warehouse. He frowned when he saw their car. Something tickled the back of his mind but he could not place where he had seen a Lincoln recently or why it mattered.

He hoped he had put on a good show for the two inspectors. Actually, he thought to himself, it was only part show. He *was* proud of the work he did here and how honed he had made his workforce. The other stuff, the secret stuff, that was just extra.

As the Lincoln departed, he thought he might have a way of easing his mind with one phone call. He trotted back up the stairs to the main office, went in, and shut the door. After a moment's hesitation, he locked it and sat down at the desk. He picked up the telephone and dialed a number.

A woman answered. "Sheriff's Department."

"Hi, Deloris, it's Larry. Is Ira in?"

"He's on another call right now, Larry. Can I have him call you when he's finished?"

"Yes, that'd be great."

"Where are you?"

"At the warehouse. Have him dial the main number. I'll be waiting. Thanks."

Watson hung up the telephone and fished a cigarette out of his pocket and lit it. As he sat and smoked, he ran a few questions over in his head. Why was Truman here, at this particular warehouse? Was it a coincidence or did he suspect something? When Edward Moore had called last night, he mentioned that the senator was in town and he might be coming by the warehouse for an inspection. Although Moore was uncertain why Truman was in town, he instructed Watson to "clean up the place" just in case he shows up and wants to look around.

"Who is he?" Watson had asked.

"He's the product of the political machine out of Kansas City. He probably got himself appointed to a committee so he could foul up the war effort and make good for his bosses back in Missouri." Watson had heard the disgust in Moore's voice. "I read about him in *Time* last year. Some people think he's doing some good, and maybe he is, but he does it by sticking his nose in other people's business."

Watson had laughed, considering the type of operation he was helping to run, but Moore had cut him off. "This is no laughing matter, Larry. We have enough people on our side looking the other way. But we don't have any Feds on our side. And I don't want some politician coming in here and messing everything up. It's too important. Do you understand?"

Watson had said he did, apologized for not staying focused, and promised Moore everything would be tidy if any inspection was necessary. Besides, he had thought, the warehouse could do for some cleaning.

The ringing telephone brought Watson back to the present. He reached over and picked up the receiver. "Moore Warehouse, Larry Watson speaking."

"Hi, Larry, it's Ira."

Watson inhaled on his cigarette and stubbed it out in the ashtray. "Thanks for getting back so soon. I've got a question or two, maybe you can help me clear my mind." He picked up a pencil and began doodling on the notepad. "I got a visit from Senator Truman and his partner this morning."

Ira Webb whistled low. "So Mr. Moore was right."

Watson frowned. "What do you mean?"

"He called me last night to tell me that Truman and a man named Hancock had checked in at the Hurley Hotel. He told me who Truman was and what he did. He also mentioned that he was going to call you and have you make the warehouse ship shape."

"Yeah, well, I did that. I took them on a tour and everything. Just glad I don't have to put on a show right now. It gets old." He put the final touches on his geometric diagram and started another. "But why would they even come here? You think he suspects something?"

"He might. That nosy lawyer McLeod picked up Truman and Hancock down in Pendleton."

With a rush, Watson remembered why the Lincoln looked so familiar. In his excitement, he broke the lead on his pencil. "Of course! Shoot, why do I have to be so dense sometimes?"

"What?"

"The car they were driving. It's a Lincoln. It looks just like the one that lawyer drives."

"Well," Webb said, "it's probably the same one. McLeod probably loaned his car to Truman. Was McLeod there?"

Watson shook his head though Webb could not see. "No, just the two of 'em."

"That's strange," Webb said. "Wonder what McLeod's up to?"

"He might be coming back with them after lunch. I managed to convince them that only Mr. Moore and Ben have the key to the books. But they want to meet Mr. Moore. He'll shut 'em down."

"Be careful, Larry. We have a good thing going on out here and we don't need any outside interference, especially from the very thing we're fighting against."

"I know, I know," Watson said, a bit exasperated. "It's just that I enjoy watching Mr. Moore do his thing. It's no wonder why his warehouse company is the biggest in the whole Pacific Northwest. He has such a way with people."

He snapped his fingers. "I just remembered one of my guys, Peter Allan, is a friend of Bumble. They were both farmers. I'm going to remind him he better keep his mouth shut or he could join Bumble. Then again, I might remind him about accidents and all the bad things that can happen in a warehouse."

"Well, just be careful, Larry. Be delicate. I'm going to see if I can't locate McLeod and find out why he wasn't at the warehouse today. Call me later and let me know how Mr. Moore takes care of Truman."

Watson said he would and he hung up the telephone. He rose from his chair and strode out of the office and down to the main floor. He saw a worker and called to him.

"Where's Allan?" Watson asked.

"In the back, unloading the latest shipment of pipe," the man said.

"I need to speak to him. In the main office."

The worker scurried off and Watson smiled. He enjoyed the power he welded here in the warehouse. He felt like Patton leading the Third Army.

He was still smiling as he walked back up the stairs to await Peter Allan.

16

Tuesday
18 April 1944
10:45 a.m., Pacific War Time

Behind the wheel of the Lincoln, Hancock pulled onto the road and headed toward Hanford. "Where to?"

"I'd like to go see the accountant, Benjamin Riley. I didn't want to say anything in front of Watson because I'd like something on this trip to be on our terms. When you find a service station, pull in and we'll borrow a telephone directory."

Hancock nodded and kept his eyes on the road. "Okay, but in the meantime, let me tell you who I met." He reached inside his coat pocket and pulled out a stick of gum. He popped it in his mouth and offered one to Truman who declined.

"While Watson's giving us the grand tour—paying special attention to you, I might add—I start to let my eyes wander. I see a bunch of men hunkered down doing their jobs. So I was surprised when I saw, in the aisle next to us, a man shadowing our moves."

"Shadowing?" Truman asked.

"Like he's keeping up with us. Well, no, like he's keeping up with me. You and Watson were three steps ahead of me. Out of the corner of my eye, I see a red flash. I glance over and see him. He's walking on the other side of a line of crates and I can only see him when there's a gap. I think that he's just doing his job but he slows down when we slow down and starts up again when we do."

"When Watson's showing us the overhead hoist, I glance again over at this man and I see him holding up a piece of paper. On it, he wrote 'Meet me in the head.'"

"That's why I excused myself while you two went upstairs. In the restroom, I see a pair of work boots in the stall so I walk up to the urinal and do my business. As I'm finishing up, the guy in the stall says to me 'You here with Truman?'"

Truman's jaw visibly clenched tighter. "How'd he know who I was?"

Hancock shrugged. "I'm beginning to think this whole town knows you're here. Besides, only one of us had his picture on the cover of *Time*. I told him yes, I'm with you and who's asking. He tells me his name is Peter Allan."

"Doesn't ring a bell," Truman said.

"Didn't with me, either. He's a friend of Bumble. They used to be farmers around here and were forced to sell their land when the government came. Having no other work, they both got jobs here." He grinned and imitated Watson's voice. "You know that Moore Warehousing is the largest company of its kind in the state of Washington."

Truman smiled. "That Watson's slick, I'll give him that. And he's obviously proud of his position." He pointed to a Gulf station up ahead. "Let's stop there."

As he pulled up to the gas pump, Hancock continued. "Anyway, we didn't have much time so Allan wanted to give me some information as quickly as possible. To make it look normal, he came out of the stall and stood in front of the urinal while I washed my hands."

An attendant came over and both men got out of the car. "Fill'er up please," Hancock said to the man and walked over to the soda machine. He fished a few coins out of his pocket and bought two Coca-Colas.

Hancock stood by the Lincoln, drank his Coke, and watched Truman step inside the station. He saw the senator pick up a telephone book, find the listing he wanted, write the address in a little notebook, and thank the person behind the counter. Truman walked over to the pay telephone and placed his call. After speaking for a few minutes, he hung up and returned to the car.

Hancock said, "Can't believe they don't have Dr Pepper up here." He handed his empty bottle to the attendant and handed Truman the other soda. "So, what's up?"

Truman gave Hancock a look that said "Not here." Hancock nodded, paid the attendant, took the receipt, and both men got in the car and drove away.

"I called Benjamin Riley's house," Truman said. "I spoke with their neighbor. They live in a duplex and share a phone line. It's true: both Benjamin and his wife are in the hospital in Hanford. We can't get to them." He shook his head. "I guess we'll just have to wait until this afternoon and speak with Mr. Moore."

"Where to now?"

"Back to the hotel."

Hancock continued. "Allan was pretty nervous, just by talking to me. He's scared that they'll do to him what they did to Bumble."

"Draft him."

Hancock nodded "Allan tells me Bumble wasn't the first to notice strange things around the warehouse."

"Really?"

"There's another worker who was head foreman early last year. Nice man. He and Allan became friends. Bumble, too. Well, one day, this guy—his name was Jacobs—just didn't show up for work. When Allan asked around, he discovered Jacobs had been transferred to the branch in Walla Walla."

"That doesn't seem strange," Truman said. "Why all the mystery?"

"Because of what Jacobs had found. Before he was transferred, he mentioned it to Bumble."

Truman opened his palms, ready for the reveal.

"He noticed two sets of invoices on Riley's desk." When Truman's face registered blank, Hancock continued. "That would be two sets of the *same* invoice. Only there was one difference. One invoice had more items listed than the other did. Curious, Jacobs went to the crate with the shipments—it was powdered milk—and counted the cartons. It matched the lower number. He gave it some time and waited to see what figure showed up on the official record. It was the lower number."

"So, did Jacobs or Bumble find out what happened to the missing cartons?"

Hancock smiled without humor. "No. A day later, Jacobs is gone. That, of course, got Bumble all a flutter. So *he* starts watching and he tells Allan. The job's a bit harder as both men were hired for their muscle and not their brains. They just unloaded things and didn't touch paperwork. But Bumble starts to invent reasons to go to the office. He starts doing his best to count shipments as they arrive. Gets Allan to do the same."

Truman shook his head. "So, Allan and Bumble think Moore is skimming off the top. But what would he be doing with it and why should it involve us?"

"To answer your second question, all you need to remember is that Moore Warehousing is the largest of its kind in Washington State. Uncle Sam has a big government operation around here and everyone needs to eat, drink, and be merry. And, in case you haven't noticed, there ain't much around here."

Truman was silent for a moment, pondering the situation. Inwardly, he was kicking himself for not seeing the connection sooner. Another good mark on Hancock's personnel file.

"While you're getting your head around that, how about I tell you the second big thing Allan mentioned to me. Of all the warehouses in the area, we know this one is the biggest. But did you know that this warehouse is the only one with an armed guard at night."

Truman raised his eyebrows. "Why?"

Hancock screwed up his face. "Struck me as funny, too.

Remember those so-called 'Mountain Men' Blaine told us about? Well, they robbed Moore's warehouse last year. Ever since then, Moore has hired an armed guard to patrol the property."

"Can't say I blame him for that. A man's got a right to protect his property." Truman looked over at Hancock. "So why'd Allan bring it up?"

"Because of the guard's peculiar schedule. If you hired a guard, what kind of hours would you ask him to keep?"

Truman thought for about a second. "Dusk 'til dawn or whenever the warehouse opens."

Hancock nodded. "Me, too, and that's what I told Allan. Turns out the guard—his name is Richard Stanley—is on duty from about eight o'clock until five in the morning. And you'll never guess who relives him."

"Who?"

"Only one of two people: Moore or his son, the happy lad we met today."

Truman looked puzzled. He was an early riser, a habit he never got over even after he left the farm life behind him. As a farmer, there was much to be said for working in the early morning hours before the heat of day sapped one's energies. But why would a warehouse owner come in so early?

He said as much to Hancock who replied, "Perhaps we should ask him when we meet him this afternoon." Hancock glanced over at the senator out of the corner of his eye. "I think our evening plans just got made for us."

"I think you're right. We'd better have a look for ourselves tonight.."

Hancock looked over at Truman. "Want Horace to come with us or stay at the hotel?"

Truman frowned. "In the daytime, for anyone to see, I don't want him near us at all. I don't want anyone to say we compromised this investigation by having a litigant influencing our decisions. But tonight might be a different story. What do you think?"

"Dunno. The company might be nice seeing as how all you and I ever talk about is the war, politics, religion, history, law, music, and literature. That leaves Horace to fill us in on, what, baseball?" He shot a grin at Truman. "Let's ask him when we get back to the hotel." He patted his stomach. "I'm starving."

Truman chuckled. "With as much food as you eat, I'm amazed you stay as fit as you do." He sat up straighter in his seat. "Of course, when this damn war started and I volunteered my services to General Marshall, I was still able to fit in my old uniform. Can you say the same thing?"

"Naw. Too much Texas bar-be-que and beer for that."

The rest of the way to the hotel, they reminisced about their war experiences in The Great War. Even though they didn't serve together, they were soldiers and still considered themselves as such. They were brothers of a kind that was greater than blood and they, and all their fellow veterans, would always be a part of that great fraternity.

17

Tuesday
18 April 1944
10:30 a. m., Pacific War Time

Toshiro Ishihara climbed the ladder from the engineering deck and found himself in the forward hanger. As he stepped through the hatch, he touched the fuselage of the seaplane. He ran his fingers along the body, feeling every nook and cranny. The wings of the plane were folded up but he still had to duck as he passed them.

His anger still burned when he saw the Japanese insignia obscured, but he hid his feelings when he saw the captain.

"Ishihara-san," Morimoto said, "thank you for joining me." Morimoto stood in front of the propeller looking toward the bow and the hanger doors. Niigata stood at attention, facing the captain. Ishihara fell in line next to Niigata.

"At ease," Morimoto said. Ishihara and Niigata complied.

"Gentlemen, you know of my contact with the American called Koishii." Morimoto looked pointedly at Ishihara. "And I know some of you do not think I should be working with him, traitor that he is.

But we are because I think it is in our best interests. By working with him, we shall cripple this one factory and, in turn, receive an asset that will enable us to gain the advantage in this war."

Ishihara arched an eyebrow.

"You have a question, Ishihara-san?"

"Yes, sir. What is so important about this factory? The Americans have thousands, if our intelligence is correct."

Morimoto smiled. "I thought you might ask that. And I order you both not to discuss the nature of this particular factory. Our morale is ebbing and I am going to need all hands to focus on our mission."

He turned and looked at the plane. He ran his fingers along the propeller blade. "Did you know that the Americans have no idea of our capacity to carry a plane inside a submarine? We have only one plane at our disposal but I remember hearing that the admiralty is going to build larger submarines capable of carrying up to three planes. The Americans are building a weapon that, according to Koishii, could destroy an entire city with a single bomb."

Ishihara and Niigata both gasped.

Morimoto continued. "But we have our own covert weapon, our seaplane. It will enable us to bring the war to the American mainland." A hint of disdain entered Morimoto's voice. "These soft Americans, they sit there, on their mainland, safe from the ravages of this war. And they build and build and build. Planes, tanks, bombs, boats. But they've never suffered what our homeland suffers." His eyes hardened and he turned to face his men. "It is time we make them suffer."

Ishihara smiled. This was the kind of thing he had wanted to do since they arrived on the American coast three weeks ago. Raiding parties and sinking fishing boats was nothing compared to actual American deaths.

Morimoto stood up straighter, almost at attention. "And you two will lead the attack on the factory that is making this new bomb."

Ishihara's smile grew wider. His heart began to beat faster. He glanced at Niigata who was also smiling, although not as effusively.

"The mission is simple. You will fly the plane to the American factory. The navigator, Niigata, will parachute into the factory. Once there, you will destroy this factory's capacity to make this bomb. You will be armed accordingly."

Morimoto turned to Ishihara. "You, Ishihara-san, will fly the plane back to the submarine." He stopped and let his words register with his men. Ishihara's smile faded a bit and Niigata's smile evaporated altogether.

Ishihara saved his fellow soldier from asking the obvious question. "Are there no plans to pick up Niigata after he parachutes into the factory?"

Morimoto inhaled deeply and looked at Niigata. "Niigata-san will be the first to lay down his life in this mission."

Niigata stood straighter and bowed to Morimoto. The captain returned the gesture.

Inside, Ishihara was shocked and hurt. True, he was a better pilot than Niigata. But he was also a better man to carry out a mission such as this. Plus, there was his family. His family needed to be avenged. And he must personally do it.

As he stood there, impassive to the other two, he began to formulate all the reasons why he should switch places with Niigata.

18

Tuesday
18 April 1944
11:30 a. m., Pacific War Time

Deputy Joe Duncan found Blaine sitting on a bench under a tree, smoking. "I've got the report you wanted on that Truman fellow."

Blaine looked up, his eyes squinting against the sun. He saw the other man standing next to Duncan. "Hello, Abe. Are you the one delivering my report?"

Abraham Carter, reporter for the local newspaper, nodded. "Yes, Sheriff. Joe called me last night. I've been working on his request all morning." He pulled out a notebook and opened it.

"Harry S. Truman, born May 8, 1884, in Lamar, Missouri. He was a farmer in Missouri until the First World War. He enlisted and became a battery captain. He returned home to Missouri, married Bess Wallace, and failed in a few businesses before becoming county judge. He is a product of the Pendergast political machine out of Kansas City."

Blaine blew air out of his mouth. "Of course he is. What politician isn't nowadays?"

Carter continued. "It was this connection with Pendergast that led him to run for the Senate in 1934, which he won. He ran for reelection in 1940 and won again." Carter paused. "But here's where you might find something interesting."

Blaine spread his hands. "I'm all ears. What could be more interesting than a crooked machine man from Missouri?"

"It's this committee he runs. The official name is the Committee to Investigate the National Defense Program but most people just call it the Truman Committee."

"What's this committee do?"

"Just as its title implies. It investigates all sorts of things related to the country's national defense. Back in '41, Truman took a trip to see if all the improper things he'd heard about were true. Like companies charging the government two and three times as much money to build inferior barracks, engines, et cetera. It was all true so Truman got the Senate to create this committee and it made him the chair."

Blaine's voice echoed his cynicism. "And now that he's got the power of the gavel, he's doling out sweetheart deals to all his pals and skimming some off the top just like everybody else." He ground the stub of his cigarette under his boot. "Politicians make me sick."

Carter cleared his throat. "Actually, no, that's not it at all. According to the articles I read, from the get-go, Truman's been very open with all his investigations. He sends out investigators, gathers evidence, and writes a report." He paused, "What do you think he does with those reports?"

Blaine shrugged. "Makes some bogus and extravagant claim against the company being investigated and blackmails the company to give him a little on the side."

Carter smiled. "Wrong. He gives the report to the company being investigated so that they have time to read and respond to all the charges in the report."

Blaine was silent for a moment. Not having anything to say, he said, "Go on."

"The committee is made up of Republicans and Democrats. Of the thirty or so reports issued thus far, how many do you think were unanimous?"

"None, I imagine, if you've got Republicans and Democrats on the same committee. Ain't no way any Democrat's going vote against anything for the Army during war, especially if Roosevelt has asked for it."

Carter smiled again. "They were all unanimous."

Duncan chimed in. "You mean to say that this Truman guy investigates a company, allows them to respond to it, and gets the entire committee to vote for it? Where's the skimming come in? Do all the members of the committee get some of the extra money?"

"That's just it, Joe. As far as I can tell, there *is* no skimming. This guy is, if you can imagine it, an honest politician. Last year, *Time* magazine had a list of influential people in Washington, D.C. and Truman was the only member of Congress on that list."

Blaine picked up a stick and began doodling in the dirt. Carter reviewed his notes. "I wrote down one last thing. This Truman Committee is so effective, there have been corporations who have turned around and done the right thing when they learned that the committee *might* investigate them." He closed his notebook and tucked it inside his suit pocket. "That's some power, right there."

Duncan said, "Sounds like you like this guy."

"I admire him. From all that I've read and from the people I've talked to, Harry Truman is a regular guy just trying to help corporations stay honest and true to Uncle Sam." Carter dropped his voice into a conspiratorial whisper. "There's even been some talk about his name being thrown in as a vice presidential candidate later this year at the convention."

Blaine scowled. "We've already got a vice president. What's FDR doing, switching the ticket again?"

Carter held up his hands. "Hey, I don't make the news, I just report it."

The three men were silent for a few moments. Carter broke the silence. "Why'd you ask for this information?"

Blaine stood up and tossed the stick aside. He hooked his

thumbs on his gun belt. "I'd rather not say. But, seeing as you've come to deliver me this information in person, I'll let you in on a little secret. Joe and I met Harry Truman yesterday."

Carter's eyes widened. "Where?" A thought came to him and his eyes widened even more. "Holy cow! Is he investigating a company around here? And in person?" He rubbed his chin. "How much trouble is that company in if Truman himself comes out to investigate. I have to tell my editor. Maybe I can get a story and...."

Blaine laid a hand on Carter's shoulder. "Abe, I don't want you to bring this matter up with anyone else right now. I only asked because we're conducting an investigation on those bodies we found in the river. Truman and two of his traveling companions drove by, stopped, we chatted, and they went on their way. That was it. End of story. Besides, I got the feeling Truman didn't want anyone to know he was in town."

"How do you know that?"

Blaine looked at Carter evenly. "I just know." He dropped his voice to a whisper. "And I suspect Mr. Truman doesn't want to call attention to himself with a big story. Might jeopardize his investigation, if you know what I mean."

Carter opened his mouth to say something then closed it. "Yeah, you're probably right. But listen, if you see Senator Truman again, will you at least ask him if I could get some time with him? It would be a great career boost for me."

Blaine nodded but his thoughts were already elsewhere. "Sure, Abe, but I don't think I'll be seeing him again. He's got his investigation and I've got mine and there isn't any connection between the two."

19

Tuesday
18 April 1944
11:45 a. m., Pacific War Time

Hancock parked the Lincoln directly in front of the hotel door. McLeod sat on a small bench, a cigarette in one hand, a folded newspaper in the other. When Truman and Hancock got out of the car, McLeod rose and took a quick walk-around his car apparently checking for dents.

Hancock slapped McLeod on the shoulder. "Don't worry, Horace, we didn't dent your car." He winked at Truman. "But we collected a lot of dust and it shows up really well on that black paint." With a finger, Hancock wrote the word "dirty" in the dust on the door.

Truman stepped toward McLeod. "I want you to know we appreciate you letting us drive your car this morning and, well, we're going to need it again this afternoon."

McLeod, who had taken out his handkerchief to wipe away Hancock's word, glanced sharply at Truman. "What? Use my car again and leave me out of the investigation? Great." His tone became mocking and a small grin broke through his overt actor-like façade.

Hancock noticed it and narrowed his eyes. "What's going on, Horace?"

McLeod's grin widened to an actual smile that brightened his face and made his eyes sparkle. "I have a case I think I can actually take to trial and win." He tossed his cigarette to the ground and stubbed it under his shoes..

"Would that be the matter Mrs. Hurley asked you about?" Truman asked.

"Yes," McLeod said, "and it's a good one."

"Do tell, Horace," Hancock said.

"Sorry, Carl, I can't do that. Attorney client privilege." Something occurred to him and he put a finger up to his mouth. "But maybe…." He trailed off, lost in an idea.

Truman and Hancock waited for McLeod to say something and, after a few moments of silence, Truman said, "I'm going upstairs to write a few letters. Let's meet in the lobby at half past twelve and have some lunch." He started for the door and that seemed to break McLeod out of his thoughts.

McLeod hooked a thumb over his shoulder "Mrs. Hurley has a telegram for you. It arrived here an hour ago."

Truman raised his eyebrows. He turned, opened the door, and walked inside, holding it open for Hancock and McLeod. Reta Hurley stood behind the front desk, poring over a sheaf of receipts and a ledger. She looked up at the sound of the bell above the door and nodded a hello to Truman.

"You have a telegram, Senator." She walked over to the shelf where messages are kept for all the guests of the hotel, withdrew a yellow envelope, and handed it to Truman.

Truman took out a small pocket knife and slit open the envelope. He unfolded the paper and read.

Washington, D.C.

The United States Senate

Harry, Need you to speak tonight at the Jefferson/Jackson meeting in Walla Walla. Also, press will be there. Give a speech about the good work being done at the naval air station there. FDR would really like for you to do this. Local sheriff, Ira Webb, will drive you. Thanks.

A. Barkley

Truman read the telegram twice and still didn't believe it. His face must have relayed his shock as everyone noticed it.

"What is it, Harry?" Hancock said.

"I have to go to Walla Walla today and give a speech." He handed the telegram to Hancock who read it.

"What?" McLeod said. "Who said that?"

Hancock said, "It says Majority Leader Alban Barkley but, since FDR's mentioned in the letter, you know where the request came from." He refolded the telegram and handed it back to Truman. The senator replaced the letter in the envelope and tucked it inside his suit pocket.

McLeod looked at Truman. "What are you going to do?"

Truman straightened his tie. "Write my speech."

* * *

THIRTY MINUTES LATER, the three men were seated at Grover's Restaurant. They ordered their lunches and sat back to wait. McLeod was still shaking his head at Truman's reaction. The senator had gone upstairs and, in less than half an hour, written an outline for a speech he intended to give that night.

"I still can't believe you're just going to get up and leave here to go give a speech."

Truman looked across the table at McLeod. "Mr. Roosevelt is the President of the United States, the Commander in Chief, and the leader of my party. If he wants me to go sell cookies for the boys overseas, I'm going to do it. I may not like it, but it's my duty to him, our country, and our party."

Hancock was used to Truman talking like this and it didn't surprise him. In fact, he felt much the same way. McLeod just nodded in agreement.

Truman filled McLeod in on the broad details of the morning.

He had been reluctant to do so but Hancock had convinced him that McLeod knowing some of the details would not jeopardize the investigation.

When Truman mentioned the name of the night watchman, McLeod interrupted. "Did you say Richard Stanley, The night watchman?"

Truman and Hancock leaned in towards McLeod. Hancock nodded.

"You're not going to believe this—I don't even believe it when I think about it—but I actually saw him one night, out in front of the warehouse."

"What do you mean 'saw'?" Hancock asked.

McLeod cleared his throat. He started rearranging his silverware. "Well…I…uh…did a, what do you call it, a stakeout."

Hancock's eyebrows rose in surprise. Truman removed his glasses and started to clean them with his handkerchief. He did this mainly to hide the smile spreading across his face. He replaced his glasses and his handkerchief. "That was an interesting thing to do. Well, what did you see?"

McLeod had rearranged all his silverware into the proper etiquette pattern and then began to move them around again. "I don't know much about actual police procedures. What I know is from the movies. But I know enough to buy a pair of binoculars." He looked up at Hancock. "I wanted to be able to see anything if, well, anything happened."

"Did it?"

"Around eleven o'clock one evening, I left the hotel here and drove up to the warehouse. Since there are no trees around here, I thought that the best place to park the Lincoln was across the highway in the gravel yard. I was actually proud of myself for being able to come up a back road and park without my headlights on." He looked to Hancock for encouragement and received a nod.

"From there, I was able to see the main bay doors of the warehouse and had a good view of that new sign. I watched Mr. Stanley conducting his rounds. He seemed pretty thorough."

"And what was his routine?" Hancock asked.

"He didn't vary much. He walked in a circle around the warehouse every seven minutes or so. Every other hour, on the top of the hour, he would go inside for ten minutes. I just assumed he was patrolling the inside or taking a break."

"How long did he stay guarding the warehouse?" Truman asked.

At this question, McLeod actually blushed and looked back down at his silverware. "I don't really know."

Truman leaned closer. "Why don't you know?"

He started rearranging his silverware. "I, uh, fell asleep."

Truman didn't move and kept looking at McLeod. Hancock put a hand over his mouth to hide his smile.

"When I woke up, dawn was just breaking. Twenty past five. I looked at the warehouse and timed seven minutes but no Stanley. I waited fifteen more minutes and nothing moved." He snapped his fingers. "But there was another car parked next to the warehouse."

"Did you recognize it?" Hancock said.

"I think it belongs to either Edward or Chris Moore. They both drive the same model car, a Plymouth."

"That's an interesting piece of information, Horace," Hancock said. "It at least gives us a rough timeline of Stanley's routine. It also corroborates what we heard from a guy named Peter Allan."

McLeod looked sheepish. "I'm sorry I can't give you a better report. But I'm a lawyer, not a cop."

Hancock stood, reached over, and slapped McLeod's shoulder. "That's okay, Horace," he said and glanced over at Truman, who nodded. "You'll get a chance to redeem yourself tonight."

McLeod looked up at Hancock, confusion on his face, then realization. "You don't mean to go out there, do you?"

"Why not? We need more information and I want to take a look myself. Besides, Harry's going to be doing his thing in Walla Walla tonight. I'd sure appreciate the company." He leaned over to McLeod and, in a stage whisper, said, "And this way, I can help you stay awake."

20

Tuesday
18 April 1944
12:30 p. m., Pacific War Time

Captain Morimoto found Ishihara and Niigata hunched around one of the torpedo tubes in the forward torpedo room. Their backs were to him and he walked into the room unnoticed. Curious as to what they were so adamantly discussing, he stood there for a few moments before they noticed him. He heard a few words out of context: "honor," "avenge," and "killing."

He didn't even have to clear his throat or do one of the numerous other tactics captains employ to get what they want. Lieutenant Niigata glanced behind him and saw the captain. The lieutenant's eyes widened slightly and he put himself to attention, nudging Ishihara in the process. Ishihara also stood at attention.

"You two seem to be discussing something rather important. What was it?"

Ishihara's answer filled the momentary silence. "Sir, we were discussing the mission and what an honor it will be to attack the Americans on their own shore."

Morimoto pursed his lips. "I see." He stepped forward, hands behind his back. "It is quite an honor, as is duty and loyalty to the Imperial Japanese Navy and the Emperor." He paused to inspect the torpedo resting in its cage. "I just spoke with Engineer Okada. He tells me that the amount of fuel in the plane after it returned a few days ago was inconsistent with the usual amount used for a reconnaissance flight."

He looked over at his two officers but neither man made any outward gesture. Morimoto continued. "Okada-san tells me that there was very little remaining in the plane's tank. And that if the flight had lasted much longer, the plane would have run out of fuel."

Morimoto glided his finger along the body of the torpedo from its propeller to its nose. "I asked him what would cause so much fuel to be expended. He said it could be many factors: strong headwind or a leak in the tank. He checked the tank and it is airtight. Headwinds are certainly a plausible explanation." He stopped walking along the torpedo body and faced Ishihara and Niigata. "Okada-san also mentioned that the extra fuel could have been expended during a take-off from the water."

Morimoto studied the eyes of his men. Both men's eyes stayed focused on the far wall. He let his last words hang in the silence.

Again, Ishihara broke the silence. "Captain-san, if I may, the headwinds were stronger than usual, both going to the military base and returning to the sub. Sir."

"Of course," Morimoto said. He turned to Niigata. "Would you concur, Lieutenant?"

Niigata nodded once. "Yes, sir."

Morimoto inhaled deeply and let the air out slowly. "That is good to hear. It reassures me that everyone has one goal on which they can focus: disrupt the American defenses and make them have to pay more attention to their homeland." He looked at each man in turn. "I would certainly hate to think that one of my officers was risking the mission by conducting unauthorized side missions."

Morimoto looked directly at Niigata, the weaker of his subordinates. "And I can count on any man to inform me of any extracurricular, correct?" The younger man didn't flinch but Morimoto noticed the beads of sweat on Niigata's forehead and above his upper lip.

Morimoto turned to Ishihara. "And, Lieutenant, next time, you will note on the official log, any occurrences of headwinds. We have a limited supply of fuel and we need to have enough for our strike against the American factory."

"Yes, sir," Ishihara said immediately.

"Very well, then. Carry on." Morimoto turned on his heels and left the room.

Niigata turned on Ishihara and glared. "You arrogant fool! The captain suspects exactly what happened. Your bloodlust is going to get us killed."

Ishihara looked at Niigata disapprovingly. "In case you have forgotten, my friend, we are at war. To die for the Emperor and our people is the noblest thing imaginable. I hope that we do die in the line of duty." He looked at the far door. "Do not worry about the captain. By tomorrow night, it will not matter."

Niigata grabbed Ishihara's shirt. "It is not Morimoto that I worry about." He pulled Ishihara closer to him. "If we are to conduct our mission, it must be in the utmost secrecy. Your unauthorized landing and murdering of those two Americans is bound to be noticed. And if it is, the Americans will be more vigilant."

Ishihara wrenched his shirt from Niigata's grasp and straightened it. "You worry too much. We have a weapon at our disposal the United States Army knows nothing about. We can strike at the heart of America at will."

Ishihara started walking toward the hatch and the crew quarters. He paused and, over his shoulder, said, "Besides, Niigata-san, there were no survivors. And there were no witnesses. You saw none and I saw none. By now, the wolves and bears will have had their fill."

21

Tuesday
18 April 1944
12:45 p. m., Pacific War Time

Theodore Frank stumbled, tried to catch his balance, and fell to the ground. Dust plumed around him. He breathed heavily, his panting created eddies in the air. He looked at his watch and he decided to rest for a few minutes.

In the silence, he sat, trying not to see the images in his head. As an artist, his mind was trained to capture every detail and render them on canvas or paper. His lower lip and chin quivered as the horrors came rushing back to him. He needed to think clearly so he took his pain and buried it deep within himself. As he sat by the shore of the Columbia River, he played out the events in his mind again. Was there anything he could have done? Was there any way he could have helped his two friends?

* * *

TWO DAYS AGO, Frank had been walking in the woods with two of his friends, Ron Garrison and Jack Buchan. It was the evening of the new moon and they had a task, a duty really. They were to go to one of the four pre-ordained drop-off sites and get their provisions.

Drop Site Four was the farthest from the main camp. The pick-up teams always hiked to the drop-off sites. It proved easier to remain concealed by staying off the roads and rivers.

The night was clear but the moonless sky required the men to use their flashlights despite the dangers of being seen and their familiarity with the surroundings. Moths and other insects bounced around the lights as the men made their way toward the Columbia. Drop Site Four was the only rendezvous where the men had to cross the river to get to the supplies. The truck driver who delivered the provisions always left the provisions in a small wooded outcropping. There was no bridge for miles and the main road was over a mile away. It was a good place to make exchanges in stealth. It only required a river crossing.

"Why does it always have to be white?" Garrison asked, pointing to the crate across the river. "Do they want to just advertise that we're out here?"

"Don't worry," Buchan said. "You can only see it from a plane, and we're not on any flight paths. That's why we chose this spot."

Garrison huffed and trudged onward.

Frank stopped. "You go on ahead. I have to take a piss."

"That makes you the lookout," Buchan said. For every one of their monthly supply runs, one man would stay back away from the others to watch for cars, boats, or planes.

Frank found a nearby tree and relieved himself. He looked up and noticed Garrison and Buchan had already begun to wade into the river. The light of their flashlights bounced off the water and lit up the trees. This part of the Columbia was wide, nearly ninety feet. A small sandbar was situated halfway between the two shores and this often served as a way station, especially on the return trip when the men were burdened with supplies.

As Frank tried to zip up his pants, his zipper got stuck. "Crap," he muttered as he tried to fix his zipper. He dropped his flashlight and he heard the small pop that meant the bulb broke. "Crap, crap!"

It was then that he heard an airplane. He looked up and, through the thinning trees, saw a dark shape flying east. One thought entered his mind: I'm the lookout. I have to warn them.

He looked over the river and saw that Garrison and Buchan had turned off their flashlights and sat, crouched next to the crate, also having heard the airplane.

In a stage whisper that didn't seem to travel very far, Frank said, "Guys, what are you doing? I can still see you so I know the pilot can still see you. Take cover."

Above, he heard the sound of the plane as it turned around and began heading back toward their position. The sound got louder and louder.

Frank took out his Zippo and, with the flame, found the piece of his shirt that was jammed inside the teeth of the zipper. He yanked the piece out, zipped up his pants, and started running toward the tree line, careful to stay inside the forest and prevent the pilot from seeing him.

He heard the splash before he saw the plane gliding on the water. He looked to his left and saw the dark shape of the plane floating on the water toward the other side of the river, where the crate and his two friends sat.

The plane was painted black but had no other distinguishing marks on its fuselage. The pilot cut power to the propeller and the sudden silence was broken only by the soft lapping of the water. The instrument panels in the plane illuminated two faces and Frank realized the plane was a two-seater, one behind the other, in tandem.

Frank wished he had carried the binoculars but Buchan had them. As his eyes continually adjusted to the night, more details came into view. From the ambient starlight he saw the forward cockpit glass slide back and the pilot stood up on the seat. With the plane still gliding toward the far shore, Frank saw the pilot climb down and stand on one of the pontoons. Then the pilot stepped off and Frank heard the small splash and swishing of water as the pilot walked onshore and toward Garrison and Buchan.

Frank's mind began to race. They were caught. He just wondered what Buchan would tell the pilot about why he and Garrison were there. Instinctively, Frank crouched closer to the ground, the tall grass easily concealing his position.

And then he heard a sound he didn't expect. It was the sound of a man screaming. It was followed by a gurgling sound. Someone yelled, "You Nip bastard!" and then another scream. This second scream was different from the first one and it took Frank's brain a few seconds to realize that the second scream and the words came from the same man.

His heart was hammering in his throat and his stomach felt empty. Without a thought, he stood up and walked behind a large tree. He hoped he could get a better view and he did.

A dark shape of a man was looking inside the crate. Frank could hear the sound of rustling and rummaging. He also saw two other dark shapes laying on the river's edge. One of the bodies still twitched.

The man crouched in front of the crate for a few moments and then stood. He walked over to the river and put his hands in the water. He then stood up and walked over to one of the dark shapes on the ground. With a great effort, the man dragged the shape toward the river.

With an audible gasp, Frank realized the limp shape was that of a man. A dying or dead man, and the body made a great splash in the river. The pilot then proceeded to kick the body farther into the river. It floated, the body's white shirt catching the starlight. Jack had been wearing a white shirt.

The silhouetted pilot did the same thing to the other body on the shore. This second body was the one still twitching and it continued to twitch as it floated away.

Frank's mind reeled at what had just happened. The pilot climbed back into the forward cockpit. Within seconds, the engine noise erupted and the plane taxied toward the middle of the river, beyond the sand bar. Frank saw something fluttering in the wind along the fuselage. He could not tell what was making the fluttering but he caught sight of a giant lighter dot underneath the fluttering thing. He made a mental note of this distinguishing characteristic and watched the plane pick up speed and lift off.

The sound of the plane faded after three minutes. But the sound that echoed in Frank's head stayed longer. It was the sound of the pilot laughing.

* * *

THEODORE FRANK REMEMBERED the sound of the laughter and, despite the afternoon heat, a chill went through him.

He reviewed his situation and the only course of action left for him. When he had joined this group, there were two leaders: one in Richland and one at the campsite. Garrison had been the leader at the campsite, someone he knew well. But Frank had met Edward Moore, the leader in Richland, only once.

For any who joined the group, there was only one real directive: never reveal the nature and location of the group or the campsite. Under no circumstances was this to be done.

Despite his dilemma, Frank still believed in the cause. He would tell no one about the campsite or what he was doing out and about in the wilderness. Unfortunately, this vow eliminated him from going to the police or just asking for help from a kindly person living out in the country. The police were obvious. They would ask questions and keep asking questions until they had his head turned around and he let slip something that should have remained secret.

But even a motorist would eventually ask questions or tell someone who would ask questions and, inevitably, things would go wrong.

No, Frank thought, there is only one thing to do: find Edward Moore and tell him what had happened. Moore would know what to do.

The problem was that Frank didn't know where Edward Moore lived. The only thing he knew about Moore was that his warehouse was located on the Columbia River.

Frank rose from his spot and looked east. Richland was in that direction. He looked to his right and found comfort in the mighty Columbia.

With a great inhale of breath, Theodore Frank put on a determined face and began walking.

22

Monday
18 April 1944
1:30 p.m., Pacific War Time

Truman ran his hands lightly over the steering wheel. "This car sure is fun to drive."

Hancock smiled sidelong at Truman. "Yeah. I'm going to have to ask for a raise after this so I can afford one."

Truman slowed the car and turned into the Moore Warehouse parking lot. The same parking space they had used that morning was still open, so Truman pulled in and killed the engine. They faced the highway and saw the gravel yard McLeod had used for his first foray into spying.

"I can see why that yard is such a great hiding place," Hancock said. "The piles of rock and dirt are high enough to obscure even a truck. Don't know about you, but, since rock yards are so common, I frankly didn't notice that place this morning."

"That could certainly help y'all tonight," Truman said, grabbing his hat. "Now, let's go see Mr. Edward Moore."

They got out of the car and walked toward the warehouse. The activity was even more chaotic than in the morning. Four flatbed trucks loaded with crates and supplies were lined up in front of the warehouse bay doors. Truman and Hancock opted for the smaller door to the right. As their eyes adjusted from the bright sun, they saw Larry Watson approaching.

The foreman extended his hand to both Truman and then to Hancock. "Good afternoon, gentlemen. I hope you had a pleasant lunch. Mr. Moore is in his office. He told me to bring you up when you got here. Follow me."

He led them up the stairs. At the top of the landing, they turned and walked toward the open door of Moore's private office. Watson paused at the entrance and allowed Truman and Hancock to enter the office ahead of him.

Expecting a space that resembled an office, both men were astonished at the look of Moore's office. All four walls were covered with hunting trophies. Taxidermied deer and moose mingled with salmon and ducks. On the wall nearest the door, a large marlin swam on the wall, forever caught in mid-jump.

There was a sitting area in the far corner with a wing-backed chair and a small table with a reading lamp. Next to the chair sat a small bookshelf with magazines and books neatly arranged. Truman noticed a few of the titles: *Field and Stream*, the collected journals of Lewis and Clark, a biography of Theodore Roosevelt, and Hemingway's *For Whom the Bell Tolls*. There was also a bookcase on the far side of the room to the left of the desk.

To their left, centered on the wall, was Moore's desk. It was a large oak desk with various office bric-a-brac dotting its surface: a pencil cup carved from an antler, a stainless steel pipe rack with a box of tobacco next to it, a desk pad with bottles of ink and a blotter.

At the desk sat Edward Moore. He looked up when Truman and Hancock entered the room, his broad smile reached all the way up to his eyes.

"Senator Truman," Moore said as he rose from the desk and

walked over to greet his visitors. He wore a heavily-starched blue denim shirt and a black tie. His shirt seemed more at home on a safari than in an office. His khakis were pressed, the only creases showing around his waist indicating that he had been sitting. Hancock noticed with approval that Moore wore cowboy boots that were polished but worn.

Moore stood about an inch taller than Hancock and he towered over Truman. He extended his hand and the senator took it. Unlike his son, Moore didn't try to break Truman's hand, instead offering a nice firm handshake.

Moore next turned to Hancock and the two shook hands. Perhaps because he was almost as tall as Moore, Hancock felt his handshake with Moore was a bit more aggressive than Moore's and Truman's had appeared.

"Mr. Hancock, isn't it?" Moore noted the Stetson and boots. "A Texan. I love that state and its rugged history."

"I'm partial to it, Mr. Moore."

Moore swept his hand to the two chairs opposite his desk. "And I hear that you used to be a sheriff's deputy. Ever give any thought to becoming one of the great Texas Rangers?"

Hancock didn't even bat an eye at Moore's knowledge about him. "Mr. Moore, every boy in Texas—and more than a few men— dreams of becoming a Texas Ranger. Truth is, I enjoyed being a deputy. Plus, the wife prefers me being close to home."

There was a twinkle in Moore's eye. "So, they turned you down?" The twinkle remained in his eyes as he stared at Hancock.

The Texan met the stare and returned it. "No, sir. I told you. I enjoyed being a deputy. Then, Senator Truman here offered me a job working in Washington. I work for Uncle Sam, do my part to help the boys overseas, bringing down big shot businessmen who think they can cheat the government. What's not to like about that?" One corner of Hancock's mouth quirked up.

In the moment of silence that followed, Hancock and Truman sat down in the offered chairs, leaving Moore standing. He spread his hands and then sat down in his chair.

He picked up the cigarette box, opened it, and offered it to Hancock and Truman. "Cigarette?"

"No, thank you," Truman said.

"I'll pass," Hancock said, pulling a stick of gum out of his pocket.

Moore withdrew a cigarette, tapped it on the desk, and lit it. "That's why you both are here, isn't it? You think there's something criminal going on." He exhaled smoke. "I can assure you, everything is on the up and up."

"Mr. Watson was certainly helpful this morning," Truman said, nodding at Watson who stood in the open doorway. "He gave us the tour of your facility and an overall scope of how much work you do for the government. It's quite impressive."

Moore nodded to Truman. "I thank you for the compliment, Senator Truman. Coming from a man with your reputation, that is a high compliment indeed." He scratched his mustache. "I imagine you see quite a bit of the country, what with your inspection trips and such. Tell me, what do you think of our little space out here in The Evergreen State?"

"When I decided to come out here, I re-read some of the passages in the Lewis and Clark journals to remind myself what they had to say about it. It's a strange sight to come from the greener lands in the western part of the state to this desert. I imagine that's why the government selected this area."

"Yes, the government and their little operation up there. I can't go to war myself and my only son nearly died in the service. I think of this as my way of giving back to the country that has meant so much to me."

"So, you're a native Washingtonian?" Hancock asked.

Moore hesitated but only for a split second. "My parents were both born in Washington. They were missionaries. I was born overseas but I am, and have been, an American citizen since birth."

"Where did your parents spread the good news?" Hancock said.

"The Far East mainly. The Philippines after the Spanish-American War, Thailand, China, elsewhere. I sometimes say that I'm from everywhere."

"Mr. Moore," Truman said, "one requirement of our inspection is a comprehensive review of the financial records. When we arrived this morning, we were told that only you and Mr. Riley have access to the books. You weren't in the office and Mr. Riley has taken ill."

"Yes, poor Benjamin. I heard about it when I got here. I was told they took him and his wife to the hospital in Hanford. I sure hope he recovers quickly. He's my only accountant and I'm far too busy with other matters to also tend to the books."

"What will you do in the meantime?" Truman asked.

"The only thing possible until Benjamin returns. I'll take care of the books and I'll delegate other matters to Christopher."

"We met him this morning, too," Hancock said, a little sarcasm lining his voice.

"Please, forgive him, Mr. Hancock. Christopher had big dreams of getting away from this small town and making it big in the movies." Moore's countenance changed a bit as he talked about his son. "It is a painful thing to see your child's dreams dashed in the split second of a bomb blast. I'm just thankful his mother wasn't around to see his decline."

"Speaking of Mrs. Moore," Hancock said, "how did she fit into your little business here?"

Moore's countenance hardened and his eyes became like steel. "Mr. Hancock, I don't consider my personal life germane for your investigation and I would kindly ask you to refrain from bringing up any additional personal matters." He closed his eyes and then opened them. "My wife died three years ago."

Looking back at Truman, Moore said, "Senator Truman, is this how you conduct all your investigations? If it is, I'm surprised you have such a good reputation."

Truman felt his temper rising and didn't like the pointed accusation. "Mr. Moore, where I'm from, it's considered good manners to inquire about a man's family. I think the same is true of Mr. Hancock's Texas. But, back to the matter at hand, we're conducting an inspection, not an investigation."

"Semantics, Mr. Truman."

Truman continued. "Since you're now present, we would like to review your books for the last fiscal year. We'll need a room in which to review the books without any interruption. In addition, we may find it necessary to interview some of your employees. I want you to facilitate these interviews if they are deemed necessary."

As Truman looked at Moore, the other man's steely eyes bored into him. From behind his spectacles, Truman returned the stare with eyes equally as steely.

Moore finally blinked and smiled. He stubbed out his cigarette and lit another one. "Certainly, Senator, you can use Benjamin's office next door. He won't need it anytime soon." He paused and sat there smoking. "If you don't mind, Senator, will you answer one question for me?"

"Certainly."

"How was it that you decided to come all the way out here, to Washington State, to conduct an inspection of my warehouse?"

The question hung in the air as Truman paused for effect. He had memorized the answer before he left the hotel after lunch.

"As you may know, Mr. Moore, I travel around the country, conducting inspections and giving speeches. I happened to be out here and am due to speak tonight in Walla Walla. It occurred to me, since I was in the neighborhood, that I should drop by your establishment and see what it is you do here to make your business so efficient. Word has reached me through official channels that, of all the companies engaged in this great project out here, yours is one of the best and most respected. With that in mind, I thought it prudent to discover the secret of your success and share it with others and help bring an end to this war all the sooner."

Moore had been silently exhaling while Truman spoke and now the cigarette hung limp from the corner of his mouth. It rose as Moore's mouth broke into a wide grin. "That's a good political answer for the reporters and the news reels." He leaned forward on his desk. "Now, just between us, what's the real reason you're here?"

Truman was nonplussed. "I just told you. At the end of our inspection, I'll bring reporters here and make a big speech about how well you do your part to help our boys overseas. I'll stand in front of your warehouse, with you right beside me, and I'll make a big show of shaking your hand and we'll all be smiling. Then, after I've told the nation what a great and efficient organization the Moore Warehouse is, businessmen from all over will come here and ask your secrets and learn how to make their own businesses more efficient and how to help our boys come home after the war."

Moore was silent for a moment, his elbows still on his desk, the burning cigarette hanging from his lips. He looked from Truman to Hancock and, with eyebrows raised, conceded Truman's point.

"Yeah, there's the post-war to think about, isn't there?" His smile was rueful. "The post-war world. This war has been going on so long that it's difficult to remember what life was like before it started."

He stood up and walked to a globe resting on a pedestal. It was printed to look older than it was, with brown to denote the oceans and matted colors for the countries. Moore spun the globe as he spoke.

"The second front in Europe will likely be the key to beating Hitler. I know the Soviets will surely appreciate it." He stopped the spinning globe and pointed at Japan. "But what do you suppose will be the key to Japan surrendering?"

Truman rose and strode over to stand next to Moore. He moved the globe to show Europe and the Soviet Union. He moved his fingers across the globe as he spoke.

"The key to beating Japan will be to beat Hitler first. We'll liberate Europe as soon as possible while we hold our own against Japan. Then, after the liberation of Europe, all of the Allies—Americans, the British, the Canadians, the Russians, the Australians, everybody—will focus their attention on Japan. And, just like Grant and the Union in the Civil War, we'll deploy overwhelming strength against Tojo's forces. We'll capture island after island and squeeze the Japanese until they surrender." He paused at the sobering reality of his prediction.

Moore nodded. "How many men will die? I have my own ideas but I'd like to hear yours."

Truman shook his head. "Too many. We've already lost close to 200,000 good men and that doesn't include the second front. The industrial facilities in Japan are still beyond the range of our bombers and, until we start striking their homeland, we have to fight them island by island. Judging by the Battle of the Solomon Islands, the Japanese fight like the dickens and don't give up easy." He tapped the globe. "If I had to guess, I'd say another 400,000."

Moore smiled without humor. "If only there was a way to end the war faster."

"I'm not sure that's possible."

Silence loomed for a moment before Truman continued. "But, Mr. Moore, let's begin our inspection and see if we can trim that number down and bring more boys home alive."

Hancock rose and walked toward the door. Next to the door was a small table. Hancock picked up a framed picture and looked at it. The picture showed a man, a woman, and a little boy. They were posing in front of a structure Hancock had never before seen. The high roof met in a steep arch with a brown and white façade in front. In the background, Hancock saw people going into and out of the structure. Most of the people in the background of the picture all wore traditional Japanese kimonos. Above the structure flew the Japanese flag.

"Is this you, Chris, and the missus going on vacation?"

"No, Mr. Hancock," Moore said, taking the picture from Hancock and looking at it. "That's the only photo I have of my parents."

"I know you said your parents were missionaries but you didn't mention you lived in Japan. How long?"

Moore eyed Hancock warily. "Off and on over twenty years. I was there when I was nine—that's this picture—and then again in my later teen years."

He replaced the picture on the table. "I know what you're thinking. Why didn't I mention Japan when I was telling you all the places I've lived in my life? I'll tell you why. Do you remember what happened to the German-Americans when the U.S. entered the Great War?"

Moore continued without giving his guests the chance to reply. "Discrimination, pure and simple. German-Americans, sometimes second and third generation, were looked upon with suspicious eyes. Some were forced to buy war bonds just to prove they were loyal to the U. S. True German names were 'Americanized' to better assimilate into this country."

"Pardon my ignorance," Hancock said, "but what do you mean by 'Americanized'?"

Moore sighed. "People changed their names to names that sounded American. For example, a Mr. Schmidt would become Mr. Smith."

"But how does this affect you?" Truman said. "You're an American."

"Yes, but I've lived in the land of our current enemy for a third of my life. There are some aspects of that culture I appreciate. I kept a correspondence with a few Japanese friends until Pearl Harbor." He walked back over to his desk and lit another cigarette.

"You wouldn't believe the stares I received when I went to the post office in January 1942 and had, in my stack of mail, a letter from Japan. The postman, in his arrogance, placed that letter—with its Japanese postmark—on top of the entire stack for everyone to see. And then, to top it all, I found that the envelope had been opened. I can only assume it was by a government official or perhaps the mail carrier. It was probably some feeble attempt to see if I was a spy."

"You can't deny a mailman's curiosity, Mr. Moore," Hancock said. "It would be the same thing if you saw a swastika on an envelope."

"So, because I have friends that are citizens of the enemy country, I'm now under suspicion? And what if that friend and I share a common goal: that all nations should live in peace?"

"No one is accusing anyone of anything," Truman said, raising a hand in the space between Hancock and Moore. The tone of Moore's last comment had a rising note to it and Truman thought he had better put a stop to the conversation before their work became compromised. "But we've got an inspection to make. If you don't mind, Mr. Moore, I want to begin as soon as possible. I have a speech to make tonight and I want to get through most of the books today, if at all possible."

The left side of Moore's mustache twitched. Truman and Hancock both saw Moore visibly get himself under control. Within a few seconds, the man was completely changed and his calm demeanor returned.

"Right this way, gentlemen."

23

Tuesday
19 April 1944
2:05 p.m., Pacific War Time

Edward Moore led the way into the adjoining office. As the four men entered, they found Moore's son sitting at the desk.

"Hello again," Hancock said as Christopher glared at him.

Edward gave Hancock a sidelong glance that Truman caught. The senator read the glance as more than mere annoyance or fatherly protection. He read it as growing dislike for Hancock.

Good, thought Truman. He made a mental note to let Hancock continue and see if he could get under Edward's skin.

"Christopher, I believe you've already met Senator Truman and Mr. Hancock." He paused, expecting a response from his son. He got a curt nod and continued. "They're here from Washington, D.C. and they'll be conducting an inspection of our facility here. Mr. Truman is convinced our efficiency can be a model for other companies to strive to greater heights and help end this war sooner."

Christopher smirked at his father's comments. While it didn't wholly undermine the elder Moore, Truman thought that the younger man's poor attitude was not lost on his father.

"Are you entering this morning's shipments into the ledger?" Edward asked, indicating the open book and invoices on the desk.

"Yes sir."

"Are you finished?"

"Yes, sir. I'm entering the last one right now. It's our grain shipment from Nebraska."

"Right," Edward said, looking at Truman. "What would we do without the Midwestern bread basket?"

"We'd all be a lot hungrier."

Everyone in the room chuckled except Christopher. Then, as if by force of will, he, too, laughed at the joke.

"When you're done, these two gentlemen are going to inspect our warehouse, starting with the ledger. Get the previous year's ledger, too?"

Christopher dropped his pen on the desk and walked over to the file cabinets. He opened the top drawer, shuffled through some folders, and brought out a ledger book. He closed the drawer and dropped the book on the desk, ruffling the invoices.

"There you go," he said and walked over to the other side of the room and sat in a chair. Clearly, he wanted to be present while Hancock and Truman reviewed the books.

"Actually, Mr. Moore," Hancock said, "we need to conduct our review of the books in private. It eliminates any hint of impropriety if this inspection turns up anything."

"Anything?" Christopher said. "What do you expect to find? We conduct our business on the up-and-up. There's no 'impropriety' here. We're above board and we do not—"

"Easy, son," Hancock said. "I didn't mean…"

"I'm not your son."

"My apologies," Hancock said, holding up his hand toward the young man. "I didn't mean anything. It's just that we've had some of our investigations go astray when it was learned that members of the company were present during the ledger reviews. It just doesn't look good. Besides, we're here on a goodwill tour, like Mr. Truman here said. We just want to get a good understanding of how y'all run this company, take some notes, and pass them on to other companies. Plus, when the reporters get here, you'll have your picture up on the newsreels."

At the mention of the cameras, Christopher's face lit up. Then, almost as fast, his face darkened as he reached up his hand and stroked the scar along his cheek.

Edward stepped over to his son and placed a hand on the young man's shoulder. "Come on, Chris, let's leave these men to their work. I want you to help Larry make a list of all our employees in case Senator Truman feels it necessary to conduct interviews."

Christopher stood. "Yeah, I'll go do that. He started walking out the door. "C'mon Larry, let's go make a list."

Both men exited the office but Edward paused at the door. "Please make yourselves as comfortable as possible. The head is downstairs and toward the northeast side of the warehouse. Coffee's in the break room, at the back of the warehouse. And, if you need anything, please don't hesitate to call me. I'll be next door."

Edward exited the room and Hancock was about to say something when Truman raised his hand to quiet him. They stood listening to Moore walk the few steps to his office and close the door. They heard his footsteps on the wooden floor until they were silenced as he stepped onto the carpet under his desk. They heard the creaking of his chair and he sat in it and then nothing.

Hancock studied the maps on the wall as Truman sat at the desk and opened the first ledger. He began to leaf through the pages. Hancock heard the pages turn faster and faster. He glanced down at Truman. "With speed like that, we may be done by supper."

"Take a look at this." He turned the ledger book to where Hancock could read it.

On each page, the standard pieces of information were listed: Item, Date, Description, Quantity, Location Shipped from, List Price, and Total Price. Hancock looked at one page and then flipped to another page. He skimmed a few more pages and then looked up at Truman. "I'm sorry, Harry, I don't see anything wrong."

"Precisely." Truman tapped a finger on the book. "There is not a single error anywhere in this book. Oh, sure, there are individual words crossed through but no line item was entered incorrectly. Does that strike you as odd?"

"Yeah, maybe." He pointed at the maps on the wall with his head. "But if Mr. Riley is as meticulous with his books as he is with these maps, that doesn't strike me as odd."

"You know I used to run a haberdashery. Invariably, there would be a mix-up of items shipped, the incorrect number would be entered. Heck, even the end of the year tallies would have some sort of reconciliation."

Hancock walked over to the file cabinets. He reached in the drawer and pulled out two additional ledgers. He placed them on the desk and opened the one marked "1943."

He quickly flipped to the last page and both men looked at it. There, in the same neat, formal handwriting of the "1944" book were the year-end tallies. There were no cross-outs, deletions, insertions, or reconciliations of any kind.

Hancock looked up at Truman. "Okay, so maybe Mr. Riley is precise with his record keeping."

"Carl, in all your experience as an investigator for me, have you ever seen a book this clean?"

After a moment's thought, Hancock said, "Can't say that I have."

"Me, neither." Truman rubbed his chin with his fingers. "We're going to have to cross check these ledgers with the original invoices. Did you see them over there?"

After reading the identification tags on all the drawers, Hancock opened one and scanned the file folders. He sighed. "They're arranged by company." He stuck his fingers inside one folder and then the one next to it. He signed again. "And, they're not chronological."

Truman took off his spectacles and cleaned them with his handkerchief. He held them up to the light and then replaced them on his face. He put his handkerchief back into his breast pocket. "Well, here's where we earn our money." He turned to the first page of the "1944" ledger.

24

Tuesday
18 April 1944
4:05 p.m. Pacific War Time

Sheriff Lester Blaine sat at his desk, tracing and retracing the four words he wrote on the legal pad. He traced each block letter with his pencil, each time the indentation of the letters grew deeper. The letters spelled out the words he had been seeking since this morning: Moore Warehouse, Richland, Washington.

Yet something was wrong. He had telephoned all the local sheriffs and asked about large-scale burglaries in recent months. He had received all negative responses. But here were two bodies, one of which had, upon his person, a packet of powdered milk and a partial invoice for powdered milk from a warehouse in Richland, Washington.

Blaine had spoken directly to Sheriff Webb of Richland and Webb had said there had been no burglaries of any large-scale items. Blaine remembered that Webb was one of the sheriffs who had asked about the inquiry and why Blaine was making it. Blaine had made up something he had already forgotten.

"Time to come clean," Blaine said as he picked up the telephone. He asked the operator to connect him with the Belton County Sheriff's Office. While he waited for the connection to be made, he lit a cigarette. The act of smoking calmed him for what he was about to do: confront a colleague.

The dispatcher answered the call and Blaine said, "Yes, this is Sheriff Blaine of Umatilla County, Oregon. May I speak with Sheriff Webb, please?" Another pull on the cigarette.

The dispatcher went off the line as Webb picked up his telephone. "Lester. What, you just like hearing my voice so much you decided to call me again?"

Blaine smiled. Humor was one way of hiding apprehension. "No, it's nothing like that. I'd like to ask a few follow-up questions to our conversation this morning."

There was a slight hesitation before Webb spoke. "Lester, you and I are cops. We both know the drill. You either had these questions in your head this morning or something has come up to lead to these new questions. As a fellow sheriff, at least tell me which one it is."

He took a pull on the cigarette. "It's the second one, Ira." Blaine leaned back in his chair and put his feet up on the desk.

"Let me guess: it ain't about some lost cattle down there in Oregon, is it?"

Blaine snapped his fingers, remembering the cover story. "No, Ira, it isn't." Another pull on the cigarette. "It's a murder investigation."

Webb was silent for a few seconds. "Who?"

Blaine chuckled dryly. "That's the thing, I don't know. One of my deputies found two bodies in the Columbia yesterday. Both males, their pockets were full of camping supplies, but no ID on them whatsoever."

"Okay, but I don't see what this has to do with me unless you're asking for assistance."

"Well, this morning, when I asked about any burglaries of large items, you said that there hadn't been any. One of the things we found on one of the victims was an invoice for powdered milk. The destination location was torn off but I traced it back through the originating company. The destination was the Moore Warehouse in Richland."

Blaine heard some rustling over the telephone and then a thump. Webb said, "Did you say Moore Warehouse?"

"Yeah."

"Tell me again where you found these men?"

"Along my side of the Columbia. The coroner said they'd been dead for two, three days. I've got as many theories as I do deputies so I was going to pay a visit to Mr. Moore and see if he could shed any light on who these men might be."

"Why you gonna do that?"

Blaine cocked his head. "Well, since these men might have stolen goods from the warehouse, I'm going to start by asking why Mr. Moore hadn't told you."

The silence on the line stretched long enough that Blaine thought the line had died. "Ira, you still there?"

"Yeah, sorry. One of my deputies just walked in and told me I'll be driving some big-shot senator to some political thing tonight in Walla Walla."

Blaine perked up. "Senator? What's his name?"

"Hang on, let me read it. Harry Truman, U.S. senator from Missouri. Know anything about him?"

Blaine stubbed out his cigarette. "A little bit. I met him yesterday. He gave me a fake name and said he sold insurance. Later, when I found out who he was and what he did, I realized why he gave an alias." He moved back to the original subject. "The reason I called was as a courtesy. I wanted to let you know that I'd be coming up your way on official business."

Webb cleared his throat and spoke. His voice had lost some of its authority. "Thanks. Listen, that warehouse is on my way home. Why don't I just swing by the warehouse and ask Moore myself. That way, you don't have to bother driving up here and you can concentrate on your case."

"But, Ira, this is my case. This is a lead that I want to follow."

"Yeah, I know, but let me help you with this. I know Mr. Moore likes to keep his public image clean. Having you show up in your patrol car with your Oregon state seal might not look good."

Blaine furrowed his brow. This was certainly odd behavior from a fellow sheriff. Whenever a sheriff called him, Blaine was more than willing to allow the other sheriff to conduct his investigation.

Webb continued. "I'll call you tomorrow and let you know what Moore says. I have to go if I'm going to do all this. Bye, Lester."

"Good-bye," Blaine said but the line was already dead. He lit another cigarette and leaned back in his chair, thinking about what had just happened.

There was no good way to describe Webb's suggestions other than a brush-off. This concerned Blaine. He was a matter-of-fact guy and operated his office in the same manner. As he watched the smoke curl within the rays of the afternoon sun streaming through his window, he shrugged. "Maybe it was nothing."

"Maybe what was nothing, sir?" Duncan asked. He stood in the office doorway, a manila folder in his hand.

Blaine waved his hand. "Never mind."

Seeing Duncan triggered something. "You've attended those party dinners with the guest speakers, right?"

"Yes, sir. I find them to be a wonderful way to get connected to the political side of our country."

Blaine screwed up his face in bewilderment. "You actually think that?"

"Yes, sir, I do. You should give some politicians a try. They're not all bad."

Blaine rose from his chair. "I'm going to give one a try tonight. I'm going to go hear Mr. Truman's speech over in Walla Walla tonight."

"What about the case, sir?"

"I'm going to sleep on it tonight, Joe. Ira Webb is going to stop by the Moore Warehouse today and talk to Moore."

Duncan hesitated before speaking. "Isn't that a little off, sir?"

"Don't worry about it, Joe. I'm taking care of it." He snapped his fingers. "Oh, one more thing. Have the coroner take photographs of the dead men. Just the faces. And have them developed tonight. I want them to be ready in the morning."

"Why do you need them? I thought you said Webb was going to talk to Moore, that he would take care of it."

Blaine scratched the back of his neck. "I have a hunch, Joe, but I don't want to say much more than that."

Duncan hesitated. "Are we going to report this matter to the Army?"

Blaine shook his head slowly. "No, not now. For now, it's still a local matter."

25

Truman and Hancock examined the books for the rest of the afternoon. Truman called out an entry and Hancock flipped through the files and found the original. He brought it to the desk and sat down opposite Truman. Hancock leafed through the file until he found the latest one, called out the number, and Truman would match it in the ledger.

A distant siren rang at five o' clock. Truman took off his spectacles and rubbed the bridge of his nose. "These numbers are about to make my eyes cross. Let's call it a day."

"Sure, Harry." Hancock replaced a file in the file cabinet. "We made good progress today. We did all of '44 and '43. We'll be able to blow through '41 and '42 tomorrow morning easy."

Truman put on his spectacles and looked up at Hancock. When he did so, he saw something on Hancock's face that surprised him. "Carl, you got something on the corner of your mouth, there. No, the left side."

Hancock rubbed his mouth. His fingers had black ink on them. He frowned. He didn't find one. "That's funny, I haven't used a pen all day." He pulled his handkerchief from his breast pocket and dabbed it on his tongue. With the wet part, he began to rub his lower lip.

"No, but you were handling all those invoices. Maybe some of the newer ones from 1944 still had some latent moisture still on them. And wetting your finger to riffle through the sheets just activated it."

Hancock held up a stainless steel stapler and used it to see his reflection so that he could wipe the last of the ink from his mouth. "It was probably the coarse ones, the ones with the blobs."

"Blobs?"

"Yeah, blobs. Some of the numbers and letters had blobs in them. You know, like a 'six' would have a blob in the circle part."

A thought passed through Truman's mind in a flash. "Show me."

"Sure." Hancock walked over to the file cabinet, opened the drawer, and found the file folder of the company in question. "It was actually in the last one we just did. It was from February 1943." He opened the file and placed it in front of Truman.

The senator moved the desk lamp closer to the invoice and stared at it. From where he stood, Hancock could see a grim smile grow on Truman's face. "Would you like to fill me in on this, Harry?"

"Has the senator found something of interest?" The voice of Edward Moore came from the office door.

Hancock and Truman were both startled and, for a second, didn't know what to do. Hancock, who was standing, decided to move in an effort to stall for time while he and Truman figured out how to answer Moore's question.

"Actually, Mr. Moore, we both admire your filing process." Hancock walked around the desk and toward Moore. By doing so, he blocked the desk and Truman from Moore's view. "Your books are very clean and precise. We were able to make great headway."

Moore smiled coyly at him. "So, your investigation is progressing?"

From behind Hancock, Truman replied, "It's an inspection, Mr. Moore, not an investigation."

"My apologies, Senator, it's just that I don't quite see it that way."

Hancock cocked an eyebrow. "How do you see it then?"

Moore gazed at him evenly. "A senator with the power of Congress behind him comes across the entire continent to request, no demand, that I open my company's private business to his eyes and that of the government. He asks that he conduct his 'inspection' of my company's financial records in private without any representative. All, supposedly, to make other companies more efficient and, thus, lose any competitive advantage I may have gained through my own hard work. That's how I see it, Mr. Hancock."

Hancock's eyes hardened slightly. "Mr. Moore, since Uncle Sam has been good enough to grant you a contract to help him conduct his business—which, by the way, is to wage and win a war—that gives him a bit of leeway to how he expects his clients to conduct their business. And if Uncle Sam chooses to create a set of rules by which everyone should follow, then he has the authority to ensure that those rules are being followed. Thus, you have the senator here conducting an inspection, investigation, or whatever you want to call it on his behalf."

The two men stared at each other for a few more moments until Moore looked over Hancock's shoulder at Truman. The senator had risen with a handful of files and was walking over toward the file cabinets.

"Don't trouble yourself, Senator. I can have Christopher or Larry put away any extra files."

"It's no trouble at all, Mr. Moore," Truman said over his shoulder. He reached the file cabinets and replaced the files. "If there's one thing my mother always taught me it's to clean up my own mess." He finished filing, closed the drawer, and turned toward Moore and Hancock.

Moore could only nod curtly. "Are you and Mr. Hancock leaving for the evening then?"

"Yes, we are," Truman said. "But we'll be back in the morning. I want to finish up the review of your records by lunch. Then, if necessary, we can begin random interviews of your employees. Would that be satisfactory?"

Moore spread his arms in defeat. "Absolutely, Senator Truman, what choice do I have?"

"Thank you, Mr. Moore. See you tomorrow."

The three men shook hands, and Truman and Hancock left the office. They walked down the stairs and were greeted by Christopher Moore. As they passed him, Hancock patted the younger man's shoulder. "See you tomorrow."

* * *

THE YOUNGER MOORE flinched from Hancock's hand as if it were on fire. He turned around and bored holes in the backs of Truman and Hancock who didn't turn around. In a moment, his father stood next to his side.

"What happened up there," Christopher said.

"I'm not quite sure," the older man replied. "When I walked in on them, they were looking at one of the invoices up close."

"Do you think they know?"

"I think they suspect something. I kept egging them on—especially that hick Texan—to let slip the real reason they're here. They didn't reveal their hand. Hear of anything out of the ordinary?"

"No, not really. We got another sickie. Peter Allan took an extra long break this morning. When Larry asked where he had been, Peter said he had stomach troubles and was in the bathroom. He left soon thereafter."

"Were Truman and Hancock here at that time?"

"Now that you mention it, yes."

Edward frowned. "Did either of them see Allan?"

Christopher shrugged. "It's possible."

Edward looked at his son thoughtfully. After a moment of silence he said, "We can't get Allan drafted, especially not with those two here." He gestured toward the Lincoln which was, at that moment, leaving the parking lot in a cloud of dust. "But we do have other means at our disposal. Come on. Let's give Ira a call."

26

Tuesday
18 April 1944
5:45 p. m., Pacific War Time

"Forgeries?" Horace McLeod said. "You think the invoices are forgeries?" He, Truman, and Hancock sat around a small writing table in McLeod's hotel room.

"We'll know tomorrow or the next day," Truman said. "Now that we know what to look for, we'll go through all the files and make a list of any suspicious invoices and quantities of products supposedly delivered. Then, we'll compare both the company of origin and the original government files and see if the numbers match."

McLeod looked thoughtful as he placed his index finger across his lips. He had a focus Truman and Hancock had not yet seen. This was the lawyer in his own element.

"But that doesn't make sense. If embezzlement can be proven by merely comparing two sets of books, why risk it?"

"Because on a cursory glance, everything looks on the up-and-up," Hancock said. "I didn't notice any irregularities in the invoices."

Truman added, "And I only knew about mimeographs and its peculiar characteristics because some of the bills that are up for a vote are copied in bulk."

"But that still doesn't account for why Moore went to the trouble of recreating an invoice with some numbers changed. Why not just skim off the top and let the original invoice stand?" McLeod paced the room, his face turned toward the ceiling. "What could he gain by faking the documents?"

All three men sat in silence for a few moments, thinking. Hancock was the first to speak. "Perhaps it had something to do with the burglaries."

"How so?" Truman asked.

"Don't know. Maybe he was worried that if the government found out about the string of robberies, they'd take away his contract."

"Possible, but unlikely," McLeod said. "Don't forget, Moore Warehousing is the largest…."

"Yes, we've heard it all day," Hancock interrupted, waving a hand at McLeod. "How could we forget it when Junior and his daddy kept reminding us? What of it?"

"Maybe he was thinking about post-war," Truman offered. "The war is going to end sometime. If he could remove from people's memories a few break-ins and still have a perfect ledger, the government would have no reason to cancel the contract."

McLeod snapped his fingers. "That's a good thought, Mr. Truman. And it begs the obvious question we have yet to ask: assuming this is true and Moore is skimming supplies and goods off the top, what's he doing with them? The post-war era might be the key."

Hancock looked confused. "Okay, Horace, spill it."

A genuine grin snaked across McLeod's face. He stood and began to pace. "The war is a constant thing in our lives. We can't get away from it. And many of us here on the home front often lament that we can only do so much. But one of the things we can do is ration. Sure, it's mandatory but most of us would do it even if it wasn't. With me so far?"

Hancock nodded. He glanced over at Truman who also nodded.

"During the war, we all do what we can: buy war bonds, write letters to our GIs, submit to government-imposed rationing. We have faith that if we do our jobs to the best of our ability, the might of our way of life will prevail and our men will come home alive. Some people build tanks, some grow grain, and some become a main supplier of all the government's needs as it builds a secret facility out in the middle of Nowhere, Washington." McLeod had reached the other side of the room so he turned around and walked back towards his jury of two.

"One such supplier sees the future and decides to do something about it, to help ensure a soft landing in the post-war economy. Because let's be frank: if your major customer is the United States Army and the war ends, the Army may not need your particular brand of service after the guns have fallen silent. Therefore, our supplier decides to take a little here and a little there, dried milk here, sugar there, or some spare tires. And he starts to stockpile them. And he waits for the glorious day of victory over our enemies."

"So, what happens when the war ends? Suddenly, we don't have to keep making planes and tanks. We can now make cars and washing machines again. Not only that, we can stop doing without sugar and nylon. But, inevitably, there will be a lag time between the end of the war and the start of peacetime production. All during this war, we civilians have been earning our paychecks but we have little to spend it on. When the war ends, people are going to be in a rush to buy everything we can't buy now." He turned back to Hancock and Truman. "And the man who has, say, a little extra stock lying around is going to fill that void. And he'll make a killing."

Hancock nodded slowly. Truman was smiling broadly.

"What do you think?" McLeod asked. "Plausible?"

"Oh, I think it's more than plausible," Hancock said, "I'd say it's likely."

McLeod faced Truman. "Senator, how about you?"

From outside, a car horn sounded two short reports. Truman looked at his watch as he stood up and walked over to the window. Parked right in front of the Hurley Hotel was a patrol car. The driver's hands were on the wheel. He turned and clapped McLeod on the shoulder. "Mr. McLeod, I think it's a very plausible explanation. And it'll be up to us to see if the facts hold it up. Good work."

Truman picked up his hat. "But I have to go wow a group of politicians and eat some semi-fancy meal probably made of roast chicken and peas." He rubbed his stomach sarcastically.

Hancock rose. "You want us to wait for you before we go out tonight?"

The senator shook his head. "I don't know how long this thing'll take. Whenever I speak at these local events, every single member of the group seems to want to shake my hand. It may take awhile. Go on without me, but be careful."

"We will, Harry, and you be careful, too. Between the three of us, I think Horace and I have the easier job."

Truman laughed at the remark.

McLeod was still beaming with delight at Truman's endorsement. "Carl will be sure to keep me in line, Senator. We won't let you down."

"I know you won't," Truman said and paused on his way out the door. "And, Mr. McLeod, call me Harry."

27

Tuesday
18 April 1944
5:55 p. m., Pacific War Time

T ruman stepped out of the hotel's front door and into the late afternoon sunlight. He shielded his eyes with his hand and walked over to the passenger door of the patrol car. He opened it and slid in the seat.

Truman reached across the center and extended his hand to the driver. "Harry Truman."

The man behind the driver's seat wore a crisp sheriff's uniform. His shirt and pants were black and he was wearing a dark brown tie clipped at stomach level with a steel tie clip. On the tie clip was a seal that Truman assumed was the seal of either the county or the state of Washington.

"Ira Webb," the other man said. "Glad to meet you." He took Truman's hand and gave it a firm shake. Even in his seat, Truman could tell Webb was a tall man, probably the same height as Hancock. His dark hair was cut short and neat. His gray eyes sat in deep sockets above high cheekbones and a firm jaw. "I got a call from the mayor this afternoon and he says you need a ride to this little shin-dig. What's a big-shot senator like you doing way out here?"

Truman placed his hat on his lap. "Just conducting a little inspection of one of your local companies. I also got a message from Mr. Roosevelt telling me to go and speak at the meeting tonight. I can't say no to the president just like you can't say no to the mayor."

Webb put the car in reverse, backed into the street, and merged with traffic. "Really? The president himself told you to do this? I'm impressed Mr. Roosevelt would even know about the Walla Walla Democratic Party meetings."

"Well, it *is* an election year, Sheriff, and, in an election year, every vote counts."

Webb smiled knowingly. "So, he's going to run again, huh?" He looked over at Truman. "Well, he'd better. We can't have any isolationist Republicans leading the military. They couldn't win this war even if they had a jar full of poison and access to Hitler's breakfast tray." He huffed in disgust. "Frankly, I'm surprised he's even holding the election."

Truman's eyes widened but he kept his gaze looking out the windshield. "Sheriff Webb, even in the midst of the Civil War, Lincoln held the 1864 election, willing to accept the results no matter what. If we suspend this year's election citing a national emergency, then we become that which we fight." He turned his head slightly toward Webb. "We have to have this election and win this war no matter who wins in November."

Webb grunted an acknowledgement. "You may be right, Senator." They discussed the war and politics until Webb changed the subject. "By the way, which company are you inspecting?"

Truman was taken by surprise with the question. "I'd rather not say at this time. I find our inspections go more smoothly when no one is prejudiced one way or another."

Webb looked sideways at Truman. "C'mon, Senator. Someone like you doesn't personally come all the way out to Washington State just to put away a small dog. It's one of the big ones, isn't it? Is it

Reinfeld's munitions plant? How about Clifford's airplane parts shop? Or it could be something in a different vein, say, like Moore's warehouse or Rutherford's railroad supplies."

Truman said, "Really, Sheriff, I'd rather not say anything at this time."

They drove on for a few minutes in awkward silence punctuated only by discussion of the weather. Truman pointed out the windshield. "Is this the place?"

Webb looked out the driver's window. "Yeah, that's it." He pulled the patrol car into the parking lot of a large two-story building. A sign above the front doors, painted in red art deco letters, read "Walla Walla Convention and Expo Hall." Quite a number of cars were parked near the entrance. Men and women were milling around the front door, shaking hands and carrying on conversations, laughing.

The sheriff parked the car and got out. Truman also got out and put on his hat. He looked at himself in the reflection of the window and checked his tie, shirt, suit, and his handkerchief. Satisfied, he turned to walk with Webb toward the entrance.

"Will you be up on the podium with me?" Truman asked.

In a loud, sarcastic voice, Webb said, "I was re-elected last year for my third term. I don't have to start shaking hands again until next year." He clapped Truman on the shoulder. "No, Senator Truman, this night is all yours."

Truman could actually hear Webb chuckle as they reached the front line of the attendees. Seeing the guest of honor, they all started applauding.

One thing Truman didn't mention was that he thoroughly enjoyed the art of politics. Smiling, he waded into the crowd. He intended to shake every hand.

28

Tuesday

18 April 1944

10:30 p.m., Pacific War Time

After his speech and after every important person had introduced himself to Truman, the convention hall thinned out. The last stragglers—usually the folks who didn't know they were not important—were milling about, in awe that they were in the presence of a U. S. Senator when Webb walked up to Truman.

"For all the talk we had in the car coming over here, Senator, you sure seem comfortable."

"I could say the same for you, too, Sheriff," Truman replied. "You seem to know everyone here." He paused to shake one last hand. "Politics can be frustrating. But when you get to the ground level, where the people are, when you get to see them and touch them and talk to them, let them tell you what's on their mind and ask if you can help, that's what makes it all worthwhile."

Webb nodded. "The only difference between you and me, however, is I have to haul in my friends if they break any laws. You can just pass a new law and get your friends out of trouble."

Truman frowned. "What is that supposed to mean?"

Webb gave Truman a disarming smile. "You know what I mean, Senator. Congressmen have palms and palms can get greased. Put it another way, take this inspection you're doing. Do you think the owner had any other answer other than 'Yes' when you showed up at his door?"

"I fear you have a hearty disapproval of the federal government and its powers."

"Comes with living out here." He motioned for Truman to start walking out of the convention hall and back to the patrol car. "There's an independent streak that runs deep out in this neck of the country and I think the folks in D.C. forget that."

They were almost to the door when they each noticed a familiar man walking toward them. Webb smiled. "Sheriff Blaine. What are you doing here?"

Blaine shook Webb's hand. He motioned to Truman with his head. "I thought I'd come and see what the senator here had to say." Blaine turned toward Truman and extended his hand. "It was a good speech, Senator *Truman*." He placed emphasis on the last word.

Truman took the hand and returned its firm grasp. "Sheriff, I apologize for the misdirection but Mr. Hancock and I were trying to keep our presence clandestine. It's been our experience that our best results are when people don't know who we are."

"You don't have to apologize to me, Mr. Truman," Blaine said, resting his thumbs in his belt. "You have a job to do and you know best how to do it. Nothing wrong with that."

"Do you have any leads on your case?"

Blaine looked toward the front of the convention hall and watched two janitors starting to remove the red, white, and blue bunting around the podium. "Funny you mention it. I might. Since I was here, Ira, I was wondering if you had a chance to call on Edward Moore this afternoon."

Since Blaine was facing in another direction, only Webb caught Truman's reaction to the mention of Edward Moore. It was subtle but obvious. Truman, for his part, was curious as to Blaine's comment. He looked at Webb for his answer. Webb scratched his chin and looked off toward the door. Truman got the impression Webb wanted to be somewhere else.

"Yeah, I did, but Mr. Moore wasn't there. I talked with the foreman and he said Moore would be back in the office tomorrow morning. The foreman asked if I wanted to speak to Moore's son and I said no, it needed to be the old man himself."

Blaine moved his gaze back to Webb and smiled. "Well, thanks for stopping by. I'm a little antsy for the answer. Are you going to stop again and see Mr. Moore tomorrow morning?"

"First thing, Lester. You have my word on it." Webb glanced at his watch. "I best be getting the senator back to his hotel so I can turn in for the night. Good seeing you, Lester. I'll call you tomorrow."

"Much obliged," Blaine said. The three men shook hands and Webb and Truman started for the front door. Webb held the door open for Truman and then followed the senator outside. The night air was crisp and cool and Truman could see a few wisps of his breath in the thin light of the street lamps. The two men walked across a near empty lot, their shoes crunching the gravel surface as they walked.

Truman's mind was whirling, trying to make a connection between Moore and the dead bodies. His heart beat fast and he could feel his pulse in his temple.

Webb unlocked the passenger door for Truman and then made his way around to the driver's side. He got into the car and fired up the engine. They drove in silence for a few minutes. Then, in a tone of shared conspiracy, Webb said, "I saw your reaction when Lester mentioned Edward Moore." He paused for effect. "You're here to investigate him, aren't you?"

Truman swallowed hard. Just like when Blaine angled Hancock into revealing where they all were staying while in Richland, he knew he was cornered. "Yes, but I still don't want to discuss the nature of our investigation thus far."

"What do you think Moore's doing?"

Truman ran his fingers along the edges of his hat. "I don't know yet, but I aim to find out." He paused, seemingly to consider how far to go. "My partner and I have a theory."

Webb looked out the window, appearing nonchalant. "How'd you first got wind of whatever Moore may or may not be doing?"

Truman looked sidelong at Webb. He actually smiled. "I like the way you put that, Sheriff. Always the politician."

Webb shrugged. "So, how was it that the Moore Warehouse was brought to the attention of your committee?"

Truman felt uncomfortable with Webb's pushiness. The sheriff's tone was noncommittal but the force of the questioning indicated otherwise. He decided to play the political answer himself.

"The committee is a watchdog to all government spending on the war. With the Hanford plant out here, I'm familiar with the Moore Warehouse. I only met Edward Moore yesterday, however. You seem to know him."

Webb chuckled. "Who doesn't know him is the better question. He's a big dog around here. Speaking of politics, he's one of those guys you always want to have your picture taken with for the front page of the paper."

"Do you know him personally?"

"No, not really," Webb said. "I mean, yeah, I've met him and had a few of those rubber chicken dinners with him but he ain't like a poker buddy or nothing." He looked over at Truman. "You know the type. Rich local man everyone sucks up to just to get him to say something nice about you?"

Truman grimaced. "I know the type."

Webb shook his head. "That would certainly change things around here if Moore were gone or sullied."

"How so?"

Webb hooked a finger between his neck and his shirt collar, pulling the collar out and stretching his neck. "Power vacuum, for one thing. Let's say you take down Moore and…"

"Sheriff, I'm not here to take down anyone. If it is proven Mr. Moore has committed any crime, he will have the opportunity to atone for his crimes. This is not a vendetta."

Webb frowned. "But isn't that what you do? I mean, with your committee work?"

"I provide the opportunity for big corporations to remember how they are so large: the American economy and the freedom it provides. I like to remind them that the best men of the younger generation are dying on faraway battlefields to protect their ability to thrive in this country. I give the companies the opportunity to do something for those men and not just to line the pockets of rich executives."

Webb grinned at Truman. "I see what you're passionate about, Senator." Webb nodded. "When you put it that way, who can say no to you? So, how are you going to expose him?"

"We'll just have to see how it plays out."

The rest of the trip back to Richland was uneventful. Through mutual, though unstated, understanding, they discussed law enforcement. Webb seemed happy to have someone new to hear his old stories and Truman enjoyed them. The patrol car's headlights provided the only light in an otherwise black night. As they entered the town of Richland itself, only a few street lamps burned faintly. Almost no traffic cluttered the streets.

Webb pulled the car up to the front door of the hotel. "I don't see your friend's Lincoln. Did he leave?"

"No, they're still in town. They should be doing a bit of reconnaissance at the Moore warehouse."

"Really? What do they expect to find?"

"Not sure, but there might be something about to happen over there." He extended his hand over to Webb. "It was a pleasure to meet you, Sheriff."

Webb took Truman's hand and shook it. "I feel the same way, Senator, if not more so. It ain't every day I get to play chauffeur to a senator."

Truman chuckled and got out of the car. He walked to the front door and saw a slip of paper taped on the door. In the glare of the headlights, he read it. In Mrs. Hurley's handwriting were these words:

.   .   .

THE DOOR IS OPEN, Mr. Truman. Please lock up after you get in.

I gave Mr. McLeod the spare key.

HE PLUCKED the paper from the door and opened it. He locked the door and made his way upstairs.

Had Truman stayed and watched the police car from the front window of the hotel, he would have seen Webb back the car into the street and make his way, slowly, north toward the town square. The brake lights flared and the patrol car pulled off to the side of the street. Webb got out of the car and walked to a phone booth. Webb placed a call, spoke to someone, hung up and got back in his patrol car. A moment later, the car picked up speed and disappeared around the bend leading out of town.

29

Tuesday
18 April 1944
11:45 p. m., Pacific War Time

"Horace, will you stop fidgeting?" Hancock whispered.

For almost an hour, he and McLeod had been sitting in McLeod's Lincoln watching the Moore Warehouse. True to McLeod's word, the rock quarry was a good place for a stakeout. The piles of rock were high enough so that any passing motorist could not see the car from the road. There was no moon in the sky so the chances of moonlight reflecting off the highly polished top of the Lincoln were zero.

Hancock had to laugh to himself. He had only known McLeod for a day in a half but he was already becoming a good friend. Ever since Truman had asked McLeod to call him "Harry"—quite a big step, Hancock knew—McLeod was like a schoolboy who had just won the spelling bee. All during dinner just kept grinning. Even Reta Hurley noticed and smiled kindly at him when McLeod told her the reason for his good mood.

"I just want a cigarette, Carl."

"Look, like I said before, every guy in the movies smokes a cigarette on a stakeout but you're not going to and here's why. First, anyone within fifty yards—and it's about fifty yards to the warehouse—would be able to see the burning tip of the cigarette. Second, it's going to get stuffy in here so we're going to have to crack the windows. If you smoke, someone could smell it. Finally, these are not Camels—my favorites—and I want to smoke, too."

For the next few minutes, Hancock used the binoculars and looked at the warehouse. The night watchman, Richard Stanley, was doing his rounds. Hancock studied Stanley's body language and, after a few complete rounds, Hancock said, "This guy's an amateur."

McLeod asked Hancock how he could tell and Hancock explained it to him. McLeod seemed satisfied and followed Hancock's lead as the Texan leaned back in his seat and began to talk baseball, politics, and anything else that came to his mind.

McLeod said, "My leg's starting to go to sleep and I'm getting tired."

"What, is my conversational manner not quite exciting enough for you?" Hancock reached over to the paper bag and withdrew a sandwich McLeod bought from Grover's. "Here, eat half of this. It'll do you good. I'll eat half of mine, too."

They sat in silence for a few minutes, eating.

"So," McLeod finally said, "do you think Harry'd say yes if FDR asked him?"

"We've been over this already tonight. Harry Truman loves being a senator. He's told me—and everyone else who has asked— that his time in the Senate has been the best years of his life." Hancock folded the wax paper over the uneaten half of the sandwich and slipped it into his suit pocket. He reached over and poured himself a half a cup of coffee from the thermos.

"Besides," Hancock continued, "Harry once told me that the job of the Vice President is to preside over the Senate and hope for a funeral. Does that sound like something he would like?"

"No, I guess not. "It's just that in the two days since I've met him, he seems like he's got a great head on his shoulders, is brutally honest, and carries himself with integrity. I mean, in some ways, he'd make a great lawyer because everything he says, you want to believe."

Hancock chuckled. "You nailed Harry. Okay, it's your turn. Let's see what Mr. Stanley is up to now."

McLeod put his sandwich down on the seat and picked up the binoculars. He began what had quickly become standard practice for the evening of reciting the actions of Stanley so the other person in the car could watch vicariously.

"Okay, here he comes around the corner. Yeah, I still see what you mean about the cigarette. I can tell he's smoking. Now he's passing underneath the one spotlight over the bay doors, he's checking the bay doors, and…hang on."

"What?"

"I don't know. He cocked his head like he heard something."

Hancock sat up straighter and squinted out the windshield. He saw the light and the outline of the superstructure of the warehouse but needed the binoculars for the detail. "Come to think of it, I hear it, too. It sounds like a telephone ringing. You hear it?"

"Yeah. But who'd be calling at this time of night?"

Hancock began to worry. If it was one thing he had learned in his time as a deputy sheriff, when a pattern has been established, any deviation of that pattern could easily spell trouble. Tonight's pattern broke when Stanley opened the door and ducked inside the warehouse.

They were silent for a few moments, waiting to see what would happen next.

Stanley reemerged from the warehouse and McLeod put the binoculars back to his eyes.

"What's he doing?" Hancock asked. His foot began tapping the floorboard.

"I don't know. He's looking around and, wait, he's going behind the warehouse." McLeod looked over at Hancock. "What do you think?"

"Let's wait a few more minutes and see what happens." He

scratched his chin, his fingernails rasping over the stubble. "But I don't like it."

Stanley was gone for about a minute until he returned to the stand under the lamp over the bay doors. He scanned the area, as if he was looking for something in particular. The binoculars were top quality and the magnification was so strong that McLeod could actually see Stanley's eyes as they searched the darkness. Stanley's eyes were so distinct that when he turned in the direction of the Lincoln, McLeod felt his heart skip a beat.

"Holy cow, he sees us!" he exclaimed and dropped the binoculars in his lap.

Hancock grabbed the binoculars. "There's no way he can see us from here." He put the binoculars up to his eyes and studied Stanley's movements.

The night watchman was walking toward their location.

"But that doesn't mean he won't see us if we don't get out of here," Hancock said. He dropped the binoculars on the seat between him and McLeod. He thought for a moment. Questions raced through his head but he put them behind the biggest obstacle of them all: how to leave the area without tipping off Stanley they were here.

He looked back at Stanley who was just about halfway across the warehouse parking lot, approximately forty yards away from their location.

He looked over at McLeod. The lawyer was gripping the wheel hard enough that Hancock could see white on the man's knuckles. McLeod stared at him, wide-eyed. "What are we going to do, Carl?"

"We're going to get outta here, but real quiet like." Hancock picked up the binoculars and put the strap around his next. He glanced back at Stanley. The security guard was nearing the tree line that separated the parking lot from the road. Thirty yards.

"Listen, Horace. The best thing for us to do is to get out of here without Stanley seeing us. Barring that, we need to make sure he can't identify this car." He gave McLeod a tense grin. "You *would* have to buy a Lincoln."

The joke brought a bit of clarity to McLeod's demeanor. He inhaled deeply and exhaled. "Tell me what to do."

"Okay, that's more like it," He took a deep breath himself. "First thing, we have to try to get outta here without him finding us. So, starting the car now is out of the question." He looked out the back window. "The back road leading into this quarry ain't but thirty or so yards away. The road's after that. I aim to roll the car in neutral until we're on that road. Then we can roll the car and pop the clutch. That way, if Stanley hears anything, it'll just be a car on the back road. No big deal."

"What, you want me to push?" McLeod said.

"No, I will. I'm bigger. And, well, there's another thing." He looked over at Stanley who had just jumped the small ditch and was crossing the road. Twenty yards.

"What's that?"

"Frankly, if we get caught, I can't be with you."

"So, you just want me to leave you here?" McLeod's voice betrayed his worry and puzzlement. He barely looked at Hancock, and then only in quick glances. His eyes were firmly set on Stanley and his approach.

"Yes and no. I'll push the car and get you out of here. We'll turn the car around as soon as we have space." He jammed a thumb in Stanley's direction. "I can evade Mr. Amateur Security Guard no problem. After he's satisfied no one's here, he'll go back to his rounds. Then, I'll slip away and meet you a mile down the road, at the four-way stop." He glanced at his watch. "Make it at 1:05."

McLeod nodded, not looking at Hancock.

Hancock rolled down his window and shoved his Stetson over to McLeod.

"What's this for?"

Hancock pointed to the dome light on the ceiling of the car interior. "Put the hat over the light while I slip out the door. After I'm out, hand it to me through the window."

Both men looked back at Stanley. He was slipping through the pylons of the wooden fence at the front of the quarry from the road. Fifteen yards.

"Okay, let's go," Hancock said.

McLeod put the Stetson over the dome light and Hancock opened the door just far enough to let him slip out of the car. Ever so quietly, he then leaned on the car door and they both heard an audible click.

Without waiting, McLeod took down the hat and handed it to Hancock. The detective took the hat and stood up. The door edged out a little and the dome light came on. McLeod inhaled and Hancock swore under his breath. He shoved the door harder and the click was louder.

Hancock looked toward the street to find out Stanley's location. The night watchman was nowhere to be found. "Okay, put her in neutral." When he heard the gear disengage, he started pushing. His boots slipped on the small gravel and he fell to his knees. He stifled a curse, rose, and tried again.

The Lincoln was stubborn and didn't want to move at all. Then, an inch, then another inch, then three. The gravel under the tires was louder than Hancock would have liked but he was committed.

He pushed harder and harder until he was jogging along with it. He stopped and made a twirling gesture with his finger. McLeod spun the wheel and the Lincoln lurched in a crude arc and skidded to a halt.

"Great," Hancock said, looking back over his shoulder to see where Stanley was. He started pushing and again. Frustratingly, the car moved only inches at a time. Slowly but surely the car picked up speed until he was again jogging behind it.

For a split second, he considered abandoning his plan of staying behind and jumping into the car with McLeod. But Stanley's voice behind him alleviated any thought of jeopardizing the evening.

"Hey, who are you? Stop right there."

With his hands still on the Lincoln's trunk, Hancock looked back in the direction of Stanley's voice. The guard's shape was backlit by the light on the warehouse and Hancock could tell he was running towards their location.

In a loud whisper, Hancock said, "This is it." He gave the Lincoln one final shove and nearly tripped in the process. He slid to a stop and then looked for the best place to hide. With the help of starlight, he found a path between two piles of gravel and a larger pile of what seemed like small boulders. Rounding the pile of boulders, he decided that height might help improve his chances so he climbed partway up the boulder pile.

Hancock saw Stanley pass the location where he had given the car the final shove. He looked over to the back road to see if he could catch a glimpse of the Lincoln but saw something that caused his stomach to drop.

In the distance, about two miles away, two sets of police lights approached their position. They must have been running silent because he could not hear any sirens.

He put the binoculars to his eyes and found the approaching police cars. He then traced the road back to where McLeod should be. Nothing.

Looking over the binoculars, Hancock saw that the patrol cars had turned onto the same back road where McLeod should have been. He cursed under his breath and looked again through the binoculars.

He heard the engine fire before he saw it. As McLeod fired the engine, he turned on the headlights. That made it easier for Hancock to find the car. It also made it easier for the police to notice him, too.

Through the binoculars, Hancock watched the two cars break out of single-file formation and start driving side by side, preventing McLeod from driving past the police cars. The brake lights of the Lincoln flared and the Lincoln swerved to miss both patrol cars. The Lincoln ended up nearly perpendicular to the road, dust visible in the glare of the police headlights.

The two police officers, one from each car, emerged and walked toward the Lincoln. Hancock saw McLeod's hands on the steering wheel. Good, he thought, keep your hands in sight.

The taller of the two deputies said something to McLeod and Hancock saw the Lincoln's door open. McLeod, hands raised, got out of the car and stepped to his left, toward the rear of the car, leaving the door open.

The shorter deputy, a stocky man with a potbelly, walked up to McLeod who appeared to be a few inches taller than the policeman. The deputy said something to the lawyer and then McLeod doubled over, having been hit in the stomach.

"Crap," Hancock whispered. His breath stirred up a layer of dust, making his eyes water. He wiped his eyes irritably and then looked through the binoculars again.

McLeod was nowhere to be seen, but the stocky deputy looked down at something Hancock assumed was the lawyer. Into the round frame of the binoculars another figure appeared. As the headlights illuminated his face, Hancock could tell it was Richard Stanley. When he rounded the Lincoln, he looked down, and Hancock noted actual surprise on the night watchman's face.

Stanley looked over at the taller deputy and the deputy said something. The taller man screwed up his face and apparently yelled at Stanley because Hancock could hear a faint sound coming from the direction of the cars.

The taller deputy pointed at both the Lincoln and Stanley, walked over, and got in behind the wheel. The shorter deputy reached down and pulled McLeod up by the collar of his shirt. The lawyer's hair, usually well groomed, fell in his face. He held both arms around his middle.

He was half-dragged, half-pushed toward the shorter deputy's car. The deputy opened the back door and threw McLeod inside. The shorter deputy got in his patrol car. He backed his car up, executed a turnaround, and drove off in the direction he had come. The Lincoln followed, leaving the taller deputy standing in front of his car, the headlights casting a long shadow along the road.

The deputy stood there, surveying the landscape. He walked around his open driver's side door and reached inside the car. He stood up and was holding the receiver of a police radio. He spoke and listened to the response. He spoke a second time, heard the response, nodded, and got in his car.

Slowly, the car began moving toward the rock quarry.

"Wonderful," Hancock said, and began to move.

30

Wednesday
19 April 1944
8:10 a.m., Pacific War Time

Hamilton Armstrong loved to fly airplanes. Ever since he was a young boy, captivated by the exploits of Charles Lindbergh, he knew he wanted to fly airplanes. There was a time, in 1927, when he insisted that his family and friends call him "Lucky," borrowing Lindbergh's famous moniker. He made model airplanes, drew airplanes, and dreamed of being a pilot. In 1941, before Pearl Harbor, he enlisted and requested pilot training. Not surprising, he had a great aptitude for piloting.

Armstrong loved flying so much he would volunteer for duties other hotshot pilots shunned. One of those duties was the morning reconnaissance flight around Hanford. Most pilots couldn't be bothered to wake early for a boring flight around this desolate region. Not Armstrong.

Like every day, he followed a predetermined route: once around the perimeter, diagonal patterns over the interior, one flyby over the residential areas, and then a final pass around the perimeter.

The sky was clear of both clouds and sand, and Armstrong enjoyed clear visibility. Except for the occasional bird, Armstrong's plane was the only thing in the air.

His first perimeter pass was uneventful. Armstrong didn't mind. He was flying. His pass over the interior yielded nothing. His flyby over the residential areas made him chuckle. All the people looked like ants and all the dormitories, trailers, and houses were like toys. Armstrong grinned and banked his plane to make his final pass around the perimeter and then return to base in Walla Walla.

As in the first pass, the perimeter was quiet. He marked all the gates and the checkpoints and he checked all the fences that enclosed most of the facility. Along the southwest side, he saw the copse of trees that grew along the banks of the Columbia River. For some reason, there was no fence in this part of the facility. And it was in this area that Armstrong saw movement.

He didn't doubt his eyes as he had better than 20-20 vision. But he was surprised to see a man walking inside the restricted area.

Armstrong reached over and retrieved his binoculars. It took him a few seconds to locate the man through the eyepieces but he finally did. The man walked east along the riverbank. The man was not in uniform. In fact, he looked like he was a lost camper. Through the lenses, the man looked up at the sound of the approaching airplane. Then the man began to run.

Dropping the binoculars to the cockpit floor, the pilot toggled his radio. "Hanford base, this is Armstrong in recon. I have an unauthorized person in the southwest quadrant. I advise sending the MPs to apprehend him, over."

"Armstrong, this is Hanford Base, are you sure it's not one of our own, over?"

Armstrong banked the plane for another pass. "Negative. The suspect is not in uniform. He started running when he heard me, over."

There was a slight pause. "Roger that, Armstrong. Scrambling now. Stay airborne and report his movements until we arrive. Over and out."

"No problem," Armstrong said to himself as he took the plane lower. He saw the man actually cower, trip over a rock, and fall onto the dusty ground. Armstrong grinned. It was always exciting to fly the plane in any manner not dictated by the rules.

He circled and flew low three more times until the ground troops arrived. Armstrong estimated an entire platoon arrived in two jeeps and a troop carrier. He saw the soldiers surround the man, all rifles raised and ready to fire.

Armstrong banked the plane and flew over the group one last time. He saw one of the officers turn his face up and salute.

Armstrong rocked the wings in a return salute. "What the hell is he doing down there, over?" he asked. He passed over the troops, who had the man loaded in the rear of the troop carrier, and banked east toward Walla Walla.

"I don't know. All we got is his name. Theodore Frank. But if you're interested, call us back later. We're going to deliver him to Major Lynch. There's no doubt the major will make him spill the beans. Over and out."

31

Wednesday
19 April 1944
8:25 a.m. Pacific War Time

As Truman returned to the hotel after eating breakfast alone, he nearly passed the front door, so deep in thought and concern was he about Hancock and McLeod. He entered the lobby and the bell sounded, startling Reta Hurley. She began to dab her eyes with a tissue. When she saw that it was Truman, she relaxed a little. "Senator, I have some bad news. Horace McLeod is in jail."

Truman's mouth dropped open. "What? How do you know?"

She wiped her nose with the tissue and threw it away. "Mildred, one of the sheriff's dispatchers, is a friend of mine. She called me five minutes ago."

Truman walked over to the front desk and placed his hat on it. He could tell she was upset but he had to ask the obvious question. "Did you hear any mention of Carl?"

Hurley shook her head. "Only Mr. McLeod." She frowned. "Isn't Mr. Hancock with you?"

"No, he's not, and I'm beginning to worry. What was the charge against Mr. McLeod?"

"Criminal trespassing." A pause. "And espionage."

"Espionage?" Truman's voice was louder than it needed to be and he apologized.

"I understand, Senator. It struck me as absurd, too. But that's what Mildred said."

Truman folded his hands on the counter. He was calmer now but his heart slammed in his chest and his mind was racing. "Okay, what other details did your friend have?"

"Not much. Mr. McLeod was brought in just after midnight."

Truman nodded. "That makes sense. Where was he picked up?"

"Near the Moore Warehouse." Her voice reflected her hardened eyes.

Truman paused. "I'm sorry, Mrs. Hurley, but you seem particularly…angry with this turn of events. May I ask why?"

Hurley breathed out slowly. She walked over to the inner office and went inside. She returned holding a framed photograph. She handed it to Truman.

Truman looked at the picture. It showed two women, one of whom was Hurley, standing outside the hotel. The other woman had Asian features. Standing next to the other woman were two small girls. Truman assumed they were the daughters of the woman based on the resemblance.

"This is my best friend, Dorothy Sakai, with her daughter Eva, the younger one, and Keiko." Hurley got another tissue and held it in her hands. "The people you don't see there are our husbands. They are the ones taking the picture."

Truman handed the photograph back. "I'm sorry, Mrs. Hurley, but I don't see how your friend relates to your reaction to Mr. McLeod's being in jail."

She looked up at him. "Did you know that her husband, James, served in the Army during World War I? And do you know where he is now? Rotting away in one of those prisons Roosevelt calls camps." She paused and wiped her nose.

"And not only that, they had to leave most of their belongings behind. Their cars, their home, their business. I gave Dorothy my suitcase. It was bigger than hers. She took it but it still didn't hold everything precious to her." She paused and looked again at the picture. "I'm keeping some of their things until they get back."

Truman didn't really have anything to say. He stayed silent as she continued.

"James and Dorothy opened a bakery on the square. They loved the place. They made the best sourdough rolls. Folks from all around would come in and pick up a dozen rolls for Sunday dinner. They were loved. Until December 7. After that, business slowed. Someone even threw a brick through the window. James had to put a sign on the front of his shop. Do you know what it said? It said 'I am an American.'" She looked at Truman fiercely. "Can you believe that?"

"Unfortunately, yes."

"I couldn't and I still can't. This is America, the land of freedom, and here we corral our own citizens and ship them off to nowhere just because they don't look like we do. And then, after all the good folks are gone, greedy Americans come waltzing in and take over things that are not rightly theirs."

Something clicked inside of Truman's head. He thought he knew why Hurley needed a lawyer.

She was looking at him. "Edward Moore is quietly buying up property formerly owned by Issei and Nise living in Richland."

Truman frowned. "Who who?"

"Issei and Nisei. Issei are Japanese-born citizens who emigrated to the United States. Nisei are the children of the Issei, American citizens. They're born here and are natural-born citizens. Moore already owns the note for their house and four others. Now, he's after James's bakery. And I'm not going to let him have it without a fight."

"Well, it seems like Mr. Moore has his hand in a lot of different pots. So, Mr. McLeod was helping you with your case? How was that going?"

Hurley placed the photograph on the main desk. "Mr. McLeod seemed to think it was going well. I offered to let him stay here for free if he'd help me with my case. He said I had a strong one, as Dorothy gave me power of attorney before she left. Not that I'm much good."

She took a deep breath and let it out slowly. "And now that Mr. McLeod's in jail, I don't have a lawyer so that bastard Moore is going to get the bakery."

Truman tapped the front counter with his knuckles. "The charges against Mr. McLeod are trumped up. There's no doubt about that. I don't think Carl would be careless and let Mr. McLeod get apprehended like that if there wasn't some good reason for them splitting up. We'll just go to the sheriff's station and talk to Mr. McLeod ourselves. I'll delay my trip to the warehouse, especially seeing as how I don't have a car."

Hurley smiled. "I've got a lot of work to do around here so you can borrow mine. It's not a Lincoln Continental but it'll get you there. Let me get my purse and then we can…."

She never finished her sentence. Truman, whose back was to the front door and window, saw her eyes grow wide with surprise. He turned and looked out the front window.

In the street, right in front of the hotel, was an old powder blue Ford pick-up. Standing next to the driver's door was Carl Hancock. He was talking to the driver. They shook hands and the driver pulled the truck back into the street.

Hancock dusted himself off and walked inside the hotel. His suit was dirty and dusty. His white shirt was soiled with what looked like mud. Even his boots and his hat were scuffed.

"Well, don't you two look like you've seen a ghost."

32

Wednesday
19 April 1944
9:00 a.m. Pacific War Time

Truman rushed over and shook Hancock's hand vigorously. Both men were grinning broadly. "Carl, it's so good to see you."

Hancock's smile faded a bit. "Thanks for the concern but I'm okay. It's Horace I'm worried about. He was picked up by the sheriff's deputies last night."

Truman and Hurley exchanged glances. "We know," Truman said. "Mrs. Hurley has been telling me about it. He's been arrested and charged with espionage."

"Espionage? How do you figure that?"

"We can't. Maybe you can."

Hancock blew air out of his mouth and looked up at the ceiling. Hancock looked over at the hotel owner. "Do you have any coffee?"

She nodded and went into the inner office while the two men sat on the hardwood bench seats opposite the front counter.

"Have you had breakfast?" Truman asked.

"Yeah. I stopped for a bite with Elmer, the truck driver who dropped me off."

Hurley returned with a cup and saucer and handed it to Hancock. He sipped the steaming brew and smiled. "Thank you." He set the cup and saucer down on the bench between himself and Truman. She wheeled her office chair through the pass-through and sat opposite Hancock.

The Texan recounted the stakeout, how well it was going, about Stanley receiving the telephone call, and then how the guard started searching for them. Hancock also mentioned how McLeod was accosted and arrested by the local Benton County deputies and how one deputy stayed behind to search for him.

Truman said, "Why do you think he was looking for you? Didn't he stay behind just to keep watch over the warehouse?"

Hancock gave a sarcastic grin. "That's what you'd think. But, no, Tall Man—that's what I took to calling him as he was the taller deputy—got in his car and started canvassing the gravel yard like he was specifically looking for someone or something."

He pointed at his boots. "These things are good for lots of things but walking on gravel and staying quiet ain't one of them. The good thing was that the patrol car made a small ruckus as it moved, no matter how slowly. I quickly decided that the piles of rock would be the first place *I'd* check so I skedaddled to some pipe factory next door to the rock yard."

Truman glanced at Hurley who sat, hands clasped together, leaning on her elbows, engrossed with the story.

"Tall Man was about to walk over to the pipe factory when we both heard cars approaching. One was a pickup, a Ford, and the other was a nice sedan. Both vehicles turned into the Moore Warehouse parking lot and stopped under the light over the bay doors. Guess who got out?" He paused for effect. "Moore and his chipper son."

Not up-to-date on their investigation, Hurley's reaction was sudden. "After midnight? What were they doing?"

Truman leaned forward, pulled out his notepad and pencil, and made an entry. "What time was this?"

Hancock looked at the ceiling. "One thirty. Chris walked over to the door and unlocked it. Edward and Tall Man stayed outside and talked. Every now and then, I'd catch a word but, basically, I heard nothing." Hancock leaned back and crossed his arms over his chest. "The way Tall Man acted around Moore was curious."

"Curious? How?"

"Body language. Tall Man stood straighter and nodded crisply. Through the binoculars, I could see Tall Man's lips. I can't read lips very well but I could tell what he kept saying over and over again. 'Yes, sir.'"

Truman raised his eyebrows. "Yes, sir? What, was he just being polite, the usual way police react to civilians?"

Hancock shook his head. "I got the impression Tall Man was deferring to someone in charge."

Hurley said, "In charge of what?"

"That's what we're going to find out," Truman said. He tapped his pencil against his lips. "What are we missing? There's something here."

"How'd you get here?" she asked.

Hancock broke into a wide grin. "By using my federal credentials." When both his listeners stared at him blankly, he continued.

"I didn't want too much daylight to expose me so I started walking back to town around dawn. About a mile or so from the warehouse, Elmer shows up. He asked what I was doing and I light bulb goes off in my head, just like in the cartoons." Hancock began to whisper. "I told him I was working undercover for the Army and he was now a part of it. I convinced him I needed his help." Hancock returned to his normal voice. "He bought it hook, line, and sinker."

Truman scowled disapprovingly.

Hancock held up his hands. "Hey, Harry, I used my gut. And it worked. I bought Elmer breakfast—don't worry, I got the receipt. And now, I'm here." He spread his arms out in a gesture made by a magician. "So, what do we do next, Harry?"

Truman sat for a moment in silence. "Even though Horace isn't a priority in our investigation, I think we need to get him out of jail.

Carl, you go to the police station and bail Horace out. Let's at least do that for him. Along the way, drop me off at the warehouse. After you've got Horace, bring him back here then come and help me at the warehouse." He looked at Mrs. Hurley. "I hope you don't mind if we take you up on your offer to use your car?"

"No problem at all. I'll be driving."

"Pardon me?" Truman said.

Reta Hurley looked at him resolutely. "You two don't have a legitimate reason for visiting him. You've only known him for two days." She pointed at herself. "But he's *my* lawyer. And I need him out."

The two men looked at each other, realizing she was right and there was no other good way. They nodded to each other and then to her.

Hancock stood and started walking across the lobby. "Well, then, that's settled. Give me a few minutes to clean up and I'll be ready to go."

Hurley looked at Truman, still working the tissue over in her hands. "You know I'm right."

Truman nodded. "Yes, I do. But just to get Mr. McLeod out of jail. I didn't want to involve too many other people in this thing, especially now that it's getting bigger."

"Don't worry about me, Senator, I'm just happy to do my part."

* * *

"Know what gets me?" Hancock said. He sat in the backseat of Reta Hurley's Model-A Ford. Truman was in the front passenger seat. "The telephone call. I mean, before the call, I was pointing out to Horace all the things Stanley was doing wrong. He was lackadaisical and, frankly, careless in his attention to his job. Then, he gets a call and, bam, the next thing we know, he comes after us like a hound dog."

Hancock waited until Truman half turned in his seat to face the backseat. "There's only one good explanation for Stanley's change in behavior."

Eyeing him in the rearview mirror, Hurley said, "Someone told him you were there."

A small twitch made Hancock's mouth go up in a smile and then it faded. "Exactly."

"But that makes no sense, Carl," Truman said. "Hardly anyone knew you and Horace were there. You, Horace, and I knew, of course. Mrs. Hurley knew you two went out but not the reason nor the destination. There was no one else."

"There's the person who delivered the telegram, sending you to Walla Walla last night," Hurley suggested.

Truman shook his head. "No, that can't be it. The telegram just said for me to go and speak. As far as the telegram man is concerned, that's the end of the story."

Hancock looked at the hotel owner through the rearview mirror. "I apologize in advance for the question, Mrs. Hurley, but did you say anything to anyone?"

She reddened slightly and Hancock could not be sure if it was out of embarrassment or anger. "I can assure you, Mr. Hancock, that I did no such thing." She paused and looked uncomfortable. "Mr. Lynch asked that I report on your comings and goings but since the invitation for Mr. Truman to go and speak arrived via telegram, I assumed that Mr. Lynch already knew. In fact, as soon as Senator Truman left with Sheriff Webb, I went out for dinner and then retired early."

Hancock looked at Truman and was about to ask him a question when he saw the senator's face. It had gone ashen. "Harry, what is it?"

Truman swallowed. "It was just a passing reference to our investigation. On the way back, Webb figured out we're here to investigate Moore. When we parked, he noticed that the Lincoln was gone and I mentioned, just briefly, where you and Horace were."

No one spoke for a few moments, letting the implications of what Truman had just said register. Hancock broke the silence. "That would explain the phone call and Stanley's sudden shift of behavior. What time did you get back to the hotel?"

"Around midnight."

Hancock nodded. "Yeah, that's about when Stanley got all Comanche on us."

"So, what are you two saying?" Hurley said. "Sheriff Webb called the warehouse to tell the security guy to go look for you?"

"That about sums it up," Hancock said. "And it also explains the deputies' hostile actions toward Horace." He leaned forward and patted Truman's shoulder. "Don't fret about it, Harry. It was an honest mistake."

Truman nodded curtly but Hancock could tell that Truman was really beating himself up over his lapse in judgment.

"Well," Truman said, "that makes our job that much more difficult. If we can't trust the local sheriff and the Army wants us out of town, who else can we trust?"

33

Wednesday
19 April 1944
9:10 a.m. Pacific War Time

"Duncan!" Sheriff Blaine's voice boomed through the station. Everyone jumped and looked toward Blaine's office. It was not in Blaine's nature to raise his voice, much less to demand someone's presence. All eyes shifted to Duncan, who rose from his desk, eyes wide, and hurried toward Blaine's office.

"Yes, sir?"

"Close the door." Blaine stood behind his chair, buckling his gun belt into place. "I just finished talking with Sheriff Webb. He talked to Edward Moore this morning and he had some interesting things to say." He looked at the deputy. "Do you know what they were?"

Duncan swallowed. He fished for something to say. "I can't think of anything, sir."

"That's because there ain't anything, according to Webb. Moore told Webb he didn't report the burglary because of PR. Can you believe that? Moore said that he'd lose his government contract if he couldn't adequately protect the goods the government's purchasing. Thus, no report of the crime, no loss of the contract."

Blaine placed both hands on the back of his chair in a visible effort to control his growing anger. He looked down at the chair and then looked at Duncan. Through the open blinds he could see most of his staff sneaking clandestine glances in his direction.

"I'm sorry, Joe. I didn't mean to yell at you. It's just that this case is already starting to get under my skin. And I got no leads."

Duncan ventured an opinion. "Sir, despite what Webb may have said, that doesn't preclude you from following the lead anyway."

Blaine nodded. "I know. That's where I'm going now." He got a cigarette out of his pocket and lit it. "Where are the pictures I asked the coroner to take?"

Duncan, hating to point out the obvious, indicated Blaine's desk. "Right here, sir."

Blaine actually laughed. "Right in front of my goddamn face. For crying out loud." He picked up the manila folder and opened it. He looked at the two 8x10s of the dead men's faces. He closed the folder. "This'll do."

He stood there, tapping the folder on his hands. He smiled a disarming smile at Duncan. "You'll never guess who Moore attributed his burglary to."

Having answered incorrectly a minute before, Duncan was gun-shy about answering again. Blaine answered his own question. "Your Mountain Men."

Duncan's mouth actually dropped open. "I always thought *I* was the only one who believed they really existed."

"Well, there appears to be two of you now. And that's your next assignment." Blaine walked around his desk and dropped the folder onto it. "Look, we all have hobbies. I like to fish and fly planes. Ted likes to make furniture and Dennis likes to play pool. It helps us pass the time."

Blaine patted Duncan's shoulder. "And I have a pretty good idea what yours is. You seem to be an expert on these Mountain Men. I expect you've made lists of names, dates of birth, all sorts of interesting tidbits over the years. Am I right?"

Duncan looked to the floor, suddenly a bit embarrassed. "Yeah."

"Good."

Duncan looked up at the sheriff. "Sir?"

"While I'm driving up to Richland, I need you to go over your lists of Mountain Men. Of the ones who, supposedly, didn't return after we got into this war, I want you to cross check them for any connection to Edward Moore."

A broad smile grew on Duncan's face. "Yes, sir."

Blaine walked back to his desk and picked up his jacket, its dark brown matched the color of his uniform pants. He reached up and buttoned his top button and fixed his black tie. He picked up the manila folder and walked over to the hat rack. He turned back to Duncan. "This is a top priority, Joe. Get to it. Radio me when you get an answer. If I don't hear from you before I get to the Moore Warehouse, I'll call you. Understand?"

"Yes, sir," Duncan said as he moved to the door and opened it. He looked at Blaine. "My, uh, *stuff's* at my house. Do you want me to bring it here?"

"Yes, but get the information first. Don't waste time driving back here. Find the information, if there is any, and call the station. Mildred will patch you through to me. Soon as you report to me, get back here. And Joe," Blaine paused, pondering how to say what he had to say, "I know most everyone has given you a hard time about these Mountain Men. Heck, I've done it myself. But if the information you have can help us break this case, you just might be the only guy around here who's hobby helped solve a crime." He patted Duncan's shoulder again as the deputy opened the door and nearly ran out of the office.

34

———

Wednesday
19 April 1944
9:37 a.m. Pacific War Time

Toshiro Ishihara knocked on the cabin door of the captain. The door opened and Morimoto stood in the doorway. "Yes?"

Ishihara bowed slightly. "Captain-san, may I have a word with you? In private."

Morimoto eyed his pilot but then stepped back. Ishihara entered his captain's quarters and shut the door. The space was tight but both men remained standing.

Ishihara got right to the heart of the matter. "Captain-san, I have a personal request. The spirits of my family demand retribution. I am the only one who can deliver it." He looked directly into Morimoto's eyes. "Captain, please give me the honor of destroying the American base."

Morimoto's eyes never wavered from his lieutenant. The stuffy air inside the submarine made the room humid and musty. He could see beads of sweat actually forming on the younger man's brow.

"Ishihara-san, you are my best pilot. I cannot allow your

personal desire for revenge to jeopardize this mission. I will need you to make more flights after tonight."

Ishihara inhaled deeply. "Captain-san, if the Americans spot our plane, there will be no other flights."

Morimoto scowled and looked about to explode when Ishihara continued. "Sir, the plane is designed from reconnaissance."

"I know what the plane was made for," Morimoto snapped. "My uncle worked in the factory."

"Yes, sir. But, if I may, the plane is not designed for combat." Ishihara stopped for a moment, wondering how far to go. On the one hand, the conversation might go in the direction where Ishihara would have to make a choice of whether or not to tell the captain the truth about the two dead Americans. On the other hand, his case would be easier to make.

"If the Americans spot the plane and send up fighters to attack, no pilot, not even the best pilot, will be able to evade the Americans. They will shoot down the plane with ease."

Morimoto considered this assertion, saying nothing.

"There is another reason. I am more proficient at hand-to-hand combat. I know it and you know it." He paused to add emphasis. "And because I deserve to avenge my family."

Morimoto's voice was even. "This is no time to have your desire for revenge cloud your judgment."

"Captain-san, my ancestors demand it. They speak to me in my dreams. They speak to me when I fly. When I am in the air, I can see them, I can almost feel them, touch them. I swore to them I would avenge them. Now, I have a chance. With your permission."

Ishihara stood at attention, watching Morimoto reflect on the request. He knew that whatever the captain said here would be final. If the captain denied his permission, Ishihara would just have to fulfill his destiny another way. He decided to lay out one last point in his case.

"Captain-san, Niigata is thinking too much. You and I both know what thinking can do to a man. He is worried that our take-off will not go perfectly. He is worried that the Americans will shoot down the plane. He is worried that the parachute may not open. He is worried that there may not be enough explosives to destroy the factory. He is worried that he will be captured by the American pigs."

Ishihara inhaled deeply and let out the air slowly. "The spirits of my family help calm me. They tell me that the plane will lift off without error. They tell me that the Americans will not know we are flying in their airspace. They tell me that the parachute will open. They tell me that I will destroy the factory. And they tell me that I will not be captured. They tell me all of these things because it is my *destiny* to do these things, to avenge the deaths of my family."

After a minute's silence, Morimoto said, "Ishihara-san, how was all the plane's fuel expended?"

Ishihara had not expected this question. He considered the matter finished. But now, he realized that his answer might hold the key to Morimoto's answer. If he told the captain the truth, the captain would undoubtedly punish Ishihara up to, and possibly including, death, despite Ishihara being only one of two pilots. If he continued his lie, however, his destiny could still be fulfilled, one way or another.

"I apologize, Captain-san, I was not entirely forthcoming with my answer this morning. There were strong headwinds on the return trip, sir. But on the outbound flight, I did circle a few locations. I apologize, sir. I am a flier trapped inside a submarine. Sometimes, when I am up there, I do not even feel the plane around me. I lose myself in the air."

Morimoto smiled but without humor. "You are a unique soldier, Ishihara, one who could go far in this navy. But you do have other talents." Morimoto nodded. "I will inform Niigata of the change."

Ishihara bowed low toward Morimoto. "*Domo arigato*, Captain-san. The spirits of my family thank you as well. I will not fail you or the Emperor."

"See that you do not. Dismissed."

Ishihara bowed again and left the captain's quarters. He walked aft toward his small locker. As he walked down the central passageway, he realized that he was already flying.

35

Wednesday
19 April 1944
9:55 a.m. Pacific War Time

Theodore Frank sat in a small cinder block room. There were no windows and the walls were painted Army white—not quite the brightness of the crayon color but not as dull as gray. He sat at a table. The two light fixtures on the ceiling lit the room with all the glaring brightness of a summer's day. Frank had had enough time in the room by himself to begin to wonder if the Army built the room based on a Hollywood stereotype or the other way around.

He was startled out of his daydream by the sound of the key turning in the lock. A man he had never seen before walked into the room. The man wore the typical Army uniform of khaki pants and shirt with a black tie folded inside the shirt. His garrison hat was folded over his belt. His hair was closely cut along the sides of his head. This only accentuated his receding hairline. His face was angular but his chin was rounded, not chiseled.

The man closed the door behind him. He didn't bother to lock it.

"Good morning, Mr. Frank. My name is Major Nicholas Lynch. I am in charge of security here at Hanford." Lynch walked over to the opposite side of the table and sat in the other chair. "You know why you are here, don't you?"

Frank was surprised at Lynch's elocution. It was quite pronounced, indicating a definite Ivy League education. Frank decided to let Lynch do most of the talking.

"You breached the perimeter of our facility. My officers inform me that, so far, you have provided your name and nothing further." Lynch leaned on the table and stared at Frank. "Would you care to break your silence with me?"

"No." Frank spoke the words distinctly and was proud of himself. As Moore and others had instructed him, allow the higher ranking officials to come in and then, only then, start negotiating. Not talking, negotiating.

"Why?"

"I have my reasons."

Lynch didn't break eye contact with his prisoner. "Mr. Frank, may I remind you, sir, that you are in a great deal of trouble. You committed a crime of trespassing. That you did it here, on this Army base, makes the penalty more severe. I could have you shot. However, it's my job to find out why you were trespassing and what you planned to do."

Frank maintained eye contact with Lynch. The major's dark brown eyes, his calm demeanor, and his precision gave Frank pause. He swallowed hard and took a deep breath.

Lynch continued. "I appreciate your cooperation, Mr. Frank. In fact, your silence will allow me to fill in the gaps. Before the war, I fancied myself a writer. Let me see if I can write your story for you." Lynch leaned back in his chair and stared at the light over the table.

"You got out of serving in the Army for some insipid reason. You were co-opted by Nazi spies and, through money or women, you agreed to help them. They told you to make your way into this Army facility to see what's going on here and report back to them.

You get arrested, they sever all ties to you, and you're labeled a spy and a traitor to this country." Lynch looked away from the light and back to Frank. "The penalty for treason is, by the way, death." Lynch smiled. "Am I close?"

Frank swallowed hard a second time. He met Lynch's eyes but his voice grew unsteady. "I am no spy."

In an animated way, Lynch proceeded. "Oh, well, I'm sorry, Mr. Frank. I guess you're not a spy because you say so. My apologies."

Lynch looked away, striking a pose like he was thinking about something and then snapped his fingers. "How about this one? You are an isolationist. You opposed the American entry into this war both before Pearl Harbor and after. You avoided the draft by, say, claiming you are a conscientious objector. Despite a direct attack on this nation, you think America should just curl up in its own nest and not engage the rest of the world. Let the rest of the world fight, leave me out of it. But our government did go to war to protect not only this country but all free countries and you just cannot stand it. You *have* to do something. What can you do? Oh, I know, you find the nearest military base and decide to sabotage whatever's going on there."

Lynch looked again at Frank. "Am I closer now?" He didn't smile.

Frank's palms began to sweat and he rubbed them on his pants. He took a deep breath before speaking in an attempt to keep his voice steady. "Look, Mr. Lynch, I…"

"Major Lynch."

"Major Lynch, I am no isolationist. I'm an American who…."

"Bullshit!" Lynch slammed his hands hard onto the table. The sound was louder than Frank expected and he jumped. The sound of Lynch's voice was also louder than he expected.

"If you were a true and loyal American, you would tell me, right here and now, why the hell were you trespassing on government land."

Lynch took a deep breath and closed his eyes. He didn't speak for a few moments and Frank began to wish that he would. The silence started to get to him and he desperately wanted to fill in the silence with some sound. The only sound either man heard was the din of activity beyond the door.

"Mr. Frank, let me tell you a few things. One, my officers and men are looking up your identity in our military and civilian records. We will find you. It would be much better for you and me if you would just tell me why you were intruding on this base."

Lynch idly traced a finger along the edge of the table. "Two, there is another possibility for you. I could have you drafted. Whatever cowardly excuse you gave to the draft board to allow you to stay home while better men than you go off and fight will not work this time. You will be drafted and I will give explicit instructions to have you posted on the front lines, either in the Pacific or in Europe. In this war, unfortunately, there always has to be a first man who goes into, say, a dug-in Japanese bunker. That man doesn't usually survive and usually is dead before he hits the ground."

Lynch paused and his finger stopped moving. "But I can't let you do that. You would be a hero, a man who laid down his life for his country. That's not in your character, is it, Mr. Frank? You are a milquetoast. You'd shit your pants at the first sight of the enemy and you'd get good men killed. No, I better not do that." Lynch looked back at Frank. "But I can."

Frank no longer wondered if Lynch could see him sweat. The beads of sweat were now running down his face in ones and twos.

Lynch smiled a smile without humor. "Have I made myself clear, Mr. Frank? I want the truth." Lynch lowered his voice to a whisper. "It will be much easier for you if you just tell the truth."

Through stammering lips, Frank said, "I can't."

"Can't or won't, Mr. Frank? There is a difference. There is a choice here. It's all up to you."

"I can't, Mister…uh, Major Lynch. I can't jeopardize the others."

Lynch's eyebrows rose. "Now we are getting somewhere, Mr. Frank. So, you are protecting someone. It must be your fellow traitors."

Anger seeped into Frank's voice. "I told you I'm no traitor."

"Well you must be. Surely you don't think your fate will be worse with them than with me? I assure you, Mr. Frank, your fate is much worse with me. This is war. I have the entire American military and the entire American government at my disposal. I can have you drafted. I can lock you up in prison and not even give a reason."

Lynch rose and walked around the table. His eyes never left Frank's until he stopped directly behind Frank, who still sat in his chair. Lynch leaned down, next to Frank's ear, and whispered. "I'm going to let you sit here and think, Mr. Frank. I know you want to talk but I have other things to do. I'll come back later. But I want to make sure I leave you with the one fundamental truth we have between us."

Frank could not see the smile but he heard it in Lynch's voice.

"I can do anything I want to you and you can't do one damn thing to stop me."

36

Wednesday
19 April 1944
10:10 a.m. Pacific War Time

Truman seethed at himself for potentially jeopardizing the investigation with his careless talk the previous evening. A nearby billboard proclaimed "Loose Lips Sink Ships."

"They also make investigations more difficult," Truman muttered as he strode across the parking lot toward the bay doors of the Moore Warehouse, the cloud of dust stirred up by the departing Lincoln partially obscuring the line of trucks that snaked around the parking lot. The wind was stronger today and curls of dust and sand flew through the air. The dust coated Truman's spectacles. As he stepped inside the warehouse, he removed his glasses and cleaned them with his handkerchief. Without his glasses, his vision was so poor that he was unable to recognize the figure approaching him until the other person spoke.

"Good morning, Senator Truman," Larry Watson shouted over the din of the diesel engines.

Truman replaced his glasses and put his handkerchief back in his coat pocket. "Good morning, Mr. Watson." He motioned to the line of trucks. "Busy, as usual, I see."

"It's always busy with the U.S. Army. Got to keep them happy to say nothing of the workers up there building the factory." Watson looked toward the line of trucks as he spoke. "It's good to be efficient and not have any obstacles blocking you from getting your job done."

Watson then noticed Truman was alone. "Where's your partner, the cowboy?"

A hundred retorts entered Truman's mind. Chief among them was to ask Watson what he was doing here at the warehouse last night. Unfortunately, the only purpose that comment would serve would be to undermine his position. He screwed up his face. He wanted to lay into Watson but didn't really have the time. Besides, he thought, I'm not sure this mule would even register the insult.

"He's on another assignment this morning."

Watson nodded and smiled.

"Mr. Moore in yet?" Truman asked, not caring that his impatience was now obvious.

"Yeah. Let me take you up there and...hey, watch it." Watson noticed one of the forklift operators hit a stack of crates, partially dislodging the top half of the stack. The crates hung precariously, ready to fall at any second.

Watson waved at his hand up to the second floor. "He's up in his private office." Watson jogged over to survey the damage and determine how to steady the crates without anyone getting hurt.

Truman realized that all the activity in the warehouse was louder than yesterday. He could not hear his own footsteps as he ascended the stairs. He reached the landing and walked the few steps over to Moore's office. The door was ajar. When Truman raised his hand to knock, he saw Moore standing at the bookcase behind his desk. The salmon mounted on a large piece of cedar had been moved like a door on hinges. Behind the cedar mounting was a safe. It was open and Moore was reading something he held in his hands.

Truman wanted to do two opposite things. On one hand, he

wanted to surprise Moore and see what came of it, knowing it would be impossible for Moore to hide the fact that he had a safe, that it was open, and that he was holding something probably not meant for Truman's eyes. On the other hand, Truman still wanted to try to conduct his investigation in as friendly a demeanor as possible. He had dealt with some antagonistic businessmen before and they were always more of a pain than necessary. Something was going on around here and Truman realized that a smooth investigation would eventually reveal the truth.

He lowered his hand and all but tiptoed back to the top of the landing. He used his peripheral vision to see if anyone on the floor was watching him. As far as he could tell, all eyes were on Watson working to avoid another accident.

Truman reached the top step and took one step down. He thought that the best course of action would be to stomp loudly so that Moore would hear him coming. At that moment, however, the truck that had been idling inside the warehouse shut off its engine. The interior of the warehouse, while still loud, softened.

The senator appreciated the quiet. He stepped back onto the landing, making sure to put his feet down harder than necessary. His deception worked. He reached the door. Without looking in, he knocked three times. He heard some movement behind the door and then Edward Moore filled the doorway.

"Good morning, Mr. Truman. Moore extended his hand. "A bit late, aren't you? I thought you were the rise-and-get going kind of man."

Truman returned the handshake. "I am. I had a few things I needed to take care of this morning, constituent letters and such."

Moore smiled. "Of course. I would imagine a senator's job is never done." He made a big show of looking behind Truman. "Where is Mr. Hancock?"

Truman expected Moore to ask this question and he had already given it some thought. For Truman himself, he started the day not knowing where Hancock was and it had worried him. Chances were, if Moore knew about McLeod being arrested—and probably even had his hand in it, Truman thought—then likely Moore would have been wondering about Hancock as well. Truman, being here without Hancock, probably gave Moore some pause, perhaps even a bit of concern. Truman decided to use this fact to his advantage.

"On another assignment. He left last night and he hasn't reported back to me yet."

Moore pursed his lips. "Hmm. I thought you conducted one investigation at a time."

"Inspection, Mr. Moore," Truman said.

"My apologies. The words seem to get jumbled up in my head."

Moore motioned Truman to enter his office. He walked over to a side table and picked up a crystal bottle. Truman assumed that the brown liquid was whiskey. Moore poured one finger worth in each of two glasses and gave one to Truman. Moore drained his glass. Truman did the same and placed his glass on the table.

"This other assignment you mentioned you had for Mr. Hancock. Pardon the forwardness, but would it have anything to do with your lawyer friend, Mr. McLeod?"

In the car this morning, Truman had chastised himself for giving away too much information to people whose trustworthiness he could not verify. Edward Moore certainly fell into that camp.

Truman put on his poker face. "No. Mr. McLeod is not a government agent. Why do you ask?"

Moore feigned surprise. "Oh, didn't you hear? Mr. McLeod was arrested last night."

Truman thought to himself it was a good thing he already knew about this or Moore would have certainly caught him by surprise. Instead, Truman raised his eyebrows. "No, I hadn't heard. It wasn't in the local paper nor did I hear it on the radio this morning. If you don't mind me asking, how is it that you know about Mr. McLeod's arrest?" Truman could tell that Moore was slightly shocked that Truman, himself, was not surprised.

Moore considered Truman for a moment without speaking. Then, giving Truman an even stare, he said, "Mr. Truman, perhaps you've forgotten who you're talking to. I own and run one of the biggest warehousing companies west of the Rocky Mountains. My distribution network is exactly the type of organization the Army needs as it builds those factories up the road. I have attended numerous meetings with high ranking Army officials, including, I might add, General Groves himself."

Moore paused, letting that fact sink register with Truman.

The senator's face remained impassive, but his distaste for Moore increased. He disliked arrogance in anyone—including name-dropping the general in charge of the operation out here in Hanford—but especially when that arrogance was aimed at him.

Moore continued. "This kind of access has its perks. One of them is knowing what's going on in the area. This knowledge enables me to operate my warehouse more efficiently and to better serve the Army. Efficiency's the thing you preach, isn't it?"

He walked over to his desk and picked up a sheet of paper. "A few years ago, we had some trouble with a group who felt it wasn't their duty to join the Army and fight. You might have heard them referred to as the 'Mountain Men.' After the Army arrived, these little incidents continued. I suggested that the Army coordinate with the sheriffs of the nearby counties and pool their efforts to gather information. Gradually, that information became a daily report. All the law enforcement officials get this report as do certain civilian entities. I'm in the latter category. In addition, other, more civilian data is collected and used to help the war effort." He walked over to Truman and handed him the paper.

Truman took the paper and read over it. The sheet listed all types of information: number of new workers arrived in Hanford, amount of food and supplies consumed during the past week. At the bottom of the page were the police reports. Truman read McLeod's name.

Well, he thought, at least the arrest is now public which means there will be a report filed.

Truman handed the paper back to Moore. "I can see where this type of information would be handy for your business. You can prepare your different warehouses for incoming shipments of things you know the Army will need. Very good. You certainly seem like a very patriotic American who does everything by the book."

Moore's mouth tightened into a thinner line that it already was. "Thank you. I just try to do my part."

In Truman's mind, he shouted, I bet you do.

Moore tossed the report back onto his desk. "So, will you be continuing the review of my books that you started yesterday?"

"Yes, I'd like to complete my review of your accounting records before I begin interviewing your employees."

Moore's eyebrows furrowed. "Senator Truman, surely you don't think that's necessary? My warehouse is running at top efficiency. Taking men off the work line just to answer a few questions seems extreme."

Truman smiled to himself. Had this been a poker game, he would have just raised the stakes.

"I'm not yet sure if interviews will be necessary. I'll know more once I complete the review of the books. Now, if you don't mind, I'd like to get started."

Truman enjoyed ending the conversation on his terms and he saw the irritation on Moore's face. Stiffly, he walked ahead of Truman, through the private office door and into the business office.

37

———

Wednesday
19 April 1944
11:10 a.m. Pacific War Time

Blaine sat inside the open driver's side door holding his police radio near his ear. He had parked around the corner from the main entrance of the Moore Warehouse. He watched the big trucks line up to unload their cargo as Duncan reported his discoveries.

"I collected all the occupations of the men who allegedly are part of the Mountain Men. I checked them for any connection and I got seven hits."

"Seven? That's a lot." Blaine got a notepad from his breast pocket and opened it on his knee. "Go ahead."

"You don't have to know all seven names. Three of them came back after Pearl Harbor and enlisted. That leaves us with four who are not accounted for: Jack Buchan, Theodore Frank, Ronald Garrison, and Eli Sale."

Blaine memorized the names as he wrote them in the notepad. "What are their connections with Edward Moore?"

"The first three—Buchan, Frank, and Garrison—all worked for

Moore before December 7th. Eli Sale evidently was a fishing buddy. I found a photo from a newspaper of Moore and Sale holding up a big marlin."

Duncan paused. "Sir, I apologize for not making the connection sooner. This is one of my hobbies and you'd think I'd know all that I have. But I didn't."

"Don't beat yourself up about it, Joe. You did good work. Now, get back to the station and bring your research with you."

"All of it, sir?"

"How much do you have?"

"Um, a couple of boxes worth."

Blaine sighed. At least he had only one hobby—fishing—that required the collection of things. His other love, flying, required only a pilot's license. "Sure, bring it all."

Blaine shut off the radio and picked up the manila folder with the photos. He walked around the perimeter of the warehouse, taking note of the hectic nature of the place, before he entered the front door. He removed his aviator glasses and scanned the interior of the warehouse. It was the typical warehouse interior with crates piled high. To his right, up a flight of stairs, were two offices. The door closest to the landing, marked "Office," was closed; the door right next to it marked "Private" was open halfway. Guessing that the private office was Moore's, he started up the stairs, a manila folder tapping his leg.

He reached the landing and knocked on the door. A large man with gray flecks in his mustache opened the door. "Yes?"

"Lester Blaine, Sheriff of Umatilla County, Oregon." He extended his hand.

The man shook the proffered hand. "Edward Moore, What brings you up this way, Sheriff?" Moore's smile seemed genuine. He gestured for Blaine to enter the office.

The office was an outdoorsman's dream. Mounted game and fishes filled the walls and shelves. "I'm working a case and I wanted to ask you a few questions."

"Does this have anything to do with the matter Sheriff Webb called me about?"

A thought went through Blaine's mind: at least he now knew Webb had actually spoken with Moore. Strike one for Blaine's suspicions. "Yes, sir, it does."

"About the invoice for powdered milk, wasn't it?"

"Yes, sir. What can you tell me about it?"

Moore walked over to the sideboard table and poured himself a finger's worth of whiskey. "Can I pour you a drink, Sheriff?"

"No, thank you," said Blaine. What he left unspoken was that he could certainly use one.

Moore nodded in a knowing way, like he knew Blaine would say that. Moore downed the liquid in one gulp and waited while the alcohol went down.

"Powdered milk," Moore said. "If only everything was as simple. You have powder, add water, and you can have milk anywhere you like and you don't even need refrigeration. Wonderful invention, don't you think?"

"It certainly has its uses. That's why the government buys it and ships it up here, so that they can give a glass of milk to all those folks working up at Hanford." He hooked his left thumb around his belt. "But why would someone want to steal milk?"

Moore walked back over and stood next to Blaine. Both men admired the mounted salmon on the wall to Blaine's right. "From what I hear, there's a group out there for whom powdered milk would be like manna from heaven."

Blaine shifted so that he was facing the salmon but also watching Moore. "The Mountain Men? You think they stole your milk?"

"It makes sense, don't you think? A bunch of people out in the wilderness with few supplies. All you need is water and there are plenty of rivers around the state to provide the water."

Blaine reached out and ran a finger along the salmon's mouth. He noticed that the taxidermist had done a remarkable job at smoothing over the place in the salmon's mouth where the hook had set.

"Fine work, don't you think?" Moore said. "That one was done by an old friend of mine, Eli Sale. He's not around anymore."

Blaine remained calm but inside, his heart skipped a beat. He shifted his weight and glanced toward the floor. The Afghan rug was a deep burgundy with a Middle Eastern pattern running through it. "What happened to Mr. Sale?"

Moore looked disgusted. "He joined the Mountain Men. And he's one of the ones who didn't come back even after December 7. Can you believe that?"

"I couldn't say. Do you think it was this Mr. Sale who broke into your warehouse?"

Moore nodded. "He'd been here many times so he knew the layout. And he knew how to get in on the nights the security guard had off."

Blaine raised one eyebrow. "You have a security guard but you give him occasional nights off? Don't you have a backup for those particular nights?"

Moore laughed dryly. "Actually, I don't. I used to stay here on those nights. So did my son. But since it had been so long since our last break-in, we got lazy. Then it hits us like a ton of bricks."

"So why didn't you report it?"

Moore pointed to the salmon. "You see this fish, here? What you don't see is how my hook ripped half of the salmon's mouth away. But it was the biggest fish I had ever caught up to that point. I was proud of that fish. So I had Mr. Sale, genius that he was with taxidermy, fix up the salmon to where he's good as new. I bet you didn't even notice the cosmetic changes, did you?"

Blaine wasn't sure where Moore was going, but he kept his face neutral. "Nope."

"And that's the point, Sheriff. Sometimes, you need a little something to smooth over a blemish in order to present a cleaner image to others. Had I reported this burglary to Sheriff Webb, he is duty bound to report it to the Army. If the Army learns that my facility is not secure, they may choose to stop using me. I can't afford for that to happen. Nor could the Army. So I do the next best thing: I make sure I have a security guard every night. I replaced all the locks on the warehouse. And one of three people—me, my son, Christopher, or my foreman, Larry Watson—scout the grounds before we lock up." Moore crossed his arms in pride. "And we've had no trouble since."

Moore laughed to himself. "I know what you're thinking: why didn't I do that in the first place? Well, as I said, we got lazy." He paused and gave the sheriff an even stare. "But we're not lazy now."

Blaine thought about all that he had just heard. It all sounded plausible. In fact, everything here seemed to be in order. "I see your point. There's one other thing you could do for me."

"What's that?"

"I have a couple of pictures here. I was wondering if you could tell me if you know these men."

Moore began to jingle the change in his pocket. "What makes you think I'll be able to identify anyone? I deal with hundreds of people whose faces tend to blend together after a while."

"My research tells me that these two men used to work for you back in 1939 and '40."

The jingling increased. "I'll certainly do what I can but I'm not sure I'll be much help."

Blaine could tell that Moore's façade had cracked a bit. He tapped the manila folder on his leg. "Here you go." Blaine handed Moore the folder.

Moore opened the folder and gasped. He looked up at Blaine. "These men are dead?"

"Do you know them?"

Moore pondered for a moment and Blaine wondered what was going on inside the man's head. Finally, Moore said, "Yes, I do. Or, well, I should say, did."

"Did?"

"Yes, they used to work for me before they went off with Eli and the other Mountain Men."

Moore tried to close the folder but Blaine held up a hand. "If you don't mind, would you please identify these two men?"

Moore pointed at the man with the beard. "This one is Ron Garrison and the other one is Jack Buchan." Moore closed the folder and handed it back to Blaine.

"Thank you, sir." Blaine was about to ask another question when Moore interrupted.

"What happened to them?" The jingling continued.

"That's the rub, Mr. Moore. I don't know. Since these men left your employment, have you had any contact with them?"

Moore's eyes darted to the salmon behind Blaine's head. "No, not since they left civilization and went to live with the bears." He looked thunderstruck. "They look bad."

"Yes, they do. They were murdered."

"Who did it?"

Blaine cleared his throat. "I don't know yet. Who would have a motive to kill them?"

The two of them were silent. When Blaine thought the silence had gone on long enough, he spoke what was obvious to them both. "One might assume someone in your organization might have motive to kill Mr. Buchan and Mr. Garrison."

"Sheriff Blaine. How dare you accuse me of...'

"Sir, I am accusing you of nothing. I merely stated that someone here, at the warehouse, might have reason to stop the burglaries altogether. I am not saying it's you. But I *am* asking if you know anything about that."

Blaine watched as Moore thought of something to say. "No, I don't." His tone was flat. "But I'll look into it. Can you be contacted at the station?"

Blaine knew a dismissal when he heard one. No matter. He had achieved all he had wanted and them some. He had the names of the dead men. He had assuaged his concerns about Sheriff Webb. And he had rattled Moore's cage. Something was bound to drop now.

"Yes, sir." He reached in his shirt pocket, pulled out a card, and handed it to Moore.

Moore took it and slipped it into his shirt pocket. "Believe me, Sheriff, I'll help you find who did this to my friends. They were good men."

Blaine nodded. "Thanks for your time, Mr. Moore. I can see myself out."

<h1 style="text-align:center">38</h1>

Wednesday
19 April 1944
11:37 a.m. Pacific War Time

Hancock drove into the parking lot and witnessed a sight that made his day. He quickly parked the Lincoln, got out, and ran.

"Sheriff Blaine!" The other man stopped and turned. He hooked his thumbs into his belt and just looked at the Texan as he approached.

"Hello, Mr. Hancock. Did you and Mr. Bruman and Mr. McLean check in okay." He stood motionless, staring at Hancock.

Hancock couldn't tell if Blaine was kidding but he shrugged. "C'mon, you know how it is. I didn't know you from Adam. And from what Horace told us, the place was crawling with spies. You would have done the same thing." Hancock waited for a response.

Blaine allowed a small smile to creep onto his face. "You're right, I would have."

They chuckled a moment, sharing the camaraderie only police

officers share. Then, almost as an afterthought, Hancock looked at Blaine. "I know why I'm here. Why are you here?"

Blaine held up the manila folder. "I needed a positive identification on the two dead men you saw the other day."

"Who here knew the names of the dead men?"

Blaine nodded in the direction of the warehouse. The giant letters spelling "Moore" cast almost no shadow in the noontime sun. "The man whose name is on the building."

Hancock's eyes widened. "Edward Moore? How did he know who the men were?"

"Remember our local myth around here, the Mountain Men? Well, it turns out that some of the men who stayed in the woods used to work for Moore. I got that piece of information from one of my deputies. You remember Duncan, the one who almost pulled a gun on you."

"Yeah, I remember. How'd he have the information?"

"Duncan's hobby is the Mountain Men. After Joe told me about all the stuff he researched, I'm about ready to give it to the Army and have them flush out these Mountain Men." Blaine paused and toed a line in the dirt. "It's just…"

"What's eating you?"

Blaine grunted. "I can't seem to get my head around the idea that now, nearly four years after Pearl, after thousands of lives lost, there are men still living out there claiming to be against the government. It just don't make sense."

Hancock shrugged. "Well, I guess they believe passionately in their cause. If you're passionate about something, you find it easy to do the things you have to do or want to do."

Blaine shook his head, not convinced. "What got me interested in Mr. Moore here was something we found on one of the bodies. It was an invoice for some powdered milk."

Hancock's jaw dropped open. "An invoice? You've got to be kidding. Invoices are the main focus of our investigation." Hancock told Blaine about the investigation so far. "Do you have the invoice with you?"

"No, I don't. I left it back at the station. Why?"

"Did it have the date, the company of origin, and the quantity listed?"

Blaine nodded with understanding. "You want me to check the original number with the number of the alleged duplicate and see if they match? But what if they don't? What does that mean to you?"

"It means that Horace's theory might be correct. He thinks Moore is skimming off the top to sell after the war."

Blaine stood a moment and said nothing. "You know what I'm looking forward to after the war and rationing? Buying a pair of nylon stockings for my wife. She's been without nylons for going on two years."

Hancock smiled. "I know what you mean. I'm looking forward to drinking a tall glass of iced tea with an inch of sugar sitting at the bottom of the glass. This sugar rationing is killing me but"—he patted his stomach—"the missus likes the results."

"You want me to give you a call when I get back to the station and let you know what figures I have?"

"That'd be great." Hancock rubbed the corners of his mouth with the index finger and thumb of his left hand. "I have, uh, a delicate question for you." When he saw Blaine waiting for the question, he continued. "How well do you know Ira Webb?"

Blaine eyed the Texan. "Why do you ask?"

Hancock still hesitated. "I don't know, but it's just a feeling, really. A hunch. Based on what happened last night, I think Webb might be in cahoots with Moore."

Blaine was silent for a moment. He looked over to the warehouse and noticed the line of trucks was actually down to two. Off in the distance, the rocky plateau that surrounded the Columbia Basin shimmered in the heat. "Tell me again how it was you and Senator Truman were compelled to come out here."

"What, you mean Horace's letters?"

"No, before that. What was Mr. McLeod's problem? Why'd McLeod call Senator Truman?"

Hancock thought for a moment. "Let's see, Horace is a lawyer and he was gathering evidence to bring against the government for taking the farm away from his wife's brother. Horace was harassed and began to feel threatened. He felt he couldn't trust anyone."

"This farmer you mentioned, what's his story?"

"Worked here. Name's Bumble. He allegedly saw some things he wasn't supposed to. He alerted Horace. Next this he knew, he was drafted."

Hancock saw Blaine smiling but not in a good way. "What?"

"That might be the key, Mr. Hancock."

"Call me Carl."

Blaine nodded. "Lester. You see, as sheriff, if I see any suspicious activity, I'm obligated to report said activity to the Army. This mandate includes any American who may be letting a little too much information slip out of his mouth. We send word up to Hanford to a guy named Lynch and the Army takes it from there. The standard protocol there is drafting and sending them overseas."

At the mention of Lynch's name, Hancock snorted. "Lynch. Now there's a piece of work."

"Actually, he's a pretty decent guy. He takes his job a little too seriously but that's to be expected and welcomed in the position he has."

"What are you getting at?"

"If the only thing Lynch needs to draft someone and ship them off is a word from a local sheriff, and if Webb needed to remove this farmer, then my guess is Webb did it by telling Lynch."

Hancock whistled softly.

Blaine kicked a pebble across the dusty ground. "Proving that's what happened will be tricky. There's no hard evidence except the written request sent to Lynch. I'd start there. Get that report then start digging." He clapped Hancock on the shoulder. "Good luck with that." He opened his car door and tossed the pictures on the passenger seat and looked back at Hancock. "Let me know what you find out. Ira's a good man but maybe he took a wrong turn. I'd like to know why. Good day, Carl. I'll be expecting your call."

Blaine started up the engine, backed out of the space, and drove away. Hancock, still dazed by Blaine's comment, turned and walked toward the warehouse.

* * *

"W**E HAVE A PROBLEM**," Edward Moore said. He was in his office. Christopher Moore and Larry Watson sat in the chairs opposite the desk. "Ron and Jack are dead."

"What?" Watson sat bolt upright in his chair. "How do you know?"

Edward nodded toward the door. "That sheriff from Oregon showed me pictures. They were in bad shape but it was obviously Ron and Jack."

Watson scowled. "What about Teddy Frank? He was scheduled to be the third man."

Edward shrugged. "The sheriff didn't mention him. Maybe he's already back at the camp."

Christopher quickly jumped to the next question. "How does that affect the camp?"

"Don't know, but one of us is going to have to go out there and check on them. It was the river drop this time. But I'm worried that someone might follow us there."

Watson said, "Follow you? Who?"

"The sheriff for one. He basically accused me of killing them. When I called him on it, he said it could be anyone in the warehouse."

"That's ridiculous," Watson said. "We're the only three that are in on this thing, at least on this side."

After a moment's thoughts, Christopher said, "We need a scapegoat, someone we can pin this on and divert attention away from us."

Edward nodded. "The lawyer, McLeod. Ira picked him up outside the warehouse last night. Charged him with espionage. That would be an easy thing to pin on him. Besides, he's been poking around here ever since we got Lynch to draft that farmer."

After a moment, Watson said, "Okay, who's going out to the camp? I can't go. I've got to bring in over a ton of grain and it's got to be shipped out tomorrow."

Christopher said, "I've got some things I need to take care of before tonight."

Edward said, "Yeah, I do, too. But this is more important. Larry, have Quinn fill in for you. We're all going out there and see what we can see."

Edward turned toward his son. "I don't think it's a good idea to come up here tonight, even though it's your scheduled time. Let's get Richard to pull another few days. I'll pay him double if he squawks."

Christopher looked crestfallen. He opened his mouth to reply but Edward stood and cut him off. "I know what I'm asking, but it'll just be a few nights. Just until all this blows over and that damn senator goes back to D.C." He looked into his son's eyes. "Chris, I'll make it up to you. I promise."

39

———————

Wednesday
19 April 1944
12:20 p.m., Pacific War Time

"Where the hell have *you* been?" Truman asked.

Hancock knew Truman was not one to yell at the people working for him, so the senator was either angry with Hancock for taking so long or with something he found in the files. He hoped what he had to say would assuage Truman.

"Getting Horace out of jail." He smiled. "I had to be a little *creative*. And I saw Sheriff Blaine."

Truman had opened his mouth at the mention of the word 'creative' then changed his mind. "Where'd you see Blaine?"

Hancock pointed with his thumb over his shoulder. "In the parking lot, just outside. Didn't you know he was here?"

"No. I closed the door just after I got started. It was too loud to concentrate and I wanted a little more privacy." He tossed a pencil on the desk and took off his spectacles. He rubbed the bridge of his nose. "I forgot to tell you, Blaine showed up at the speech last night as well. He asked Webb about speaking to Moore. So, what did you and Sheriff Blaine talk about?"

Hancock stepped inside the office and closed the door. He pulled up a chair next to Truman and sat down with his arms on his knees. "Harry, we may have a bigger problem that duplicate invoices and embezzling." Hancock laid out all the evidence, circumstantial though it was, concerning Webb and Moore. He also included Blaine's suspicions about Moore's involvement with the dead men.

Truman listened to it all. His glasses remained off, his thumb and forefinger squeezing the bridge of his nose. His eyes stayed closed until Hancock finished.

Putting his spectacles back on, Truman asked, "Tell me again about this invoice Blaine found on the dead bodies. What was it for?"

"Powdered milk. It was dated earlier this year, February."

Truman leafed through pages in his notebook. He found what he was looking for and then proceeded to look in a stack of files sitting on the desk. He pulled one file from the stack and opened it.

"Here it is. February 1944. The duplicate copy here lists fifteen cases. We'll call Blaine later and find out how many he shows on his original invoice."

Hancock gestured toward the duplicate invoice in Truman's hand. "I don't get it. If they're skimming off the top, what were they thinking in making all the duplicate invoices? Didn't they figure someone like us might come around looking for them?"

Truman raised a finger. "Ah, but they are not all wrong. I pulled twenty-five of these duplicate invoices. I got the telephone numbers from the invoices and called the original shipping companies. Fifteen of the duplicate invoices matched the figures given to me by the company representatives this morning. That's sixty percent correct. So, the odds that someone conducting an audit that would strike upon the other forty percent is rather small. Then, of course, Moore can just say it was a typo."

Hancock shook his head. "But what if an auditor catches two or three that are wrong? You can't claim 'I typed the wrong number' three different times."

"The odds are against that happening."

Hancock shrugged. "Okay, so what do we do now? Do we start building a case against Moore?"

"That will take some imagination," Truman said. "One way to do it, of course, is to wait until the war's over, when Moore produces all these civilian goods when no one else has them. That would certainly make our job easier." He scratched his chin absently. "Did you know Mr. Moore has a safe in his office?"

"Where?"

"It's part of the bookcase directly behind his desk. There's a mounted fish that swings open to reveal the safe."

"How do you know? I can't imagine that's part of the tour."

"When I came upstairs this morning, his door was open and I saw him reading something. Not wanting him to know I knew about the safe, I stepped back a few feet and then stomped my feet in an obvious way. When he came to the door to meet me, everything was back in its place."

Hancock cracked his knuckles. "You know, I talked with a bank robber once. He told me how to open safes. Why don't you give me a crack at it? You never know what might be inside."

Truman shook his head. "Any evidence you found wouldn't hold up in court or to public scrutiny."

Hancock grinned one of his devilish grins. "But it wouldn't have to. All we have to do is find out what's in the safe, get a court order to search the premises, and 'find' the safe during our search. Then, if the evidence we know was in there suddenly turns up missing, we can pressure Moore to give it to us."

Truman gave Hancock a sidelong glance. "Sounds like you've done this kind of thing before."

"Let's just say I've known it to work." He smiled as he spoke.

Truman grunted. "I hope it doesn't have to come to that. I'd prefer a different approach, a less questionable approach."

"Okay, what about cross referencing the duplicate invoices with the official police reports?"

"How so?" Truman asked. "What would that prove?"

"If we can tie the dates of the duplicate invoices that have wrong numbers to the dates that Moore filed the police reports, then we can establish a connection."

Truman looked skeptical. "I don't think that would get us anywhere."

"No, but it would certainly help us." Hancock ran his fingers through his hair. "I just wish we knew where all this stuff was going."

"I have a theory about that. Let me see if you have the same one." Truman opened his notepad. "The earliest date I have where a discrepancy exists is December 18, 1941. It was a shipment of Army tents. The Army ordered one hundred tents but only eight-nine were listed on the duplicate invoice."

Hancock frowned. "December 1941. That's right after Pearl. That seems a little odd."

"Don't forget, the draft had been in effect for over a year by that time. We had men already in uniform and being trained." He ran his finger along the list. "The next one I found was later the same month, December 30. That invoice was for blankets. Two hundred ordered, one hundred eighty delivered."

Hancock leaned his chair back on the two rear legs. He put his hands behind his head and stared at the ceiling. "The next one, please."

"January 14, 1942, for Mason jars. Forty-two cases ordered, thirty-eight delivered." The Texan still stared at the ceiling, his brow furrowed in concentration.

"January, 30, 1942, cast iron skillets, fifty ordered, forty-seven delivered. February 7, 1942, dehydrated beef, seventeen cases ordered, fifteen delivered. March 2, 1942, Sterno heaters, sixty cases ordered, fifty-eight delivered. March 22, 1942, powdered milk, twelve cases ordered, ten delivered. April 1, 1942, bar soap, thirteen cases ordered, eleven delivered." Truman looked up from his list. "What do you make of all this?"

Hancock, still staring at the ceiling, said, "With the things you listed there, it kind of sounds like someone is going camping." He looked at Truman.

Truman nodded. "And, after about May 1942, almost all the discrepancies involve food items."

Hancock landed his chair back on four legs. He ticked off the items on his fingers as he spoke. "If I'm getting what you are saying, we have one, a man skimming off the top, two, most of the stuff can be used in camping, and three, we have rumors of a group of people living in the woods trying to get away from the government and the Army." He looked at Truman questioningly. "Is that what you got?"

Truman nodded.

"Okay, then, what do we really know about these so-called Mountain Men? A group of men and women who don't like the idea of Uncle Sam drafting their boys in peacetime so they flee civilization as a protest? Sounds like a bunch of isolationists, if you ask me."

"You're damn right. What kind of people would turn their back on America? President Roosevelt saw what was happening, knew that we weren't prepared—just like in 1917—and did something about it."

"And, after Pearl, some came back and some didn't." Hancock shrugged. "That's all I know." He held up a finger and reached for the telephone. "But Blaine said one of his deputies, the one who nearly pulled a gun on me, was some kind of amateur expert. Let me call him and see what he knows."

Hancock reached the dispatcher and asked for Blaine. After speaking with Blaine for a minute and posing the request, Blaine called Duncan to the telephone. After an awkward hello, Hancock started with a little flattery.

"Deputy Duncan, Sheriff Blaine tells me you're the expert on the Mountain Men. I think only you can shed some light on some questions Senator Truman and I have."

"Thank you, sir. Listen, I apologize for nearly drawing my weapon on you."

Hancock laughed. "Never mind that. You didn't know me from Adam. For all you knew, I was some crazy reporter looking to break a big story." In a bit of a conspiratorial whisper, Hancock said, "Besides, I would have done the same thing myself."

Hancock laughed and allowed the younger man to laugh as well, albeit uncomfortably. With the flattery out of the way, Hancock got down to business.

"I need some information about these Mountain Men. I understand why and when they went. What can you tell me about the efforts made to find them?"

Duncan cleared his throat. "There were a total of three search parties sent out before the Army arrived. The first two were conducted about a month after the draft law went into effect and the men started to be drafted."

"People around here don't like the elected representatives in Congress telling them what to do. And that goes double when it involves the young men of the community. Editorials were written, meetings were held, and there was talk of getting the state governments of Oregon and Washington State to step in. That didn't work out seeing as how it's the federal government versus the state government. The federals win every time."

"So a group of men started talking. They wondered if the government would come look for them if they left town. Secret meetings were held and preparations were made to try it as a test run. A good number of draft-age men were included in this group. One night, they all just disappeared."

"Just like that?" Hancock asked.

"Just like that." Duncan's voice was getting excited. Hancock realized there was a good chance that no one had ever asked Duncan to tell all he knew. "But the townsfolk soon figured it out. Initially, there was broad support for the move. Then, gradually, support waned."

"Why?"

"Think about it: you got the Mountain Men whose draft-age men were not being drafted and you had townspeople's sons who were. The fairness question came up. So, those left behind pressured the local sheriffs to create search parties."

After looking at the notes he had taken, Hancock said, "You said there were a total of three search parties before the Army arrived. I can guess the result. Tell me what happened."

"The result was pretty obvious. The Mountain Men were not found. Despite the pressure from the townspeople to find the Mountain Men, the first two search parties cost a lot of money, in time and material. With no results, there was a split. Some people wanted to call off the search and others wanted to continue. By this time, two to three months later, there was some anger starting to develop. When all the law enforcement agencies didn't mount a third search party because of the money involved, a private search party was formed."

"What do you mean, 'private'?"

"A search party not sponsored by any governmental agency. It was a group of hunters who supposedly knew the area well. They announced that they would go out and search the wilderness for these Mountain Men. And it was only today, after Sheriff Blaine asked me to do some research on the Mountain Men and any connection to Edward Moore, that I turned up Webb and one of Moore's hunting buddies, Eli Sale."

Hancock made a note on his notepad. He wrote Moore's name and drew a circle around it. Then, he started writing other names and drew circles around them. He put Moore in the center and, after a few moments, had a small web.

"Are you saying that Moore was a part of the third search party that looked for these Mountain Men? Let me guess: they found nothing."

"Right. And that was the last time a search was made until the Army arrived in late '42. And you're going to like this. When they learned about the Mountain Men, they wanted to mount their own search party, using men as well as planes. Guess who they hired to help?"

Hancock was starting to think Moore had his finger in every pie around here. "Moore."

"Close. Eli Sale. Edward Moore, of course, went with him as did Christopher Moore. Webb wasn't involved with this search as it was limited to the military and their civilian guides."

"And they found nothing."

"Yes, sir. Which was strange because of the random burglaries that started in early '42."

Hancock put his hand over the receiver and asked Truman, who had resumed his search of the files, "Harry, where's that list you were reading from?"

Truman pointed at the desk and Hancock slid the paper over in front of him. "What's the first burglary you have attributed to the Mountain Men?"

Hancock heard some papers rustling. "February 1942, dehydrated beef, from the Moore Warehouse. The next one was for six cases of oranges, stolen from the Ferguson Warehouse, March 1942."

Hancock made a note on Truman's list. "What's the next one?"

"April 1942, bar soap, two cases."

Hancock put another mark on Truman's list. The senator, who had come over to stand behind Hancock, looked puzzled. "I'll tell you in a minute, Harry."

To Duncan, Hancock said, "Deputy…"

"Call me Joe, Mr. Hancock."

"Okay, Joe, you can call me Carl. As a follower of these Mountain Men, what was the key detail that led you to link the Mountain Men with these burglaries?"

"The owners of the warehouses blamed them. It was in the police reports and the papers."

"So, from the beginning, these random burglaries were attributed to the Mountain Men by folks like Moore and other warehouse owners." Hancock thought for a moment. "If you were to graph the dates of these robberies, is there a time when, say, the frequency of the burglaries tapered off?"

More rustling of papers. "Yes, around the time the Hanford facility started to be built. The burglaries were frequent until late last year. There may have been more burglaries but either they weren't reported—which is Sheriff Blaine's assumption—or they were not attributed to the Mountain Men and, thus, I didn't note them."

Hancock sat for a moment in silence. "Lester, are you still on the line?"

"Yes," Blaine said, "I'm here. What do you think, Carl? I think we have enough for a warrant."

"I think so. But there's one piece of this puzzle that will make our job easier."

"What's that?" Blaine asked.

"The military," Hancock replied.

"Okay, I don't follow."

"It's like this. If Moore's dirty, then him getting Webb to make an official report to Lynch to get Bumble drafted is a crime. It would not only void his government contract, it could land him and Webb in jail. I think Mr. Truman and I need to go talk to Lynch and see what Webb or Moore told him to get Bumble drafted."

Hancock looked up at Truman who nodded. Hancock continued. "If we can establish that Moore used the power of the federal government for personal gains, we have an easy case. And it'll open up the Moore Warehouse to intense scrutiny. Lester, let me talk this over with Harry and we'll call you back."

"Okay," Blaine said and hung up.

Hancock hung up the telephone. "You get all that?"

Truman nodded. "Enough. And I understood the last part very well."

"So, you agree we should talk with Lynch?"

"Yes." Truman grabbed his hat. "Let's go."

Hancock saw the blood begin to seep into Truman's face. Quickly, Hancock added, "Maybe with you and I both leaving the warehouse for a while, Moore will breathe a little easier. He might get sloppy."

"I doubt it. He's covered his tracks pretty well."

Hancock read Truman's face. The senator had something more to say. "Okay, Harry, what is it?"

Truman let out a great sigh. "Carl, it's bad enough that we're fighting a war in which a few bastards decide to pick the government's wallet while young boys are dying. But this is something different. This," he put a finger to his lips, "this is near treasonous.

And it's all for money. If all of this is true, Moore and his cronies have no honor."

Truman started to put all the files back into the file cabinet. Hancock helped. "I don't know about you but I'm hungry. Why don't we go see Lynch after we eat?"

Truman nodded in agreement but said nothing.

"Any idea about how to get Lynch's attention? If he's inside Hanford, we can't exactly knock on his door. And if we call him, he'll just hang up on us."

Truman smiled. "Oh, there's a way to get his attention."

40

Wednesday
19 April 1944
2:55 p.m. Pacific War Time

The tall clear glass of ice water sat on the table in front of Theodore Frank. He watched it so fixedly that he saw beads of condensation form on the sides of the glass. A thick ring of water surrounded the base of the glass where it met the table. Every now and then, one of the beads would start to move down the glass toward the table. It would move slowly, catch another bead, and then speed down the side of the glass. Frank was so thirsty that he imagined he heard the 'plop' when the bead of water touched the table.

Frank paid no attention to Major Lynch who sat opposite him, watching him. The Army man had not spoken a word since he came into the room with the tall glass of water. He had set the glass down, pulled up a chair, and sat.

Frank had tunnel vision. He only saw the glass. Everything else was in a haze but the glass, with its cool refreshment, remained in clear focus.

Abruptly, Lynch reached over and picked up the glass. There was an audible pop as the liquid seal around the base of the glass broke. Lynch brought the glass to his lips and began to drink. The ice cubes tinked the side of the glass. As he drank, drops of condensation fell from the glass and spotted his pressed khaki shirt and black Army tie. Frank watched, horrified, his mouth open, as a small line of water trickled from the side of Lynch's mouth and worked its way down his cheek.

Lynch drank the entire glass of water. "Ah, that really hit the spot." He looked over at Frank, his eyes and mouth smiling. "Would you like a glass of ice cold water?"

"Yes, please," Frank said. His voice sounded dry through cracked lips. He had not had anything to drink since yesterday evening.

"I bet you would. I bet you'd like to lick this glass, just to wet your lips. I bet you'd like to lick the table where that water ring is." He motioned to the place where the glass had sat. "I bet you're just dying for a drink. I don't know about food, but I bet a drink is exactly what you want right now. Am I right?"

Frank just nodded.

Lynch reached into his pocket and pulled out a bandana. He leaned over the table where the drink had been and wiped up the water ring leaving only a wet smear. He then turned the glass upside down and allowed the few drops still in the glass to fall on the floor. He shook the glass and more water beads went flying. He wiped the glass dry with the bandana and sat the now-dry glass on the table. He put the bandana back into his pocket and looked at Frank.

"All you have to do, Mr. Frank, is tell me what you were doing walking around a restricted area." The smile had left Lynch's eyes.

Frank was about to answer when there was a soft knocking at the door.

"What is it?" Lynch asked, clearly perturbed.

A man stuck his head into the room and motioned for Lynch to meet him by the door. The man spoke so softly that Frank was unable to hear anything substantial. But he heard Lynch's reaction.

"Who the hell does he think he is? I don't care if he's a United

States Senator or Jimmy Stewart, he can't come inside a restricted area." He cursed and then looked back at Frank.

"Mr. Frank, you're going to have to hold your answer for a little while. I have something else I need to take care of." He walked over and picked up the glass, wiggling it in his hands. "All you have to do is talk and I'll fill this glass up with the sweetest water you've ever tasted."

Lynch regarded Frank. "And I don't want to hear anymore of this 'Let me make one phone call' shit. I'm a reasonable man. I'll listen." He cupped a hand on either side of his head in a stage-like gesture. "I'm all ears."

Lynch turned on his heal and left the room. As soon as the door closed, Frank went around to the other side of the table, the side where Lynch had shaken out the water. To his chagrin, all the drops of water had dried. Tired, thirsty, and alone, Frank just sat on the cement floor.

* * *

"SENATOR TRUMAN, what exactly do you want?"

Hancock heard the irritation in Lynch's voice. Next to Lynch was another man, a lieutenant judging by the uniform. They both walked toward Hancock and Truman, who stood at one of the gates that led into the Hanford facility. Two soldiers stood guard as well as the officer in charge, who had telephoned for Lynch.

"We have something I think you should know."

"What, possibly, would I want to know that I don't already know?" Lynch stood just behind the gate, his hands on his hips.

"I think it best discussed in private. May we speak in the guard house?" Truman indicated the small, one-room structure just inside the gate.

Lynch eased a smile from his mouth. "You would like that, wouldn't you? To be able to say you got into the base when everyone else was denied admittance."

Hancock looked sidelong at Truman. The senator's mouth was a tight line. "It's not like that at all, Major. We have information that we think you should hear."

Lynch put a finger to his lips. "Let me guess: it has to do with your investigation into the embezzling charge against one of the biggest assets we have out here in Hanford." When he said the word 'embezzling,' Lynch placed special, and unflattering, emphasis on that word.

Truman inhaled deeply and was about to let Lynch have a piece of his mind when Hancock interrupted. "Major, we think that you may have been involved in a crime."

Hancock's comment actually took Lynch by surprise. Lynch lowered his hands from his hips to his sides. He noticed the soldiers' eyes looking at him. He took two steps forward and put his face inches away from Hancock's despite the Texan's height advantage.

"Sir, you better withdraw that last comment or I will have you taken away and sent to the front lines where you can do some actual good."

Unfazed, Hancock smiled. "That's exactly what we want to talk to you about. May we have a few moments of your time?"

Lynch glared at Hancock for a few moments longer, neither man breaking eye contact. The major turned on his heels and all but marched over to the guard house, the lieutenant right at his side. With a flick of his wrist, he beckoned Hancock and Truman to follow him. They did so and found themselves in a small room, with a desk with a telephone.

Lynch beckoned Hancock to close the door. "I don't appreciate you making inflammatory comments about me in front of my men. Had you been anyone else, I would have…"

"Drafted them?" Hancock said. "Like you did to that farmer?"

Lynch screwed up his face. "What is it with you two and this farmer?"

"Do you mind if we ask you a few questions about the procedure you use to have someone drafted?" Truman asked.

Lynch let out a huge sigh and nodded. "If you promise to leave after I answer whatever *little* questions you have."

"Of course," Truman said. "Tell me what happens when you draft someone."

The major said, "They get shipped to boot camp then moved to one of the theaters of operations." Lynch smiled at his non-answer. Truman grunted and Hancock chuckled.

"Are you asking how I actually recommend someone for drafting?" He walked over to the north window and looked out toward the Hanford area, giving Truman and Hancock his back. "Around here, it's rather easy. We have a secret operation going on. And it's extremely important it stay secret. Most of the people working here don't know the nature of this project. If they did…" He turned toward the two investigators. "Well, let's just hope that doesn't happen."

Hancock said, "What exactly *is* going on here? Why all the secrecy?"

Lynch put on a thin smile. "It's top secret and, well, you both don't have the clearance."

There was an awkward silence in the room. Hancock considered pressing the case but decided against it as it was not germane to their investigation. He could see the struggle on the senator's face as Truman came to the same conclusion.

"Fine," Truman said. "Back to Mr. Bumble. Why'd you draft him?"

"Because he was a threat to this operation."

"And how did you reach that conclusion?"

Lynch sighed again. "Sheriff Webb made a report. In this report, he laid out all the evidence and supporting testimony to convince me this farmer was up to no good."

Hancock took up the questioning. "Did you actually see this report?"

"No."

"Why not?"

"Sheriff Webb called it in. He outlined it for me over the telephone. The written report can be filed at a later date."

"Did you ever receive Webb's report?"

Lynch spoke slowly. He didn't like saying what he had to say.

"No, I didn't. But with the secrecy around here, that's not always necessary."

"So, what you're telling us is that he called you with a request and you acted on that request?"

Lynch nodded.

"What if we told you that the request and the report were compromised?" Truman said.

Unease flashed across Lynch's face. It was gone in a second but Hancock saw it nonetheless. "In what way?"

Truman spoke in a matter-of-fact tone. "It's our assumption Sheriff Webb is using the power of his office and yours in conjunction with Edward Moore to embezzle goods from the government."

Hancock delivered the punch line. "And you drafting Mr. Bumble, a witness, was part of this plot. It served to eliminate him from talking to anyone."

Lynch was silent for a few moments. Hancock saw concern and deep concentration in his eyes. "What's your proof?"

Hancock looked to Truman who looked back at Hancock. "Well, actually, nothing concrete, at the moment. But we have strong suspicions." Hancock briefly explained their findings in the warehouse files and Blaine's suspicions that the dead men found in the Columbia worked for Moore.

Lynch's lieutenant spoke up for the first time with the obvious question Truman and Hancock had already grappled with. "If Moore is stockpiling goods for the post-war years, where's he keeping it?"

"That's our biggest question," Truman said. "But don't forget: he owns a series of warehouses in Washington State. He could just move them around from warehouse to warehouse and no one would be the wiser."

Hancock continued. "And it's our thought that the two dead men were somehow working with him to keep the goods away from the government's eyes."

Lynch clapped his hands together and rubbed them together as if he were warming them. "Okay, gentlemen, I've heard enough. I have to help win the war. I don't have time to play Holmes and

Watson with nothing more than conjecture. If you don't mind, I have work to do."

Truman looked aghast. "But this *is* important work. Our government, *your* government, is being defrauded. Moore is stealing from the American people."

Lynch looked at Truman evenly. "You don't know that for sure. And to say it anywhere other than here would be slander. Without evidence, you can do nothing." He snapped his fingers, acting like he just remembered something. "You could go back to D.C. and leave us alone. How about that?"

Truman snapped. "I'll go back when I'm damn good and ready, sir. And when I do, it will be with a report, on the evidence I find here and about the willingness, or lack thereof, of people involved in this investigation."

Lynch spread his arms and tapped the side of his head with a finger. "Let me guess how this might go, Senator Truman. You make a report and list me as, say, an unresponsive party. Let's say this report goes all the way to the top, to President Roosevelt. You know what he's going to do? He's going to defer to Secretary Stimson and do you know what the Secretary is going to do? Defer to General Groves, who, in turn will defer to Colonel Matthias. Now, you've met the colonel and, since this is a security matter and I'm in charge of security, you know what's going to happen?"

Lynch waited just long enough for Truman and Hancock to start to wonder if he was going to finish them. "Nothing. Absolutely nothing. We have a delicate operation going on up here and, like it or not, embezzler or not, Edward Moore and his resources are a big part of it. Now, unless you have some sort of concrete evidence that implicates Mr. Moore directly, I suggest you stop bothering me and let me do my job."

It was Lynch's smugness that irked Hancock. He wanted to deck the man but knew it would not further their cause, no matter how rewarding it might feel. He tapped Truman's shoulder. "Okay, we got the picture. As long as whatever it is you're building is moving forward, you can step on anybody and anything and it's okay."

Truman stood his ground for a few moments. "That, sir, is the kind of thing we're fighting against in Europe." He turned and walked out of the guard house, banging the door open as he left.

Outside, Hancock, despite his larger stride, had to trot to keep up with Truman. The senator was grumbling. "You know, Lincoln had imbeciles like this. That's probably why it took him four years to win the Civil War."

"Harry, all we need is some evidence. If we have incontrovertible evidence of a crime, it can't be ignored. If Lynch won't do anything about it even with the evidence, we'll take it to the top."

"But we don't have any evidence."

"There is the safe." They stopped at McLeod' car, staring at each other over the top of the car. "I can crack it. We can do it tonight. What do you think?"

"Carl, this is getting ugly."

"Yes, but we didn't make it ugly. Someone else did. We're just playing the cards dealt to us."

Truman considered. "Okay, let's do it. Tonight. You want to include McLeod?"

Hancock shook his head. "No, but I think I'd like to ask Lester and see if he'd be willing to sit with us. I wouldn't ask him to go in with me, just be there, with us, in case something goes awry."

Truman opened the door and slid in behind the wheel. Hancock followed suit on the passenger side. "If something goes awry, it'll take more than a local Oregon sheriff to fix it." He started the engine and put his hands on the wheel. "I'm fine with Sheriff Blaine and his deputy coming along provided he does one thing."

"What's that?"

Truman grinned. "Join us for a poker game tonight."

* * *

LYNCH SAT in the Army jeep next to his lieutenant as it bounced back to the main security station in Hanford. The dust the tires kicked up didn't bother him. He kept thinking of what Truman and Hancock had said, the accusations they made. He looked at it from every conceivable angle. It all came up to one conclusion, the conclusion he already gave: No evidence equals no further action on his part.

And, yet, here he was, still thinking about it. That annoyed him. Despite what he thought of Truman's actions, he knew the senator's reputation. He conducted his hearings in an honest, straightforward manner. He had stated, on many occasions, that he was not out to second-guess military men. He was there to help the country win the war. Given all that he knew about Truman, Lynch doubted the senator would be lying.

He sighed. It would be best to cover all the bases. After his lieutenant brought the jeep to a stop, Lynch jumped out. "Lou, as the chief security officer, I need to go through the motions of studying his accusation. Call Webb's office and get him to deliver the report. Have him do it in person. I want to have a chat with him."

"Yes, sir," the lieutenant said and started to walk away.

Lynch grabbed his arm. "And Lou, keep this between us. I don't want word getting out that I'm taking the senator's side, especially with the men who overheard the accusation. Please go out there and remind them, in no uncertain terms, to keep their traps shut. Do you understand?"

"Yes, sir."

"Good. Now get to it."

41

Wednesday
19 April 1944
4:00 p.m. Pacific War Time

Edward Moore, Christopher Moore, and Ira Webb stood on the small rise that blocked the view of the Columbia from the highway. They had arrived in three separate vehicles: Webb in his cruiser, Edward in his 1939 Chrysler New Yorker, and Christopher in his 1940 Chevrolet Special Deluxe convertible coupe. Below them, incongruous to the gentle beauty of the river and the surrounding woods, was the evidence of the murders. Two large bloodstains matted the sand and grass. The small crate that contained the month's supplies was opened but full, a few packets of powdered milk scattered around the ground, evidence that whoever killed Garrison and Buchan was not interested in theft. From each large bloodstain was a trail of blood that ended at the river.

They walked to the riverside in silence, their boots crunching dry grass, Webb leading the way. He indicated the opened crate and restated what they all knew. "This thing's still full. If this was a robbery, this crate'd be gone or empty."

Edward nodded and walked around the area. Avid hunter that he was, he was interested in the footprints on the ground. "Chris, can you remember what kind of soles were on the boots we gave them last year?"

Christopher walked over to stand next to his father and crouched down on his haunches. He surveyed the footprints and pointed to one pair of tracks. "That's them. Judging by the size of the print, I'd say that was Jack. He was over six feet tall."

"I agree," Edward said. He picked up a small branch and pointed at another set of footprints, these leading to the other side of the crate. "That would make those prints Ron's."

Webb had come to stand next to them. "Look how both sets of prints seem to just come out of the water. Did they swim across?"

"Yes," Edward said. "At this drop site, we thought it best to have the pick-up team wade across the river so as to not leave a trail or a scent. It's one more piece of security for the camp."

"I see your point," Webb said. He cocked his head, studying the prints. "Okay, so Jack walks on the left side of the crate and Ron on the other. Then, this third set of prints arrives, also from the water. Those prints don't match these other two."

Edward looked at Christopher. "Did we send everyone at the camp the same boots?"

Christopher nodded "Easier to hide the same types of boots. This third pair doesn't match any that we gave them."

"Could the folks at the camp have received any supplies from another source?" Webb asked.

"Not that I know of," Edward replied. "We're their only source of supplies, both food and everything else. They kill game but that's obvious."

Christopher rose and walked toward the river's edge, following the trail of the third set of prints. "So if this person was not a part of our team, then he must have come from the river. And he probably came by boat."

Edward looked at the water's edge and studied it. Most of the area where water met land had the usual smooth surface that one would expect. "Here's Jack's prints, Ron's prints, and those of the third man. And this is where his boat landed. You see the jut onto the shore?"

He pointed at a smooth crevice carved into the muddy bank. It was about four feet long and its edge descended into the clear water.

Edward continued. "Here's where he jumped from the boat onto the shore. These prints are deeper than the rest. He must have caught Ron and Jack by surprise."

"Don't these men carry weapons?" Webb asked.

"They have weapons. Now, whether or not they brought them with them as they traveled is a different story."

Christopher snapped his fingers. "The lookout! We require all our pick-up teams to travel in groups of three and one to stay back, just in case of an emergency."

Edward turned to look across the river. "He would have been watching from the other side. C'mon, let's go check it out."

Father and son waded into the river. Their long shadows, cast by the late afternoon sun, rippled along the surface. They reached the sand bar and continued walking in the water. They reached the other side and started looking for a good blind spot where the last member of the pick-up team would have stationed himself.

Edward said, "Who was the watchman for this group?"

"Teddy, Walter, or Keith." Christopher stopped and crouched down. "Look."

Edward saw a set of footprints leading along the riverbank toward the east. The prints were of the same boot type as those across the river, indicating that this was where the third member of the pick-up team sat and watched his friends murdered.

"How long ago did that sheriff say Ron and Jack had died?" Christopher asked.

"About two days in the water and he found them on Monday. So, four days ago."

"We've instilled in everyone's mind that the secrecy of the camp is the most important thing. If anyone is caught, we are not to divulge the location of the camp or that it even exists."

"What are you getting at?"

"Look at the tracks. They are not going back to the camp. They are going to Richland. To tell us what happened."

Edward considered what his son had just said and its implication and nodded. "It took us just under three hours to drive here. It would take a man on foot three to four days to make his way back to Richland if he followed the river."

"Right. That's today. And I'm placing my chips on the fact that he'd go right up to the warehouse."

"But he couldn't do that in daylight," Edward said. "He'd have to wait until after dark so as not to call attention to himself. Either that or call Larry once he got to a phone."

"If he was able to call," Christopher said, "we would have already gotten a call." He waited a moment before continuing. "I think someone should go to the camp and someone should go back to the warehouse and wait." He looked up at his father, his eyes squinting in the sun. "I'll go to the warehouse."

Edward looked at his son. "I've told you, we need to wait until Truman and his partner leave before we have any more late night activities. Last night's arrest is proof that they were at least looking for something. We'll all go to the camp and then return to Richland. We need to keep Stanley as guard tonight but we're going to have to let him on everything. That way, if our man shows up, Stanley can help him."

Irritated, Christopher stood and started to cross back to the other side of the river. "Fine. There's nothing more we can learn over here. Let's go back and clean up." Edward stood for a moment longer then joined his son.

As they reached the sandbar and looked toward Webb and the murder scene, they both noticed something on the crate. Up close, it appeared like a red smear. From farther away, its true shape was revealed.

"Chris, do you see what I'm seeing on that crate?"

In a quiet voice, his son answered. "Yes, I do."

They cross the second part of the river, hardly taking their eyes from the side of the crate. They didn't notice what Webb was doing off to their right until they walked onshore.

"Over here," Webb said.

Edward and Chris looked at each other and Edward shook his head. They walked over to see what Webb had found. He pointed at a second smooth crevice just at the water's edge and under the water. It was parallel to the larger, more prominent crevice.

"I paced it off," Webb said. "It's five feet, give or take. It's also the same size as the other one. Webb's voice filled up the silence. "These marks were made by a float plane."

"Shit," Edward said, his voice softer than even he expected. "This might be worse than we thought."

Webb looked puzzled. "Worse than what? There seems to be clear evidence that a person in a float plane landed here and killed our friends. There's not a lot of float planes around here for civilian use. You two have one, of course, but it shouldn't be too big a problem finding out which plane was in the area. We can use flight plans and pinpoint likely suspects and then go question them."

Edward said, "No, Ira, you don't understand. I don't think this was a local crime. I think this was an act of war."

"What the hell are you talking about?"

Christopher pointed to the side of the crate. "Take a look at that."

Webb scrutinized the crate, moving his head this way and that to try to get a different angle. Both father and son could tell the sheriff was confused. "What is that?"

Edward said, "It's the Japanese character for revenge."

Webb's eyes widened. "What the hell?"

They all contemplated the implications of what they were seeing.

"We have to report this," Edward said. "And not just to the police. We have to tell the Army."

"Tell them what?" Webb asked. "That there's a Japanese plane flying around Washington State? That's impossible."

Father and son exchanged a glance.

"You know what telling the Army means, don't you?" Christopher asked. "It means questions and more questions. Why were you out where you were? Why were you near a murder scene? Questions will lead to more inquiries and the one Truman's conducting will seem like nothing." He paused and looked at the other two men. "It means the camp will probably be exposed."

No one spoke for nearly a minute, each man realizing that years of work was starting to crumble around them.

"There's no choice," Webb said, "We have to tell Lynch. My radio's out of range right now. We'll need to get closer in order to find a signal."

"Wait," Edward said. "We have to do something else first. We have to go to the camp and tell everyone what's happened. We need to prepare them for the inevitable."

"I agree," Christopher said. "I'll go on ahead and you two…"

"No," Edward said, "Ira needs to go, and in his patrol car. That way, if anyone sees him, it'll be in a police car and fewer suspicions will be raised. Besides, it'll add weight when it comes from the sheriff." He paused, pain lancing across his face. He looked at his two companions. "I guess we couldn't hide them forever."

Webb nodded. "Yeah. You go on back and drive straight to Hanford. Tell Lynch all that you know and what you've seen and what we suspect. He'll know what to do." He kicked a small rock and it ricocheted off the crate, causing a loud knock. "Damn Japs! How the hell did they get here? I just hope I get to see one 'cause I'll put a bullet in his brain!"

42

Wednesday
19 April 1944
5:48 p.m., Pacific War Time

Nick Lynch stared down at Theodore Frank. Lynch's hands were flat on the table and the security chief's face was inches from his prisoner.

"I give you pencil and paper to write your confession and all you think to do is draw a stupid airplane? What kind of trouble do you think you're in? You've been arrested by the *military* police. The president has decreed I don't even have to tell you why you're being held." He straightened up and put a hand over his heart. "But out of the graciousness of my heart, I told you why."

Lynch turned his back and started pacing. "But no. You have to turn into Pablo Picasso. I bet it's your favorite airplane from when you were a kid, right? You're probably reverting back to your happier childhood memories. That's probably a good thing." He turned back to Frank. "Because where you're going, those are the only good memories you'll have left."

"It's not like that at all, Major," Frank said. His throat was parched from the lack of water. "If I were to tell you what you want to know, I would be betraying those to whom I swore an oath."

Lynch looked disgusted. "Oh, would that be your Nazi friends?"

Frank looked confused. "What are you talking about?"

"You're a spy. If you and your so-called friends are not for the United States in this war, you're against it."

Frank looked at Lynch evenly and spoke in a voice stronger than he had ever used that day. "My friends *are* Americans. And I am not a spy."

Lynch regarded Frank with a skeptical look. "Prove it." He took a more conversational tone. "Mr. Frank, all you have to do is tell me why you were on restricted government land. Surely you can see my dilemma. In the absence of all other evidence, I'm forced to make only one conclusion: you were up to no good and we caught you. Now, unless you tell me something I don't know, I'm going to lock you up for a very long time."

"I've told you something already. Just look at the drawing."

Lynch looked down his nose. "Mr. Frank, I don't have time for games." He walked over and picked up the notepad. "I see a plane. Oooh, and it's got pontoons on it. Wow. That's some imagination you have there."

Lynch ripped the drawing of the plane out of the notepad and threw the pad back on the table in front of Frank. He crumbled up the drawing into a small ball and started tossing it from hand to hand. He turned toward the door. "Try again, Mr. Frank."

Two officers, standing on either side of the door, held the door open for Lynch and followed him out into the hallway. One, Louis Ross, was Lynch's second-in-command. The other, Ken Seaborn, was the unofficial warden of the holding area.

Seaborn said, "You want me to up the ante with this guy, rough him up a little?"

"Maybe," Lynch said. He tossed the ball of paper between his hands. "But let's give him the night to think it over. I'm guessing that another day without food or water will wear him down."

Lynch tossed the ball to Ross who caught the ball rather clumsily. Lynch rubbed his eyes and temples and let out a great big sigh. "Any word from Webb's office?"

"Still nothing," Ross said. "One of the deputies said Webb was out on a call."

Lynch scowled. "On a call? What the hell does that mean? With the Army here, all he has to do is catch people speeding."

Ross shrugged. "You want me to call again?"

Lynch started walking down the hall and Ross and Seaborn fell in step with him. "No, I want you to send a man over there. Have him wait there for Webb to get back. The minute he gets back, I want that report. I don't care what time it is."

"What are you going to do?" Ross asked.

"I need something different to think about tonight." He looked at Ross. "I'm going to go catch a bite to eat and then head to the Hurley Hotel."

"What's at the Hurley Hotel?" Seaborn asked.

Lynch didn't answer immediately and Ross just nodded. "I understand, sir. You want to see what Truman's plan is."

"I'm curious. It'll break up the monotony of this place. I'll be there in an hour so leave a message at the front desk for me if Frank starts talking."

"Yes, sir," Ross said and Lynch turned and walked away down the hall.

"What was that about?" Seaborn asked.

"It's the thing with that senator investigating the Moore Warehouse. Truman thinks the owner of the warehouse is swiping stuff from the government but he doesn't have any hard evidence. Lynch basically told them to not bother him unless they had evidence. From the looks on those boys' faces, they were going to go find some."

Ross looked down at his hands and saw the ball of paper. He regarded it for a moment then slipped it into his pocket.

Seaborn pointed at Ross's pocket. "Don't forget: you have to file that. It's evidence."

"Right, sorry," Ross said and pulled the wad of paper from his pocket and started to smooth it out. "And even if they do find something, I don't know what good it'll do."

"Why's that?"

"The Moore Warehouse really helps this operation run efficiently. If it's true what Truman is saying, I'm not sure what Matthias or Groves will do."

Ross looked at the drawing. He turned it right side up and considered it for a few moments. "That's funny. I don't recognize this model plane."

Seaborn gave a dismissive wave. "Frank's just a civilian. To him, all planes probably look the same."

"Let's ask Randy. He knows all the aircraft we have. Let's see if he knows the model of this plane. It's probably just a recon plane Frank saw while he was traipsing around the river. It's got pontoons, you know."

"You're right," Seaborn said. "But still, why in the world would Frank draw this picture when he's been arrested for spying?"

"Beats me," Ross said and started walking down the hallway.

* * *

"Boy that sure hit the spot. Thanks." Burt Osborn patted his stomach. He wore wrinkled khakis and a white shirt with sleeves rolled up to his elbows. An off-white undershirt peeked out under his unbuttoned collar. The scientist repeatedly swept his hands through his brown hair to get it off his forehead. In his shirt pocket were a couple of pens and the outline of a cigarette pack.

Osborn was about the same height as Koishii, thinner now than when the project at Hanford started. The pressure of the job and doing what they were doing didn't do well for the health of many of the scientists. Osborn had confided in Koishii a few times, although the scientist never revealed the true nature of the work.

The restaurant was crowded for a Wednesday night. Construction workers sat with army officers, soldiers ate with men who were Osborn's fellow scientists. The entire room was an egalitarian example of life in America, a snapshot of the melting pot nature of the country. Koishii smiled and nodded to people he knew. Osborn did as well. There was a pang deep in Koishii's gut that nagged at him. He pushed that pang deeper inside himself.

"It's the least I could do," Koishii said. "How are things going at the site?"

Osborn leaned his elbows on the table and took a sip of coffee. "The construction work is fast and furious but a man's got to have some down time. Maybe this weekend? Wanna go down to the river, drop our lines, see what we catch? "

Koishii smiled. "Sounds good."

The waitress brought the check and Koishii snatched it from her hands. "This one's on me. And so's the beer and pool down at the tavern." He stood, left a few dollars on the table and made his way out of the restaurant. Osborn followed.

On the sidewalk, the friends walked side by side. Dusk was near, the sun halfway down on the horizon. In the eastern sky, the dark blue of night already backdropped stars. Couples and groups of people milled about, walking to restaurants or the movie theater, all seeking to escape the pressures of the day for just a few hours before they all repeated the process again the next day.

In his chest, Koishii's heart hammered. He had rehearsed in his mind, over and over, what he intended to do and how to subdue Osborn. Now that the time was here, he got nervous.

Osborn looked at Koishii sideways. "You got something on your mind. What's up?"

The American traitor smiled at his friend. "Nothing. Just wanted you to know I appreciate your friendship. Here, let's take my car. I parked it out back."

Koishii turned and walked down the windowless alley between the restaurant and a barber shop. He slipped his hand into his pocket and felt the metal box. With his fingers, he opened the box and put the wet cloth in his hand. He pulled his hand out of his pocket and kept it close to his side.

"Here, let me unlock the door for you," Koishii said, gesturing for Osborn to walk ahead of him around to the passenger side.

Koishii had told himself not to look at Osborn's face as he

subdued him. He feared he would not be able to do what he had to do if he saw the man's eyes.

When the scientist skirted past him, Koishii wrapped his stronger left arm around Osborn's neck. He kicked Osborn's knees out from underneath him and dropped with the scientist as he fell to the ground. Koishii's right hand brought the rag of chloroform up to Osborn's face and held it in place.

Osborn put up a decent fight despite being outweighed by forty pounds. He twisted left and right, trying to get the rag away from his face. During a twist, Osborn's eyes locked on Koishii. The look was one of fear, anger, and surprise. Koishii met his friend's gaze with one he hoped was impassive. Inside his soul, however, he was crying.

Desperately, he grabbed a handful of Koishii's hair before the American kneed his friend in the back. The muffled cry from Osborn allowed more of the gas to get into his system. Osborn's fingers loosened and left Koishii's hair, his arm falling into the dirt and gravel. His body slumped, and Koishii followed it all the way to the ground.

Trembling with adrenaline, Koishii stood up and looked around. He saw no one. He replaced the rag in the metal box and put the box back in his pocket. He unlocked the trunk of his car and moved the two bags he had already packed. With a great effort, he managed to dump the unconscious Osborn into the trunk. With a short length of rope, Koishii tied Osborn's hands in front of him and stuck a piece of tape over his mouth.

As Koishii closed the trunk, he took several deep breaths. Tears began to sting his eyes and he viciously wiped them away. "No," he said, "no tears for the enemy. He is no longer my friend. He is a prisoner of war."

43

Wednesday
19 April 1944
7:55 p.m., Pacific War Time

Lynch hesitated only once before he knocked on the hotel room door. He heard rustling and the sound of a chair scraping along the wooden floor. Taking a step back, he waited. After a few seconds, Carl Hancock opened the door.

"Major Lynch, this is an unexpected pleasure. Come on in." He held the door open for Lynch who strode inside the room in all but a formal marching stride.

Around a circular table sat Truman, a sheriff and a deputy wearing the uniform from an Oregon county, and a fourth man, impeccably dressed that Lynch assumed was the lawyer, McLeod. In front of each man was a small pile of money, coin and paper. From a quick glance at the piles of money, he could tell Truman and the sheriff had won the most while the lawyer's pile was almost gone.

Truman rose and greeted Lynch with a firm handshake. "Good evening, Major. Would you like to join us?"

"As long as you have some cash to lose to these two," Hancock said, gesturing to Truman and the sheriff.

"Thank you, I'd like that," Lynch said.

Everyone got up and adjusted their chairs to make room for a sixth position. Hancock went out of the room and brought back a chair for Lynch. The security chief reached in his wallet and pulled out a few dollars and set them in front of his spot.

Truman made the introductions. Everyone shook hands and sat back in the chairs. Lynch was surprised at the warm welcome he was receiving and laughed to himself. Perhaps these guys were not so bad after all.

Hancock spoke first. "Can I be the one who goes ahead and asks the obvious question: why are you here?"

Lynch smiled, opened his mouth, blew out breath, and then closed it again, considering his next words. He stared at his pile of money. "Senator Truman, I've been thinking about what you said this afternoon, about Webb and his connection to Edward Moore.

Hancock and Blaine exchanged glances. Truman remained still.

"I did a little digging," the major said. He motioned to the bottle of whiskey next to Hancock. "May I have a nip of that?"

"If you keep talking," Hancock said, "you can have the rest of the bottle." He slid a glass over in front of Lynch and poured a good two fingers. Lynch threw back the entire contents with one practiced flip of his head. The heat burned his throat but it felt good.

"Thanks. I've been trying to get a hold of Webb since this afternoon. It seems he's on some kind of assignment. Out of town."

"That's nothing out of the ordinary," Blaine said. "I leave town regularly on police business."

"I know it's not strange. It just irritated me so I had to start digging elsewhere. I ended up calling Colonel Matthias. He was here when we started building out Hanford and I wanted to find out what he knew about Moore. Turns out quite a lot."

"Back in early '43, we needed to survey the entire area to determine where to build certain structures. That's when we learned about this Mountain Men business."

Blaine said, "Deputy Duncan here is our local expert on the

subject." Duncan tried to hide his smile but Lynch caught it just the same.

Lynch continued. "We made one great attempt to locate said fugitives and we received some local assistance. When the Army mounted its search parties, a group of local men offered their services. They were avid hunters and knew the area quite well. They were also members of the first two search parties conducted in '40 and '41."

Truman said, "Moore and Eli Sale?"

"Among others. Not Webb though."

Duncan piped in. "Are you referring to the fact that Moore and Sale led a team and had no Army officers with them?"

Lynch regarded Duncan with a cross between irritation at being interrupted and admiration for the deputy knowing the answer. Much of the nature of the search party is classified. Lynch made a mental note to find out how Duncan knew so much.

He nodded once. "That's right. And when all the teams reported nothing, there was no independent means to verify that Sale's and Moore's team did, in fact, find nothing."

"The one thing I was never able to determine," Duncan said, "was the range that Sale and Moore covered. Where was it?"

Lynch gestured with his hands. "North and west of here. More north, really, where the desert gives way to the usual type of geography people associate with Washington: mountains, streams, valleys, greenery."

"Just the place for a bunch of people to live off the land," Hancock said. "So why did you just figure this out today?"

"My job is rather busy. By the time I was assigned to this position, the Mountain Men had faded to myth, despite the burglary reports that occasionally popped up."

"We have a theory on that," Truman said.

Lynch smiled. "I'm sure you do. Moore and his warehouse are very important to our work. I might even go so far as to say irreplaceable. Everyone before me gave Moore a pass and I did, too." Lynch spread his hands. "So, that's what I have. It's circumstantial at best. But it was you, Senator, who really turned me around."

Truman eyed Lynch warily. "How so?"

"I asked a few higher ups about you. They all commended the job you're doing even if they won't admit it in public. Most of all, you seem to be an honest politician, a rare breed to say the least. You and Mr. Hancock were so adamant that I decided to try seeing things from your shoes and assumed what you were saying was true. It explained why I never received a written report from Webb. It explained why his deputies all defer to him on that question. No one at the station seems to know anything about that report." He looked at McLeod. "It also might help explain how it was you were charged with espionage."

McLeod looked down at his cards and then back up at Lynch. "I help people get out of jail. I've never spent a minute inside a jail that I didn't know I could leave at just a word to the guards. I don't ever want to do that again."

Lynch looked back at Truman. "So, given that I'm here and telling you what I know, how are you coming along with the task I assigned you this afternoon?"

Truman was silent for a moment. "Carl has an idea about acquiring evidence. It's a little unorthodox. Why don't you tell him, Carl?"

Hancock explained his idea about breaking into the warehouse and seeing what was inside the safe. He also explained how the safe may have some evidence directly linking Moore to the dead men Blaine found. At the mention of the dead bodies, Lynch looked over at Blaine.

"You didn't report that, sheriff. Why?"

"Because it's still a local matter. It is a murder investigation and doesn't require any military involvement."

Truman looked from Blaine to Lynch. He cleared his throat, heading off any immediate confrontations. "Major, why don't you join us on our reconnaissance mission tonight? It might be fruitful. We leave in ninety minutes."

"Sure. I'm working on one case but I don't have anything more to do with it until tomorrow." He tapped the table. "Deal me in."

44

Wednesday
19 April 1944
8:15 p.m., Pacific War Time

The part of the crew responsible for the seaplane stood at attention in front of Captain Morimoto. He could tell they all waited expectantly for his order. He told them that this was likely the last mission with the seaplane but he didn't want any sentimentality to impede their tasks. He held up his stopwatch and instructed them to beat their own best time of seven minutes. Morimoto gave the order and his crew moved as one, a well-oiled machine inside a larger well-oiled machine.

His men rose to the occasion.

The submarine surfaced and the forward hanger opened. The crew hollered and yelled at each other as each step of the process was completed. The crew rolled out the plane, its wings folded. They unfolded the wings, extended the rear stabilizer, and adjusted all the proper joints and sockets. All as one, the seaplane crew set the plane onto the catapult located on the foredeck and primed the launching mechanism. Their task complete, they all lined up and saluted Morimoto. He stopped the watch and looked at the time. Six minutes and fifty-one seconds.

The captain beamed with pride and returned his men's salute. Despite the pitching sea, the men did a remarkable job of remaining upright on the deck.

Morimoto nodded to his first officer and the younger man barked a command. From inside the hanger, Ishihara and Niigata strode forward. Morimoto stood just inside the hanger door and inspected his men. Niigata, as pilot, wore a clean uniform, markedly pressed and pristine. For all his frustration with the type of soldier the Empire created, Niigata was facing his destiny with honor and was dressed the part. Morimoto smiled. He would have done the same thing.

"For the Emperor," Morimoto said.

"For the Emperor," Niigata replied and saluted. Morimoto returned the salute.

The captain moved to Ishihara. He, too, was dressed in his formal uniform. Morimoto had suggested to Ishihara that a black coverall might be more appropriate but Ishihara declined. He knew the mission, he had said, and he knew how it was going to end. He wanted to be wearing his finest when he destroyed the American facility.

Over his uniform were the straps of his parachute. Around his waist hung a belt of grenades. Ishihara stood at attention, the rocking submarine barely affecting him. Morimoto marveled at the youth and vigor of this young man. He had been like that once and fancied himself still that way. But time and war had a way of tearing one down, eroding one's age prematurely. Morimoto felt old. Ishihara was still young and vibrant.

"Ishihara-san, you will make the Emperor proud today. You will make me proud to have been your captain. Please, do me the honor of one final request."

Ishihara looked at Morimoto. "Sir?"

"Tell me the truth. I am sending you to your destiny. Please repay me with the truth."

Ishihara nodded once. "Sir, I landed and killed two Americans.

And I loved it. Three more American deaths and my family will be avenged"

Morimoto nodded and said nothing for a moment. He had assumed as much but not the killing part. Why else would Ishihara have landed the plane?

With a suddenness that caught everyone off guard, Morimoto struck Ishihara with the back of his hand. The sound of the surf drowned out the sound as soon as it happened. To Ishihara's credit, he didn't even touch the place on his cheek reddened by Morimoto's fist but remained at attention, his eyes focused on the horizon.

"Were this any other situation, Lieutenant, I would have you killed on the spot."

"Yes, sir. It was a chance I was willing to take." He turned his eyes to look into Morimoto's. "I and my family thank you for helping me avenge them."

The captain took a step back. "That day has come, Ishihara-san."

Ishihara stood straighter and saluted his captain. Morimoto returned it and then nodded. Ishihara and Niigata marched toward the seaplane. As he passed the rear of the fuselage, Ishihara stopped. He looked at the space where the giant red dot representing the rising sun of Imperial Japan had been intentionally obscured by black tape during their reconnaissance missions. He reached up and tore off the tape and flung it into the air.

Morimoto's mind completed the image of the Japanese flag. The imaginary flag fluttered in the wind, keeping pace with the pitching of the submarine. His heart filled with pride for his country and for men like Ishihara.

Ishihara turned back to face Morimoto and saluted again. Morimoto saluted Ishihara and the young officer turned and climbed into the second of two seats.

Morimoto watched as the crewmembers scurried around the aircraft, checking every last detail. Everyone stood back in the hangar as Niigata started the propeller then scrambled into the cockpit. The wind gusted back into the hangar. Morimoto held onto his hat with one hand. He nodded to his first officer and he signaled Niigata.

With a great force, the seaplane shot off the submarine's bow. As soon as it cleared the catapult, the plane dipped toward the ocean's surface before righting itself.

Morimoto soon lost the plane in the night. But the image of the Imperial Japanese flag still burned into his eyes.

45

Wednesday
19 April 1944
9:25 p.m., Pacific War Time

"I have to hand it to you, Carl," Truman said, "this was a good idea."

They stood in front of the two large rectangular windows of the pipe warehouse facing north and the Moore Warehouse. One of the few trees in the area grew right next to the windows. The light from the Moore Warehouse cast a shadow on the face of the pipe warehouse wall, obscuring anyone from the warehouse noticing Truman's party.

"I'll have to tell Horace about Stanley's route tonight. Last night, he was all impressed with Stanley's pattern until I showed him all the problems. I think Stanley got some new instructions."

"Are you referring to him walking across the street and checking the rock yard?" Blaine asked.

"Yup. That wasn't on the route last night. And you can tell he's taking his job a bit more seriously now."

Lynch said, "How are you going to cover that open area undetected? I'm guessing that's about two hundred yards or so."

Hancock, who had put on his darker suit and removed his tie, pointed at the little drainage ditch on the Moore Warehouse side of the road. "The way I figure it, I need to do it in two groups. First, when Stanley's on the other side of the rock yard, I'll run and hide in the ditch. As Stanley passes behind the warehouse, I'll scoot across the parking lot and go in before Stanley comes back around to the front. That's four minutes if his timing stays the same. Once inside I'll go to the main office window—the one there on the second floor—and signal y'all with my flashlight. Morse Code"

Everyone nodded. Hancock continued. "If Stanley holds true to his schedule, he only goes inside the warehouse every two hours. I guess that's his break time. And I seriously doubt he would have a key to Moore's private office. As long as I can get in there without Stanley seeing me, I'll be in the clear. Even if I have to be there for hours, it'll be better to be safe."

Truman looked at his friend. "Are you ready for this, Carl?"

"You're damn right I am. I've been waiting for some action since Moore started stinking. And ever since you mentioned the safe, I've been dying to see what's inside." He made fist. "I want to nail this bastard."

* * *

The blip appeared on Jack Bower's radar screen while he was getting coffee. When he sat back down at his station, the blip was a quarter of the way across the screen.

Bower took a sip from his coffee and burned his tongue. Cursing, he set down the cup and picked up the list of flights for the evening. For the second time in two days, he found no flight plan listed for that time.

The blip moved west-to-east, now past the halfway point.

He double-checked the flight list one last time. Confirming that no flights were scheduled in this area at this time, he picked up the telephone. Without hesitation, he dialed the number for his commanding officer.

"Captain Arnold, this is Bower on radar. We may have a problem."

As he waited for the captain, Bower noted the time he noticed the blip in the log. He was composing a short history when Arnold arrived.

"What is it, Jack?"

Bower pointed at the screen. "This is the second time in two days I've seen a plane flying in the area and it's not on any scheduled flight plan. Yesterday I called all surrounding airfields and none of them launched or accepted any unscheduled flights."

"Have you called those airfields tonight?"

"No, sir. I called you first."

Arnold gave a curt nod. "Call all the airfields west of here. Verify that no flights took off this evening. And call the airfields east of here and find out if they are expecting any flights. After that, report back to me with your findings."

"Yes, sir. Where will you be?"

"In my office." Arnold scratched the back of his neck. "You say this is the second time you've seen an unidentified blip on the radar? What happened the first time?"

"Whatever it was flew from west-to-east and then, about ten minutes later, another unidentified blip traveled from east-to-west."

Arnold pursed his lips. He looked at the screen. The blip was almost out of the range of the radar, still traveling east. He looked at the clock on the wall above Bower's station.

"It's exactly 9:49. Call the airfields and then call me in eleven minutes. I want to know if whatever it is comes back just like it did on Monday."

He tapped Bower's station. "Let's make sure this thing is legitimate before crying wolf."

* * *

Randy Connolly looked up at Ross and Seaborn and shook his head. "I don't know this plane. Are you sure the prisoner drew it accurately?"

Seaborn looked at Ross who said, "Sure. He's had the notepad for almost the entire afternoon. All he did was draw this picture. Why do you ask?"

Connolly traced along the page where Theodore Frank had drawn the plane. "Well, for one thing, most of our sea aircraft have three pontoons, one in the middle and one each on the wings. The U.S. doesn't have but one seaplane with two pontoons and this ain't it."

"How do you know this is not one of ours?" Ross asked.

"Easy. Look at the tailfin area. The one we have—it's a Northrop N-3PB—has a vertical stabilizer and tail rudder that forms one continuous line from the top of the fuselage toward the bottom. The one drawn here has a stabilizer and rudder that are different sizes. Different tail feathers means different planes."

"Okay," Ross said, "go on."

Connolly circled the struts holding the pontoons to the plane's fuselage. "Look at these struts. Our planes have a solid piece under the body of the plane that holds the pontoons. This plane has three struts." He leaned closer to the drawing. "And if what this guy drew is accurate— this guy does good work—then the cowling is something completely different than we have."

Seaborn looked lost. "In English, please."

"Sure. The engine isn't one we make."

Ross said, "You keep saying we, meaning the U.S. What other nations have seaplanes?"

Connolly chuckled. "Which country doesn't? You name a country, they have a navy. If they have a navy, they'll have seaplanes."

Seaborn said, "But why would this prisoner decide to sketch a seaplane when he's been arrested for espionage and spying?"

Connolly looked at the two men. "That's a very good question."

46

Wednesday
19 April 1944
9:55 p.m., Pacific War Time

Hancock stood in the shadows made by the façade of the pipe warehouse and gazed across the road at the Moore Warehouse. Despite the quiet night, he could not hear Stanley's footsteps as the night watchman made his rounds. Good, Hancock thought, then he won't be able to hear mine.

He watched as Stanley marched his pattern across the Moore Warehouse parking lot. Stanley crossed the road at a trot and slowed to a walk as he reached the entrance of the rock yard. As soon as Stanley was on the far side of the rock yard, Hancock ran. The only evidence of his presence was the dust his boots kicked up. He made it across the two-lane highway and threw himself into the ditch. He stilled his breathing and waited for the night watchman to pass. He hoped the dust cloud he made would dissipate before Stanley came back across the street.

Stanley emerged from the shadows and walked back across the road. Hancock heard the man whistling but couldn't discern the tune. Hancock risked a glance and saw Stanley standing under the light illuminating the front of the Moore Warehouse, a lit cigarette dangling from his lips. Hancock wished McLeod could have been there to prove to the lawyer that one could see the smoldering light of a cigarette from a very long distance.

Stanley resumed his walk and passed along the east side of the warehouse and into the shadows. Hancock could not see him, even though his eyes were adjusted for the dark. After about three minutes, he saw Stanley's silhouette backlit by the light on the rear of the warehouse. Hancock stepped out and started to run as fast as he could in a pair of cowboy boots. He reached from the front door and glanced at his watch. Three minutes until Stanley rounded the front of the warehouse. Hancock smiled. Plenty of time.

* * *

Bower looked at the clock. It read 10:04 p.m. He had decided to give the mysterious blip and additional five minutes just in case there was something in the air that slowed it down. He noted the time in his log and was about to call Arnold when the captain strode up behind him.

"Bower, why didn't you call me? Status."

"No sign of the plane, sir. I gave it an extra five minutes and still nothing. All airfields reported that no flights have left tonight." He looked up at Arnold. "What next, sir?"

Arnold picked up the telephone on the adjacent desk and dialed the operator. "Continue monitoring. And note everything. I'm calling all airfields to be on alert for an unauthorized plane flying in the area. It would have to be on a new moon night."

The operator answered and Arnold said, "Connect me with the main security office at Hanford ASAP."

Bower could do nothing but watch Arnold.

Finally, Arnold said, "Yes, Private Pierce, this is Captain Arnold, commanding officer of the Delta radar station. I'm alerting you to the fact that there appears to be an unauthorized aircraft heading your way. It's out of our range. Monitor radar and see if you can pick up the signal. It left our scopes about fifteen minutes ago. I'm about to call Pasco and Walla Walla and alert them as well."

He listened for a moment and then nodded. "We'll continue monitoring. Thank you." He hung up the telephone.

"Keep watching that screen, Bower, and tell me the instant you see anything."

"Yes, sir."

Arnold cursed under his breath.

"What is it, sir?"

Arnold waved him off. "It's probably nothing. A drill maybe. But it just doesn't feel right, you know?"

"Yes, sir, I feel it, too," Bower said and turned back to the radar screen.

* * *

Ross and Seaborn glared down at Theodore Frank. Initially, the prisoner had not quite smiled when the two men came into the room without Lynch. When Ross slammed the drawing down in front of him, however, whatever semblance of a smile he had vanished.

Ross spoke first. "Tell us why you drew this plane. What does it mean?"

Frank stared at the drawing then down at the floor. His mouth opened but nothing came out.

"Look, Major Lynch isn't here right now so you got us. Why does a man in your position draw an airplane when he's been arrested for espionage?"

"I am no spy." Frank's voice was halting, cracking dryly.

"That's what you keep saying. And, frankly, I'm beginning to wonder. How would a spy know about a plane like this?"

Concern crossed Frank's brow. "What do you mean by that?"

Ross looked at Seaborn and they made a mutual decision. Seaborn took the lead. "What can you tell us about this plane? Did you see it recently?"

Frank looked down at the floor again and his lip began to quiver. "Yes," he whispered.

"Okay," Seaborn said, "that's progress. Where?"

Frank didn't answer.

"We can assume it was near some body of water unless you saw it in the air. Did you see it on the water or in the air?"

"Both," Frank said. He looked up at Seaborn. "I saw it fly, land, then fly off again."

Ross raised his eyebrows. Seaborn nodded to Frank. "Okay, that's good. Thank you. That's the first answer you've given that gets us anywhere. Which body of water?"

Frank's lip continued to quiver. Out of Frank's sight, Ross was signaling Seaborn to increase the pressure. Seaborn shook his head and continued in a soft voice.

"Mr. Frank, since you were on foot, there are only a few bodies of water around here a plane can land on. Did you see it land on one of the lakes?"

Frank shook his head.

Ross chimed in and took a cue from Seaborn and spoke gently, like a lawyer leading a witness. "Well, we found you along the Columbia. There are a few places where a plane could land." He bent down to Frank's level. "Did you see the plane land on the river?"

Tears began running down Frank's cheeks. "Yes."

Ross frowned at Seaborn who shrugged. "What's with the waterworks?"

Frank quietly sobbed and Ross stepped over to stand next to Seaborn. He glanced down at the notepad and noticed that Frank had written two names: Ron Garrison, Jack Buchan.

Again, Ross leaned down to Frank's level. "Who are Ron Garrison and Jack Buchan? Are they friends of yours or fellow spies?"

Seaborn scowled at Ross for breaking the mood that was finally getting answers. However, Frank burst out with a voice loud and with anguish.

"They're dead! He killed them. The man in that plane killed them."

Ross and Seaborn were startled by Frank's words. Seaborn stepped to Frank's left and kneeled down next to the prisoner. "Look, Mr. Frank, we want to help. Honest. We *can* help. Just tell us what happened."

Frank's inner dam of resolve finally burst. He told Ross and Seaborn about "camping" in the woods near the river. He told them how the strange plane landed on the water and glided over to the bank. He told them how the pilot jumped out of the plane and murdered his two friends. He told them how he heard the sound of laughter before the plane took off and flew west.

Ross had picked up the notepad and jotted notes during Frank's story. Seaborn slid the drawing over in front of Frank. "That's quite a story, Mr. Frank. In the morning, we'll send a team out to this location you told us about. And we're going to get you some food and water. Did the plane have any unique characteristics that could help identify it?"

Frank sniffed and wiped his nose on his sleeve. "It was too dark to see much detail. I think the plane was green." He looked at his drawing. "Oh, I missed something." He motioned for Ross to give him the pencil and the other man did so. Frank drew a circle on the back part of the fuselage, just behind the tandem cockpit. He shaded the circle. "There was this circle painted on the back. It appeared to be red. It seemed odd and I…what is it?"

Ross and Seaborn were looking at each other, eyes wide with terror. Seaborn spoke first. "You don't think…"

"Can't take the chance. Put the base on alert." Ross turned to Frank. "Did you get a good look at the pilot?"

"No, I didn't. It was across the river and I…"

"Fine. When did this happen? Tell me exactly."

Frank opened his mouth to reply when the door opened. Ross looked up and said, "What is it, Private Pierce? We're in the middle of an interrogation."

"Sorry, sir. With Major Lynch offsite, I thought you should know that we just received a call from the Delta radar station. The CO there claims that an unauthorized aircraft entered his airspace and was heading east."

"Shit," Ross said and ran out of the room.

* * *

HANCOCK WAS PROUD OF HIMSELF. He managed to reach the front door, pick the lock, slip inside, and make his way up to the main office in time to see Stanley walk across the street and into the rock yard. He pulled out his flashlight and signaled 'All clear.'

He didn't have much difficulty with Moore's private office lock either. Even though there were no windows in this room, Hancock preferred not to turn on the light. The light of his flashlight made the various animal heads and bodies look eerie.

He made his way to the bookshelf behind Moore's desk. He moved the fish and his light shone on a dull gray safe with a combination lock. Needing both hands, he set the light on the desk and put his ear to the safe. He began to spin the dial and didn't notice his flashlight rolling off the desk. In the near total silence, the crash was deafening.

He cursed to himself and picked up the light. He stood stock still, listening for any sign that Stanley was making his way inside the warehouse. It was in this position that he saw another bookcase, this one the size of a door, begin to swing open.

* * *

NIIGATA OPENED a radio channel and sent one predetermined coded message. He wanted Morimoto to know that this part of the mission was a success. He didn't mind that, by doing so, he would be more of a target. He knew his mission and he was carrying out his orders to the letter.

Niigata smiled at himself as he watched Ishihara fall into space, the parachute opening like a flower. He thought Ishihara would have appreciated this particular message: The spirits will be avenged.

47

Wednesday
19 April 1944
10:30 p.m., Pacific War Time

Through binoculars, Nick Lynch stared at the window of the Moore Warehouse. He saw no movement. He slid the binoculars down to the ground level and found Stanley, walking his route. Lynch turned from the window and handed the binoculars to Truman. "Still nothing."

Truman took the lenses and started watching.

Blaine stood next to Truman, his thumb hooked into his gun belt. Lynch sidled up next to Duncan and asked the young deputy a question that had bothered him since earlier that day. "How was it you came to link the dead men with Moore?"

Duncan rose an inch taller as he straightened his back. "Well, sir, I can't take all the credit. It was Sheriff Blaine who pointed me in the right direction."

Without turning from the window, Blaine said, "Go ahead, Joe, you can take the credit. It was your research that gave us the link."

Had there been a light in the room, Lynch would have seen Duncan blush.

"Thank you, sir." Duncan explained how he had searched for a link between the suspected Mountain Men and Moore. Duncan also explained how he figured out which of the seven Mountain Men tied to Moore had returned after Pearl Harbor.

The entire concept of the Mountain Men confounded Lynch. "What kind of people are these Mountain Men? Are they all outdoorsmen?"

Duncan shook his head. "Hardly. The one named Garrison was a lawyer. There's an artist named Frank who drew pictures for magazine advertisements. The one named Buchan is an accountant. The one named…"

Lynch's entire world shrank down to two things. Duncan continued speaking but Lynch didn't hear him. Duncan said there was a person named 'Frank' and was an artist. Theodore Frank, instead of writing out a confession, drew an intricate picture of an airplane.

He stopped Duncan from reciting his list. "This 'Frank' person, what's his first name?"

"Theodore," Duncan said. "Why?"

Lynch's mouth went dry and he felt a lightness in his stomach. In the gloom of the office, it took a few seconds to find the telephone. He picked it up. "Deputy, I think you may have helped two cases today. I'm holding a Theodore Frank at my station. And he drew a picture—a very detailed picture—of an airplane."

He dialed his station and started talking as Truman said, "Uh-oh."

Lynch stopped talking for a moment and they all looked toward the Moore Warehouse.

A light was in the upstairs window. Silhouetted on it was a person they all assumed to be Hancock judging by the size of the man.

"What's he doing?" Duncan asked. He looked over toward where Stanley was walking around the rock yard. "Doesn't he know Stanley will see him?"

They were all wondering the same thing when Hancock began flashing his flashlight. At first, they saw no pattern. Gradually, it became clear: three short flashes, followed by three longer flashes and three short flashes again.

"Is that…" Duncan began.

"Yes," Truman said and made his way to the door. "It's an SOS call."

"Go on ahead," Lynch said. "I'll catch up with you after I talk to my men back at the station."

Blaine and Duncan drew their weapons. The two officers and Truman raced out of the door. As the three men crossed the road, two pairs of headlights came into view. Despite the urgency of Hancock's signal, they slowed and turned to look at the newcomers, hands held up to shield their eyes from the glare. Both cars pulled into the parking lot. A police cruiser stopped with its headlight framing Truman, Blaine, and Duncan. The second car, a sedan, stopped in front of the trio, effectively blocking their way toward the warehouse. The three newcomers exited their vehicles and walked toward them: Edward Moore, Christopher Moore, and a man in uniform.

"Ira?" Blaine asked, his vision still clouded by the headlights.

Webb tipped his hat toward Blaine. "Sheriff."

"What the hell is going on here?" the sound of Edward Moore's voice boomed in the quietness. He looked at the three men in his parking lot. His eyes didn't linger on Duncan but he recognized Blaine and then Truman. His shoulders sagged.

"Senator Truman. I guess when you can't find any real evidence during your regular *investigation,* then you stake out an honest businessman's establishment and hope something happens."

Moore bumped Duncan as he strode toward Truman. He stopped in front of the senator, the headlights illuminating both men's profiles. The taller Moore looked down at Truman.

"I'm not going to stop until you are impeached and removed from office. And I don't care how high I have to go. I know many men in powerful positions. After I'm done with you, you won't be able to get a job as a janitor. It's too bad you're too old to be drafted. At least then you could do some good."

Truman opened his mouth to retort but Moore spun around and glared at Blaine.

"Sheriff, I also know quite a few influential members of the Oregon state legislature. I'll be sure to speak to each and every one of them about your hounding me."

Richard Stanley trotted up. "Evening, Mr. Moore. What's going on here?"

Moore whirled on Stanley. "I should ask you the same thing. I hired you to stand guard over my warehouse and, for two nights straight, I have spies outside my business."

Truman had had enough. "Look here, Mr. Moore. I have more than enough suspicions to investigate your entire warehouse. And there are many questions you need to answer. What about all those duplicate invoices? Where is all the merchandise you embezzled? What about your connection to the Mountain Men? What do you know about how those men died?"

The sound of Christopher Moore's laughter filled the air. "It doesn't matter now. Since you 'spies' have been caught in the act of espionage, we'll just have to report you. And we have the word of a true, law-abiding sheriff, on our side as well." He shook his head in contempt. "You picked the wrong man to spy on, *Senator*."

Edward Moore beamed with pride at his son. "That's right, Mr. Truman. We have you and there's not a damn thing you can do about it. No matter what you say now, I win. I'll just claim that everything you say is just a figment of your imagination."

"Is this a figment of his imagination, Mr. Moore?" The voice belonged to Carl Hancock. Everyone turned and watched as Hancock walked into the radiance of the headlights.

His visage surprised no one. What made everyone's mouth hang open was the figure next to him: a young Japanese woman.

* * *

Toshiro Ishihara finished stuffing his parachute under a rock outcropping. On his descent, he had considered just leaving his parachute where it landed, so confident was he that he would be able to carry out the mission even if the Americans knew he was there. He had dismissed the thought. He knew the outcome of this night for himself but decided to make it easier. Were he to leave his parachute out in the open, an American pilot would be able to see the white silk from the sky, even at night.

He withdrew from his pocket the map the American traitor had drawn. He spat at the thought of the dishonor the American brought upon himself. Koishii fancied himself a Japanese citizen. Ishihara almost wished that he could meet the American now. He would run a knife through him.

Ishihara oriented himself by the stars. He looked at the surrounding area and fixated on his target. He judged the distance to be three to four miles.

He turned on his flashlight and, in its red glow, looked down at the map one last time. He had memorized the map before the flight but it was good to study it now that he was on the ground.

About the only thing that American traitor was good for, Ishihara thought, was that he could read, write, and speak Japanese. The traitor identified Ishihara's target: Reactor 100-B.

Ishihara didn't know what a reactor was but he guessed it was the place where the bombs were made.

Ishihara hoped Niigata's sacrifice would give him enough time to make his way to his intended target. He put the map back in his pocket and started to move.

48

Wednesday
19 April 1944
10:50 p.m., Pacific War Time

The young woman wore a simple black dress that went down to mid-calf. Her black shoes were highly polished and there was a red ribbon holding her hair back from her forehead. She walked over to where Edward and Christopher Moore stood.

Edward Moore said, "Keiko, what have you done?"

Keiko looked at him then back at his son. With a suddenness that surprised everyone, she slapped him across the face. "Traitor! And to think I once called you *Koishii*. No more am I your beloved!"

Edward stepped forward. "What's the meaning of this?"

"Tell him, Chris," Keiko screamed. "Tell your father what you have done or, by God, I will!"

Koishii's hand went to his face. The sting of Keiko's blow still burned. He blinked back the tears that began to form in his eyes, determined not to show pain or weakness. He then realized that he was in a position with only one outcome.

Truman was the first to break the silence. "Ma'am, who are you and what are you doing here?"

"I am an American, just so you'll know, born and raised. And, even though it's still technically in effect, I stopped being his wife as soon as he told me what he has done."

Truman looked at Hancock to see his reaction. Judging by his calm demeanor, Truman could tell that the Texan already knew.

Edward stepped forward and took Keiko's arm. "Okay, everyone, let's all…"

She wrenched her arm free and spun on Edward. "No, Edward. Your dutiful son has something he wants to say to you." She looked at her husband. "This is your last chance, traitor. Tell him, tell everyone here, or I will."

"What is she talking about Chris?" Edward's voice took the timbre of a father.

Before Christopher could respond, Lynch burst into the glare of the headlights. "We've got a report of an unidentified aircraft in the area. My prisoner"—he looked at Duncan—"Theodore Frank saw an airplane matching the description of a Japanese 'Glen' seaplane."

At the mention of Frank's name, Edward spun on his heels. "Ted's alive?"

Lynch nodded. "It was his drawing that led my team to put two and two together. But I still can't figure out how a plane that small got so far inland."

Keiko spat on the ground. "This traitor knows."

Lynch noticed Keiko and drew his weapon. "Who the hell are you?"

Christopher stepped in front of Keiko. "This is my wife, Major Lynch. Lower your gun.

Keiko stepped out from behind Christopher. "No, Major, arrest this traitor now. Do it before he escapes."

Edward turned to his son. "Chris, what the hell is she talking about?"

Christopher Moore surveyed his position. His back was to the warehouse and his car. Osborn, still unconscious, lay in the trunk. As he looked ahead of him, his father was to his right. Webb stood inside the open door of his cruiser. Hancock, who had walked over to Truman, stood next to Blaine and the deputy. Lynch stood behind Truman, his gun raised.

He looked down at the ground and toed a line in the sand. He stepped over it and slightly behind his father, thus partially blocking Lynch's aim. He chuckled and looked over at Keiko. "I know what I have done is right. Why don't you tell them? Let me just hear it spoken in your wonderfully lilting voice."

All eyes turned toward Keiko, exactly as Christopher wanted. As she began to speak, he slowly reached into his pants pocket and gripped his pistol.

Her eyes focused on Edward. "It seems that your warped sense of right and wrong has poisoned your son. He's working with the captain of a Japanese submarine off the coast. They are planning on sabotaging the Hanford base and kidnapping an American scientist."

Edward spun around to face his son. As such, he completely blocked the line of sight not only for Lynch but also for Webb and Blaine who had drawn their weapons along with Duncan at the mention of the treason. "Tell me it isn't true. Tell me you've not betrayed our country."

Christopher rounded on his father. "Our country? Would that be the same country that imprisoned its own people just for being different? How can you say that? I've spent hours and hours listening to you pine for your one true love that's still in Japan, married to another man. All because your parents, paragons of Christian virtue that they claimed to be, were just as bigoted as everyone else in this country.

Edward's eyes moved between disbelief and anger. "Son...I...it was a different time, a different place. It could never have worked out for Miko and me."

"Is that you talking or the pious bastard that was your father?"

"Don't insult my father. He was a good man." Edward took a step toward Christopher and the younger man backed up.

Christopher withdrew a gun from his pocket and aimed it at his father.

"Don't come any closer. There's a letter on mom's bureau. It's all in there."

"Well, I'm here now. Why don't you tell me?" Edward's voice took on parental authority. He took another step toward his son who stepped back again.

To the police officers and Lynch, Christopher said, "Put down your guns or I'll shoot him. I'm getting out of here and I'm bringing Keiko with me. This is not your fight."

Weaponless, Truman said, "Like hell it's not our fight."

"Do it!" Christopher shouted.

"I can't do that, Chris, and you know it," Webb said. He stood behind his open car door, gun trained on Christopher.

"What, you suddenly grow a conscious, Ira? Decide to start being a cop again?" Christopher took a few steps to his right, putting his father and wife between him and Webb. From his new location, he surveyed his position. He realized he needed a distraction and found one.

In a split second, he turned the gun on Duncan and fired. What he had counted on happened. Everyone not holding a gun instinctively ducked. He took an additional step to his right and fired at Lynch, grazing his cheek. The major yelled, grabbed his face, and fell to the ground.

Knowing his father was still blocking a clean shot by Webb and Blaine, Christopher decided Webb would be less likely to try to shoot at him for fear of hitting Edward. Christopher ducked low and aimed for Blaine's foot, hoping to incapacitate the sheriff. But the foot was not there.

Flames bloomed from Blaine's gun. Christopher pulled back and avoided a killing shot. Instead, the bullet ripped through his left bicep, taking a chunk of flesh with it.

The combination of Edward ducking and Christopher being hit gave Webb, who didn't flinch when the gunfire erupted, a clean line. All Webb did was adjust his aim downward and pulled the trigger.

Christopher intuitively knew his cover was gone. From his position with his left knee and right foot on the ground, he lunged left and threw himself into a roll. Webb's bullet impacted the only part of Christopher that still touched the ground: his right foot. The bullet embedded itself within the steep tip of his work boot. The pain was sharp, but the lead slug didn't penetrate his foot.

But Christopher's roll gave him a moment of luck. He rolled in front of Webb's car. To shoot again, Webb had to move to his left and around the open driver's side door to get another clean shot. In that instant, Webb, instead of backing up a step and keeping his gun trained on Christopher to go around the car door, raised his gun to his ear and stepped around the door, unknowingly blocking a clean shot by Blaine. As Webb was lowering his gun again, Christopher fired twice and hit Webb square in the chest. Webb went down and his gun fell three feet from Truman, who had taken cover next to the patrol car and behind Webb.

Christopher continued to fire at Blaine who had been behind Webb. Blaine ducked and rolled toward the rear of Webb's cruiser. All at once, Christopher's pistol clicked empty. That was the moment Hancock had been waiting for.

From his position at the front of Christopher's car, the big Texan took three steps and put everything he had into his punch. The blow took Christopher by surprise as he held his empty pistol in his right hand and the full clip in his left. Hancock's blow landed along Christopher's right ear and face, sending lightning across the younger man's eyes. He saw stars but he also saw Hancock's rearing back for an additional punch.

Christopher crouched and rolled forward. Hancock's swing hit only air and spun him around. Christopher continued with the roll and stood up. He jammed the clip into the pistol and cocked the gun. Hancock was sprawled on the hood of Webb's patrol car and Christopher raised the gun to shoot the Texan.

The side window of his car shattered into pieces as a bullet from his right missed his chest. Christopher ducked and the hesitation allowed Hancock time to roll off the hood and around behind the car.

Christopher looked to his right and saw Truman, standing on

the other side of the open door of Webb's cruiser. He smiled as he raised his gun to kill the senator.

A blur crashed down on Christopher's right arm, disrupting his aim. The bullet landed harmlessly in the dirt. Another blur was his father's fist as it landed square in his jaw. The force caused Christopher to stumble backward and his gun hand grazed the broken glass of the destroyed window.

Edward stood still and leveled a hand at Christopher, palm open. "Give me the gun, Chris before anyone else gets hurt or killed!"

"I can't do that! You know I can't. Above all else, loyalty is supreme."

From behind Edward, Blaine yelled, "Moore, get out of the way."

Edward spread his arms. "I know about loyalty, Chris. You are my son. I want to protect you. Put down the gun and we can work this thing out."

Christopher raised the gun and aimed it at his father. "I'm leaving. Don't try to stop me." In a flash, he aimed the gun just past Edward's right side and fired. The rear tire of the patrol car burst. Over his shoulder, Christopher yelled, "Keiko, get into the car."

"No." The sound came from the far side of his car, the side closest to the warehouse.

Incomprehension furrowed Christopher's brow. "I did this for you, for us, so we could be happy back home in Japan."

She stood up from behind the car and, in a voice that was neither yell nor shout but as crisp and clean as a winter's day, said, "I am home."

Her words sliced through Christopher. His heart skipped a beat and, all at once, his world crumbled.

Edward said, "She's made her choice. Now, make yours. Put down the gun and we can work through all of this."

Tears formed in Christopher's eyes and his father's image looked as if it were raining. "No. You choose. It's your choice now. You're blocking them from killing me and me from killing them. What's more important? Family or a country that has betrayed the ones we love?"

Edward Moore's chin quivered. Tears welled in his eyes. A single tear flowed down his cheek. When he spoke, his voice was soft. "My son, this isn't what I wanted. I love you, but in light of what you've done…." His voice trailed off as he stepped aside.

49

Wednesday
19 April 1944
11:20 p.m., Pacific War Time

"Now this is flying!" Despite the urgency of the mission, Hamilton Armstrong loved opening up the plane and flying full tilt.

Armstrong and his entire squadron had scrambled and took off within fifteen minutes. They were in such a hurry that they were given their orders only after they were airborne. Their commanding officer had told them that an unauthorized aircraft was in the vicinity of Hanford. It was a seaplane and should be considered extremely dangerous. Upon contact with the seaplane, the orders were to open fire and take it down.

Each pilot was given a specific route to follow. Armstrong had the northernmost route, a path that would take him north of the Columbia to the plateau ridges that surrounded the entire Columbia basin.

Armstrong inhaled deeply and took a firm grip on the stick. He felt the plane and its vibrations. It felt natural. He banked and flew north.

* * *

NIIGATA'S RETURN flight had gone uneventful. After Ishihara had jumped, Niigata banked the plane westward and had set a course toward the Pacific. He kept an eye out for anything out of the ordinary. So far, he saw no sign that the Americans had detected him.

In previous flights, Niigata noticed that most of the coastal communities had blackouts in effect. As he flew inland, however, farther away from the ocean, the communities gradually got brighter and brighter.

For a reason unknown even to himself, Niigata had decided to fly back to the submarine on a route more to the north of previous flight paths. He kept the plane lower to the ground so as to avoid detection.

Despite the moonless night, he could tell he was about to enter a small valley. He could see the darker outline along the horizon but what also helped him were the fires lit on the ground. His first thought was of forest fires set off by lightning. But there had not been any rain for nearly two weeks.

Curious, he slowed the seaplane somewhat to give him additional time to survey the fires. What he saw bewildered him. A group of people were milling around. Niigata saw tents, small houses made of wood, a well, all the accouterments of a small community. The light of the fires came through the trees and he realized that the only reason he could see these people was because their firelight illuminated them from the ground. Had Niigata's plane had a searchlight, he probably would not have been able to see them through the tall trees.

Puzzled as to why a group of people would be out in the woods, Niigata had a moment of independence for the first and last time in his life as a member of the Imperial Japanese Navy. He knew Ishihara had removed the camouflage covering the rising sun on the seaplane's fuselage. He also knew he would make it back to the submarine. What was the harm in buzzing the Americans and letting them know a Japanese plane was flying over their own land?

He threw the seaplane into a large bank and came around again, this time from the west. He flew lower than before, to ensure the Americans saw the rising sun.

He was grinning and laughing.

* * *

AT THE CAMP, Nancy Frank had finished packing her family heirlooms, including her husband's drawings, when she heard the sound of an airplane. She looked at all the fires her group had lit to help them see while they prepared to leave and realized that time was shorter than she realized. The plane was probably looking for them.

She saw the plane fly over the encampment and she ran to a clearing to get a better look. Warren Douglas, the leader of the group dubbed the Mountain Men, trotted beside her, eyes gazing upward. They both were not surprised when they heard the plane turn around and approach again. They looked at each other and hugged.

A dozen more of their family and friends surrounded them and looked skyward. The light of the fires cast shadows of the trees on the far side of the valley.

As the plane made its return pass, Nancy heard someone running toward them. She diverted her attention away from the sky and saw one of the hunters running towards them. In his hands, he carried his hunting rifle. He was screaming something the woman could not understand until he got closer.

"Everyone get down! It's not one of ours. It's a Jap plane!"

Most of the people gasped and scrambled for cover. Nancy and Douglas simply crouched low to the ground. She saw the hunter kneel down and raise his rifle. She turned and saw the plane extremely low to the ground.

The first thing she noticed was the pontoons. She realized Sheriff Webb was right about his suspicions of a rogue Japanese plane in the area. The second thing she noticed was the large red rising sun painted on the fuselage. Only later would she recall the name the American GIs gave that symbol: the meatball.

The last thing she realized before the hunter fired was amazement that, by the light of the fires, she could actually see the pilot's face. He appeared to be smiling.

The hunter got off three shots. What happened next astonished everyone.

* * *

THE JAPANESE ENGINEERS had designed the Yokosuka E14Y1 for reconnaissance and the ability to be carried by a submarine. The plane was light and could easily be stored inside the submarine. As such, it was far from bulletproof.

If the hunter had a hundred shots, it would have been impossible to duplicate his first and most accurate shot. Knowing the pilot's body was situated under the cockpit, the hunter aimed not for the cockpit but at the place on the fuselage where the pilot would be if the outer skin of the plane was invisible. The bullet passed through the paper thin outer shell and landed in Niigata's abdomen. The immediate reaction was that he involuntarily pitched forward and his hand slipped from the stick.

During his pass, Niigata held the plane level and low. As his hand slipped from the stick, the plane's nose dipped toward the tree line. As low as Niigata had been flying, there was little room for error. The left pontoon nicked a treetop and broke off. The plane lurched forward and part of the propeller shattered. Without the stability of two pontoons and a propeller, the seaplane dipped further toward the ground.

A second treetop struck the left wing and sheared it off, throwing the rest of the plane into a spin. The force of the spin broke the fuselage into two pieces. The front half of the Yokosuka E14Y1 continued to crash through the trees until it struck the ground and exploded. The tail of the plane hung suspended in a tree.

Nancy shrieked and covered her eyes. After a few moments, she looked at the burning half of the plane. "What does this mean?"

Douglas looked at her. "Our life here is over." He pointed at the flaming plane. "And our duty begins. Bring me the radio."

50

Wednesday
19 April 1944
11: p.m., Pacific War Time

Two shots rang out in quick succession. Hampered by Truman's poor eyesight, the bullet from his gun sailed high and embedded in the warehouse wall. Blaine's shot, much more precise, took off a piece of Christopher's right ear. He screamed and put his gun hand to his ear. A third shot sounded as he realized his error. The third shot whistled over his head. But this shot came from his left.

He looked in that direction and saw Hancock, gun in hand, aiming for him. Again, Christopher tucked and rolled forward, putting the body of Webb's car in front of all three of his assailants. Looking under the car, he saw Hancock's boot and aimed for it. The shot missed its mark but Christopher heard the Texan curse and scurry to the rear of the patrol car.

Still using Webb's car as cover, Christopher scampered in front of his car and came around to the driver's side. There he saw his wife, hunkering down and trying to avoid being hit. He held out his hand. "Keiko, come with me. We can be together forever."

"Go to hell," she said and spat in his face.

Something erupted within him. He nearly pulled the trigger and shot her right there. Instead, he hit her across the face with the pistol. Everyone heard the sound of her nose breaking. A scream gurgled in her throat. In her confusion, she stood up, lost her balance, and reached out her hand to steady herself. She regained her bearings and stumbled away from Christopher leaving a bloody handprint on the rear windshield. As he watched her run from him, Christopher's heart turned to stone. He raised his gun, fully intent on shooting his wife in the back.

The shattering of the driver's side window brought him back to reality. Blaine had moved to a position behind the door of Webb's patrol car, not ten yards away. Truman and Hancock, both still positioned at the rear of Webb's car, aimed their guns at him. Christopher realized in the next few seconds, he would either die or be on his way to his destiny. He wanted to make it to the submarine, to be back in Japan. He inhaled deeply, closed his eyes, and made his decision.

He would live.

He fired off three shots in rapid succession. He opened the car door, not bothering to close it, and fired up the ignition. He slouched down in the seat to make himself a more difficult target. Above him, five shots passed through the car.

Christopher fired a few more rounds at Webb's car. He gunned the engine and threw the car into gear. The car lurched forward and sped out of the parking lot and onto the road.

* * *

"DAMMIT, WE LOST HIM!" Truman put the smoking gun down on the hood of Webb's patrol car and removed his hat to wipe his brow with the back of his hand. He looked down at Blaine who knelt next to Webb. "How is he?"

"Dead," Blaine said.

"The deputy's still alive," Edward Moore said. Dust had caked his face but Truman could see dried rivers of tears along his face. "We need to get an ambulance here."

Richard Stanley, who had actually run around the backside of Christopher Moore's car during the shooting, started running toward the warehouse. "I'll call."

"Forget the ambulance," a groggy but still coherent Lynch said. "We need to put out an alert for him. And I need to get to Hanford." A large gash on his cheek seeped blood and it ran down and stained his collar.

Hancock said, "C'mon, Nick. I'll take you. Need any help getting back over there?" He hooked a thumb at the pipe warehouse.

"Hell no, cowboy." Lynch led as both men ran back toward the pipe warehouse. Seconds later, the engine sounded, gravel fanned into the air as Hancock gunned the engine and turned the Lincoln to Hanford.

Blaine stood. "Chris Moore can't hope to escape. As soon as we call this in, we'll have roadblocks over every highway, farm road, or dirt road. He can't get out."

Truman spun around and faced Edward. "Can he pilot a plane?"

Edward looked glum. "Yes, he can. I own an airplane. It's at a private airfield about seven miles from here."

Blaine said, "Mr. Moore, call Ira's station." He started to move across the street when a radio message through Webb's police radio stopped him. "John Brown, this is Denmark Vescey, the cherry blossoms have wilted." Expressionless, he looked at Truman.

The historian part of Truman's memory triggered with the references to "John Brown" and "Denmark Vescey" and made the assumption that the message must be a code. John Brown had led a raid on the armory at Harper's Ferry, Virginia, in 1859, with the hopes nearby slaves would follow. None did and Brown was executed. It was one of the last harbingers before the Civil War. Vescey was a former slave who had purchased his freedom and was accused of trying to start a slave revolt in South Carolina in 1822. He was executed prior to the planned insurrection.

The historical irony of those particular code names wasn't lost on Truman. He looked at Edward. The other man's face was ashen.

"Not now, not so soon," Moore whispered. He ran forward and slid in the driver's seat of Webb's patrol car. He picked up the transmitter. "This is John Brown. Go ahead, Denmark."

"Mr. Moore," the male voice on the other end of the radio said, "we've been discovered."

Moore lowered his head and closed his eyes.

Blaine made a guess. "Are those your Mountain Men friends?"

Moore nodded, his hair hanging in his face. "But not the kind you think."

Truman approached the cruiser. "Mr. Moore, your son's a traitor. Who the hell's on the other end of that radio?"

Moore, his shoulders slumped with the burden of secrecy, looked at Truman. "Make no mistake: they *are* a group of Americans. They have every reason to fear our government." He sighed. "They are my friends. And they just happen to be of Japanese ancestry."

Blaine and Truman exchanged glances but any additional words were cut off when the voice on the radio continued. "But there's something else. There was a plane, a *Japanese* plane."

Moore's head shot up. He looked at Blaine and Truman.

"Where?" Truman asked.

Moore asked the question. The response initially puzzled them. Moore rephrased the statement to get clarification. "You shot down the plane? How?"

"Fukiyama did it. He saw the markings on the plane during its first pass. On its second pass, he shot at the plane and hit either the pilot or some part of the machinery because it crashed. The explosion has caused a forest fire. We've already seen American planes circling. I think the Army's coming."

Moore put his face in his hands. "I'm sorry, Warren, I really am."

"Don't worry, Mr. Moore," Douglas said. "We all knew, deep

down, this day would come. You gave us two years of freedom. For that, we'll always be in your debt."

Deputy Duncan groaned. Blaine snapped back to the situation at hand. "Mr. Moore, we still need to apprehend your son. Call Webb's station. Stay with Joe until an ambulance arrives. In the meantime, I'm going after your son. We're still the closest unit to that airfield." He started running toward his cruiser parked at the pipe warehouse.

Truman matched the sheriff's pace.

Blaine stopped. "Senator Truman, I don't think it's a good idea for you to go with me."

"Shut up, Lester, and get in the car. I'll man the radio while you drive like a demon and we'll *both* get that son of a bitch."

51

Wednesday
19 April 1944
11:25 p.m., Pacific War Time

Christopher Moore brought his car to a halt at the main hangar of the airfield. He killed the engine and laid his head on the steering wheel. Everything hurt and he thought he might pass out. He took his belt off and made a makeshift tourniquet for his arm. He heard footsteps and looked up through the windshield.

"Hi, Mr. Moore. I have your plane ready and..." The young man's voice trailed off after he got a look at Christopher. He put up his hands when Christopher pointed the gun at him. "Hey, Mr. Moore, what is this? I..."

"Help me get the man in my trunk in my plane." He opened his door and got out of the car. The young man stood motionless.

Christopher opened the trunk and the young man gasped. "Who is that?"

"Prisoner of war," Christopher said. "You get his arms, I'll get his legs. And hurry." When the other man didn't move, Christopher cocked the gun and pointed it at the other man's head. "Do it!"

The young man snapped out of his state of fear and reached inside the trunk and grabbed the unconscious Burt Osborn from under the arms. Christopher pocketed the gun and grabbed Osborn's legs. The two of them moved the short distance to the Moore private plane. The younger man heaved the still unconscious body of Burt Osborn into the passenger seat.

"Tie his hands to the seat in front of him," Christopher said, leaning on the plane, weak from the exertion and adrenaline. He wiped his brow with his dirty handkerchief and saw something out of the corner of his eye.

A police car, lights flashing, siren blaring, sped along the far side of the airfield, straight toward the hangar.

* * *

"There he is," Truman shouted above the siren.

Blaine glanced toward the hanger. "I'm not sure we can get there in time. We may have to call in Army air support for this. Every plane here is civilian. No weapons."

Truman was silent for a moment. He looked toward the hanger where the Piper Cub started to taxi toward the runway.

"Turn that siren off, Lester," Truman said.

Blaine complied and then Truman continued. "I know this sounds out of left field but my guess is that Moore's flying to the submarine. There's probably some predetermined rendezvous point. What if we let him lead us there and then we can get the sub, too?"

Blaine shook his head. He braked and tires squealed as he turned the car into the airfield and straight for the hanger. "I don't know, Harry. That seems awfully risky. I just as soon shoot the bastard out of the sky and let the Navy take care of the sub."

"But the Navy's missed the sub for as long as it's been out there. Didn't you say you can fly a plane?"

Blaine looked at Truman out of the corner of his eyes. "Yes. Why?"

"Let's get a plane and follow him. We'll radio back to the Army and Navy once we have identified the sub's location."

"That's a damn fool idea, Harry."

"You got a better idea for getting Moore *and* the sub?" He pointed down the runway where Moore's plane was lifting off.

Blaine brought the car to an abrupt stop right in front of the hangar. "Let's go."

Both men scrambled out of the car and ran over to the man standing in the doorway of the hanger. The man was pointing toward the departing airplane and spouting gibberish. "Chris Moore had a man tied up in his trunk. He made me help him. I couldn't help it."

"Don't worry about it, son. I'm Sheriff Lester Blaine of Oregon. We're going after him." He pointed to the row of planes inside the hangar. "Which one is ready to go?"

52

Wednesday
19 April 1944
11:45 p.m., Pacific War Time

Hancock sat in the main security office in Hanford and felt utterly useless. There was a bustle of activity all around him but there was nothing for him to do.

He heard Lynch firing off order after order. Lynch, gauze patch on his cheek, had sent out three companies of men to seal off the crash site and contain the fire. Hancock overheard the first reports from the field about a group of people out near the crash site. The group appeared to be Japanese. He had also heard about the casualties.

Oblivious to the activity, Hancock strolled around the main office, looking at all the paraphernalia on each individual desk. On one he saw a sketch drawing of a seaplane and realized this must have been the one the prisoner had drawn. He looked at it and noted that the drawing was, indeed, good.

Having nothing else to do, Hancock decided to see if he could fill in the gaps of his investigation. He found the holding cells and looked through the small windows until he found a room with a single man sitting at the table. Hancock entered the room and shut the door.

"You must be the man named Frank," Hancock said.

"Who are you?" The man's voice cracked with fatigue.

"Carl Hancock. I'm a special investigator for Senator Harry Truman's committee. We came out here to investigate some strange things at Edward Moore's warehouse and stumbled onto this." Hancock hooked a thumb over his shoulder in the direction of the door. He walked over to the table and sat down opposite Frank. He placed the drawing on the table. "I was wondering if you could fill in some details to the story the Senator and I have constructed."

"I guess the game's up now, huh?"

Hancock nodded. "You're one of the Mountain Men, right?"

"Yes. So were Ronnie and Jack."

"The dead men. Sorry for your loss. So, how did a group of men who hated the peacetime draft become a front for hiding a bunch of Japanese-Americans?"

Frank smiled. "That was all Mr. Moore's idea. From the beginning, he was with us. But, because of his high stature in the community, he couldn't join us. So, he provided us with supplies. You know about his childhood years spent in Japan?"

Hancock nodded.

"Anyway, Mr. Moore has always admired the Japanese way of life. He even fell in love with a Japanese girl and wanted to marry her. His parents didn't approve and prevented him from marrying the girl. Soon after that, he came to Seattle and started working. Years later, he builds this great warehousing empire across the Pacific Northwest. But he still can't get over the first broken heart."

Frank chuckled dryly. "Truth is I admired the Japanese way of life myself. Now, that don't mean I wanted to join them."

Hancock was silent for a moment, allowing the other man his private thoughts. Idly, he spun Frank's drawing around under one finger. Every few revolutions, the drawing would be right side up. As Hancock continued to look at the picture, something tickled the back of his mind. He could not quite put his finger on it until he replayed Frank's last words.

Hancock leaned forward. "What do you mean by 'they'? Is that the general 'they' as in the enemy?"

Frank shook his head. "No, I mean the 'they' that killed Ron and Jack. From the plane." Frank pointed at the drawing. "There were two men in the plane."

Hancock stared at Frank. In his mind, Hancock tried to recall if the field reports he overhead mentioned a pilot or pilots. He stood and sprinted out of the room.

He ran straight up to Lynch who was talking on the telephone. Hancock didn't wait for a break in Lynch's conversation. "How many bodies did your men find in the plane?"

Lynch put a hand over the receiver. "What? Carl, I'm in the middle of a…"

"How many bodies did you men find in the plane?"

Lynch frowned, Hancock's question still not registering. Hancock held up the drawing in front of Lynch's face and pointed toward the cockpit. "It's a two-seater, Nick. How many bodies?"

Hancock saw clarity enter Lynch's eyes. He handed the telephone to a staff sergeant and called out, "Ross, how many bodies were in the plane?" Lynch's voice was so loud in the room that everyone stopped and looked at him.

"I think they said one," Ross said.

Lynch's mouth tightened. "Don't think. Verify." He looked at Hancock who returned his stare. Hancock could feel his heart sinking before Ross even relayed the question back to the field. For a few tense seconds, most of the activity in the room ceased.

Everyone in the room heard the soldier from the field answer the question: "One pilot, sir. The other seat is empty and the canopy isn't broken, as would be consistent with the person being thrown from the seat."

"Dammit!" Lynch said. He ran both his hands through his hair and looked at the ceiling. All the activity in the room started up again as people continued with their tasks.

"Nick, look," Hancock said, "can't we narrow down possible

targets? We know Moore is in cahoots with the Japanese. With his access, chances are he'd know enough about this area to at least give the Japs a list of best places to commit sabotage."

Lynch looked at him. "It's not that easy, Carl. Hanford is about 670 square miles of area. That's half a million acres. I'd need Ike's army in Europe to canvas this area in the time we have."

Hancock smiled reassuringly. "But there has to be a main target or two. I mean, those tall buildings out north of here seem pretty important. What about those?"

Lynch sighed. "Yes, they're very important. They're the most crucial things around here." He turned toward Ross. "I want every sentry around"—he eyed Hancock and then continued—"the reactors to report in. I want every available platoon stationed around all the reactors. I want reports every minute."

"Yes, sir," Ross said and relayed the orders. Lynch started to bite his fingernails as the reports were delivered.

* * *

OUTSIDE OF THE structure known as Reactor-B, Ishihara crouched behind a line of trash cans. As far as he could tell, no one yet suspected he was there.

Overhead, planes circled. Alarms and sirens blared in the distance. He realized that Niigata must have been discovered. He returned his attention to his prey.

The sentry was on alert, his rifle in a ready position. But he was still looking outward. Ishihara had already breached the sentry line and was now, in essence, behind enemy lines.

Ishihara took out his knife and held it at the ready. As the sentry paused to retrace his steps, Ishihara stepped toward him. With his left hand, Ishihara covered the sentry's mouth and with his right, he slit the sentry's throat. He cut hard and deep, severing the man's windpipe, carotid artery, and vocal cords. The sentry went limp and Ishihara let him fall to the ground. Ishihara picked up the rifle.

That was three Americans killed for his family of five. Only two more to go.

* * *

"Sir, the sentry at Reactor B doesn't respond. I've tried twice now."

Lynch pointed to Ross. "I want double the manpower at Reactor B now. But remind the men of the delicate nature of the building. No unnecessary firing."

Hancock pulled out Webb's pistol he had kept and checked the load.

Lynch put a hand on Hancock's arm. "What do you think you're doing?"

Hancock re-holstered his gun in his jacket pocket. "I'm coming with you. You can think of me as one of your men for all I care." He looked Lynch squarely in the eyes. "But I want to help nail this bastard."

The fury in Hancock's voice was all Lynch needed. "Okay, you're with me."

53

Wednesday
19 April 1944
11:55 p.m., Pacific War Time

Burt Osborn awoke. His head ached. He tried to touch it. For some reason, his hands could not move. Through fluttering eyelids, he saw why. His hands were tied together and they, in turn, were tied to the seat. He looked up and realized he was in an airplane and it was night.

He looked over at the person piloting the plane. It was Christopher Moore. Osborn tried to speak but found tape over his mouth.

Christopher reached over and removed the tape over Osborn's mouth.

"What the hell's going on?" Osborn shouted.

Moore stared straight ahead. "You're a prisoner of war. I'm taking you to a Japanese submarine.

Osborn stared at Moore in horror and bewilderment. "What? Why?"

"Because they need your assistance."

Osborn opened his mouth but no sound came out. He tugged at his bonds but they held fast. He looked over at Moore in disbelief.

Moore continued. "Your knowledge of that big bomb you're making, I'm delivering you to them so that you can help them build one of their own."

"Like hell I am!" Osborn tugged again at the ropes. "Look, Chris, there's no way on God's green Earth that I'm going to help the Japs build anything to use against our boys. You can take that to the bank."

Moore smiled but without humor. "There are ways to make a person talk."

They said nothing for the next few minutes. Osborn looked at Moore's condition. The young man had a belt acting as a tourniquet, he was bleeding from his ear, and he appeared to be crying.

"You suddenly grow a conscience? We can turn back, you know. You've not done anything yet."

Moore looked over at him. "You don't know what I've done."

"What have you done?"

Moore wiped his eyes. He flexed his hands on the stick. "Not only am I bringing you to them, they're launching a raid at Hanford. And I helped them."

"You son of a bitch!" he tugged violently at his bonds. "What in blue blazes are you thinking? You know that we need to build our bomb before the Nazis do. If they beat us to it, we're done for. Our freedom will die."

"Freedom?" Moore yelled. "Whose freedom?"

"American freedom, you idiot. It's being on the side that's right."

"On the right side? The Americans are on the right side? How can you tell? We get reports of the Nazis shipping Jews and God knows who else to camps and we do nothing. I don't even want to think about what happens next. Those are the enemy. And we hate them for that."

"But right here, in our own country, our own state and cities, Americans are shipped off to camps just because they look like our enemy. They vote, they speak English, they pay taxes, and they're just like you and me. So what if their names are Sakai or Inouye? They're *Americans*."

Osborn sighed. "Yeah, we get it a little wrong every now and then. But this is still the best damn country on Earth."

"'Every now and then'? You got the slaves, the Indians, the Chinese, the Japanese, the Irish. You want me to go on?"

Osborn shook his head. "We aren't perfect. But we're still a hell of a lot better than Hitler's krauts or Tojo's rice eaters."

Moore threw a fist out at Osborn and hit him squarely in the nose. Blood started to seep down around his lips and into his mouth. Osborn had to wipe the blood off on his sleeve as his hands could not reach his face.

"Don't you ever say that about the Japanese again! They're good people. I was born there. And I'm going home."

"I *am* home, you son of a bitch," Osborn said. He spat blood in Moore's face. The result was another punch to the face.

Again, they said nothing to each other. Finally, Osborn said, "I thought we were friends."

"We are, were."

"Well, which is it? 'Are' or 'were'? Either way, friends don't give friends over to the enemy."

"They're not my enemy. They never have been. I've heard enough of this." Moore let go of the stick and grabbed Osborn's hair and held it firm. With his other hand, he brought the cloth with chloroform up to Osborn's nose and mouth.

Osborn, for his part, was not without a fight. He banged his head and Moore's hand on the back of the cockpit wall, causing Moore to lose his grip on Osborn's hair. Then, Osborn thrashed from side to side, denying Moore a clean point of contact with the cloth.

In the end, however, Moore gained the upper hand. He elbowed Osborn in the temple and stunned the scientist. Moore was then able to apply the chloroform. The dosage was not as high as the first time so it took a few minutes for Osborn to lose consciousness.

In the meantime, the Piper Cub drifted off course. Moore settled back in his seat and was about to reset the course when he looked out of his window. He saw nothing. He readjusted his course and continued toward the Pacific.

* * *

"Do you think he saw us?" Truman asked.

"Don't think so," Blaine said. "I've kept her higher than Moore's plane. When I saw the plane drifting to port, I moved us a bit to his starboard. I think we're alright."

Truman gestured at Moore's plane. "Why do you think they drifted?"

"Well, if I were that guy and Moore told me what he was up to, I'd jump."

Truman nodded. "I think I would, too. Or do anything in my power to get away. Or crash the plane. Ain't no way in hell you get me to even serve them tea."

54

Thursday
20 April 1944
12:05 a.m., Pacific War Time

Lynch gathered his officers around him. Hancock stood with the other officers. They were all outside the main door of Reactor B on the northern edge of Hanford.

"Listen, I want to make this perfectly clear. What we are building here will help us end this war. What we are building here will bring our boys home alive. Above all else, we need to make sure this project stays on schedule. We don't want the Nazis to build one of their own and use it on us. I don't want anyone just firing willy-nilly at anything in there. We can't just throw grenades and hope the roof caves in on the Jap. We have to find him and kill him *without* damaging the building. Make that crystal clear to all your men. Understood?"

Everyone grunted an affirmative.

"Okay. Let's move. We all enter in sixty seconds. Mark."

All the officers returned to their predetermined locations. Lynch had surrounded the reactor with six platoons. Each platoon was responsible for one section of the interior of the reactor. Lynch's plan was to fan out his men and keep them stationary after securing an area. That way, the only places unchecked would be places the Japanese soldier would be.

Lynch looked up at the building in front of him. Reactor 100-B was a large structure with multi-tiered levels, looking somewhat like the top of the Empire State Building but without the tower. Lynch had reminded his teams that the initial construction was due to finish in the next couple of months. If the commando was able to destroy any part of this structure, the whole project could be jeopardized.

He looked at his watch. The second hand reached the top of the dial and he motioned with his pistol to move out. Hancock walked next to him.

Before they reached the front door, a single shot rang out. A soldier not twelve feet away fell to the ground. The soldiers in Lynch's team crouched and scattered. They looked up at the open window but there was nothing to see.

Lynch was about to give the order to move ahead when he caught sight of Hancock running toward the front door. The tall Texan's gait covered the ground in half the time it would take Lynch to get there.

He knew he could not call out to Hancock for that would give away his position. The only thing to do was join him. "Follow the cowboy," Lynch said to his team. He stood up and ran for the door.

* * *

HANCOCK REACHED the door and opened it, crouching and pointing his gun into the open area. He saw nothing. He heard footsteps behind him and saw Lynch run up next to him. Other soldiers followed.

"What took you so long?" Hancock asked.

"I wanted you to roll out the red carpet, cowboy. See anything?"

"Nope. But I'm glad you decided to keep the lights on. Makes our job just a teensy bit easier."

"Didn't want to make it too hard."

Hancock could hear the humor in Lynch's voice but the security chief face was all business. "What now?"

Lynch directed to of his officers to move on both the left and right hallways. To Hancock and his third officer, he said, "We go straight to the reactor and secure it."

Hancock fell in line to Lynch's right. Both men held their pistols at arm's length and at the ready. Every so often, a member of Lynch's team would break off and remain behind.

Lynch raised a hand and stopped his team at a door. He motioned for silence and motioned for Hancock to cover him. Lynch grasped the door handle and burst through the door. Hancock was right on his heels aiming for a head shot. The other men streamed in behind him.

Hancock stood just inside the doorway and stared at the strangest thing he had ever seen. He knew enough about this facility to gather that it was designed to make a bomb. But he expected the interior to look similar to other bomb-making factories he had inspected.

He stood in front of a wall, several feet tall. But the wall was not solid. It had innumerable small holes bored into it. On either side, he saw pipes leading to the top and behind the wall. In the middle was a type of scaffolding and, judging from the wheels underneath the platform, the scaffolding could move up and down along the face of the wall.

"What in God's name is this thing?"

Lynch stood off to Hancock's left. "All you need to care about is that it's going to bring our GIs home alive."

* * *

Ishihara peeked around the wall he used as a cover. He had judged correctly that the interior of this building contained the most important part of this bomb factory. It was the strangest factory he had ever seen. But if what the American traitor had said was true, this bomb was unlike any other bomb ever made.

The soldier he had shot outside as the Americans moved in had made four dead Americans to his family of five. One more and his family would be avenged.

Ishihara saw every man but one wearing a uniform. The one not in uniform was taller than the rest and he wore boots and a cowboy hat. Ishihara chuckled to himself. He had seen some American movies and knew that this man must be some sort of cowboy. What was more appropriate than killing a cowboy to avenge his family? And he was standing right in the middle of the room.

He looked left and right and marked where he would move next. He rested his arm along the pillar, steadied his aim, and fired.

* * *

HANCOCK DIDN'T EVEN HEAR the shot. The bullet hit him above the heart and lodged in his clavicle, splintering it. He fell face forward but had enough gumption to throw out his right arm and absorb most of his weight. Still, his head cracked on the cement floor and he saw a red haze as he rolled over on his back and looked up at the lights. His hat rolled on its top, rocking.

"Carl!" Lynch shouted.

One of the soldiers fired off a shot at a darting blur of khaki and a chip of cement flew off of the pillar. Lynch ran to Hancock's side.

"How bad?"

Hancock tried to sit up but failed. "Not bad." He coughed and blood spattered Lynch's shirt. He smiled. "Okay, maybe." He motioned up to where the shot originated. "Go get the bastard."

Lynch took another moment to examine Hancock's clothes. Though he tried to hide it, the look on his face said more than words.

He pointed at two men. "Get him over there, out of range." To the other pair of soldiers, the major waved once. "Follow me."

Two of the men reached down and hooked their hands under Hancock's armpits. They yanked his torso up. The investigator groaned with the electric jolts of pain that coursed through his body.

He blinked away the pain, willing himself to stay conscious. He focused on his Stetson which rested on the middle of the floor. Only when he reached the wall and the soldiers propped him up against it did he note just how much of his own blood was smeared on the floor.

Hancock reached in his jacket and withdrew his handkerchief. He dabbed his mouth, looked at the handkerchief, and saw the blood on it. The amount of blood and its brightness wasn't good. The pain in his shoulder burned with each heartbeat. Every beat of his heart seemed to shoot fire through his veins. His breathing started to become shallower.

"You boys better go get that son of a bitch," Hancock said. He willed his voice to remain strong. It complied. "I'll be fine."

"I don't think you'll be fine," said the soldier to his left. He was brawny, his shoulder muscles straining the seams of his uniform.

"Maybe. Maybe not. But in either case, you can do more good chasing the Jap than you can babysitting me." He coughed. Blood sprayed on the ground. A pang of realization settled him. It simultaneously made him angry, sad, and scared.

He noticed that the two soldiers to his right and left were scanning the room but on the ground level. Hancock looked up and examined the spaces between the cement pillars on the second and third levels.

Behind one pillar, Hancock saw the Japanese soldier. The man's khaki uniform was bright against the gray cement walls. He didn't know where Lynch or any of the other soldiers were although he could hear their boots pounding on the floor. He inhaled and tried to speak but he felt liquid in his lungs. He coughed again.

Hancock raised his gun and fired.

His aim was off and the bullet ricocheted off a metal stair.

But what he saw tumbling down to the ground made his wife and children flash before his eyes.

* * *

FROM HIS NEW VANTAGE POINT, Ishihara looked down to the ground level. He saw the blood smear and the cowboy sitting up against the wall, still alive. He was about to fire again when he had a different idea.

He reached down to his belt and took off a grenade. He thought that killing five Americans would only equal the deaths of his father, mother, two sisters, and an uncle. Why not take more?

He pulled the pin but then had to duck as the cowboy saw him and fired. Too late for the cowboy, Ishihara thought, and tossed the grenade down to the floor.

He heard the grenade land on the cement floor and bounce up. What Ishihara didn't count on was the combination of the cowboy's shot and the origin point of the grenade to be calculated so quickly. Ishihara never even saw the man who shot him. The bullet entered Ishihara's stomach and exited through his spine. His legs were paralyzed before he even hit the floor.

The shouts of the Americans sounded far away and Ishihara realized his hearing was fading. He still held his pistol and he raised it with a shaking hand. An American soldier came into his view. Judging by the strips the man was a major.

Ishihara smiled. A major would count as two.

The gun felt incredibly heavy as his body began to shut down. It was all he could do to hold the pistol. He didn't even have the strength to pull the trigger. Not that it mattered. The American major simply kicked the gun out of Ishihara's hand. His arm fell to the floor. He could not move it.

Ishihara's eyesight began to fail. He could see the faces of his family. Ishihara didn't fear death; he feared he would not be able to avenge their deaths. He began to move his other hand toward the grenades on his belt. The American officer kicked that hand away and kneeled down on top of it.

The gaijin's face filled Ishihara's entire vision, blotting out the visages of his family. In his mouth, Ishihara tasted blood.

The gaijin leaned closer to Ishihara's ear and whispered the last thing Ishihara ever heard. *"Temae-wa janjitsu feiru."* Today, you failed.

* * *

WHEN THE SOLDIERS next to him saw the grenade, they did what every soldier is trained to do: they scrambled away from the deadly weapon. Their boots scraped on the concrete floor as they ran away and ducked for cover.

Hancock couldn't scramble. He could barely move. Each breath proved a dreadful combination of pain from his injured body and the feeling of liquid in his lungs.

Despite his physical condition, Hancock was still seeing his family in his mind's eye when the grenade hit the concrete floor and bounced toward him. He figured that one second had already elapsed. Two seconds remaining.

He saw his wife on their wedding day. He saw his daughter on the day of her birth; then on her wedding day. He saw his son, as a boy and then all grown up, wearing a Texas Rangers' uniform.

Hancock smiled. "I'll be damned."

The grenade skittered across the floor toward his position.

In all the personal memories flooding his mind, Hancock almost admired the Jap commando. He was pretty damned accurate.

One second remaining.

The next second slowed and everything for Carl Hancock became crystal clear. He saw his family and they were all smiling. He saw newsreel footage of the war and explosions. He saw dead Americans lined up on battlefields. He remembered his time in World War I and all the death he experienced as an infantry soldier. He remembered how he just wanted all the death to end.

He looked up and saw the giant wall in front of him. In his mind, Lynch's words rang out: "What we are building here will help us end this war. What we are building here will bring our boys home alive."

He decided to do his part for the boys overseas.

Carl Hancock slumped over and covered the grenade with his body.

Zero seconds.

55

Thursday
20 April 1944
12: 25 a.m., Pacific War Time

Captain Jim Gordon stood on the bridge of the destroyer *U. S. S. Cheyenne*. He scanned the dark Pacific horizon and saw nothing but a black line.

"Report."

The navigator looked up at the captain. "Nothing, sir. Are you sure this isn't a drill?"

"This came straight from the top. Any word from the *Nantucket*?"

"No, sir. They're three miles to port. Last report was five minutes ago." The navigator thought for a moment. "Sir, what are we looking for?"

The captain's eyes remained fixed out the window. "A Jap sub, Woody."

"Holy crow!" Woody exclaimed. "How the hell did it get here?"

"That's a damn good question. But one thing's for certain: it ain't getting out."

* * *

Captain Morimoto also scanned the horizon but his gaze was trained toward the sky. He had kept the submarine surfaced and the lights off. The inky water splashed over the white-painted steel. Not for the first time did he wish his sub was painted gun metal.

He had ordered his communications officer to monitor American air waves. The communications officer knew a little English, enough so that he could understand if the Americans had been alerted to their presence.

As Morimoto stood atop the conning tower, he felt a tapping on his foot from the open hatch on the deck. He looked down and his communications officer was beckoning him down into the ship.

"Captain, there is something you must hear," the officer said. He climbed back down the ladder and Morimoto followed him.

The communications officer handed a pair of headphones and Morimoto put them on. What he heard alarmed him but didn't really surprise him. The American traitor thought too much of his own military ability. Morimoto knew better.

"This is Senator Harry Truman. I am in pursuit of a Piper Cub aircraft piloted by Christopher Moore, a traitor. He has a hostage. He is trying to rendezvous with a Japanese submarine. I am requesting any air or naval assistance to stop this plane."

Morimoto dropped the headphones. He switched on the intercom and sounded an alert. All activity in the submarine ceased as every sailor stopped to listen to Morimoto.

"We have to take aboard two allies. They are coming in by airplane. They will land and we will retrieve them without the Americans discovering us. This mission is vital to the Emperor and the preservation of our way of life. Do all in your power to make sure this mission succeeds."

He switched off the intercom and toggled the red alert klaxon. To his engineer, he said, "Prepare for a crash dive. Are the batteries charged?"

"Fully."

"Good." Morimoto turned to his gunner. "I want fore and aft

torpedoes at the ready. If that message is received by the Americans, we will have destroyers and cutters and planes down on us in no time."

"Not if we shoot them out of the sky." The gunner's eyes showed a clear desire to go hunting.

The captain smiled. "I agree. Order your gunners on deck."

Morimoto motioned to his signalman to follow him to the conning tower. Both men climbed the ladder and looked out into the night.

There was about ten minutes of tense waiting. Every man on the submarine did what all men under combat do: they thought about family, they thought about their country, they thought about their nation, they thought about what they had to do.

The signalman saw the lights first. He tapped Morimoto's arm and pointed toward the eastern sky.

Three red lights—one on each wingtip and one atop the tail fin —moved among the stars. Morimoto scanned the sky and found the second, fainter set of three lights.

"It looks like they are flying higher to avoid detection. Do you think our ally knows he is being followed?"

"Not likely. Flash the signal and we will verify which plane turns." Into his intercom, he relayed the orders to the gunnery officer: shoot down the higher plane.

The signalman flashed the prearranged signal. The plane flying lower veered off its course and made its way toward the submarine.

* * *

"Do you see anything out there?" Blaine asked.

Truman scanned the horizon out his side windows and down at the vast black ocean. "I can't see the water, much less the Jap sub."

"Switch channels and try the radio again."

Truman repeated his message. The radio crackled with a response. "Senator Truman, this is the *U.S.S. Cheyenne.* What is your heading and bearing?"

The grin across Truman's face was never bigger. "Good to hear you, *Cheyenne.* We are flying at 9,000 feet, three thousand above the suspect. We cannot see the submarine but he is expected to…wait, he's changing course."

Blaine continued to fly in his westerly pattern. He and Truman both looked down at the new direction Moore took his plane.

"*Cheyenne,* this is Truman. The plane has changed course and is appearing to land on the water." Truman toggled off the radio and pointed down to the water. "Lester, what are those flashes?"

"Tracers!" Blaine shouted as bullets screamed past their plane.

* * *

The navigator on the *U.S.S. Cheyenne* toggled the intercom. "Captain, we have them!"

Gordon hustled to the bridge. "Status, Woody."

Woody pointed to where a stream of tracer bullets had just lit up the sky. "Tracers came from that direction."

"Tracers?" Gordon asked. "What are they shooting at?"

The communications officer, Jasper, spoke up. "A second plane, sir. There's a Harry Truman on board. He said the first plane has an American traitor that is trying to rendezvous with the sub."

Gordon looked through his binoculars. "Well, tell him to get the hell out of there. We'll take over from here. Woody, full speed ahead. Jasper, radio the *Nantucket* with the coordinates. Gunner, ready the forward torpedoes and charges."

Jasper relayed the messages, first to the *Nantucket* and then to Truman. He pushed a button so that everyone in the bridge could hear Truman's response. "We're hit. Heading back to shore for an emergency landing."

The radio crackled then Truman came back on for a final message.

"Give'em hell, *Cheyenne!*"

56

Thursday
20 April 1944
12:33 a.m., Pacific War Time

Christopher Moore slowed the plane as much as possible but the impact on the water still threw him and Osborn forward in their seats. Both men looked up out of the cockpit. The dark shape of a conning tower blocked the stars.

Water seeped through cracks and joints. The plane listed to starboard and Osborn's window looked directly into the ocean.

Osborn, his hands still tied, realized his only course of action: do not let Moore deliver him to the Japanese alive. He looked to his window, the only barrier from a gush of seawater rushing into the cockpit and sinking the plane. Without another thought, Osborn slammed his head against the window. It cracked and more water trickled into the cockpit.

Christopher saw what Osborn was trying to do. "Hell no you don't. I've come too far. I will not let you die on me."

With that, Christopher unsheathed his knife and cut the rope holding Osborn's bound hands to the seat. He dragged his friend out through the pilot door.

Osborn's head was muddled with the force of the impact but he still had his wits about him to see what was happening. He swallowed seawater and started to cough and sputter. Christopher held onto the rope still binding his hands.

Osborn started to thrash and tug violently at Christopher's grasp. He managed to break free from Christopher as he heard two splashes.

On both sides of him, Osborn saw Japanese sailors wearing life jackets. They bobbed in the water and swam towards him. The only thing left to do was go under and not come up. He didn't even hold his breath.

A few feet underwater, strong hands gripped his hair and pulled. The pain made his shout and water went into his lungs. Osborn breached the surface and coughed. Through blurry eyes, he saw a rope thrown down and affixed to his hands. With a powerful heave, he was dragged from the water and deposited on the deck.

He rolled over on his side and let the water run out of his mouth. He saw other sailors pull Christopher from the water and throw him unceremoniously onto the deck as well. Despite his attire and shaky legs, Christopher managed to stand. "Permission to come aboard, Captain?"

The captain slapped Christopher across the face. He said something in Japanese that Osborn could not understand. However, when the captain pointed out to sea, Osborn understood.

Making its way toward them were two destroyers.

* * *

THE INTERIOR of the submarine stank of sweat and smoke and machine oil. Despite all that he had been through, Osborn wondered how the Japanese sailors could take it.

He and Christopher were hustled to the main crew mess area and thrown onto a bench. The captain motioned to a sailor to stand guard. Osborn noticed that Christopher was clearly upset. Osborn assumed that Christopher considered his treatment to be unjustified. Good, thought Osborn, traitors don't deserve any special treatment.

Over the intercom, Osborn could hear orders fly back and forth. Knowing not a word of Japanese, he was lost. He looked at Christopher. The red print of the captain's hand was still visible on the younger man's face. "Hey, buddy, since you speak the language, how about filling me in a little. The suspense is killing me."

Christopher threw Osborn a hurt look. He touched the place where the captain had hit him. He acted like a dog that had been spanked. "The destroyers are coming at us from two sides. I think they're trying a crash dive to see if we can lose them."

"I hope not."

The alarms and shouts were loud. Osborn wondered how any good action could come from such harried activity. The submarine changed angles as it dove under the water. Pots and pans began sliding against their restraints. Osborn and Christopher had to hold onto the fixed tables for balance. Their guard grasped the door frame and it was at that moment Osborn first noticed the guard's sidearm.

The captain delivered another order via the intercom and almost all motion and action stopped. Osborn said, "What's up?"

"You'd better hold on tight. Depth charges have been launched."

Seconds later, great explosions rocked the submarine. The lights flickered and a valve released steam. The guard reached up and closed the valve. From the rear of the submarine, Osborn heard a loud clang. He guessed that something had just broken. The smooth churning noise the engines had been making began to sound strained. Smoke started to billow through the aft bay.

Christopher was thrown against the bulkhead while Osborn fell off the bench and to the feet of the guard, who slipped and fell over Osborn. The guard regained his footing and kicked Osborn in the ribs, motioning him back on the bench. Osborn shot the guard a furious look but complied.

Osborn overhead the captain gave a frantic order. The constant thrumming that was the submarine's diesel engines stopped. The only sound was the creaking of joints and the breathing of scared men.

In the silence, every man could hear the destroyers circling, searching with sonar for their prey. Osborn whispered to Christopher. "Are those the destroyers?"

"Yeah. I don't think they can hear us."

"How long can we stay quiet down here?"

Christopher asked the guard. "The batteries are fully charged. We could be down here an hour or so."

Everyone sat in silence. Osborn stared at the guard's gun. He noticed how it lay in its holster, how he might open it and get the gun with his hands still tied. He studied his bonds and realized that there was no way to untie the ropes in time.

For all his scientific knowledge, he didn't know how sensitive the Navy's sonar equipment was. He wondered if they would be able to hear gunshots through the hull. He decided to test just how sensitive the Japanese were to being quiet. He started coughing, loudly, and doubled over.

Christopher glared at Osborn. "Shut up, will you? Do you want them to hear us?"

Still coughing, Osborn fell to the floor, next to the feet of the guard. Uttering something Osborn hoped was a curse, the guard bent down to lift Osborn up off the floor. Osborn went limp and then stiffened as he coughed. The result was that the guard had to use both hands to drag him up off the floor.

That was the opening Osborn had wanted. In one move, he unsnapped the guard's holster and slammed the guard up against the wall. With his arms pinned by Osborn's body, the guard was unable to prevent Osborn from unholstering the pistol. Osborn swung his right leg forward and knocked the guard's feet out from under him. The guard fell to the floor.

Osborn turned toward Christopher Moore and brought the gun up to bear. Without thinking or saying anything, Osborn started pulling the trigger. He emptied the magazine before two other sailors tackled him. They kicked him and punched him, knocking a tooth out and splitting his lip.

He looked at Christopher Moore. The traitor's eyes were open, staring at him. His chest was still rising, slightly, so Osborn knew Christopher was still alive but not for long.

"Yes, you son of a bitch, I want them to hear us."

* * *

THE SONAR OFFICER on the *Cheyenne* looked up at Captain Gordon. "Sir, I think I just heard gunshots."

"Do you have a fix on the source?"

"Yes, sir."

Gordon toggled the intercom. "Launch all remaining charges at this mark now." He stepped out of the bridge and looked aft. He saw the white splashes each charge made as it entered the water. He stepped back into the bridge. "Radio the *Nantucket*. Bring them about to our location and tell them to drop charges. We are not leaving here until I hear that baby crack."

* * *

MORIMOTO SLID down the ladder from the bridge as soon as he heard the gunshots. His face was drained of color. He strode back to the mess area. He saw two of his men holding a bloodied Osborn. He also saw the American, Koishii, Christopher Moore, dead on the bench, the traitor's blood flowing down the bench and onto the floor.

In English, the captain said, "You realize you have just signed your death warrant?"

"As long as I can take you and your damn submarine with me, I'm okay with that."

The captain regarded Osborn with a serious air then nodded to the scientist. Everyone heard the sound of additional depth charges splashing in the water.

Osborn said, "I would assume the Navy knows the depth now?"

The captain shrugged. "Not necessarily. But they know the location. All they have to do is keep dropping the charges. Our engines are damaged and, even if they were not, I cannot start them up as that would make too much sound. So, this is it."

Osborn nodded but didn't smile.

"Mr. Osborn, you know why you were abducted, do you not?"

"Because of the work I do."

"If you please tell me one thing: is this bomb you are making really as devastating as Mr. Moore said it is?"

Osborn regarded Morimoto. He brought his bound hands up to his face and wiped away the blood that ran down his cheek. "What did he tell you?"

"He never really said. All he said was that this one bomb could change the course of the war."

Osborn pursed his lips and nodded once. "I see." He laughed dryly. "Damn fool didn't even know what he was dealing with." He looked at Morimoto, a gleam in his eyes. "Can you send out a radio signal at this depth?"

A depth charge detonated too early and above the submarine. The ship shook and Morimoto reached out a hand to steady himself. More lights flickered. From somewhere deep in the sub came the sound of metal creaking. He shook his head.

"Truth is no one really knows what kind of bomb it will be. But all indications are that one bomb will be able to destroy an entire city."

Morimoto looked down toward the deck and nodded. "Then you will win the war."

The last things Captain Hiroyuki Morimoto, Burt Osborn, and the crew of the Japanese submarine heard were the sound of exploding depth charges, the cracking of the hull, and the onrush of seawater into the submarine.

57

Thursday
20 April 1944
10:45 a.m., Pacific War Time

Harry Truman sat in Colonel Matthias's office across a table from the colonel and Major Lynch. He was haggard. After Blaine had managed to land the plane on the beach, the two men had been picked up by the Army. After learning about Hancock, Truman insisted he be driven back to Hanford only to be denied admittance. The attempted sabotage of the Hanford reactor caused an immediate lockdown of all unauthorized personnel. Truman had been told to go back to the hotel and get some sleep.

He didn't sleep. He started writing his committee report of all that he and Hancock had discovered and assumed. He included Edward Moore's embezzling, Christopher Moore's treachery, and the fugitive Japanese-Americans living in the restricted zone on the western coast. He put it all in the report and managed only an hour's worth of sleep.

"Why can't I see Carl?"

Matthias said, "It's just not possible at this time."

"What's his condition?"

"We can't say."

"Can't or won't?"

Matthias shrugged. "All unauthorized personnel are being denied admittance to Hanford."

Truman spread his hands around the room. "But I'm *in* Hanford now. Why can't I get a straight answer from you? What happened to him? Why can't I see him? What am I going to tell his wife?"

"Leave that to us, Senator," Matthias said.

Lynch said, "Senator, since we had our *training accident* last night, security has been beefed up, especially since we're having such a distinguished guest as you visit us."

Trumas narrowed his eyes. "'Training accident'"

Lynch slid a folded newspaper across to Truman. The senator picked it up and unfolded it. He scanned the front page, trying to determine why it was so important. Below the fold, on the right side, was this story.

TRAINING ACCIDENT CLAIMS PILOT LIVES, Starts Forest Fire

Last night, in a routine training exercise over Richland and Hanford, events took a dreadful turn. Pilot Brad Bartlett and his navigator, Leo Spencer, lost control of their plane and crashed. Their last act of heroism was to avoid the populated areas of our fair cities and fly north to crash in an unpopulated wooded area north of the Columbia. The resulting explosion started a fire that burned several dozen acres before the Army Corps of Engineers contained the blaze.

The two men were awarded posthumous Purple Heart awards. Their names will be specially mentioned in today's speech by Colonel Franklin T. Matthias.

TRUMAN LAID the paper back on the table. "But that's a flat out lie. That's not the way it happened at all. It directly contradicts my report. After my committee publishes the report, everyone will know the truth."

"There will not be any report, Senator Truman." The voice was not that of Matthias or Lynch. A portly man, dressed in a formal Army uniform of a dark blazer over khaki pants, walked into the room. Both Matthias and Lynch rose and saluted. Truman rose as well but didn't salute.

The man returned the salute and faced Truman. He extended his hand. "General Leslie Groves."

Truman shook his hand. "I know who you are, general." All four men sat.

Groves got right to the point. "We can't have you writing, submitting, or publishing a report, no matter how much truth it has in it."

"Why not?" Truman blurted. "That's my job."

"And our job is to win this war."

"I'm trying to *help* you win the war," Truman persisted. "As I've told you military brass types countless times, my goal is not to bog you down but to make everyone accountable and…"

Groves held up a hand. "Save it, Senator. I'm not your constituent."

"Like hell you're not. You're an American and the American people are my constituency and my work speaks for them."

Matthias spoke up. "The general's right, Senator. We can't have you making a report about anything that happened here."

Truman tapped the table as he spoke. "Why the hell not?"

"Because," Groves said, plastering a photo-op smile on his face, "if you were to make a report about all that went on here this week, the press would get a hold of it. They would come here and start asking questions. Someone would discover the important work we're doing here and print it in a newspaper. Then, a Nazi spy or a Jap spy would read the newspaper and report back to Tokyo or Berlin and let everyone know our little secret. There goes our biggest weapon: surprise."

He sighed. "Besides, we already had a damn Jap spy *inside* the facility. You cannot possibly imagine how much damage he could have done." He glanced at his two subordinates. Truman got the impression the debrief with Lynch and Matthias would not be pleasant.

Groves leaned on the table. "You're a good senator, Mr. Truman, and a good American. You fought for this country in the last war and you know what it's like to lose a man in battle. What we're doing here will *save men's lives*, theirs as well as ours. I know you can appreciate that. You love this country. I know you will see the right thing to do, the honorable thing, and do it."

Groves straightened in his chair. "You're a lover of the classics. Think about what Cincinnatus did."

Truman responded promptly. "Cincinnatus, like George Washington, was the commander of an army. Both men chose to give up power, thus gaining more power. But I don't see how that relates here."

"Because you now have the power," Groves said. "You can make your report. It's in your power to do so. But you will have greater power and respect if you choose not to. It's for the greater good."

Truman opened his mouth to respond then closed it. He was silent for a moment. He knew Groves was right. He took a deep breath and let it out slowly and nodded.

"I've already written the report. I'll not submit it to the committee."

Lynch said, "I'd prefer if you burn it, Mr. Truman. It's safer that way."

"I can do that." Truman looked at Matthias. "Did we get confirmation that the Navy sank the submarine?"

Matthias nodded. "Yes. Reports from the field are that both destroyers heard the sound of the hull cracking. They're still patrolling the area and we've called in the Coast Guard but she's as good as gone."

"And the kidnapped scientist?"

"Down with the sub, I'm afraid."

"How are you going to explain that to his family?" Truman asked.

"Like we do all accidents here," Matthias said. "Although this one will have a bit more fluff to it. Word is there were gunshots that tipped the destroyers to the sub's location. I don't know what happened down there but I hope to God that Osborn blew a hole in that traitor."

"What about Edward Moore? Will he be brought to justice?"

Matthias deferred to Groves. "Not now. His warehouse is still the biggest in the area. Frankly, despite what he did, we still need him. As soon as the war's over, we'll prosecute. But I don't imagine folks will be too interested in that."

Truman's mouth hung open. "What? So he gets off scot free?"

Groves spread his hands. "It's war, Senator. We have a need. He fills it."

Truman looked at Groves, then Matthias, and then Lynch. "So that's it, then. We have an embezzler that walks free, a group of American citizens who are about to be shipped off to one of our camps for no other reason that they are of Japanese ancestry, two dead men and two dead soldiers, and I still don't really know what happened to my partner. And I'm just supposed to walk away and say nothing?"

Groves spoke for all three officers. "Yes."

A thousand things went through Truman's mind, all of them inflammatory. He saw the handwriting on the wall. He read it clearly, understood it perfectly, and hated it completely.

He sighed. "Well, since I'm here, I might as well hear your speech this morning, Colonel. I'm looking forward to hearing what you'll have to say about those two dead soldiers."

Matthias looked at Groves who nodded. Matthias said, "Mr. Truman, you can't attend the speech this morning."

Truman's eyes hardened. "Why?"

"Because of your growing notoriety. For all the reasons General Groves spoke about why you can't submit your report, you can't attend the speech. You attend the speech, the press sees you, asks you why you're there, and the entire cycle spirals out of control again."

Lynch pulled out his cigarette case, looked at Truman, and replaced it back in his shirt pocket. He smiled at Truman. "We have everything under control here, Senator. We don't need anyone or anything to rock the boat. We survived last night by the skin of our teeth and luck. Let's hope that's all that happens between now and the end of the war."

Truman reached into his suit jacket and withdrew his handkerchief and began to clean his spectacles. He finished and put on his glasses. "Since we're talking about the end of the war, what say I just keep my report and publish it then? It would be a testament to the American resolve that we overcame this attempt on our military strength."

Groves shook his head. "I'd prefer this little episode just be lost to history. Few people know the real story and, if no one says anything, future generations will never know about it."

With his foot, Truman scooted the trashcan from its position next to the desk to in front of him. "May I borrow a light?"

"I thought you didn't smoke," Lynch said, handing Truman a Zippo lighter.

"I don't," Truman said. He withdrew from the interior pocket of his coat a small stack of folded paper. He lit the lighter and put fire to the papers. He held the paper as it burned and then dropped the smoldering heap in the trashcan. He handed the lighter back to Lynch.

Truman regarded the three men in front of him. "You boys ever read *Meditations* by Marcus Aurelius?"

They all shook their heads.

"You should. I never went to college but you can learn all you need to know about mankind in books. There's a passage in the *Meditations* that seems about right today. It goes like this: 'First, do nothing thoughtlessly or without a purpose. Secondly, see that your acts are directed toward a social end.'"

Truman rose from his chair and the other three rose as well. "I'm going to call every day until I hear news about Carl. And you let *me* be the one to tell his wife." Matthias nodded and Truman picked up his hat.

"What are you going to do now?" Lynch asked.

"I'll go back to the hotel and pack. Then, I'll take the train back to Washington. I have a lot to think about. And I think I'll stop and see my mamma back home."

Lynch smiled at Truman. "Senator, what do you think about the rumors you might be nominated as vice president?"

Truman turned back toward the three officers. "Gentlemen, there are a dozen men who are better qualified than I am to be Mr. Roosevelt's vice president. I don't think there's a chance in hell they'll pick me, which suits me just fine. I've never been happier than I am now in the Senate."

He tapped his hat with his hands. "In all my travels across the country, I hear just about everyone say that they're just doing their part to help the boys overseas win this damn war and come home. If, by some deranged act of fate, they pick me to run with Mr. Roosevelt, I'll do what everyone else does here at home: I'll do my part and serve."

Senator Harry Truman put on his hat and walked out of the office.

EPILOGUE

Thursday
9 August 1945
6:45 p.m., Eastern War Time

"M r. President?"

Harry Truman sat at the president's desk in the Oval Office. Around him were microphones for the radio address to the nation he was to deliver later that evening. Scattered papers covered the desk. He was marking changes to the speech in pencil when he looked up and smiled broadly.

"Carl Hancock!" Truman said. He rose from the chair and walked around to greet his former partner. The president clasped the Texan's hand with both of his and shook it vigorously. "How are you doing?"

"I'm fine, Mr. President. How was Potsdam?"

Truman's smile faded. "I'm speaking about that in a few minutes. Between you and me, I'm glad I'm back." Truman remained silent for a moment. "Carl, you wouldn't believe the devastation over there in Germany. I don't know which is worse: destroying a city with a hundred bombs or just one."

Hancock nodded. "I read about another one today, at Nagasaki. With the Russians in Manchuria, Japan's got to surrender any day now, right?"

"That is my prayer.

"As long as we got these bombs, we should use them. They'd use them on us in a heartbeat."

Truman motioned Hancock to the two chairs opposite the president's desk. He sat in one and Hancock sat in the other, placing his Stetson on his lap.

"I wrote a letter to Senator Russell of Georgia today," the President said. "He feels the same way. I don't like killing all those innocent civilians just because their government is run by stubborn mules. But I'm the President of the United States and my job is to save as many American lives as I can. And if I can also save Japanese lives, so be it."

"I understand, Mr. President."

Truman crossed his legs. "Carl, tell me something: back in Hanford last year, after you were shot, did Lynch tell you about what they called the Manhattan Project?"

Hancock looked evenly at Truman and didn't blink. "I didn't speak about that day until news of the Hiroshima bomb was released. Only then did I tell Louise that was the reason I was shot: protecting the Hanford project. I'm proud of that." Hancock straightened in his chair. "Yes, Mr. President, he told me. He felt he owed me for my actions even if the grenade was a dud."

Truman nodded. "You're a good man to keep that secret."

The Texan scowled. "It was weird keeping it from you. Was it true Mr. Roosevelt never told you about the bomb?"

The President sighed. "No, he didn't. Mr. Roosevelt ran this office a different way than I do. I don't hold it against him. It was the way he liked it. Hell, I wasn't even told the truth about the bomb on that awful day when Mr. Roosevelt died. Stimson gave some cryptic remark about a big project. Funny how secrets are kept in this town."

Hancock gave a sidelong glance. "How'd you know about the grenade?"

Truman grinned. "One of the perks of this job is that I can find out almost anything. After V-E day and all that mess was sorted out, I saw Groves one day. It was when he briefed me about the bomb. It occurred to me to find out the whole story about everything out in Hanford."

"And?"

"Well, I found out about what you did. Actually, it was Lynch who came to Washington and told me himself. I don't care that the grenade didn't go off. Carl. That was a remarkably brave thing to do. You will be commended."

Hancock waved a hand at Truman. "I was just doing my part."

"I know. And I'll see you rewarded for it."

"Now that the war is winding down, what's going to happen to Edward Moore?"

Truman exhaled air through his nose. "Just as Groves predicted: nothing. Even though the war is almost over, we still need to make more atom bombs. We have to keep Stalin in line. So, Moore Warehousing continues to operate. But I'm going to see to it that Mr. Moore is denied *any* future government contracts."

Truman leaned back in his chair. "About the only good thing Mr. Moore did was buy up all that Japanese-American property. Once those folks are allowed back out of the camps, he'll give it back to them. That was his plan all along."

"Well it sure didn't look that way."

Truman started to clean his spectacles. "You talk to Horace recently?"

"About a month or two ago. He still wants me to go back out there and fish. Someday, I just might. The Army offered to discharge Mr. Bumble. He decided to stay in. Thought he could do more good in the Army rather than out of it. He lost an arm at Iwo Jima."

Hancock continued. "I still write Lester often. He promoted Duncan to chief deputy. The folks in Webb's county renamed the sheriff's station after him."

Truman put his glasses back on his face. "I'm enjoying the reminiscences but that's probably not why you came here, is it?"

Hancock traced his finger along the arm of the chair. "No, sir, it's not." He looked at Truman. "I've decided to retire from government service, specifically your old committee."

Truman leaned down and placed his elbows on his knees. "Why? I thought you liked it. Louise liked you doing it, too, right?"

Hancock looked over at the president's desk and the microphones. A few technicians scurried around making sure the connections were secure. "Yes, she does but I want to do something different. I'm going to join my friend Andrew Taylor's private investigator firm."

Truman laughed. "What, you're going to be all Sam Spare or something? What prompted the change?"

Hancock shrugged. "I don't know. The war's winding down so the committee work will dry up soon. Louise and I have made a life here in Washington. We like it. Anyway, it won't be like the movies. All Andy does is take pictures of men who cheat on their wives and, occasionally, he gets to impersonate important people when the need arises. Sounds like a nice change of pace."

"With your penchant for trouble," Truman said, "I don't think you'll be slow for long."

"We'll see."

An aide approached Truman. "Mr. President, one minute until air time."

"Thank you, Charles." Truman rose from his seat. Hancock stood as well. "Carl, why don't you stay and watch me give this little speech. After that, you can join me upstairs for a drink. How's that sound?"

"Very nice, Mr. President. Thank you."

Hancock watched as his friend, Harry Truman, President of the United States, straightened his tie and adjusted his handkerchief. A moment later, a dozen reporters came into the Oval Office, flashbulbs lighting up the ceiling.

Hancock stepped over to one side to allow more room for the photographers and reporters. He watched as the President sat in his chair and picked up his speech. The President's countenance changed. Hancock saw Harry Truman but he also saw something else. He could not put his finger on it.

One of the reporters angled up to Hancock. "Can I get your name and your relationship to the President?"

Hancock looked at him. "I'm nobody special, just an American who is honored to call the President my friend." He turned back toward Truman and found the word he needed.

It was presence. Harry Truman was where he needed to be. Harry Truman was where the *nation* needed him to be.

Carl Hancock beamed at his friend.

The aide counted off the final second and then pointed.

President Harry S. Truman began to speak: "My fellow Americans…"

The End

AFTERWORD

Treason at Hanford has an interesting origin story, and I owe its beginning to a friend of mine who asked a simple question.

Back in summer 2005, I worked as a technical writer for a computer company. Down the hall was a guy I had seen passing in the hallways, but, since we worked on different projects, we didn't have much contact. Gradually, I learned his name was Doug Warren, he was a science fiction geek like me, and we shared common interests in films, TV shows, and books. Slowly but surely, we got to know each other and a friendship grew.

One of the things we both discussed was the idea of writing a book. But in those days—pre Kindle, pre indie publishing—it seemed monumental. Sure, I had written a Master's thesis, but a book of fiction? And if we finished them, we lived in Houston, Texas. How would we even get them published?

First things first: the book had to be written.

I'd like to say I had this burning desire to write a book since I was a youth, but that wasn't me. Even as Doug and I discussed the idea of writing our first, respective novels, I cannot consciously remember ever gearing up to do it.

Until one day Doug came to my office and asked me a question: "Would you read chapters of the book I'm writing?"

Again, I have no memory of what I thought at that moment, but I distinctly remember my response: "Sure, if you read chapters of mine."

We nodded in agreement. The pact was made. But, you see, while Doug had already started on his novel, I faced a challenge: I had nothing.

I did, however, have an idea.

I'm not sure exactly how the idea of a novel featuring Harry Truman came to me, but it did. The summer of 2005 was a mere six years since I had graduated from the University of North Texas with a Master's Degree in history. I had read David McCullough's wonderful Truman biography and the man from Missouri was and remains one of my favorite presidents. However I came about the idea, I started working on the book during a family vacation to Waco, Texas, in the last week of July 2005.

Not knowing how to write a novel, I fell back to the one thing I knew how to do: write a history paper. I purchased a composition book—the kind with the black-and-white mottled print—a bunch of index cards, multiple pens in different colors, and post-it notes. From there, I set about outlining the story.

One of the first scenes that came to me was when Carl Hancock steps out of the Moore Warehouse with Keiko Moore, the wife of Christopher Moore, the American traitor. I didn't know who they were yet. All I saw was two people, a man and a woman, in silhouette, surrounded by other shadowed figures. As a rookie fiction writer, I made a decision that ended up being one of the best decisions about the entire book: I resolved not to write that scene until I got to it, chronologically.

That was July 2005. I didn't write the scene in question until months later. Talk about anticipation. When I finally arrived at that scene, I remember being very excited. The words simply flew through the keyboard and onto the page. I know other authors talk about writing scenes out of order. For me, I'm a chronological writer. Start to finish. Thus, I started at the very beginning.

The process Doug and I established was simple. Every Wednesday, we'd meet at the cafeteria for lunch. We'd bring fresh pages—typically a chapter—and the marked up chapter from last week. While we ate, we'd discuss each other's book, the choices we'd made, and options for changes. His novel turned out to be *Devon Blake and the Starship Crash*, a middle grade story about a youth and his friends who get stranded on a planet and have to survive. It's a fun science fiction adventure book and I enjoyed reading and discussing it.

The motivation of having something every Wednesday became a good milestone. I remember a few times—before I learned how to carve out time in my day to write—of staying up late on a Tuesday just to have fresh pages the next day. It was always a crushing thing to admit you missed a deadline and didn't have anything new to deliver.

Along the way, another co-worker of ours joined our group. Darrell was writing a gritty crime story, so it turned out to be fun reading three books in three different genres.

It was sometime in January 2006 when Doug and Darrell asked me a question about my book. By that time, I was at least halfway through the novel. I had a corkboard in the guest bedroom with different colored note cards pinned in order. The color-coding proved crucial because I'd be able to see if a certain character had been off stage for a few chapters. I wrote everything in Word on a then-not-quite-old Mac laptop, the one that looks like it was designed by Batman.

Their question seemed simple: what were the Japanese characters doing while all the American characters were on stage? I probably rattled off everything I had mapped out.

"Put all of that in your book," was their common response.

Really?

Yeah.

At that point, I halted forward progress on the narrative and went back and wrote all those smaller scenes with Morimoto, Ishihara, and Niigata. I think it's a better book for it.

As the spring of 2006 wore on, I could see the end of the

tunnel. Naturally, my thoughts turned to publication. In those pre-Kindle, pre-ebook days—I know ebooks existed, but indie publishing wasn't a thing yet—the only option was an agent. But who? And where would I meet him or her?

Turned out, there was a local mystery conference in Houston on Father's Day weekend 2006. I knew little, but I assumed that if I pitched to the agent at the conference and they said yes, I needed a completed manuscript. There was my big deadline. I backed it up a bit, and circled 1 June 2006 on the calendar. That would give me two weeks to revise and edit.

I met that 1 June date. My very first novel was complete.

Now, I'll admit that each and every time I complete a manuscript, there is a feeling of euphoria, of accomplishment, and of celebration. But there is nothing like writing "The End" on your first book. That feeling remains a high point of my writing life.

I met the agent at the conference. She listened to my pitch, intrigued, and asked for the first hundred pages.

Are you kidding me? I got a yes?

I did. And I sent it off. I was already dreaming of being on the bestseller list. Don't all rookie writers think that?

And waited. And waited. And waited some more.

Ultimately, the agent passed. I found another in 2007, but, after another year, she and I amicably parted ways.

And then nothing for another five years. I started another book —a modern crime story set here in Houston—but it ultimately died on the vine, unfinished. I finished nothing for five years until I completed what turned out to be my first published book, *Wading into War*, in 2013. By that point, the indie publishing revolution was on and I started my own company to publish my books on my own. I moved forward and rarely looked back.

But what about that first book, the one with Harry Truman?

I decided to re-read and revise it, but as I prepared this book for publication, my thoughts naturally drifted back to 2005 when Doug stepped into my office and asked his question. It was the one event that sparked me to write my first book, and I thoroughly enjoyed sharing the journey with him. It made me miss him all the more.

Doug passed away in 2015. It was sudden and shocking for me and his family. It was at his memorial service where I stood and told the assembled mourners what Doug meant to me. That was also the day that I decided that if *Treason at Hanford* were ever to be published, I would dedicate it to my friend.

Thanks, Doug, for asking that question eighteen summers ago.

Scott Dennis Parker
    October 2023

ABOUT THE AUTHOR

Scott Dennis Parker lives and works in his native Houston, Texas, and is the author of eight books and numerous short stories and novellas.

With a childhood in the 1970s and 1980s, Scott knows what it's like to have three TV networks, lots of great music, and a little film called Star Wars. He revels in all of pop culture of the 21st Century and has written about it for more than a decade on his blog: Scott-DennisParker.com

He is one of the inaugural members of Do Some Damage, a group blog focused on crime fiction, where he is the Saturday columnist since 2009. You can read his posts and those of his fellow writers at DoSomeDamage.com.

Connect with him on Facebook, Twitter, and Instagram.

Visit ScottDennisParker.com to learn about other books, join the mailing list to keep up-to-date on new books, and connect with him on FaceBook, Twitter, and Instagram.